PRINCE KRISTIAN'S HONOR

Book One of
The Erinia Saga

TOD LANGLEY

Prince Kristian's Honor

Published by Wheatmark®
610 East Delano Street, Suite 104
Tucson, Arizona 85705 U.S.A.
www.wheatmark.com

International Standard Book Number: 978-1-60494-304-7
Library of Congress Control Number: 2009928867

www.TodLangley.com

Dedicated to Jennifer, the Queen of Patience.

Stories of Fantasy are nothing more than the retelling of our own triumphs and sad, sad tragedies.

CONTENTS

1

QUEST'S END

"Do you still dream of me, Cairn?" she asked.

The cold was so bitter that anyone would have trouble finding the strength to go on. After several hours in the storm, the man had lost some of the feeling in his fingers and toes and could feel an icy pain working its way up his back. His chest ached, and his throat was raw; his eyelids were almost frozen shut. His body was sore, and yet, his mind remained clear. He knew where he was and where he was going.

"Will you always dream of me?" she insisted upon knowing.

The voice in his head comforted him and kept him focused. He pushed the numbness out of his mind and continued walking north, further up the mountain trail.

He pulled his thin, black cloak tighter against his body, trying to keep warm as he guided his horse up the narrow valley. It was just after sunset when he was finally forced to dismount and lead them both through the growing snowdrifts, some so high they threatened to force him back with his purpose unfulfilled. He was determined to see this through and was closer to completing his quest for revenge than he had ever been. No winter storm, no matter how cold or terrible it might be, was going to keep him from finally ending it.

"*I should be there to keep you warm,*" she teased with a whisper.

Would she talk like that? Cairn asked himself as he tried to pick up the pace. *Was his love ever that forward? Yes, sometimes she was,* he remembered. There was no happiness in thinking of her, though. There was only pain and sorrow.

Cairn tried to put her out of his mind for the moment to check his surroundings for signs of danger; he could not let anything steer him from his destination now. Three dead men in the foothills south of the valley were the latest proof of his determination and skill. *It had been easy to kill them,* Cairn reminded himself. He had hunted each of them down, stalking them like animals, slaughtering them like goats. The rest of his prey would not be as easy to kill.

He looked at the mountains around him, but he could discern little. It was dark and gloomy. The little bit of light there was reflected off the heavy snowfall, highlighting the narrow path with an eerie glow. The skeletal branches of the nearby trees reached out to him like the desperate arms of his dead parents. They silently begged for Cairn to help them, but it was too late for that. He could do nothing to save any of them.

The northern wind was so fierce that even the larger branches were frozen solid. Weighted down by ice and snow, they broke off and fell shattering on the rocky ground close by. Cairn could not hear their fall over the sound of the howling wind, the cold wind that made it hard to keep going. The jagged mountains themselves protested the unnatural storm, echoing the vengeful sounds of the wind back at him.

Cairn pulled his scarf up higher to cover his scarred cheek and started walking again.

"*Just keep walking, my love, and remember me.*" Cairn could never forget.

It was the harshest winter any of them had ever experienced, and they all regretted their decision to visit the tavern this night but not because of the storm. Settlers of the small mining village of Worndale had gathered in the town's only inn, the Mother's Vein, to forget about the storm as well as the rest of their bad luck. The sign out front smacked the side of the wall, knocking snow from the roof as the storm continued unabated. Normally, the tavern was filled with laughter as trappers and miners tried to forget their problems, talking about the gold still hidden within the mountains. The rough men normally joked with each other and drank away what little coin they still possessed. They thought about better times.

Tonight, however, the tavern was deadly quiet. The villagers sat nervously eyeing those that had invaded their peaceful sanctuary. There were ten soldiers sitting amongst them and all wore black armor with red-smeared crosses painted on their chest plates. They had come into Worndale late in the afternoon carrying broadswords and maces and demanded food and drink.

No one knew why they had come to their isolated part of the world, and the villagers really did not care. They simply wanted to be left alone. The soldiers, or more likely marauders, had burst into the tavern just as the storm hit the mountains, demanding the innkeeper serve them. They were evil men, full of anger and cruelty.

The villagers gave them plenty of space as they plopped down on chairs throughout the room. A few tried to escape when it was obvious the soldiers would not be leaving any time soon. One poor fool was immediately beaten and thrown back toward his table by the brutes; he tripped over his chair and fell to the floor, crying out as his elbow slammed into the wood. His shout seemed to annoy one of them, and they gathered around him. They were determined to force their brand of fun on all of the tavern's occupants, and no one would be allowed to leave.

"Where do you think you're going?" one of the soldiers asked, pointing at the nervous man that tried to scramble away from him. The villager's eyes opened wide in fear as two men grabbed him again, laughing cruelly.

"Come. We're going to play a game," one of them said.

"But we're missing a key player," the other man added. "Ever heard of Dead Man Swinging?" They laughed together as the villager squirmed between them.

"We'll drink a toast to those that didn't make it up this sorry mountain," the one called Hefler cried out.

"To Pierren, Oril, and Dag," his friend shouted back. "May the snow bury them so we don't have to." Hefler and the others laughed.

The frightened villager tried to break loose, but Hefler hit him hard with his fist. The man cringed, cupping his bloody nose with his hands. He watched in horror as Hefler's companion grabbed a rope from his pouch and started making a noose.

A HALF MILE DOWN THE snow-covered trail from Worndale, Cairn continued struggling against the wind and the snow, but he knew he was close. His breath froze in the air as soon as it left the cowl of his hood, but he ignored the storm completely and made a final push north toward the lights in the village. The solitary man had traveled far and never stopped to think about the hazards to his own welfare, but he suddenly felt a slight hesitation. He had always believed in his mission, and one way or another it would finally be over, but he was not as confident as he had been that he could see it finished. Cairn was not nervous or frightened … he had trained too long and hard for that. He was eager to kill those responsible for his loss, but he had no way of knowing if he would be successful.

"Better to die tonight than to keep on living," he whispered.

The voice in his head giggled. *"I love you, Cairn."*

"Not now," Cairn told himself. "I've got to stay focused."

He started searching for the men he had tracked for the last several weeks. Cairn walked up the one road in Worndale looking for signs of danger. They had to be here somewhere, he knew.

"They'd never face a storm like this in the open. They would seek shelter." Halfway through the town, he spotted lights shining out from under the shuttered windows of the Mother's Vein. He noticed several horses tied to the front porch and upon closer examination was able to tell they belonged to those he was searching for. He heard a man's harsh laugh and a woman crying. This was definitely the place.

He tied his horse up separately from the others, making sure the knot was secure but could be easily undone. Cairn did not like leaving his horse exposed in the storm like this; he was not like those he hunted, but he had no choice. He patted the animal's neck to say thanks and possibly good-bye and then crossed the porch slowly. Cairn paused in front of the tavern, hesitating for a moment … to make certain he was prepared … and then he opened the door and entered. The commotion inside abruptly stopped as they looked to see who was foolish enough to interrupt their cruel sport.

Cairn quickly scanned the room to ensure there were no immediate threats. Thick, greasy smoke floated around his head, but it did not keep him from seeing the occupants clearly. On the left side of the tavern, he saw a small hearth with a fire spreading its light out into the main room. Soldiers and villagers occupied six round tables, unevenly spaced across the floor. A bald man sitting near the hearth abruptly ended the song he was singing and looked at him pleadingly. A body hanging from a nearby rafter was swinging slightly back and forth. The man at the hearth kept getting tapped on the shoulder by the dead man's boot. He looked up at his dead friend in shock, but was afraid to move or stop the body. Cairn guessed the soldiers had strung one of the villagers up to set an example. One of them laughed and gave the body a rough push.

"If it stops swinging, you've got to get the next round," Hefler shouted to his companion.

Two more soldiers looked up from their table to stare threateningly at Cairn but then turned back to their drinks. Obviously, Cairn was not seen as any real threat. He turned his attention briefly to those nearest him. Villagers sat huddled together at their table, frightened and worried. They did not look up, afraid they might accidentally draw attention to themselves. The villagers did not know Cairn and feared he might be another soldier that would do them harm.

At the bar counter on the right side of the room, one drunk soldier turned only momentarily toward him to make sure everything was alright before resuming his drinking. He was trying to keep his balance and was only able to stand by leaning on his axe handle. The bartender, an older, plump man wearing a gray smock under a beer-stained apron, quickly shook his head, warning Cairn to leave before it was too late, but he was distracted by the pleading of a young woman. At the back of the room, two more men were trying to rip the skirt off a young girl near a stairway leading up to a second floor.

Cairn ignored that particular situation and continued to search for the man he was looking for. A group of men were gambling with stones at the very back table. They were so intent upon their game that they paid him no attention. He let out a deep sigh and then shut the door. He was committed to ending this … tonight. Cairn's gaze remained fixed on the one he had come for; he was one of the men at the back table and seemed oblivious to Cairn's sudden appearance.

The soldiers returned to what they were doing, as if the shut door was a signal that the stranger was just another stupid villager, not worth the bother. The two would-be rapists lifted the poor young barmaid off the floor and manhandled her up the stairs.

"Father," the girl begged for help, reaching out toward the barkeep.

A moan escaped the man's mouth as he rushed toward the back of the room. "Not my girl, please, not my girl."

The soldier at the bar grabbed him and put a dagger close to his face. A menacing snarl and a shove were more than enough to force the owner back. "They can poke her or I can poke you and a few others with this."

The man waved a rusty blade at the innkeeper's face. The man with the lute struck a few uneasy notes hoping to ease the situation, but the leader of the marauders looked up from his game and snarled at him. He then laughed as his men joked about what they would do to the girl.

"Come, lass, let me show you what a real pike looks like," one of the men on the stairs shouted.

The girl sobbed, reaching out a final time to her father. He raised a hand feebly back toward her, but did not move from his spot. The old man looked around at the intruders to gauge what might happen if he tried to stop them from raping his daughter. He let his hand drop back down to his side with a defeated sigh. The drunken soldier grinned in triumph and shoved him back toward the bar.

"I need another drink," he demanded.

The leader of the soldiers finally sighed and then grimaced. He waved his spiked glove around the room, counting, "One, two, three, six … ten, twelve. Fourteen. Fourteen." He shook his head in disgust.

"That's why this is happening to you. That is why we have come. Because you are weak and we are strong. There are fourteen of you in here. There's probably another twenty hiding in their homes. If you had any courage, you'd attack us. Sure, some of you would die … a lot of you would die. But you would win."

The man nodded toward the stairs. "And she would be safe. But you won't do it. You won't move your scared asses off those chairs to help an innocent, young girl. And that's why we're here."

He scratched his matted, black beard and sighed in pity. Then he casually picked his stones back up off the table and asked, "Whose turn was it any way?"

"*Do you still dream of me?*" the voice asked Cairn again.

"Of course," he murmured back to the voice.

Cairn took a step deeper into the room, knowing he had found his man. He was their leader, and Cairn meant to kill him. He began to move slowly toward the back of the room.

He stopped at the table directly across from his enemy, scrutinizing each of the men carefully. One person, a local man, obviously did not want to be in the game. He looked up at Cairn nervously as if to determine what stone he should play next.

Two of the black armored soldiers sat to either side of the villager, their sheathed broadswords resting casually in their laps. On the far side of the table sat another black-armored man. He was the one that had taunted the villagers. He was the one in charge of the soldiers, and Cairn focused all of his attention on him.

He was a Belarnian officer, and Cairn noticed his armor was better maintained than the other soldiers', though somewhat dented. His face was riddled with old scars and bore a permanent scowl. He wore a red cloak with black fur trim and had a helm of similar design setting on the table in front of him. On top of the helm rested a pair of spiked, leather gloves.

Cairn hesitated, staring at the gloves, as if reliving a deeply buried memory. Lost in the impossible past, he struggled to maintain his composure as the man across the table deliberately ignored him and continued to play out his stones.

Images of fire and smoke and cries of pain, agony, and grief emerged from somewhere deep inside him. It almost seemed that Cairn swayed, hypnotized by the rhythm of the cries in his mind. He first saw a thatched roof on fire. The yellow flames quickly sprang from the roof to the surrounding walls and structure, engulfing everything in its intense heat. Cries for help and screams of terror and pain echoed through his mind as he turned away from the blazing house to look for survivors. Every house in the village seemed to be on fire. People ran in all directions screaming in agony as flames ate at their bodies. A woman's voice screamed in terror, "Cairn ... Cairn ...."

"*Remember.*"

"Are you drunk or just another stupid villager?" The comment and the immediate laughter of the other two soldiers at the table brought Cairn out of his trance.

He stared at the leader again, prepared to follow through with his promise of revenge.

"You're Garnis," Cairn said softly. It was a statement not a question. "You're a Belarnian lieutenant and serve the Prince of Belarn." This got the attention of everyone at the table.

The one named Garnis set his remaining stones down and looked at the stranger closely for the first time. Cairn was tall and slender and dressed in tattered, black clothes. Little could be discerned about him other than his eyes and the small flash of brown hair escaping the folds of his scarf and hood. The leader briefly scanned him for weapons and finding none focused back on his eyes. Garnis was unsettled for a moment; there was something familiar about the stranger. He had seen this man before, but could not remember where they had met. The officer could not figure it out and it bothered him more than he liked.

Trying to play off the mystery of the stranger and his eyes, Garnis said, "So? Many have come to know of Garnis. Unfortunately for them, the wrong way. Unless you want to end your life like they did, I suggest you crawl away."

The slight attempt at humor caused low grumbles of agreement from Garnis' men.

"I would have you know my name as well," Cairn said, standing a little straighter.

"And what might that be? Are you the village idiot? Are you the son of an important miner? Perhaps you are the King of the Mercies … isn't that what you people call these cursed mountains? You people make me sick. You've lived here for too long without control. You've forgotten that your allegiance is to Belarn. Well, we're here to help you remember.

"Now, sit down or I am going to string you up and gut you. We'll use your intestines for replacement strings on that lousy musician's lute." The singer heard them mentioning him and plucked the wrong note, filling the tavern with a sharp *twang*. Again, Garnis' taunts made his men laugh. The rest of the tavern, finally catching on to the drama unfolding before them, turned in their chairs to see what would happen.

Garnis looked around at his men, seeking encouragement in his name calling, laughing along with his soldiers. Then Garnis looked back at Cairn. The Belarnian officer looked into the stranger's eyes, and he suddenly remembered him.

But it was too late.

"My name is Death," Cairn promised him. Suddenly, the ebony

handle of a dagger was protruding from Garnis' throat. The officer's eyes opened wide in shock. He had not seen the stranger pull the blade from his cloak or the swift flick of his wrist that sent it flying toward him faster than anyone could track.

Garnis was being strangled to death, the blade completely blocking his air passage, but he could not get anyone to help him. Villagers' mouths dropped open in surprise, and soldiers looked on in drunken silence; no one seemed to understand what was happening. The soldiers shook their heads in disbelief, trying to shake off the effects of the ale and wondering what kind of man would have the audacity to murder a Black Guards officer.

Garnis tried to say something, but no word would ever escape his lips again. Slowly, his eyes lost focus, and he blinked hard in a vain attempt to refocus on Cairn. His head began to wobble, and he reached out across the table to grab his killer. The officer failed and fell away from the table, his facing turning blue. The last thing he saw were the dirty boots of the villagers he had terrorized.

"My name is Death," Cairn repeated in a low but determined voice. He deftly pulled a slender, two-handed sword out from the depths of his cloak and moved to take care of Garnis' men. The remaining two soldiers at the table fell back with their throats cut before they could even get their weapons free of their scabbards.

Cairn's movements were so quick and precise that the remaining soldiers hesitated before attacking. The four soldiers behind Cairn formed a tight wedge and prepared to hack at him with all of their weapons at once. He spun smoothly to one side, deflecting the blow of the lead soldier while returning a diagonal slash across the guard's face. Cairn then moved to his left to dodge the downward swing of a wicked mace while swinging his own blade in a wide arc that sliced open the stomach of one of the other guards. He moved so quickly around the soldiers that all they saw was a blur of motion.

He took advantage of every available opening. As he turned back to his right to face the remaining soldiers, he saw that only two remained. One man lay crumpled on the floor at Cairn's feet trying to keep his guts from bursting out through the large gash he had made. Another was dead, his face a bloody ruin.

Cairn cut down the other two men just as easily. They did not know how to work together, and he parried one man's sword into the cross guard of the other soldier. He then used quick, jabbing strikes into the first man's neck and then into the other man's unprotected armpit. The two quickly fell, their life's blood pumping out through punctured arteries.

Shocked at how easy it was for this stranger to kill his friends, the drunken guard at the front of the tavern just stared at him. There was a hint of confusion and despair reflected in his eyes.

Cairn did not hesitate, and he launched himself at the clumsy man who waved his axe wildly in front of him. Cairn swung his sword in a backhanded motion that easily deflected the attack. He landed lightly on the floor allowing his momentum to carry him forward; he tucked and then rolled right past the man. Before the Belarnian soldier could turn and face him, Cairn cut across the back of the man's legs, severing his hamstring muscles and forcing him to his knees. Cairn quickly and efficiently jabbed his sword into the man's back as the guard knelt on the floor in front of the villagers. The guard's axe dropped from his hands as he clutched at the steel protruding from his chest.

Not wasting a second, Cairn jerked the sword free of the dead man and moved behind the stairwell as the villagers looked on in amazement. The two soldiers upstairs with the owner's daughter, confused by the commotion in the main hall, came rushing down looking for signs of danger. They were pulling their clothes back on as they started to see the devastation below. Cairn jumped out from beneath them and thrust his sword across the steps in front of the down-rushing soldiers, letting their momentum cut their legs out from underneath them. The two guards lay crumpled on the floor, moaning and holding onto what remained of their lower legs.

Again, Cairn moved over to finish them off, jabbing his sword through their leather armor and into their hearts.

He scanned the tavern looking for any other threats before he walked back toward the center of the room. Seeing only shocked faces, he wearily lowered his guard. Then he walked over to Garnis to see if he was truly dead. Convinced that his quest was finally ended, he closed his eyes and let out a deep sigh of relief.

"I will never forget," Cairn promised her.

After only a brief moment, he walked back toward the front of the tavern. He paused near the door and looked around at the surprised faces of the villagers. His scarf had fallen away, and they could see the terrible scars that had ruined one side of his face, three parallel cuts that had not healed properly went from his right eye down to his chin. Cairn put the scarf back in place and then turned to the innkeeper. He nodded once at the old man, pulled the hood of his cloak back over his head, and opened the door to leave. Just as he was about to close the door behind him, Cairn thought he heard all of them let out a long-held breath.

He looked past his horse into the night, confused about what to do. For the first time in many years, he had no idea where to go. Cairn hesitated, reflecting on his past and struggling with the terrible memories. Then he finally guided his horse down the street away from the town. The snow quickly concealed him from the villagers that rushed out of the tavern to watch him disappear into the storm.

THE WIND STILL BLEW FIERCELY through the mountain valley, forcing him to huddle under an outcropping of rock only a few miles from Worndale. He found little wood that would catch fire, and he knew the best thing for him to do was to continue down the valley away from the village. Cairn was anxious to leave the mountains, but he was cold and exhausted. He looked at the fire trying to keep warm but felt a chill running through his entire body; it touched every part of his soul.

Cairn frowned. "It's not the storm that makes me feel so cold," he complained aloud.

But there was no turning back now, he thought.

"I am what I am," he whispered.

He had finished his quest for revenge. The years of intense training and hunting had paid off. He had made good on the promise he set six years ago, and there was a certain sense of accomplishment and relief in the fact that it was finally over. He could sleep now. After six long years, he would finally sleep and let the past go.

"It's over now. It's over. It's over." Cairn kept telling himself this as he ran his fingers lightly over the scars that covered the right side of his face. He stood and began pacing around the small fire, clenching and unclenching his fists in an attempt to control his rising emotions.

"*Do you still dream of me?*" she asked him again. She asked him that a thousand times every day.

Unable to restrain his anger and pain any longer, he suddenly turned his face to heaven and shouted.

"Julia! Julia!"

It was the first time he had let his emotions run their course in six years, but it did not relieve him of his grief. He fell to his knees and gave in to the desperation that engulfed him.

2

ERINIA

The storm that hit Worndale finally pushed its way east out of the mountains and into the plains that surrounded the seas of central Erinia. Heavy gusts of wind forced the dark waters of the Utwan Sea to crash against the harbor walls of Belarna, threatening to destroy the city's small fishing boats. Rain flew sideways as it slammed into buildings and homes, frightening the occupants. Only the towering, black stone walls protecting the city seemed capable of withstanding the fierce onslaught.

The old citadel was a mighty fortress, ringed by strong walls and massive, round turrets. The black stones used for the walls were native to the craggy beaches along the Utwan Sea. People passing under the massive gates and into the city never forgot the horrible stories of their ancestors. How could they when every stone surrounding them was black?

The guards on top of the bulwarks huddled down behind the stone, trying to hide from the wind and rain. Several guards looked behind them fearfully at the palace, cursing their bad luck. They could see a single dim light through the rain and the mist coming from the house of their king. Then the guards turned away to hide behind the stone again as the wailing wind and rain almost blew them off the wall.

"The sorcerer has unleashed the fury of the Mercies," one of the guards moaned.

"He meddles with things that are best left alone," another Belarnian added.

"Maybe he unleashed some of the magic that was supposed to protect the treasures of the spirit folk," the first man suggested. "Now they're pissed off and we're feeling their anger."

"The spirit folk are far to the south, and they've never meddled in our affairs," their sergeant said, shaking water from his soaked coat.

"They say they've been around a thousand years and they've never come out of their woods." The older guard gave up on the futile attempt with his coat, cursing and only half listening to the superstitious men.

"Maybe they never had a reason to until now," one of them suggested.

"I think our prince is an evil man. The whole world will soon turn their attention on us," the other complained.

The sergeant came over quickly and slapped the man hard across the face. The younger guard fell back, shocked by his leader's sudden anger.

"Prince Ferral has done more to give us back our pride than anyone has in the last five hundred years. We were great once. We controlled magic and Belatarn showed us favor. Then the Erandians with their superior attitudes and cavalry thought they could put us in our place. They thought they could bring us into line and rule us like they ruled all the other kingdoms. We defeated them once, using the same magic that Ferral now possesses. We took control, and we dominated Erinia," the sergeant spat out the last word.

"But we were overconfident and boastful. We lost our magic, and the Erandians defeated us. We lost everything we had, but we will reclaim what was ours … with Ferral's powers and leadership," the sergeant said with reverence in his voice.

The soldiers were unsure of what to say or do. They simply nodded and tried to huddle even closer to the wall.

THE SOUND OF HEART-WRENCHING SOBS reverberated through the dark halls of the palace. Two guards that wore the blood insignia of their prince were dragging an old, whimpering man out of the audience chamber. The sound of his feet skidding along the floor echoed off the high arched ceiling and columns that lined the way to the throne.

"You committed treason, old priest. You accused me of heresy and witchcraft in front of your pathetic congregation. Well, I accuse you of worshipping a weak god!"

"I have done nothing! Nothing! Please, I beg you, please don't!" the old man pleaded.

"Cut out his tongue so that no one will have to listen to his treasonous words again," the angry voice called out.

The priest's urgent cries could still be heard even after he was taken from the room. The sound of harsh laughter quickly drowned out the condemned man's wailing. The laughter rang out shrilly, continuing on past reason.

A man and woman lounged on the top of a small dais enjoying their cruel game. They had just gotten rid of the last priest that opposed the return of Belatarn. The two sat in the oversized, royal chairs languidly, not caring about the craftsmanship that went into making them. The man dressed in black satin clothes trimmed with gold and green casually draped a leg over one of the armrests. He was in his thirties but somehow looked older. His black hair and mustache hung limply from his scalp and lip. He was too thin and looked too weak to hold the huge silver goblet that was in his hand.

As if by the direction of an unseen master, he stopped laughing and took a long gulp from the cup. He stared into oblivion for just a moment as if to remember what was so funny, and then, in a rage his body did not seem capable of, he threw the goblet across the room to smash against the mantle of the fireplace. The dripping wine seemed to add new life to the smoldering embers and large gouts of orange and red flame quickly erupted.

The action amused the man, and he began to laugh again pointing at the fireplace. This time, the woman next to him joined in his amusement.

"Very nice, my love," the woman purred.

The witch was stunning and seemed an odd match to her weak-looking lover. Dark red hair and a pale, smooth complexion highlighted the sharp features of her face. Her lips were a dark red color, almost the color of blood. Rebenna smiled and then laughed. She seemed to cackle rather than give way to true laughter as she reached over and began kissing him on the neck.

The Prince of Belarn quickly grabbed her long hair and pushed her face toward his. He forcefully kissed her as if there was little time left in the world. And it seemed as though he would quickly move to take more than kisses when he was interrupted by a voice.

"Are you that anxious to take my place, Ferral?" an old, frail man asked as he entered the room from a side door. He was too old to walk on his own anymore and had to be carried in a chair by servants. Ferral was annoyed by his father's unexpected presence.

"Aren't you dead yet," the prince muttered in obvious contempt. He kissed the woman again ignoring his father.

"I am still King of Belarn, Ferral, and while I am king, no bitch of yours will sit in your mother's chair!" Loyal servants cautiously approached the dais to ensure the woman stepped down. They looked up to Ferral for approval before taking a final step forward. The prince smiled and signaled for the guards and his lover to leave him and his father alone.

Rebenna stepped down from her lofty place and bowed deeply to the old king; she acted hurt by the man's harsh words but moved with a seductive saunter that ensured all their attention was focused on her. She gave a tight-lipped smile to her lover and then turned and walked out in grand style. Rebenna threw her arms around the servants escorting her and laughed as if she were going to a party. The closing door echoed with a dull thud as they left the father and son alone.

Ferral smiled and said, "Isn't she beautiful? She reminds me so much of Mother."

King Farras looked at his son in bitter despair. "Of all my sons, Ferral, you are the one I least wanted to succeed me."

"Father, I'm hurt by your words. Haven't I always tried to bring glory to our house?"

"Your glory is not what this kingdom needs or wants! Why do you openly strive to turn all of our neighbors against us? Do you not see that this will ruin Belarn? We have struggled for almost three hundred years to regain some of the power we lost."

"Five hundred years ago our empire rivaled any in the world. The people of Erinia knew and feared us and soon they shall again," Ferral declared.

"Your mind is as weak as your body," his father said, dismissively. "Go ahead, play your little power games. Amuse yourself with your witch and your foolish cult. Your zealots won't help you change anything."

"Father," Ferral replied, "why are you so cruel to your only son? Every cunning thing that I've learned was from you … by the blessing of our god, Belatarn, of course."

"Belatarn is dead. The magi lost their powers five hundred years ago," the king replied. "Instead of wasting time reviving a dead religion, you could have been helping me against the Erandians."

"Do you really think that a few border wars will accomplish anything substantial? The only thing you will accomplish is wasting more resources. The Erandians may be arrogant, but they are strong. Only with the help of Belatarn will we be able to create an empire capable of dominating the world." Ferral's dark eyes lit up as he spoke.

The king shook his head. "Religious fanatics don't win wars, Ferral. I thought you would at least have learned that much from me. If you want to have a kingdom to rule after I am gone, you will follow my lead.

Politics can be as threatening as any war and can do as much harm as any army. We shall defeat the Erandians through intrigue and sabotage, not by rushing them with a thousand suicidal idiots."

"There are the loyal followers of Belatarn, and then there are those that deserve to die. The Erandians especially deserve death. Those meddling fools have influenced our world for too long. It's time they realized we don't want or need them. It's Belatarn's will that all non-believers die, and I'll be his messenger."

The king sighed in disgust. "Were your brothers here to see you throwing away …." The prince jumped out of the chair and leaped off the dais to stand in front of his father.

"My poor brothers," the drunken prince said as he reached down to pat his father's hand, "are dead." His lower lip curled out in a mocking pout. "I grieved over their tragic deaths for a long time. What are the odds that two sons of a great king would die such horrible deaths? Aron drowned in the sea by his own nursemaid when he was only three years old. And Dael, your eldest and heir to this great kingdom, killed in a terrible hunting accident just a few years ago. Would you have thought Fate could ever be so cruel? I assure you, Father, I exacted a terrible revenge upon Aron's nurse as well as those that hid her from us! Now if I could just find where that evil boar is hiding."

For the first time, the king seemed to realize what his last remaining son was responsible for and what had happened to his family. His shock turned to grief as he lowered his head in despair.

"I am still the king," he repeated firmly, "and while there is still breath left in me, you will not lead Belarn back down the road to destruction. You must be stopped!"

The prince was surprised by his father's vow. He weighed the odds of killing his father right there, but decided to wait a little longer. Ferral yawned and stretched, "Oh, Father, our conversation has bored me to the point that I can hardly stay awake."

"It's more likely you have been in the cellars again and are drunk," Farras snapped.

"Yes, more likely at that. Wine!" Ferral ordered.

In response, a small, frail woman stepped out from behind a column. Farras was so startled by her presence that he almost jumped out of his chair. The beautiful girl, dressed in a simple light blue gown, slowly crossed the floor carrying a pitcher of wine and a goblet. She was slim and wraithlike. Her long black curls shined and reflected the light like a raven's wing. The servant's beauty was rare. Her eyes were a dull gray, like melting ice, the king thought, but her face held no expression at all. In fact, upon closer examination the king realized her skin was too pale. Her arms and hands were the same color as her eyes. Even her lips held a tint of blue.

"What kind of abomination is this," the king demanded as he stared wide-eyed at her.

"She is beautiful isn't she? She is my greatest achievement. Do you know how long it took me to transform this poor, little peasant girl into a proper lady of the court? Not to mention bring her back from the dead," Ferral snickered, patting his father on the shoulder. The prince liked to keep her close by as a constant reminder of his early victories over those that might stand against him. He had kept her hidden from his father, though. Ferral had decided to reveal the extent of his powers now because it was too late for any of them to stop him.

"My God, what have you done?" Farras asked. A deep foreboding filled him as he looked in horror at the dark hair, slender figure, delicate features, and complete lack of life within her.

"Not your God, my god … Belatarn has rewarded me many times for my devotion," he snapped. Ferral paced around his father as he stroked his beard smiling. "I have been studying hard over ancient documents for the last ten years, and I have made several discoveries. I have gained much power, Father."

"Evil power, Ferral. Power that will destroy you and everyone else along with you. I told you nothing good would come of your experiments," Farras countered still looking at the dead slave girl.

Ferral smiled. "These powers will help Belarn influence the rest of the world. Those that might have stronger armies will be afraid to use them out of fear of what I can and will do to their people. They will surrender to me or they will watch helplessly as their kingdoms are destroyed."

The girl's monotone voice interrupted their argument, "Kill ... me." The prince looked in amazement at the girl and then burst into laughter. "She does that from time to time. I have no idea how she manages it."

"I knew you were experimenting with dark magic, but I never thought you would go this far, Ferral. You're evil. You are truly evil, and you must be stopped." The old king seemed to gain new strength from his determination. He looked straight into Ferral's eyes and added, "I will stop you."

"Good night, Father. I hope you sleep well," Ferral said as he turned away from Farras. To himself he added, "I hope you sleep very well."

Farras impatiently waited for his servants to return as he sat uncomfortably next to the young woman.

"Kill ... me," she said again. There was no emotion in her voice, no inclination of expression on her face. Yet, the king realized these were not the most terrifying things about her. He looked into her eyes again and saw how dull and lifeless they were and wondered if there was a soul inside that beautiful body. "Kill ... me."

3

THE ESCORT

The sun had just come up over the mountains in the east as the mounted soldiers of Erand rode towards the coastal kingdom of Duellr. The cavaliers, dressed in their light gray coats and red pants, carefully scanned the trees on either side of the road. Their heads constantly moved from left to right, the long horse-hair braids decorating the tops of their helmets switching from one shoulder to the next. The land the company was riding through was famous for its beautiful fields of wheat and shaded woods, but the cavaliers took no chances in these dangerous times, especially considering the importance of the escort mission they were on.

The lieutenant in charge of the advanced guard stared with contempt at the man riding in front of his formation. All morning long, Mikhal Jurander had tried to convince the prince of Erand that for his own safety, it would be better if he rode with the main body a mile behind them. The prince ordered him back to his company with a sharp rebuke every time the young officer tried to broach the subject. So,

Mikhal resigned himself to the task of ensuring, as best he could, that the prince would not be surprised by an ambush.

The cavalry officer was convinced that Belarnian spies were keeping track of the company's eastward progress and had sent a squad of his soldiers ahead to scan the sides of the road.

"Look for assassins or anyone that doesn't belong in the area," Mikhal ordered.

When the prince demanded to know what the soldiers were doing, the young cavalier had simply answered that they were going ahead to ensure that no locals would impede his travel. That was the one time Mikhal had seen the prince smile.

"What a pompous jerk," Mikhal thought.

"Good morning, lieutenant. How are you fairing this beautiful day?"

Mikhal instantly recognized the voice as his commander came up from behind. "Sir, I would feel better about my orders and my chances of accomplishing them if 'His Royal Highness' would listen to reason and stay with the main body."

"Well, he is such a fine-figured and good-looking man, it would be a shame to hide him in the middle of a formation where his devoted followers could not see him," the captain responded, waving his hand with a royal flourish. Mikhal's mood began to lighten.

Mikhal Jurander was the brightest, young officer in the cavaliers. He was selected over a hundred volunteers to be an officer in the finest cavalry regiment in all of Erinia. At only twenty-two years of age, Mikhal was one of the youngest officers ever so honored, and he was also one of their best soldiers. Mikhal did not look like most Erandians; he had blue eyes and short blonde hair. He was also taller and slimmer than most of the other soldiers.

There was something different about the way he carried himself; Mikhal was a natural leader. He had overcome much to get into the regiment. Most of the officers in the cavaliers were hand-selected as youths from the richer families in Erand. That he was able to make it this far despite coming from a farming settlement showed how much potential Mikhal had already demonstrated. Mikhal continued to maintain his discipline and humility even after achieving what he had always wanted. This was why Mikhal was well liked by all of the men. Some day they knew he would be a commander in the unit.

For now, he only wanted to be more like his own commander, whom he respected above all others. Captain Alek Hienren had a great sense of humor, and the seasoned officer was always able to put his men at ease, no matter how much stress he was put under.

"You know, Mikhal," the commander started, "the king spoke privately with me one night before we set off on this little adventure. He called me into his personal chamber where he was sitting in his favorite chair warming himself by the fire and he said to me, 'My son is an idiot.'"

"No?" Mikhal cried out. Startled by his outburst, he quickly looked ahead to make sure the prince had not overheard.

"'My son is an idiot,' he told me, and I could not help but laugh! I had to immediately regain my composure for fear of being thrown into a cell next to the church where they chant all day. But he just smiled at me and said that if I could ensure that his son reached Duellr in one piece and proposed to Princess Allisia then he, in turn, would ensure that I was handsomely rewarded," Captain Hienren chuckled adding, "So you see, Lieutenant Jurander, my financial freedom depends on you keeping a cool head."

"Were it only so easy," Mikhal responded. The prince was sitting straight up in his saddle, oblivious to the conversation behind him. He looked as if he were in a parade, passing adoring subjects. *The imaginary crowd must be applauding his heroic feats with great enthusiasm*, both officers thought.

"Captain, come here for a moment." The two officers were somewhat unsettled to hear the prince's voice. The captain sighed and then grudgingly rode up to the prince.

"I am concerned about the lack of planning that I have, so far, seen in regards to our campsites."

"I'm sorry, Your Highness, but I don't understand."

"We've been on the road for three days now, and every night we have found the most inhospitable, out of the way locations to sleep. I am sure that your men are quite thoroughly discomforted and would appreciate a more relaxed campsite."

Obviously, the prince was leading toward something that he had already decided would be best for all of them. However, Alek also knew the selection of campsites had been left up to Mikhal. Mikhal chose every site thinking only of the prince's safety. Alek had no idea how he was going to make their prince understand.

"Your Highness, our locations for resting are chosen to ensure your safety. My men understand the importance of this mission. You must reach Duellr safely and propose to the princess, thereby ensuring Erand and Duellr join forces against the growing threat from Belarn. Besides, my men are used to much worse than this. Thank you for your concern, but they can manage." Alek hoped he had clearly outlined the reasons for the necessary security measures. He also wished that just once the prince would act more like a soldier than the spoiled child that he was.

"Well, I've heard there is a village not too far from the main road. We could be there by midafternoon. I bet your men would enjoy the opportunity to drink a mug of ale." The prince either did not understand their situation or he did not care.

"Again, I appreciate your concern for the welfare of the company, but to stop in a village would not only delay our progress, it would also put you at unnecessary risk from spies and even Belarnian assassins." The curt manner Alek used to speak with the prince, like they were at court, was about to tear the commander apart.

"Belarn! You must have been subjected to the false propaganda of my father and his overdramatic council. The royal family in Belarn has no control over any of its subjects, let alone control over its army. But, now that you have brought it to my attention how concerned you are for the safety of this company, I wonder how capable the cavaliers really are."

Alek ignored the provocation. "Your Highness, I'm just a soldier. I don't understand politics, but your father does. If he believes it's important for you to get to Duellr to marry their princess then I must believe he knows what he's doing," Alek explained.

"My father must have thought of everything then," the prince replied sarcastically.

"Maybe she'll be beautiful, and you'll be the luckiest man in Erinia," the commander joked.

"Not likely. Ever met a thin Duellrian?"

"Well then, maybe she can cook," Alek suggested happily.

"Your humor is not infectious, commander. I find nothing funny about being ordered to marry a fat, spoiled child," the prince snapped.

Spoiled is something you would have in common, at least, the officer thought but did not say. Instead, he tried another approach.

"Sometimes, our duty must …"

"Stop! Don't lecture me about duty, Captain Hienren. My father has taught me more than I ever wanted to know about the subject." The young man turned in his saddle to look at the officer.

"Do you know how many opportunities we have wasted with Belarn? How many border wars have they started that we could have finished? Our duty was to protect our lands not let those mongrels ravage it. Where was my father's sense of duty then?" he asked, almost shouting.

The commander was taken back. "I apologize, Prince Kristian. It was not my place to lecture you."

The prince was about to say something else, but held his tongue. "Just show me the way to a place where I can have a drink and a little privacy. I've felt the eyes of your men on my back since we entered the woods."

"There is no reason for you to be out in front of everyone," Alek said.

"Never let it be said that I didn't set a proper example for the men, Captain," the prince replied.

"They're cavaliers. They know what right looks like," the commander shot back. The angry look the prince gave him let the officer know he had gone too far. "If, Your Highness would like to lead the way toward this village, my men will try, as best they can, to protect you. If you have nothing further for me, I must inform my officers of the change."

The prince smiled, "No, Captain Hienren, you are dismissed."

The cavalry commander had never felt such hatred toward anyone before, but as he trotted away from the prince, he started to laugh remembering the king's words, "My son is an idiot."

By the time he reached Mikhal, he had a huge smile on his face. He announced, "We'll be stopping in a village this afternoon. The prince seems to know the way." Alek headed back toward the main body.

Mikhal looked forward at the stiff back of his prince and frowned. He would have to send someone to the village to check it out. "Damn him," he swore, and then he called for his sergeants.

Prince Kristian of Landron heard the lieutenant call for his subordinates. When he thought no one was watching, Kristian let his shoulders slump forward. He sighed, looking down at his gloved hands in frustration.

"Duty," he told himself. "Duty."

"When will you learn this lesson, Kristian?" he remembered his father berating him one day. "Someday you will rule this kingdom, and you must understand your duty."

"I'm trying, but part of what you're saying doesn't make sense," Kristian had complained. "You talk of duty like it is an abstract thing. Something I will encounter during a quest, but it isn't like that. It's something I face every day."

"Oh, Kristian," his father replied in a patronizing way. "You've never had to face a true challenge … nothing that has tested you as a man or a ruler. One day I hope you begin to understand," the king replied.

"One day maybe you will understand me," Kristian mumbled as he left the room.

Kristian looked back down at his tight grip on the pommel and forced himself to let go. Frustrated, he looked behind him wondering why it was taking the lieutenant so long to get his men on the right trail toward the village.

Kristian figured they would nave no choice but to follow him if he led them on. He spurred his horse hard and did not look back.

THE ERANDIAN ESCORT CROSSED OVER into Duellr late the next day. The road snaked up through the wooded Disam Mountains for many miles before it crested at the Tarin View Pass. It was a bald mountaintop with two small hills. The road went through the saddle of the two hills and provided a fantastic view of the Duellrian capital. Argathos was still miles away, but from where Mikhal stood, they could see its magnificent spires and palace towers reaching to the sky. The sun reflected off the Tarin Ocean, highlighting the yellow walls of the city.

Argathos was a crowded, bustling trade center. The city covered many of the foothills that sloped down from the Disam Mountains toward the ocean. The patrol noticed several large merchant ships anchored in the protected bay. Others were moored along the docks that littered the harbor. People hurried about loading and unloading the ships that were bound for the Old World.

If there was ever a city in Erinia that might reflect the culture and architecture of the Mesantian kingdoms than it has to be Argathos, Mikhal Jurander imagined. The escorts had all stopped to gaze in wonder, including the prince.

Eventually, their eyes shifted to the cliffs north of the capital, to the seat of Duellrian power. The palace grounds were on a small rise atop the cliffs that overlooked the Bay of Argathos. The castle was small compared to those in Erand, but more beautiful because of the care demonstrated in its architecture. Terraces and balconies jutted out from the three-story home so that guests would have outstanding views of the ocean. The most spectacular part of the palace was rumored to be a wall of glass that faced east. The blue stained glass was a magnificent sight that all travelers commented upon.

Mikhal sighed, glad they had made it safely and that his mission would soon be over. He did not even care if he saw the window or even stepped into the palace, as long as he did not have to look at the prince for a while.

4

The Prize and The Gift

The halls in the Belarnian palace were dark and cold. The servants had finished their chores hours before and quickly retired for the night. Many of them felt an evil chill penetrate their clothes, and they quickly abandoned the darkened hallways for the safety of their small chambers. Several windows were ajar, swinging in the heavy gusts of cold wind that blew into the castle. The only sign of movement was the heavy curtains that flapped like war banners into the center of the hallway. The only sound was an evil whisper in the wind, warning the frightened to stay in their rooms and keep the doors bolted.

There was one, cloaked in darkness, who took pleasure in all of this. Prince Ferral casually walked down the main hall that went through the royal family's living chambers while everyone else hid and prayed that the evil would pass them by. He smiled like a man that had finally gotten his hands on the prize he had always sought. Tonight was his night.

Tonight he would begin to change the world. Soon everyone would know and fear him. Only one thing remained undone. He stopped and turned to the door on his left. The two guards standing to either side of the door looked at him nervously. After only a moment's hesitation, the last of the king's loyal guards stepped aside. "You have saved more than just your lives tonight," Ferral replied darkly.

Black clad men emerged from behind the columns and drapes near the prince as soon as the door was unlocked. Their shadows quickly slipped into the room. The Prince of Belarn smiled and then entered and shut the door quietly behind him.

His father appeared to be asleep, unaware of what was coming. Pulling the silk screens aside, Ferral could see that his father was awake, quietly awaiting his son. Ferral smiled in anticipation of what was to come.

"My last act as king is to curse you, Ferral. May you die never realizing your plans. May you die the type of death you deserve. May you die and go to hell! Now do what you came to do and kill me quickly." The king closed his eyes and patiently waited for Ferral's henchmen to finish him. He was surprised to hear Ferral's voice instead.

"Yes, Father, you will die tonight. A new age is upon the land, an age that I will usher in, but I'm afraid you will not die as soon as you wish. This will not be an easy night for you." With a small gesture of his hand the shadows swarmed around the bed. The king tried to sit up but was quickly pushed back down. A hot cloth containing a pungent, sticky substance was shoved into his face. The king gasped for air, the substance filling his lungs and burning his nose and lips. Finally, the king's body went limp.

THE KING AWOKE IN A poorly lit room he had never seen before. His wrists were strapped down to the sides of the cold stone table he was lying on, and he could not sit up. Looking around him, the old king found many disturbing artifacts decorating the room. Hundreds of bones, including dog, snake, and even human skulls, littered the many shelves.

Acrid orange smoke from an incense burner filled the air making other observations difficult, but he could at least see one other terrible sign of his son's unholy magic. On the wall to his left, a faded symbol painted in blood clearly represented the dark god, Belatarn.

It was a symbol of everything the surviving people of Belarn had tried to forget about their dark past; the rise of Belatarn and his lesser gods represented a time when devout loyalty to the demon-god was expected and fear controlled the country. The symbol on the wall was the classical representation of the Dark One in his treelike form. Five points made of branches and roots formed the outline of a face within an oak tree. The eyes were replaced by ancient letters; they were in a language that Farras would never have known existed if his son had not mentioned it in his fervor for the cult. The letters stood for Belatarn and his closest demon, which Ferral claimed to be the god's most favored servant. The ancient symbol for chaos replaced his mouth, and the king could foresee that Ferral's "new age" would represent chaos very well. The king finally tore his eyes away from the evil sign, hearing footsteps approach from a door on his right.

The door opened, and Ferral and Rebenna entered the round room. The woman had on a simple, yet revealing red dress that accentuated her curves. She carried a covered tray over to the cluttered table next to him. After setting the tray down, she leaned over to examine the king's bound wrists and feet, making sure he could not get free. She smiled, confident that he could not move; Rebenna knew what was about to happen. She ran a finger seductively along his leg and up to his chest where she smoothed out his sleeping garments and then bent down to kiss him. Rebenna continued to tease the old man despite his refusal to return her kisses. Moving to his neck, she nibbled on his ear until she found his ear lobe. She bit him, laughing naughtily, and then with the viciousness of an animal, she bit deep into his ear with her front teeth and jerked back as hard as she could. The king cried out in pain as she pulled the flesh from her mouth and licked her lips.

Ferral laughed in genuine amazement as he continued to make preparations around the room.

"Oh Rebenna, you naughty witch! I'm sorry, Father. It has been a long time since I properly disciplined her. I'll make sure to do that tonight." Rebenna laughed as she held the king's ear in one hand and tauntingly flipped it with a finger.

Farras let out a sob. "She's a perfect match for you, Ferral. She's just as evil as you are. You will both burn in hell for your witchcraft." Ferral chuckled as he turned away from the shelves at the far end of the room and looked at his father.

"Witchcraft? Please, Father, give me a little credit." Ferral walked over to the covered tray and removed the red scarf. "Do you think a simple witch like Rebenna could bring a beautiful girl back from the dead and keep her from rotting?" He cringed as he thought of what rotting flesh might smell like, and then he smiled.

"No, Father, you will be proud to know that your son is a true sorcerer. I am the first in a new order of magi. The most powerful one in the world. What? You doubt my abilities? You need a demonstration?" Ferral let out an exhausted sigh. "Very well, but I don't think you are going to like it." The prince took a jeweled bone dagger from the tray and held it before the king. The bone blade was dull gray and came to a curving point. The handle was also made of bone but inlaid with gold and rubies. Ferral seemed very fond of the knife. "This will hurt a little."

Suddenly, with a force that matched the hate in his soul, Ferral raised the dagger high above his head and plunged it into his father's heart. The king gasped for air as if he were drowning, reaching out for Ferral. The king fixed his eyes on his last remaining son; blood was smeared over his lips and teeth. There was no hint of despair or fear in his eyes, only anger, as he tried to reach his son's throat. Then he died.

Ferral was furious. In his greatest hour of triumph, he wanted to feel the elation of taking the throne. He wanted to see his father suffer; he wanted to see fear in his eyes. The prince had waited patiently for so long, studying his dark magic, and now, the power would finally be his … but the old man had been stubborn until the end. Ferral pulled the dagger free of the king's chest and stabbed him again and again.

Rebenna stood next to him watching in glee as blood flew from the dagger to hit the skulls on the walls. The mad son abruptly stopped, realizing how critical his timing was, and unfurled the scroll he had laid on the tray. The prince nodded and smiled, quickly scanning a passage. He grabbed a golden goblet and filled it with his father's blood. Ferral looked into the cup and swished the blood around contemplating what he was about to do and then took a deep gulp. Ferral began to pray as blood dripped from his mustache and beard.

"Oh, mightiest of all gods, know that I am your most faithful servant. I live to serve you, and I will be the one to restore this world to the chaos you have long waited for." Looking to the ceiling, Ferral raised the cup in a toast and implored Belatarn. "Give me the strength I need to destroy our enemies. Give me the strength to conquer this world and claim it for you!"

The sorcerer began to chant in a long dead language, his words a blur of guttural phrases followed by high-pitched whines. It was a queer mix of the barbaric with the elegance of a sad song. Ferral did not know how his god would answer his prayer, but he expected something grand, something that would show him he was favored above all others. He waited several moments in anticipation. Nothing happened. Ferral began to tense, unsure if the spell would actually work.

When nothing happened, he became angry. Ferral threw the goblet at Rebenna. She barely dodged the cup as it flew past her head, shocked by the turn against her. The cup hit the wall and spilled the blood across the stone surface. Ferral shouted at her as the red liquid ran down the wall. He ran around the table and grabbed Rebenna, slapping her across the face.

"Bitch! You lied to me. You lied. I've killed him and risked everything I had to gain because of you and your prophecies. You know how hard it was to get that knife and scroll. You were there. It took me years to decipher their language."

Ferral threw her across the body of his father and began pummeling her as she struggled to get off the bloody corpse.

"You kept telling me I would obtain unlimited power, and that I would control more than just this pathetic kingdom. All I had to do was wait for the right moment." Ferral slapped her again.

"Wait, My Lord. Just wait. All the signs pointed to this moment," she implored.

"I should have known better than to trust a skulking whore. What did you have to do to get the scroll and dagger, I wonder? How many of those cursed folk did you sleep with? 'See the glorious future', you said. 'Take the throne and pledge your allegiance', you said. I could have killed him as soon as my brother was dead. I could have taken control then, but you kept urging me to revive the religion. Your prophecies are all lies."

He pushed her back down when she tried to get off the altar; the blood from the cup still ran down the wall as he continued beating her. Much of it had already dried, turning from red to brown, forever staining the stones.

Where the blood first hit the wall the color continued to darken. The spot changed to an even duller stain until its edges could no longer be defined. The color changed from red to brown to black. The bloody spot grew darker and darker until the depths of the wall were no longer discernible and it looked as though you could fall through it into another world. Then the blackness began to swirl, becoming a fluid whirlpool swallowing more and more of the wall.

At first, the prince did not notice the changes as he continued beating Rebenna. A gust of wind emanating from the black whirlpool hit Ferral in the face and he stopped to look. Ferral threw Rebenna away from him sending her crashing into a bookshelf.

A soft buzzing followed the wind out of the blackness, growing from a low whisper to a loud swarm of angry insects as the sound increased. Voices within the buzzing cried out in agony and terror, their eternal pain causing everything in the room to shake.

Rebenna screamed as the voices wailed louder and louder. Some warned them to run while others screamed that it was already too late.

From inside the darkness, an image emerged, rapidly approaching the surface of the whirlpool. The image became the shadow of a human and grew larger and larger as it approached the portal. The evil aura the creature projected made even Ferral cringe as he stared at the winged and horned monster that was preparing to enter his world. A clawed hand reached out from the wall, grasping for something to cling to. The demon pulled itself free by clutching at the edges of the stone surrounding its magical doorway.

First, the other hand appeared probing the air in front, making sure there were no obstacles in its path. Then slowly the creature's horned head emerged. Its face was contorted in pain as it struggled to pull itself free of the abyss. Yellow glaring eyes rolled back in the creature's head as it screamed in anger and pain from the agony of crossing over the barrier between its world and Ferral's. The naked monster lay crumpled on the floor, hugging itself and trying to forget the pain.

Rebenna vomited as the disgusting fumes and ooze dripping from the demon reached her.

Finally, regaining some of his composure, Ferral cautiously approached the creature. "Has my god answered my prayers and sent you to serve me?" he asked warily.

The creature chuckled menacingly as it attempted to stand. Ferral was then able to discern the monster was a female. Although she was built more like a Herculean man than any woman Ferral had ever seen, the creature definitely had other features that were common to all women. The demon stood and looked at the sorcerer, though it was still bent over from pain.

"I am here because my master commands me to *assist* you. Do not even begin to think that you have any control over me, mortal. If my master wishes that you have what you desire, than I shall grant it."

Looking at Rebenna, the demon smiled revealing its many razor-sharp teeth, "Very pretty, Ferral, very pretty and … frightened, too. Leave us, wench." With a snarl that made Rebenna cry in fear, Ferral's lover backed out of the room and ran down the hallway out of sight.

The demon smiled in satisfaction. Turning her gaze back on Ferral, the demon said, "Killed your own father in the hope that my master would help you advance your pathetic skills? You risked a lot to gain something you have no idea how to control."

"I am the greatest magi in the world. I brought you here, and I can send you back. I demand greater respect from you," Ferral declared.

"You will demand nothing," the demon snapped, advancing on him. "In fact, I may not help you at all if you do not complete the ritual and give me the gift." She turned her glare away from the prince and eyed the king's body hungrily.

"What do you mean? According to the scroll, I have done everything required for the ceremony," he claimed, defending his new skills. He then saw her staring at his father's body.

"Your translation was incomplete," the demon snapped. Frowning in disgust, Ferral turned away from the demon giving into her demands. He could hear her tear and rip at his father's body as she hungrily devoured bits of flesh. Once the sounds stopped, he looked back, but the hideous creature was gone. The horned skull was replaced by long waves of blonde hair. The leathery wings had turned to ash and fallen away, and the yellow eyes had changed to a piercing blue. Where the evil demon had been there was now a slender, beautiful woman standing before him.

She is much too frail to be the same monster just threatened me, he thought. Ferral stared in astonishment at her beauty. Standing there naked, she wiped the blood from her chin and pulled long blonde hair from her face.

"You think I am disgusting don't you? You think that I am just a lowly minion of our master. Remember that when you become like me, there will be many things you will have to do that you will hate yourself for. Call it ... punishment if you like." Her body began to shift back into the monstrous demon again. The woman grabbed her middle in pain.

She quickly turned back to Farras' body to consume more flesh. Again Ferral heard her lips smacking as she bit hungrily into the corpse. Events were unfolding too fast even for him. He left the room for a breath of fresh air, but he disagreed with the demon. He would regret nothing.

5

THE ROYAL BARGAIN

The court announcer drove his staff down heavily on the marbled floor three times, signaling the arrival of honored guests. "Your Royal Highness, and people of Duellr, I present our most esteemed guest. Having ridden far to seek you out and ask you an important question, one that will forever change our lives, I present to you, the royal heir to the throne of Erand, Prince Kristian of Landron."

The courtiers of Duellr welcomed the handsome young prince into their capital with thunderous cheers. Many exclaimed that he looked very impressive in his fine clothes and armor.

"He looks like a true hero," one blushing courtesan said to another.

"I heard he had to fight his way out of an ambush single-handedly on the way here," said another. "And look, not a scratch on him! He must be the greatest swordsman to ever live."

Alek Hienren almost laughed out loud when he heard these comments as he escorted the prince down the central walkway toward the king of Duellr and his children. Nothing was farther from the truth. A mob had gathered to force the prince and his companions out of town after the prince had nearly killed a drunken villager over an insult to his honor. The cavaliers had quickly formed up and ridden east toward the capital to ensure the safety of their prince.

The prince had threatened the villagers, "Someday I'll return, and when I do, I'll not forget how they treated me, their future king."

Later, Alek had the pleasure of telling him the village was not in Erand. They had crossed over into Duellr several hours before sundown. The prince had admonished him for not keeping him informed of their current location.

Prince Kristian walked slowly, emphasizing the importance of the occasion as he advanced toward the royal family. Alek had to admit that the prince knew how to swagger. He carried his helmet and gloves in one hand, and the other rested casually on the hilt of his saber. He did not smile or nod or give any sign of enjoyment at being here, though. In fact, Alek knew he was furious at having to go through with this. Finally reaching the king, Kristian quickly kneeled and rose again.

"Your Majesty, I bring you greetings from my father. It has been long since the two of you met in Erand, and he wishes to know how you are and if you still stand firm in your resolve." The prince wasted no time in cutting through the tedious court greetings to the real reason he was here.

King Justan the Seventh, in his purple and white robe, looked more like an overstuffed cushion than his future father-in-law, Kristian thought. He grimaced as he noticed the son was just as obese as his father. He assumed his future bride was just as hideous, but before he could get a good look at her, the king waived a hand in acknowledgment. Although displeased by the prince's apparent reluctance to partake in the ceremony, the king smiled and returned the greeting.

"Welcome, Kristian, I am fine. In fact, I feel better now that you have finally arrived. My resolve has not changed. I still oppose Belarn … openly!"

A loud cheer erupted from the gathered crowd. Cries of 'Down with Belarn' and 'Hang the Prince of Belarn' could be heard throughout the crowd. The king raised his hand to quiet them. He looked back at the prince expectantly.

Realizing the king was waiting on him to propose a treaty that would bind his kingdom and Duellr together against Belarn, Kristian finally looked to the left of the king to see his future bride. He could barely hold back his grimace until he saw the beautiful young girl standing before him. Princess Allisia was very unlike her father or brother. She was small and delicate. With long auburn hair, green eyes, and olive skin, she looked more like a beautiful clay figurine shaped by a gifted artisan than the offspring of the king of Duellr. She wore a simple light blue satin gown that highlighted her slim build and accentuated her thin gold crown. Pearl earrings dangled from ears that barely showed through the wavy hair falling over her shoulders.

Kristian was confused. He was certain someone had told him the princess was not even worth looking at. For a brief moment, he felt a glimmer of hope that things might work out after all. Kristian had been certain that he was doomed to an unhappy marriage to someone that did not love him, but the beautiful girl standing above him commanded his complete attention. Was the princess someone that he could marry and enjoy his life with?

Allisia felt the prince's stare and turned to look at him, but she did not return his smile. He noticed her icy glare and wondered what he might say to win her over.

The king stood there expectantly, waiting for Kristian to say something. Kristian had planned to say as few words as possible, wanting to get it all over with quickly, but now he decided he needed to say something grand to capture her attention. He did not want to be too hasty in his words to his … new family.

"Belarn is the true enemy of all decent people, Your Majesty. News of their king's death and his evil son's ascension to power traveled across the land like wildfire, beating even us here. Many know, as I do, that he's a mad sorcerer bent on dominating the entire continent. None of us will be safe from his schemes."

Alek rolled his eyes looking up at the ceiling in disbelief. Just two days ago, Kristian had scoffed at rumors that the prince of Belarn was planning to wage war on Erand. *True, more and more reports were reaching them that the Prince of Belarn was planning to usurp the throne,* Alek admitted to himself, *but what made his own prince suddenly change his stubborn mind?* The cavalryman could not wait for this ceremony to end so that he could get away from the fool.

Kristian continued his rhetoric, "None of us will be safe unless we combine our forces to defeat this madman. Alone he may well be able to hurt some of us." Obviously, the prince did not mean Erand, Alek thought, "but together, representing all of Erinia, we will surely destroy Belarn in the name of God." Courtiers again cheered, praising the valiant prince for his courage. He looked back at the king's daughter to see if she was impressed by his speech. She raised an eyebrow questioningly as if challenging him to keep his word.

"Your words are strong and bare great importance," the king said smiling. "And they mirror my own feelings. I have long thought that we must unite against the evil prince of Belarn."

Kristian paused for a moment, faking careful consideration before he turned to the gathered crowd. "Then let us unite, king of Duellr. Let Erand and your own kingdom stand together to destroy our common enemy. In the name of my father, the king of Erand, I propose a treaty between us. One that I hope will not only see us through the dark times ahead but will forever bind our great kingdoms together." He turned back toward the king and his children and said, "And to seal our treaty and ensure the bond between us lasts forever, I ask for the hand of your daughter in marriage. I hope the love we will share as husband and wife will lead the way for all of our people throughout the coming age."

The crowd hushed as the king looked to his daughter. Seeing the great hope that was in his eyes, the young princess realized her fate was already sealed. Her father needed this treaty not only to keep Belarn in check but also to shore up their own kingdom. Trade relations with the Old World were worse than they had been since the wars between them over five hundred years ago. Her father was looking hopefully at her. It was her duty to help ensure the welfare of their people. She nodded her head in quiet acknowledgement, but refused to smile back at the man that would be her future husband.

The king's smile widened as he turned back to face the crowd. He raised his hands in a grand gesture and repeated, "May your love lead the way for all of our people throughout the coming age."

With that final symbolic phrase, the gathered crowd cheered louder than before. Hats and scarves were thrown into the air as bells rang in the distance. The bells signaled to everyone within the city that the treaty was final and that a royal wedding would soon occur.

"There will be a feast at the end of the week to celebrate this momentous occasion. On the following morning, you two shall be wed."

Prince Kristian and his captain quickly bowed before leaving. The last look Allisia had of her betrothed was of him strutting out of the hall, his back straighter than what looked comfortable. She frowned in disappointment, knowing the rest of her life would be spent with a self-centered, uncaring bore.

ALLISIA SAT ON THE LIP of her favorite fountain, tossing pebbles into the murky water. A stone maiden held a vase in her hands that poured water into a pool full of lilies. The statue always appeared so benevolent to Allisia, but she knew there would be no wishes granted for her today. She could not help but feel sorry for herself. Her ladies-in-waiting had assured her that Prince Kristian would take great care of her. Besides, he was wealthy and handsome and that was enough to satisfy them.

"What do those giggling, foolish girls know?" she accused her reflection as she threw another pebble into the water. "I know what he's really like." Allisia had known for quite some time that her father planned to marry her off to ensure a treaty with another kingdom. When she learned that it was to be to the prince of Erand, she hired her father's couriers to do a few other tasks while delivering messages to the neighboring kingdom. She found out what he looked like, what he acted like, and most importantly, what others thought of him. Allisia knew her life was ruined when she found out that even his father feared Kristian was beyond hope. She loved her own father very much and did not want to disappoint him, but she had often thought about running away and forgetting all about the prince of Erand.

She was startled to hear a voice interrupt her contemplation. "Isn't it customary to throw coins in a fountain if you want to make a wish? Surely, the king's daughter is not so poor that she can't afford a few coins instead of pebbles?" The prince's sense of humor did not amuse her, and she did not turn to greet him. Though he sensed he was not welcome, Kristian sat beside her and tried to comfort her as best he could. "You will like Erand. I'm sure of it. There are fields of grain that look like golden seas and forests that stretch for miles. There is space enough for everyone ... even for the lesser classes. Here, I feel trapped by the hills and the ocean. You could explore the expanses of Erand your entire life and never see all of it."

Allisia was offended by his comments of the one place she had known for eighteen years. She finally turned to look at him. "I have never seen another land, My Lord. I am sure there are many beautiful places that I will never see. But this is my home. I grew up here, and I love it. I don't want to leave it," she said defiantly. "And I think you're mocking it."

Kristian tried again to win her over, unsure of what he had done to ruin things this time. "I'm sorry. I meant no offense. Your city is a magnificent wonder. So many people have come together here because of the trade you share with the old kingdoms. It is a great cultural experience for me. And naturally, with so many people in one place there is also bound to be a significant amount of ..."

He smiled, acting innocent, as he looked back at her, but Allisia was gone. Kristian stood in embarrassment, looking for her. He challenged her, running to catch up to her before she disappeared behind a shrub wall. "Are all ladies in Duellr this rude? Do they just get up and walk away from a conversation whenever they want ... from one with their future husband?"

Allisia wheeled on him in anger. "Rude? You assume much if you think I wish to marry you. I don't. You're going to take me far from the one place I know and love. And you offended me by insulting my city and my people. I don't believe you know what rude is, otherwise, you wouldn't act as badly as you do." She looked up at Kristian with contempt in her eyes; she stood there impatiently with her hands on her hips demanding an answer.

Kristian fumed at her. He retaliated in the tone he used with everyone that was beneath him. "You assume that I proposed our marriage out of genuine concern for our future. In fact, I opposed it. If it were not for my father's insistence, I wouldn't be here at all. Marry a pretentious, naïve princess whose only wish is to stay hidden in her own father's house? Indeed."

Completely taken back by the prince's sharp words, Allisia almost slapped him. Kristian immediately regretted saying them. He could see the scared and hurt look in her eyes and was instantly sorry. Allisia turned away from him and started to leave. He grabbed her arm gently but firmly and turned her around. He hesitated before speaking.

"Wait, please don't go. I am sorry. Look, I admit that I oppose the treaty because I don't feel that Belarn is the threat our fathers do. But when I saw you standing beside your father, for the first time, I felt something good might come from this agreement. I didn't mean what I just said. I'm scared, too." It was hard for him to swallow and even more difficult to continue, but Kristian could see that Allisia was not satisfied. "I know you don't love me, but maybe with time things will change. I don't wish for us to spend the rest of our lives acting like this."

"And I am afraid that is as much as I can hope for. I am the king's only daughter and must help Duellr in any way I can. And I love my father." Allisia lowered her eyes trying to hide her sadness. "Well, there is the celebration at the end of the week. Perhaps we can start over then."

She curtsied and took her leave before he could reply. Kristian watched her run into the palace through a small door near the fountain.

"Why did I say that?" he asked himself, ashamed of his actions. He walked out of the courtyard and headed for the lower part of the city, not knowing the answer.

6

WITHOUT FRIENDS

The next day, the Erandian prince was walking down a narrow street far from the palace. Kristian did not even know how long he had wandered through the back streets of the capital. He was lost in his thoughts, carefully reconstructing his first conversation with Allisia. Sometimes he said things he knew were wrong, but Kristian could not explain why he said them. He regretted disturbing her. Kristian had only meant to introduce himself, but things were much worse now.

He was confused and angry, feeling too many emotions all at once. Kristian hated his father for forcing him into this marriage. Yet, now that he had met Allisia, he was not displeased at the thought. Allisia was beautiful and seemed more mature than the other girls her age. She might be defiant and argumentative, but at least she did not immediately give in to him like everyone else did. Allisia captured Kristian's imagination the way no other woman ever had.

He was angrier with himself then anyone else. There had been a small chance that they could be friends, but Kristian had ruined that chance in the first few minutes alone with her.

Kristian also felt contempt for Captain Alek Hienren and his officers who constantly seemed to garner respect from their men. Yet, Kristian wished he was more like them. He had practiced every day to be one of them, but he would never get the chance to prove himself worthy of that kind of respect, and he blamed his father for the way he acted. Still, he wished he had spent more time with his father before he had left.

Emerick was a hard man to love. The king had fought back against Belarnian aggression his entire life, and he wanted to make sure his son was prepared for the growing conflict. Kristian knew his father meant well, that he only wanted to make sure Kristian was ready to lead their country, but he neglected everything else a father should do with his son to make sure it happened. The last conversation they had with each other had been heated. Kristian had threatened to walk out of the Duellrian court without asking for a marriage to seal the treaty.

Kristian sat down on a bench outside one of the shops, defeated. The storefronts rose up around him, cluttered but still magnificent. The buildings were all sorts of colors and many had windows full of merchandise. The stores seemed to lean toward him, pressuring him to make decisions. He stared at the fine clothes inside one of the shops and frowned. He wanted to wear something new and grand for the celebration, but nothing suited him. They reminded him of his failures at court and in life.

"May I sit with you?" a lovely but unexpected voice asked. Kristian stood astonished to see Allisia standing next to him. She looked even more beautiful than he remembered, standing there with her arms full of parcels. She was wearing a green dress with a simple design. She did not have her crown on, but an ornate comb fashioned to look like a butterfly decorated her hair. Kristian hurried to take the packages from her as he sheepishly gestured for her to sit. Neither of them spoke for a while as they sat and watched the people hurrying by.

"I've got to admit," she said, breaking the uneasy silence, "I've been watching you for some time. Why are you so much more and less than you seem? I mean, how is it that you can act so rudely, hurting my feelings, and then walk aimlessly through a strange city obviously upset about what happened?" Allisia laughed at Kristian's complexity, and strangely it made him feel better. He tried to laugh with her but barely managed a chuckle. The prince could think of nothing to say to explain his behavior.

"What are you really like, Your Highness?" she asked, truly puzzled.

"Please, call me Kristian. I want so much to apologize for my actions. I really want us to be friends."

"That would seem appropriate since we are to be husband and wife." Allisia paused uncertain of how much to tell him. "I have a confession. I paid my father's emissaries to spy on you while they were in Erand."

"For how long?" Kristian asked, afraid she had gathered enough damning information to hate him forever.

"Oh … several months." Kristian grimaced. "I only wanted to know what you were like. I can't stand the possibility of marrying someone I don't know."

"I suppose you've heard enough to be forever disappointed in me," he said.

Allisia laughed again. "I'm afraid that most of what I heard was not good. But some of it was. They told me you were very handsome, strong, and …"

"Yes? And?"

"Well, wealthy."

"Is that all anyone has to say about me?"

"But it's clear that you care about what people think of you. You're a complex person, I think." Her brows furrowed as she tried to figure out her betrothed. "That has to mean you want to be liked, that you want to have friends."

"I have no friends," Kristian said feeling sorry for himself.

"Why do you say and do the things you do? If you truly want

friends, why do you abuse those around you?" she asked. The prince shook his head, not knowing the answer. Allisia scooted a little closer to him. "Tell me all about yourself."

Kristian was taken back. "Here? Now?" Her smile was enough to get him started. He began hesitantly, describing a few fond memories from childhood, but before he knew it, Kristian was describing every bad event he could remember.

In all of Erinia, Kristian could think of no one who could understand the way he felt. No one could understand what it was like to grow up with a mother and father who paid little attention to their son. Both of his parents were too busy to spare time for him during the day. They were, however, concerned about his education and potential. Kristian's parents ensured that the best scholars taught him everything he would need to know except how to interact with others; they were afraid of turning their kingdom over to a son incapable of leading Erand in the direction they wanted. The only people Kristian was allowed to see as a child were teachers who had forgotten what it was like to be a young boy. He was forced to read the history of Erand, Belarn, and other kingdoms instead of being given time to play with children his own age.

At first, Kristian defied them all by escaping to the army barracks whenever there was an opportunity. He loved spying on the cavaliers as they trained. For hours he would sit on a bale of hay high up in a stable and watch the cavalrymen conduct inspections or practice with their weapons. Once he had seen the entire unit marshaled. Never before had he seen men dressed so magnificently. The cavalrymen were wearing their best uniforms and highly polished armor. They sat upon well-groomed horses at rigid attention. Blue and gray banners snapped in the wind, and Kristian felt a great longing to be one of the soldiers. As he grew older, the prince began to realize that he was doomed to spend the rest of his life engaged in diplomatic affairs. His trips to the barracks became less frequent as he lost all hope.

He began to study in earnest the things the scholars were trying to teach him. In a very short time, he learned to scrutinize everything they lectured him about. He read so many conflicting versions of history that he no longer believed much of what he was taught. They constantly tried to impress upon him the proud heritage of his kingdom. There was no greater kingdom in the world, they said convincingly. Ever since Salin transformed the undisciplined mob of farmers into a powerful army, the rest of the world had left the affairs of the newer kingdoms to Erand.

The educators soon became disgruntled as Kristian accused them of altering significant events in Erandian history. They never successfully convinced him of the way things really occurred. Kristian challenged them to prove there ever was a man named Salin. Eventually, they gave up on the skeptical prince.

It was during this challenging time in Kristian's life that his mother died. Kristian had never been close to his parents, but when she died, it seemed that he lost a part of himself also. He began to drift even further away from those near him. What little bond was left between the king and his son finally broke. Kristian became unruly and defiant. Servants and tutors refused to work for or with him, and soon no one in the castle wanted to associate with him. The young prince did not mind. He did not care what people thought of him anymore. In contempt, he threw the teachers out of the palace and claimed the royal library as his own. There, where no one dared disturb him, Kristian would read for hours, losing himself in documents. In his spare time, however, a single palace maid or gardener would see the prince secretly grooming his horse or practicing with a saber. These lucky few saw the prince as few others ever did.

"And now, I am twenty years old. I know I treat others poorly sometimes, but it's only because I feel like I'm a victim, too. If I've treated others harshly, I guess it was because that was what happened to me when I was younger."

Allisia tilted her head in sadness. "Poor Kristian, you certainly had a terrible childhood, but you have to realize that it wasn't just those around you who were responsible. You must take responsibility for your actions ... and for your words. No one forced you to behave badly. We always have a choice."

Kristian shook his head in sad agreement. "Yes, Allisia, we do. And I will give you a choice. I will find a way for the treaty to hold without you having to marry me. I will talk to your father and ..."

"I have a choice, and I already made it." Allisia said looking into his eyes. "As you said, maybe someday we will love each other. Or at least get along well enough to live with each other," she said laughing.

Kristian smiled. He liked seeing her like this and hoped the moment would last longer. "For now, I just hope we can be friends. Will you allow me to start over? Can I take back my words to you at the fountain yesterday?" Allisia gave a little smile and nod.

"Yes," she replied, "but what about the way you have treated others? The way I have heard you treat your escorts. What about them?" Allisia was not going to let him out of trouble too easily.

Kristian shrugged indifferently. "It's too late. I know they all hate me. I'll never be good enough in their eyes." Hoping to change the subject, he asked, "But what about you? What was your childhood like?"

She shrugged in response. "There isn't much to tell, actually. I never knew my mother. She died giving birth to me." Seeing that Kristian was about to comfort her, she continued. "I regret that I never got to know her, but I love my father and brother very much. My whole life has revolved around them and my home by the ocean."

She went on describing the things she loved the most like her favorite wildflower and song. She loved to sit on the rocks not far from the palace and watch the waves crash into the cliffs below.

"There is nothing more reassuring to me than the smell of the ocean. I will miss it."

Kristian was uncomfortable with where the conversation had gone. He felt ashamed for taking her away from her home, but he also began to see Allisia as a friend. She was an incredible young woman not just a beautiful princess. For one so young, she was able to pick out the most discerning details in everything she saw, and she was very intelligent. Allisia could identify almost every variety of plant she saw by both the Duellrian name and its Old World name. She loved to read tales transcribed by priests because she felt that in many of them there were underlying themes of sadness and love. Kristian commented that they at least had one thing in common, their love of reading. She agreed. They continued their conversation, telling each other their pasts, their likes, and their dislikes.

When Kristian began to relax and feel more comfortable around her, he decided to share one more thing. "I feel like I'm under immense pressure to succeed, but I don't know what the task is supposed to be. I feel like there are expectations placed on me, but I don't know what they are," Kristian tried to explain. He knew his words were not accurately reflecting his frustration.

"We are both under great pressure. We're expected to marry and be happy and somehow unite our kingdoms so that our fathers can deal with Belarn. That is a lot of stress put on us," Allisia responded.

"I don't even believe in the reason we are supposed to unite our countries. Belarn is not a threat, and Erand could have dealt with them a long time ago," Kristian declared.

"Your father has convinced mine that Belarn is a very real threat," Allisia said.

"I think it's all about politics." Kristian reached inside his coat pocket and pulled out a folded piece of paper. "I … I want to be completely honest with you, Allisia. If we are to be married, I want us to understand one another."

"I want that, too," Allisia agreed.

"This is a letter that I received the day I arrived here. I want you to read it." Kristian handed the paper to her.

"Kristian," she read aloud, "I trust you reached Argathos safely and without delay. Give the king of Duellr and his people our respect and gratitude for their hospitality.

"I hope your future bride is beautiful," Allisia continued. She saw Kristian nod in agreement to his father's concern, and she smiled, "and that she is ready for a grand ceremony. I am also looking forward to your return. This old place could use a few little ones running around to brighten up the place."

"I also hope you understand how important this treaty is to our kingdom and to your future. I know I can count on you." Allisia re-folded the letter and handed it back.

The questioning look she gave Kristian showed she did not understand what he was upset about. "In the first part," he explained, "my father is really saying 'I know you reached the capital because the cavalry commander has sent continuous reports back to me.' Alek Hienren is my father's appointed guardian and shepherd.

"He then reminds me of my duty to put on a good show for your father so that I earn his trust and ensure he does not back out of the treaty." Kristian stood and began pacing as he became more agitated.

"And the part about getting back fast and having children ... that's to secure the treaty and make sure Erand has leverage over Duellr."

"Don't you think you might be reading into this a little too much?" Allisia asked.

"And he closes," Kristian continued, "by reminding me again about the treaty because he doesn't trust me to go through with this. I'm surprised he didn't come here and hold our hands to make sure we got married. He might even stand over our bed the first night to make sure we ..." He suddenly stopped, embarrassed.

Allisia stood and came close. "You're thinking way too far into the future. How can you maintain this level of self-imposed pressure? I think the most important thing is for us to get to know each other and to be happy. If we can do that, who cares what our fathers get out of the bargain? Do you want children?" she asked.

"Of course. I want lots of children," he replied.

"How many?" she asked again.

"I don't know," Kristian said, starting to laugh. "It's all too much to take in right now."

"Yes, it is," Allisia agreed, "but it's more enjoyable to talk about our future than a letter from your father." They laughed together for awhile and then shifted the conversation toward the ceremony. Kristian was apprehensive, but Allisia told him how simple it would be. He looked forward to seeing her again and getting a chance to dance with her. Allisia smiled, her face turning red.

Finally, Allisia said she had to leave. Kristian did not want her to go, but he did not try to stop her. He enjoyed the conversation and would always remember it. They said their good-byes, exchanging hopeful glances at each other. Allisia also promised that they would talk more before the ceremony. Then he remembered that he still had to find something to wear, and Kristian moaned in misery.

MIKHAL JURANDER WAS SITTING ON the edge of his cot cleaning his boots while he listened to the company's oldest sergeant, Truan Langwood, share a war story with some of the newer men. The young officer snorted as he heard the old soldier embellish his version of the Battle of Marker. He had heard Truan tell the story before, but it never seemed to amaze Mikhal how much better the tale became with each retelling.

"And there I was ... standing next to the commander. There were only a few other Erandian cavalrymen still alive. We looked out past the fog from the hill we were defending and saw nothing but our own dead and hundreds of the bodies of Belarnian infantry." He looked at each of the young men listening to him before he continued. "And as we counted the numbers of our dead, an ear-splitting sound pierced the fog. It was a Belarnian march-horn signaling the advance. From just beyond the limits of our vision, the sound of hundreds of horses could be heard approaching our position."

"And just how many Erandians were left on the hill?" inquired a young soldier.

"There were five of us left. And no one had a mount. We faced certain death at the hands of our enemy, and we were prepared to meet it. So, as they began to charge us, I turned to the commander and asked, 'Sir, what reward will you give me for taking their damned flag and presenting it to you?'"

Mikhal laughed as he watched Truan put a boot up on the edge of a cot as if he had just climbed the highest peak in the Mercies and planted an Erandian flag at the summit. "The commander looked at me seriously and said, 'Son, you grab that flag, and I'll give you a day off.'"

"A day off?" one soldier asked in disbelief. "Is that all?"

"That's exactly the same thing I said to him. And he replied, 'Killing the enemy is your job, cavalier, I expect no less of you than for you to do your duty at all times.'"

"So what happened? How did you escape them?"

"Well, let's just say that the next day I could be found enjoying my day off in the arms of one of the most beautiful women in Erand!" Soldiers throughout the hall cheered at his words. Alek Hienren had just arrived from the palace and added his own comments.

"Liar! I happen to know that you spent that entire day in the arms of your wife and she is definitely not beautiful." The gathered soldiers laughed and cheered for their commander, as well. Mikhal stood to greet his captain as he approached the crowd of soldiers. The other two officers quickly came over to their commander to see how the plans were coming along. Lieutenant Hanson, a tall and strong man from the southern plains of Erand, was recently accepted into the cavaliers from the regular army. He was always quick to point out the fact that he was from the south where men were born to be great warriors. Mikhal knew he was capable of taking on any soldier in the company, but he sometimes doubted Hanson's ability to lead without being rash. The other officer, Romlin, was the youngest of the four officers. His father was an advisor to the king and had at one time been a decorated cavalier. Romlin always pushed himself hard to be the best of all of them; he wanted his father to be proud of him. He was a capable cavalryman and would someday be a commander, but he tended to worry too much about what other people, especially his father, thought of him.

"Well, sir, what happened?" Hanson asked. Mikhal looked into his commander's eyes to see if he would tell them everything. Their commander had gradually withdrawn from his junior officers ever since the prince had almost gotten them killed in the Duellrian village. He still joked with them and the rest of the company and never neglected to correct them if they were doing something wrong, but lately he had stopped making fun of the king's son. Mikhal and the other officers had anxiously waited every evening while on the road to Duellr for their commander to sit with them and do his best impression of the prince. Obviously, even Alek's patience had worn thin. He was ready to ride home again.

"The treaty is final," Alek replied. "There will be a party to celebrate the unification of our kingdoms and the coming wedding of our prince to Princess Allisia." Mikhal and Hanson exchanged concerned looks when their commander added, "Yes, you are formally invited. And yes, you must go. So ensure that your dress uniform is taken out of your packs and get the wrinkles out. And make sure you take a bath tomorrow." Alek looked at Hanson to ensure the southerner understood. They all laughed while Hanson looked down at his boots, embarrassed.

"Indeed, I have heard that southern Erandians don't bathe as frequently as the rest of us. Is that true?" an unexpected voice asked from the doorway. The gathered officers and soldiers turned to see Kristian standing there with his arms crossed in front of his chest and a questioning looking on his face. Taken back by the prince's sudden entrance, Alek took a few moments to gather his thoughts before calling the barracks to attention. The commander quickly approached the prince, attempting to head him off while the rest of the company stood motionless.

"My apologies, Your Highness, had I known you wanted to conduct an in-ranks inspection, I would've prepared the men. I'm afraid they're not ready for you." Alek hated being caught like this. He had not done anything wrong, but he knew the prince would never understand. Instead, he was surprised to see the prince smile as he took off his gloves and approach the gathered cavalrymen. Alek followed the heir of Erand not knowing what to expect.

Mikhal and the other officers remained at rigid attention, looking straight ahead as Kristian approached their little group. They tried not to move, afraid of calling unnecessary attention to themselves. Kristian approached Hanson and looked straight into his eyes. The other two sighed as he passed them.

"Lieutenant Hanson, isn't it?" he asked. The man looked surprised, and it took him a moment to regain his composure and reply.

"Yes, sir," Hanson barked out, unintentionally revealing how nervous he was. Realizing how uncomfortable he was making them all feel, Kristian patted Hanson on the shoulder and turned to Mikhal.

"I've heard that the hard work you southerners are used to makes you more accustomed to your smell, but surely you'll bathe for the pretty girls that you'll meet tomorrow night? Otherwise, I fear that even my betrothed may run away." A few soldiers laughed and even Mikhal smiled before he remembered how much he hated the prince.

Hanson stared in disbelief as he realized he had become the brunt of another joke. The rest of the cavaliers remained at attention but became more relaxed as they saw a side of the prince they had never seen before. "Relax, gentlemen, please relax." Kristian said as he turned to Mikhal. "Actually, I came to say thank you to you, Lieutenant Jurander. You completed a challenging task in getting me here … I know how difficult I can be. Thank you." Mikhal was shocked and could think of nothing to say or do and could only nod. Kristian hesitated a moment, a genuine smile of respect and appreciation on his face, and then he moved on to the other soldiers.

As cavaliers began to relax their stance, Kristian moved from cot to cot shaking hands and chatting with them. Everywhere he went, cavaliers smiled or even laughed at the prince's comments. Mikhal looked questioningly at Alek who could do nothing more than stare at their prince and shake his head in complete disbelief.

Romlin tried to get in on the fun and walked up to Hanson handing him a bar of soap. "Here, you might need this one as well as your own." Fuming, Hanson grabbed the younger officer by the shirt and dragged him toward the door. Mikhal laughed and shouted encouragement to Hanson as the burly southerner took Romlin outside to teach him a lesson. "But everyone else got away with it!" Romlin shouted as he grabbed at the doorway, refusing to leave.

"Yes, but they outrank me. I can pummel you and not worry as much about punishment," Hanson replied as he ripped Romlin's grip from the door and took him outside.

Mikhal could hear Romlin pleading in the distance. "It was just a joke. I'll polish your boots. I'll clean your uniform."

7

A Royal Celebration

Kristian looked in the mirror and frowned. He had finally purchased garments from a tailor that Allisia had recommended, and he hoped the new clothes would impress her. The over-pleasing tailor assured him these clothes were designed after the most popular fashion in Duellr. The tight-fitting pants and billowy sleeves seemed a bit too feminine to the Erandian, but he wanted very much to win the princess over.

"Well, if this is what all the nobles of Duellr are wearing, then I will wear it, too," he finally told his reflection in the mirror. He had chosen black pants and a black leather vest to offset the less manly appearance of the outfit, though.

Now that Kristian was back in his room and had tried on the clothes, the only thing he saw as he looked in the mirror was a fool. He still felt out of place and uncomfortable, even with the personal touches he had added.

"She'll see right through me. She won't like the clothes, and she'll hate me even more for trying to be someone I'm not." Kristian cursed his bad luck. "Maybe they're right. Maybe I am an idiot." He knew how the cavaliers felt about him. Their feelings toward him would never change. Even if he continued to mind his manners, as Allisia had put it, Kristian was not sure the cavaliers would ever respect him the way they respected Alek or Mikhal.

His last conversation with Allisia immediately came to mind. Kristian was walking through the gardens late in the morning, hoping to catch her there again. He hoped to talk to her one more time before the celebration. She was there, sitting at the fountain and looking at the flowers floating in the water. Kristian felt a moment of hesitation, afraid to interrupt her. He was beginning to realize how different Allisia was, that she was more than just a beautiful woman.

She knew she was being watched and turned to smile at him.

"I hoped I would see you again before it was too late," she told him.

Kristian felt bold and said, "You are very beautiful, and I hoped to see you, too." He had tried to say it both as a compliment, after all she was stunning, and to put her at ease. His smile quickly faded as Allisia stood and frowned at him.

"I am glad that you find me attractive, but I hope that isn't the only reason you are agreeing to this," she warned him.

Kristian quickly shook his head. "That isn't what I meant."

Allisia raised an eyebrow, challenging him.

"I mean there is much more to you than just looks," Kristian added. Allisia smiled, enjoying her game at his expense.

She laughed and then said, "It's not about how I look that's important. My face doesn't reveal my true character. My mettle is demonstrated in my resolve and by my actions. I know I can be stubborn, but I think I'm also intelligent, reasonable, and forgiving … and my challenge is to get you see that."

"There must be something to that," Kristian replied, "because you are the only one that has ever wanted to be my friend."

"Maybe I'm looking beyond the handsome features at the true mettle within," she suggested.

He smiled, as he lay there, remembering what she had told him. Kristian truly wanted Allisia to be his friend; it was the only thing that mattered. He figured in his head, however, that by the way he was pushing her, she was just as likely to hate him by the time the party was over.

Kristian fell back on the bed and moaned, not knowing what to do about his appearance. "Hello, Your Highness, I'm Prince Idiot." He said mockingly as he rolled over and tried to hide under the pillow. Then he remembered the last thing she had told him; perhaps things were starting to get better. Anything seemed possible when he was around Allisia.

Frustrated with his own indecisiveness, he turned onto his side and looked aimlessly at the wall. The cavalry sword he had secretly gotten when he was a boy hung over the back of a chair next to a newer, jeweled saber. It was an old blade, having lost its high polished shine many years ago. Kristian had practiced with it every day as a youth. He had always taken pride in owning it. Kristian's parents never found out about the sword; he had hidden it from them since the beginning. He always kept it at the bottom of a chest and pulled the sword out only when he wanted to get away from everyone. Kristian smiled as he remembered those quiet moments practicing in the garden. It was one of his few fond memories as a boy.

He did not know why he had brought it along; maybe it was a small act of defiance against his father. No, that was not it, Kristian realized. The older sword reminded him of what he wanted to be. The jeweled sword his parents had given him would easily break during a battle, but the cavalry sword would hold up well during a duel. It was a plain-looking weapon, but its metal was strong. Kristian thought about Allisia's words one more time, agreeing with her. There was more to him then what he had so far shown those that knew him.

Making one last decision about his appearance, Kristian chose the older sword and headed for the door, leaving the more ornate saber behind.

MIKHAL PACED OUTSIDE THE THRONE room along with the other Erandian officers as they waited for their prince. They hated official ceremonies. They constantly felt the necessity to check their uniforms for faults. Although no one here would know if something was amiss, the fact that they would be scrutinized by Duellrian military officers, and perhaps even by some beautiful, young ladies, made them all feel uneasy. Romlin slapped Hanson on the back to let him know he was finished scanning him for wrinkles and dirt.

"If you just ruined my coat, I will take you back outside, Romlin," Hanson threatened. Offended, Romlin carefully backed away to let the big southerner cool off. Mikhal smiled as he watched the two make fun of each other. "You did do a good job on my boots, though."

Alek looked down the hallway again cursing under his breath. "Where the hell is he?" he demanded. His junior officers shrugged in ignorance. No one had seen the prince the entire day. All of them had decided it would be best to wait for their prince to arrive and lead them into the party. Prince Kristian was almost out of time. Waiting nervously, Mikhal looked down at his feet again to make sure there were no scuffs on his boots and then straightened out his gray dress coat.

It was decorated with gold-overlaid buttons down the center; Mikhal felt the cavalier uniform signified the simple and hard life they led while also showing everyone else they were skilled soldiers. He took great pride in caring for all of his equipment. Mikhal had spent the greater part of the morning polishing his saber, ensuring there were no fingerprints on the scabbard or blade. Fingerprints always seemed to lead to tarnishing on the polished metal and Mikhal could not stand a tarnished blade. Mikhal's sword was awarded to him by the commander of the cavaliers when he was selected to join the unit. All officers were awarded a saber upon their selection, so it was not that special, but to Mikhal, it represented his dreams coming true.

Mikhal was also awarded a red sash to tie onto his scabbard after proving himself a hero in a small battle on the border between Erand and Belarn. The sash was normally awarded only to senior officers who had shown a high level of dedication or bravery, and Mikhal took great pride in wearing it. He only wore it when attending special events like tonight and absently toyed with the material as he thought about the dance and, hopefully, some very pretty Duellrian ladies.

Mikhal spent most of his time as a young boy training for the opportunity to become a cavalier. He worked every night at his small town's granary to earn extra money. Mikhal saved everything he earned so that he could one day buy a horse. Once he found one he thought was perfect for him, Mikhal started every morning by riding and then grooming his new friend, Champion. Even while working, Mikhal daydreamed about riding down a villain while mounted on his new charger. Or he would dream of dueling with the leader of an opposing army for the Honor of the Cavaliers. Mikhal was often scolded for not paying attention to his chores. It rarely helped to wake him from his dreams. Someday, Mikhal knew he would be a cavalier and nothing else mattered.

Mikhal had no official military training when he finally joined the Erandian army. Starting out as a foot soldier, he worked hard to learn everything his sergeants taught him. He spent extra hours dueling with his instructors and constantly asked questions about military tactics, especially cavalry tactics. After serving only a year as an infantryman, Mikhal's commander had seen enough to know that he was an exceptional soldier and leader. Mikhal was commissioned as an officer in the service of the king of Erand after another year of studying with men his own age but from much higher classes of society. Mikhal's first assignment was back in the infantry, but he was quickly transferred to the cavalry. Mikhal finally realized his dream after two more years of hard work and training. He was screened for admission and welcomed into the cavaliers by a board of unit commanders.

The rest was a blur. Mikhal could not remember a single week he and his men were not patrolling the borders of Erand for at least the last eight months. Nothing else exciting happened after that small battle, yet he refused to let his men's training slacken. Mikhal's platoon trained hard six days a week, and the young officer was proud of them. He knew that if they ever had to fight again, no one would be able to stand against them.

Mikhal was startled out of his reflections by the approaching sounds of hurrying steps coming down the passage. Kristian entered the room with a rush of wind behind him that sent drapes flying.

Kristian simply nodded, cutting short their greetings, and said, "Okay, is everyone ready?" After the four officers nodded back to him, the prince straightened out his new clothes one last time, took a deep breath, and opened the doors to the sounds of courtiers and music.

Alek noticed that the throne room was specially decorated for the evening's celebration. Ropes of ivy intermingled with roses were wrapped loosely around the pillars that lined the walls. Bouquets of wildflowers that grew in the mountains surrounding Argathos were amazingly arranged around the many added candelabras. The candlelight was reflected off the glass dome roof and made the commander feel like he was walking toward the Gates of Heaven. Even the rugs that had been present the day before were removed, revealing a highly polished marble floor. The floor itself was a beautiful work of art. Various shades of blue marble had been placed in the center of the floor and were arranged to reflect the beauty of the Tarin Ocean. The blue colors swirled and faded to light green, perhaps representing the eastern coastline that was the foundation of Duellrian success. In the center, a golden sea serpent's head emerged between foaming waves.

Most amazing to them was the large window on the far wall. The stained blue glass spanned the entire side of the ballroom and reached up to the tall ceiling. The cavaliers stared in amazement at the palace's intricate details and beauty.

With Kristian leading the group, the five men walked past hundreds of courtiers toward the king of Duellr and his two children. Mikhal felt like everyone's eyes were on him instead of the prince. He tried to look professional but felt more like a stiff corpse that had just walked out of its crypt. Hoping that he was not making a complete fool of himself, he slowed his pace a little to calm himself. None of the officers had ever seen this many people gathered for a celebration before.

Hanson smiled as he looked over to his left and saw a large table full of food and wine. "At least this evening won't be a total loss," the southerner whispered.

The five soon arrived at the place where the king and his family were waiting. The king was dressed in blue and white satins with a wide green sash wrapped around his large middle. He smiled at the men as they bowed deeply in a gesture of respect. His son, Justan, looked too much like his father. The heir of Duellr was only a few years older than Mikhal, but instead of being fit, he looked like he had wasted most of his time eating and drinking. The king's son also smiled as he nodded toward the Erandians. These large men were soon forgotten by the Erandians as they looked at the princess. Allisia was wearing a silk gown that matched the color of her light green eyes. Her auburn hair was bound in several places by small white roses attached to ribbons that hung from her hair and gently rested on her bare shoulders. She tried to hide her embarrassment by playing with the bouquet of flowers she held in her hands. She pretended not to notice the stares of the men.

Kristian was stunned by her beauty, and he was sure that his lower jaw was about to hit the marble floor when he suddenly realized that none of the noblemen were wearing a style of clothes that even closely matched his own. His amazement at Allisia's beauty turned to embarrassment, and he lowered his eyes in shame. He felt like such a fool.

Allisia saw the prince's reaction and mistook it for disappointment in the way she looked. She, too, lowered her eyes fearing she and Kristian would never become close.

They were pulled from their sulking by the king who proposed a toast in honor of the two kingdoms that opposed Belarn. He also asked

God to bless Prince Kristian of Landron and Allisia to ensure their marriage would be filled with love and plenty of children. The Erandians were surprised to also hear the king give thanks to the cavaliers for their dedication in ensuring Kristian reached Duellr safely.

After drinking to the toast, Mikhal and the other two lieutenants slipped out of the king's circle and headed for the banquet table. Hanson almost knocked his friends over as he reached the food first, grabbing a platter in each hand. Romlin started to berate the bigger man for his unrefined manners, but something drew Mikhal's attention toward the gathered crowd. He had the eerie feeling that someone was staring at him, and he wanted to make sure there was no danger. Amid the dozen circles of men and women talking and laughing, he spotted a beautiful woman with blonde hair looking right at him. He could not tell how long she had been standing there, but it excited him, and he suddenly felt the urge to go to her. Before the young officer could move, the tall and slender woman smiled at him and gathered her red cloak tightly about her. She left the hall through a side door. Mikhal tried to follow, but he lost sight of her in the crowd. The woman was even more beautiful than Princess Allisia, and the cavalryman wished he had moved quicker to catch her before she left. He frowned in disappointment when he realized he probably would not see her again. Mikhal had never been in love before, and he had always had trouble relating to Erandian women. Even when he was a boy, he had been too shy to talk to girls. Now that he was twenty-two years old, he was still unable to feel comfortable around them. Mikhal was torn between two different classes of Erandian society … the one he was brought up in and the one he was forced into by his rank in the military. It was hard enough to understand how he was supposed to act around the other officers; it was impossible for him to figure out how to talk to women. Instead, Mikhal had focused his energy on training, but he often wished he had at least known one woman more intimately.

The distant sound of rolling thunder brought Mikhal back from his thoughts. *A storm must be approaching from off shore*, he thought, looking out the massive window toward the coastline. Sighing, he turned around to see Hanson threatening to pummel Romlin with a turkey leg if he did not stop nagging him.

"You eat as much as your cows," Romlin exclaimed pointing at the bigger man's plates of food.

"I have never owned a cow. I may look like a farmer, but my family is as noble as yours. And yes, I eat a lot, and if you don't shut your mouth right now, I will eat you!" The southerner raised the drumstick menacingly as courtiers turned toward the three to see what was happening.

"Both of you shut your mouths before I have you flogged. You're embarrassing us. Now act like the officers and *noblemen* you're supposed to be." Mikhal never used his rank to order his friends around, and he was not sure if they would listen to him, anyway. Mikhal was, officially, their superior and second in command of the company. It was important for them to realize this, in case anything ever happened to their commander. He was surprised and glad to see them both stop and lower their heads in silence. "That's better." Hanson put the drumstick back on his plate and continued to scan the table for more food.

"And Hanson, leave some food for the other guests," Mikhal added.

The king continued to receive his guests as he introduced his future son to his subjects. He was so happy about everything that he did not see Mikhal's mysterious woman approach to pay her respects. The woman became engulfed in her dark red cloak as she kneeled before the king, Kristian, Allisia, and her brother, Justan. Kristian sensed something was wrong as he continued to stare at the woman hidden underneath the red fabric. "I have come, king of Duellr, to pay my respects to you and the prince of Erand on behalf of King Ferral of Belarn." Lightning flashed above the glass roof as Kristian's eyes widened in horror at the impossibility of what he was seeing.

The beautiful woman slowly transformed, growing more than three times her original size. The cloak still managed to hide everything from their view, but it was obvious that the thing underneath was no longer the beautiful woman. Bulging muscles could be seen even through the thick fabric, and a deep hideous laugh filled the throne room.

The king was horrified and could not move. He could only stare at the looming figure that was rapidly approaching. In an instant, the monster had him. The demon grabbed hold of the king's head with one massive, clawed hand and twisted it fiercely until there was a loud snap. Before anyone could react, the demon pulled the king's head from his body and tossed it onto the blue marble floor. Blood sprayed all of those nearby including Kristian and Allisia. The courtiers screamed in panic and ran toward the doors as the king's headless body rolled down the dais. They did not know what was in the room with them but were certain their lives would soon be over.

The king's children were right next to the thing. Allisia stood frozen. She tried to scream, but nothing would come out between her tightly closed lips.

Struggling to overcome his shock, Kristian pulled his saber free and prepared to send the thing back to hell. The evil creature turned on him as he finally moved into action. It crouched within its cloak, preparing to attack; before it could spring, a loud clang spun the monster around. Alek stood over the king's dead body. He had used all of his strength to drive his blade through the creature, but when the blade hit the demon's scaly flesh, it shattered. The cavalry commander looked into the fierce yellow eyes and fell victim to the demon's ability to cast fear and doubt. He tried to move out of the creature's path, but his legs would not move. It swatted effortlessly at the captain sending him across the room. Then it turned its attention back to the prince of Erand.

Sweat ran down Kristian's face as he looked into the folds of the creature's hood. Although he could see nothing in there but an impenetrable darkness, he knew it was smiling at him. Kristian was paralyzed by fear. It bowed to him in a mocking gesture, laughing. Then, from its crouched position, Ferral's demon launched at him.

The monster's attack was stopped in midair by the thrust of a spear at its abdomen. The demon rolled away from Kristian lithely and sprang back up in a crouched position anxiously looking for the new attacker.

The hood had fallen back, revealing the demon's face. The monster was horrifying to look at, its face full of horns and scales. Its slitted yellow eyes were looking for the person that had interfered.

With a determined look in his eyes, Mikhal carefully maneuvered into a defensive position between his prince and the demon. He braced for another charge, holding what remained of the spear in his hands.

The demon hesitated, lowering its defenses as it looked at the young cavalry officer. For a moment Mikhal thought he saw the beautiful blonde woman again standing before him. It hesitated, unsure of what to do. The monster moved as quickly as storm clouds flying across the plains. The demon brushed Mikhal's side but did not kill him as it came at the prince. It knocked Kristian over and snarled at Allisia. She was in shock and paralyzed by fear, but as the demon stopped to look at her, she suddenly screamed in terror. The demon reached out and grabbed her arms.

"No!" Kristian shouted as he sprinted toward them.

Allisia fainted, and the monster scooped her up, running toward the stained glass window. The demon was about to crash through it, but then abruptly turned around to face Kristian. Its face contorted in pain, stretching back into a more feminine shape. It was hideous to watch, this transformation from hell spawn to beautiful woman, but it lasted only long enough for it to utter a few words. The demon's deep-throated voice was barely understandable.

"Do not attempt to follow. Do not attack Belarn. You have seen our power. Do not provoke us further," the demon warned.

It seemed as if that was as much control as the monster could muster. The demon's face quickly transformed back to the hideous mask of something from the abyss; it howled in anger before smashing the glass with its clawed foot. It readjusted its hold on Allisia's limp form and then plunged into the darkness.

Kristian and Mikhal reached the broken window a moment later, staring out into the stormy night. There was no trace of Allisia or the demon. Lightning flashed and thunder boomed as the two looked back at each other.

8

DELIBERATIONS

Mikhal sat slumped in a large oak chair within the council chamber. This was where the advisors informed the king of the problems the territories faced. At any other time, it would have been a privilege for him to be included among the men seated in the room, but after the attack, he could care less. After the murder of the king and the kidnapping of his daughter, the room was now being used to determine what should be done next. Alek sat next to him but was even less aware of his surroundings than his lieutenant. A bandage was wound tightly around his head. He tried to maintain focus on the problem, but ever since the demon had thrown him against a pillar, Alek had faded in and out of consciousness. The commander managed to order Romlin and Hanson back to the barracks to alert the men and prepare them for whatever orders might soon be coming, but that was as much strength as he could muster. Mikhal had started off with them as well, but Alek quickly stopped him and requested he stay in case he passed out again. The young officer was reluctant to sit in on such a meeting but decided that waiting for hours with the others in the barracks would be much worse.

Now he sat at a long polished table watching Duellrian officials argue with the Erandian prince about what to do. The kingdom's resolve to fight Belarn had significantly diminished with the death of their king. The councilors now argued that both time and deep thought were needed before committing to anything.

Kristian paced the length of the table, shaking his head in disagreement to the suggestions of the old men across from him. "No, no, no! We can't wait. Even now we are wasting time. As we debate about what to do, this demon is probably taking the princess to Belarn for who knows what purpose. I have only a small force with me, but I am willing to ride with them to free her. How can you calmly suggest we wait and see what this madman's plans are?"

The king's chief advisor stepped forward, trying to assure the prince. "My Lord, please understand. We have lost our king. His son is still in shock and unable to make such a heavy decision."

"He's likely cowering instead of taking on his responsibilities," Kristian replied under his breath.

Mikhal was disgusted with Kristian. The prince had continually insulted their hosts instead of trying to find a viable solution to their problem. He did not know what Kristian was thinking, but Mikhal thought he was too ready to attack with no real plan of what to do. Kristian seemed to have changed for the better in the last few days, at least toward the cavaliers. He was more open and concerned about the challenges of leading. *Maybe the positive change was the influence of the princess*, Mikhal thought.

Mikhal noticed that Kristian was even personable with the officers, and he began talking with Alek about the current affairs of Erand. The young officer and his captain both hoped their prince was finally coming around. Now, Kristian was even more bitter than before. He was quick to anger and even quicker to judge the actions of others.

Mikhal feared the demon's attack had permanently and irreversibly changed their prince. The cavalier saw how the prince had frozen when the monster looked at him. They did not know what Kristian had seen. Maybe it was his death or his inability to destroy the monster. Whatever the prince saw, it had left him feeling inadequate in some way. His failure was an insult to his sense of honor. *Perhaps,* Mikhal thought, *Kristian felt like a coward, and it was that feeling more than anything else that was driving him to encourage a hasty attack.* Mikhal feared the cavaliers and all of Duellr were about to march for the sake of his prince's honor rather than to save the princess.

"But how was I able to resist the demon?" Mikhal asked himself. Everyone commented how it had struck such a terrible fear into them that they could not move. Even Alek asked Mikhal if he had looked into the demon's eyes.

"I've never seen anything more terrible. Ever. It was like looking into the depths of hell," his captain commented. Mikhal had no answer. He had simply acted to save the prince by attacking the monster. Mikhal tried to remember the demon's eyes but could not. He did not remember anything terrible like Alek or Kristian. In fact, whenever Mikhal thought of the demon, he found himself thinking of the beautiful woman he had seen earlier.

"Besides," one old man attempted to point out to Kristian, "this direct act to destroy the entire leadership of our kingdom indicates to me that Belarn plans to attack us, very soon." Several other officials nodded in agreement. This time even Mikhal sneered in contempt. For Belarn to attack Duellr, they would have to either sail across the Forsian Sea and then along the Jennd River to Duellr or cross the largest kingdom in Erinia ... Erand. In either case, Duellr would not be surprised or overwhelmed by Belarn. These old fools were using their fears as an excuse not to act.

The advisors seemed relieved when the kingdom's highest ranking officer, Admiral Clarind, finally entered. The old seaman looked weary as he introduced himself to Kristian and his officers. His eyes reflected a doubt that Kristian did not understand. Finally lowering his eyes, he sighed and then turned to the table and spread out a large map of the eastern coastline and the adjoining territories to the west.

"I have twenty ships that can be ready by tomorrow evening. If we act now, we can reach far inland before the winter storms arrive." The gathered councilors gasped in shock as they listened to one of their own suggest they invade Belarn. They shouted in dismay, demanding to know on whose authority he planned this outrageous scheme. Duellr established a policy of non-involvement after their lands were devastated by the Kingdoms of Mesantia hundreds of years ago. As an active trader between the old and new worlds, they had learned to prosper without incurring the wrath of any kingdom that could someday come back and destroy them again. The people only supported the king in his initial decision to stand against Belarn because they believed they could get away with supporting Erand with just war materials and gold. They did not want to commit their own forces in a direct conflict, which might put them at odds with other kingdoms they traded with. Now, one of their most trusted and respected advisors was recommending their ships and men be used to attack another, more powerful, kingdom.

"The heir has completely left the decision to me. He is quite incapable of making any decisions on his own at this point, and I am afraid that even when he recovers, he still might not be able to act in time to save Allisia." The great seaman towered over the assembled men, his chin jutting forward, challenging the advisors to argue with him on his right to act on behalf of the new king. His eyes sharpened and seemed to regain clarity, and he wished he could smile. For years these politicians had delegated and deliberated, always opting to wait for further developments rather than take the initiative and act in the best interest of the kingdom. Admiral Clarind counted his navy as one of the finest in the world. They knew the waters between Erinia and Mesantia better than any other force. They constantly risked their lives crossing through terrible storms and defending their cargo against Mesantian pirates, and they rarely surrendered the latter to those who tried to steal it. He was outraged by the audacity of one evil prince who thought he could cripple a kingdom by killing its king and stealing their princess. He did not plan to let the king's death go unanswered, nor did he plan to leave the fate of the princess in the hands of these fickle fools.

Kristian's concentration began to waver, and his memory of what had happened when the demon attacked began to resurface. When the demon had come for him, he could not move. He wanted to, he knew what he had to do, but he could not move. Kristian was paralyzed with fear. If Mikhal Jurander had not acted quickly and bravely, the demon would have torn him apart as easily as it had killed the king. Kristian was embarrassed and ashamed of his inability to save Allisia. The acknowledgment made him angry, and he swore that he would find a way to fight back against the demon and the Belarnians. He owed it to Allisia and to himself.

Kristian also wondered what his father would think of all this. *Was he right, after all, about the threat from Belarn?* he asked himself. *Will he think his son somehow failed him?* Kristian wondered if there was anything he could have done different to help Allisia. Couldn't he at least have found enough strength to break the demon's spell so that Mikhal would not have had to save him? He was sure it made him seem like a coward to the young lieutenant.

He knew they were judging him; their eyes told him that he had not lived up to their sense of duty and honor. There was something to that, Kristian realized. He did not truly understand those concepts. They eluded him, and it was frustrating that others seemed to accept the terms so blindly. But his heart told him his anger and frustration were about more than just his slighted honor. Allisia was the closest thing to a friend that Kristian ever had. She was willing to give him a second chance when no one else, including his mother and father, were. The prince was not sure if his feelings for her were love, but there was something there to build on, and he did not want to lose her. Allisia deserved better than this, and he would continue to fight for her.

Admiral Clarind looked back at Kristian and his cavalry officers. "These ships are fast and capable of carrying all of your men and horses plus most of our army. If we sail tomorrow and head north toward the Jennd River, we should reach the Forsian Sea within a week. From there, we will move quickly to seize a port on the west side of the Forsian and land on Belarnian soil. Within two weeks, we can be at the gates of Belarn, tearing down the walls around that evil man's castle." Kristian nodded, admiring the man's boldness.

"Excellent. I'm sure that Captain Hienren and his men will be ready well before tomorrow morning." Kristian hesitated as he heard someone cough beside him.

"We have a small army in comparison to our ally, Erand. We do not have the power to attack Belarn on our own," one of the ministers told Clarind.

"Erand has thirty thousand soldiers that it will commit," Kristian promised. "I swear that my father will send them to reinforce you. Together we will remove the evil men responsible for this attack, and we will form a new government in their country. A government that will ensure peace and stability in the region."

"Are you sure Erand will send soldiers? It will be a bloody day for us if they do not," the minister declared. Everyone leaned forward eager to hear what Kristian would say, including the cavaliers.

"I speak for my king and my country. We will fight with you to get Allisia back," Kristian swore.

"Excuse me, Your Highness, but may I suggest something?" Mikhal asked, trying to keep his voice steady as he spoke to the gathered officials.

Turning to see what was wrong, Kristian saw the cavalier anxiously waiting for permission to speak. He quickly nodded for the officer to address the council, wary of what the cavalryman might say. "There is no doubt we can be ready by tomorrow, and the speed of your ships can't be matched by a forced march back through the mountains and Erand all the way to Belarn. But once we reach the Forsian, the cavaliers should disembark."

Kristian was about to dismiss the plan, but Mikhal continued before he could be stopped. "We should disembark for two reasons, Your

Highness. First, Brekia is only two days ride from the river. By sending a messenger to your father, he could be made aware of our intentions and possibly send reinforcements in case of a long siege. Second, and more importantly, the cavaliers could ride ahead of the main force and secure the port before the ships arrive. We can use surprise and speed to our advantage, saving many lives that would be lost in a battle at a hostile harbor. If the ships attempted to seize the port without the support of ground forces, the battle could turn disastrous." Mikhal finished his proposal looking first at his commander and then his prince for approval. Alek smiled weakly and nodded, impressed by Mikhal's quick thinking. The prince, however, seemed doubtful.

It was the Duellrian officer in charge of their army that influenced the acceptance of Mikhal's plan. General Aphilan nodded insightfully. He smiled as he saw the events unfolding in his mind. "Yes, it's a good plan. We will need to preserve our forces for taking Belarn. The quicker we take the port, the quicker we can reach the enemy's capital."

Clarind looked around the table at the other officials to answer any remaining questions. The feeble council members frowned and murmured, but they had lost the argument, and they eagerly waited to be released. He was about to dismiss everyone when the main door opened and the new king walked in.

Concern flashed across the faces of the Duellrians as they looked at the ashen and pale color on their new sovereign's face, King Justan the Eighth. Stumbling into the room, the new king looked around to see the faces of his father's aids. His eyes were bloodshot, and his hands trembled visibly as he approached the table. Leaning against the back of a chair for support, the young man swallowed to moisten his mouth before addressing them.

"It is true that I have authorized Admiral Clarind to act on my behalf in this matter." He smiled wanly at his father's friend. "I have come here to ensure that his judgment is not questioned on this matter. I have come to say that I will be going as well." The officials shook their heads in disbelief. Even the admiral felt it was not a good idea for the new king to accompany them. The seaman gently clasped his hand and urged him to reconsider as he moved closer to the grief-stricken man.

"My King, I understand your reason for wanting to do this. I know how much you want revenge, but the kingdom needs you to give them hope. I fear this is not the end of the bloodshed in Duellr. If you leave, no one will be able to stand up to those who would destroy us." The advisors and even Kristian and his officers nodded in agreement.

Color briefly returned to Justan's face as he chuckled at the thought of the kingdom's dilemma as his personal responsibility. "No, Admiral Clarind, you are wrong. You were a great friend to my father," he paused to steady himself, afraid that he might pass out, "but I'm sure everyone is aware that I am not fit to be king. Not now, maybe not ever. It was my father's hope that Kristian and Allisia's child might succeed him on the throne with me or even Allisia acting as regent until he was old enough to rule on his own. My father dreamed of a stronger kingdom able to influence the Old World and, thereby, increase our wealth and power. Now that Allisia is gone, it cannot happen, and that is why we must get her back safely. The kingdom will be best served by these officials until we return."

Turning to Kristian, he looked directly into the other man's eyes, judging the motives locked inside. "I loved my father and love my sister very much. I know I am not anything compared to you as a great leader … but please understand that I have to go with you. She is my sister."

Looking at Justan, Kristian could not help but see the poor young man trapped beneath the weight of his responsibilities. Justan was truly not fit to accompany them, and Kristian was concerned he would slow their progress down. He thought about Justan's right to see his sister rescued, and a part of Kristian urged him to accept the new king. Without knowing why, he shook his head in approval. Admiral Clarind reluctantly agreed.

The gathered assembly closed by shaking each other's hands and wishing them good luck. Mikhal and Alek were the last to leave the room. Mikhal felt a slight chill along his neck as they looked at the map that was still laid out on the table. The two seas, the Forsian and Utwan, took up much of the drawing. A black dot along the eastern coast of the Utwan made his stomach turn. It was Ferral's stronghold, Belarna. He quickly turned to help his commander back to the barracks. There was a lot to do before they sailed the next day.

9

NO ESCAPE

Allisia awoke slowly, finally escaping her nightmares. She forced her eyes open, afraid that she was still trapped in the darkness of her dreams. She tried to sit up, but a heavy weight kept her down. It was as if chains pinned her to the bed, but she finally started to realize where she was. She blinked several times to make sure her eyes were actually open, but everything was covered in darkness. Moving her hands across her body, she found that she was not bound by chains but by several layers of silk sheets. She was lying in a large bed, and by the feel of the material, she was not in a dungeon as she expected.

The light from a candle blinded her before she could discern more. Allisia heard, more than saw, a figure open a door across from her and quickly enter. The lone figure lighted more candles and then hesitantly approached the bed. Allisia's sight finally returned, and she began to see the slim and beautiful figure of a woman in a dark red robe. The woman poured water into a cup from a nearby pitcher and then turned and smiled at her reassuringly.

Allisia suddenly recognized her. It was the demon … her father's murderer. She screamed in terror, lashing out with her hands and feet, feebly trying to push the monster away. Smiling demurely, the demon raised a finger to her lips, commanding Allisia to silence. Allisia stopped screaming abruptly, afraid of what the demon might do if she disobeyed. The princess fought to keep her sanity as she cringed away from the monster on the far side of the bed.

The demon woman sat on the opposite side from her, smoothing out her red dress and cloak. Allisia wondered why the demon was so quiet now. It was completely different from the monster she had seen earlier, and it unsettled her. She began to question the terrible things that had happened as she looked back at the creature that had killed her father. The only thing she remembered from the previous night was the face of a beautiful woman with dark blue eyes and long blonde hair. And then the demon's hand had changed as it reached slowly toward her father. The delicate hand grew mangled and clawed, the skin turning a mottled gray. The hand rested on her father's head, the claws sinking into the skin near his temples. Effortlessly, the demon's hand twisted, snapping his neck. Allisia remembered hearing a soft pop and then there was blood everywhere. She remembered watching the woman bow deeply in a gesture of respect. That was a cruelty Allisia would never forget. She was terrified of the creature, but the demon woman appeared to be calm and unthreatening. The monster handed her the glass of water, urging her to drink.

"It was a long journey here for you. Drink the water. It is not poisoned," she said calmly. She looked expectantly at the princess waiting for her to do as she was told. Allisia looked hesitantly at the water before deciding; poisoned or not, she was thirsty. *Perhaps dying from poison might be better anyway,* she thought. She quickly drank the water, finding she was even thirstier than she imagined. The empty cup was clenched between her hands as she looked distrustfully at the demon.

"It was not easy for me to do. You will not understand that, but I do not expect you to understand." The demon woman leaned closer to the princess, sending cold chills through the young girl's body. Realizing she was unsettling Allisia, the demon slowly backed away. "I think you will find your accommodations are not as bad as they could be. You will, of course, be locked in this room, and there are guards right outside the door." The demon saw Allisia quickly look toward the window, and she added, "They are barred, and we are hundreds of feet above the courtyard. Escape is impossible. Do not bring down harsher punishment upon yourself by trying anything foolish." The demon stood, turning one last time to look at the young princess. She smiled and said, "And do not try to harm yourself. The place where you would go is much worse than this."

She glided back across the room and shut the door behind her. Allisia could hear the lock fall into place and was certain she was trapped with no hope of escape.

THE NEW KING OF BELARN paced across the dais, constantly looking toward the door behind the throne. He had sent the demon to the princess's chamber to check on her condition. He was unsure what affect her health would have on his plans, but he thought it better to ensure her well-being, for the moment, than to kill her. Ferral was initially exhilarated by his newfound powers in the black arts, but he was reluctant to experiment further. The sorcerer-king simply did what the demon advised him; he was afraid he might destroy himself by abusing the magic he had been given. That restraint was quickly eroding.

The demon, in its grotesque warrior form, was incapable of logical thinking; the monster served only one purpose. It had been given strength to destroy whatever got in the way, and it fed off the fear of its victims, giving it even more power. The demon, in woman form, was a schemer and was constantly calculating the outcome of events. The beautiful creature devised a plan that she assured Ferral would prevent Duellr from aiding Erand. The red robed woman promised that with the deaths of Duellr's royal family and the heir to Erand's throne there would be no one left in the world capable of preventing him from mastering the powerful magic he sought or from conquering Erinia. Things did not appear to have gone according to plan.

Ferral had made a few changes in the citadel while the demon was gone. Belatarn was re-established as the official religion. The One God priests quickly vanished as did many others that opposed Ferral's actions. The purge was necessary. Belarn would become strong again if it followed the old ways, the mad man assured them. He had waited anxiously for the demon to do what it had promised. Ferral waited an entire week, growing more impatient. When the demon returned, it was furious that things had not gone well. The monster went on a rampage, killing two guards as soon as it entered the palace.

Later, the woman had calmly reappeared to inform him that her mission had not been completely successful. The king of Duellr was dead, and the heir was so dumbfounded by the tragic death of his father that he was incapable of leading his kingdom. However, for some reason that the demon woman did not offer, the prince of Erand still lived. In fact, he would most likely raise an army to move against Belarn very soon. Ferral was unable to control his anger. If they came too soon, he would not have the time he needed to prepare for the next ritual. The demon promised him even greater powers if he sacrificed the princess and moved his army out to destroy the lands of Erinia.

The demon woman reassured him, "You will have the ability to raise the army you need to destroy anyone that dares interfere with your plans. Our Master will be especially pleased with you when you offer the princess as a pledge of your eternal servitude."

Ferral instantly moved to prepare for the princess's sacrifice, but the demon stopped him. Ferral would have to wait. Belatarn would tell him when to kill her.

Reluctantly, Ferral agreed to wait, in order to appease his god. He still remembered the demon woman's puzzled look after he mentioned their god's name. When he repeated the name, she smiled knowingly and left to check on the girl saying, "Call him what you will."

Now, Ferral paced the throne room floor, anticipating her news. He also worried about what he would do if Kristian's army arrived before it was time to sacrifice Allisia. He had not easily won over the leaders of Belarn's army. Most of the generals had mysteriously vanished one evening after telling him they would not marshal their soldiers to fight Erand. It took him two weeks to regain control, placing trusted leaders from his personal Black Guards unit into key positions within the army. They were now ready to march, but he was unsure about what they could accomplish. If he ordered the attack against Erand now he might succeed in destroying his enemy, but his capital would be left defenseless against Kristian's forces.

"However, leaving them here may prove just as disastrous," he said out loud. He knew his own men were no match for the better-trained Erandians. If he wanted to see his plans come to fruition, he would have to destroy his enemies by using his new powers and the element of surprise. Finally, he shrugged, deciding to do nothing for the moment.

Except with Allisia. He smiled, thinking of the pleasure he would have in toying with her mind. She would remain alive until she was called for by his god even though she would beg for death.

Still walking back and forth, he did not notice his wench, Rebenna, move past him to drop down on the throne. "I think you are misled. The demon woman calls no one master and will destroy us. Kill her. Kill her now, before it is too late," Rebenna demanded. She smiled as Ferral finally noticed her.

Quickly moving to her side, he grabbed her by the wrists and flung her down the steps of the dais. Fuming, he pointed a single finger at her and warned, "Do not push me, Rebenna. I am more powerful now than you ever thought possible. You are here because I allow you to be. Do not assume to be in my confidence any longer." His eyes reinforced the threat, but Rebenna would not give up. She crawled seductively across the floor toward him.

"But my love, it was me who foresaw your coming to power all those years ago. I have been your constant guide. Will you throw me away now after everything I have done for you? What I can still do for you?" She slowly stood up and approached the king. Throwing an arm over his shoulder, she kissed him. "Have you forgotten how well I please you? I have given you everything I have to help you."

"I have not forgotten what you showed me," Ferral murmured as he smiled, "but answer me this then, Rebenna. What good are you to me now that I have everything you had to offer? I warn you, be careful or you will be lucky to remain as a servant girl."

Laughing, he motioned toward a dark corner of the throne room where a single figure stood constantly waiting for her master to give her an order. Incapable of rest, never to be released, the beautiful girl with pale features and raven hair stood as still as a statue. She sensed that her master was using her as an example. Standing motionless in the dark shadows, the servant girl tried to move. She tried to run away, scream, cry … anything that would set her free from her curse, but she knew it was futile. She had been trapped in her body for what seemed like an eternity, and there was no hope of ever escaping.

10

QUEST'S BEGINNING

The armada was large. Twenty-five Duellrian corsairs, in close formation, were heading north. They were sleek fighting ships used to patrol the coastal waters in search of pirates. They had twin masts, one slightly taller than the other, and a total of three massive sails that caught the wind and pulled the ships through the water with ease. Three towers broke the silhouette of the hull, at the fore, midship, and aft parts of the ship. Each tower could hold five bowmen or a small catapult. The ships were long and maneuverable and were designed for close quarters combat, but they would work just as well carrying the Duellrian army. More than the navy's ships were needed, though. The massive army, with its food supplies and war materials, required many more vessels to carry them on their journey. Admiral Clarind had several merchantman ships drafted into service. They had larger holds for the men, horses, and supplies. They could not maneuver in the way the corsairs did, but they did not have to. The navy was out front of the rest of the fleet to protect them from any other surprises Ferral might have.

The river that was only a short distance north of the Duellrian capital would lead them into the interior of the Erinian continent. The Jennd River was wide and deep, and Admiral Clarind had no reason to believe their journey would be delayed.

Kristian and his one hundred cavaliers and ten thousand Duellrian soldiers now waited anxiously for the voyage to end and the invasion of Belarn to begin.

KRISTIAN STOOD AT THE BOW of the fourth ship in the formation, looking past the gloomy mist and sleet toward land. He strained his eyes to catch glimpses of the mountains that guarded the mouth of the Jennd River, waiting impatiently for the fleet to turn inland. For two days, the combined forces of Erand and Duellr had sailed north along the coastline toward the river. The first day proved to those that doubted the speed of the vessels that they were going twice as fast as the army could have moved on foot. The Duellrian ships with their tall masts and large sails had caught the prevailing winds and cut the waters like finely honed blades. Hopes were high among all the men on Kristian's ship, and he felt certain they would succeed. He was unsure of himself, but he knew the cavaliers and the Duellrian army would be more than a match for Belarn. His only concern was for Allisia; she had to be saved.

"Ferral will hang for what he has done," he promised.

The second day, however, had shown them just how bad things could get. With the rising of the sun, dark, ominous clouds swiftly moved over the mountains from the west and out onto the ocean like a wall of malice that struck the ships with immense force. The storm was cold and foreboding. Strong winds and hail slammed into the ships without warning, forcing the crews to tighten the sails and double the personnel on deck. The waves became so turbulent that three men were needed to hold the wheel and keep Kristian's ship on course.

Unaccustomed to life at sea, Kristian and many of the cavaliers became ill. Retching over the side, Kristian wished Admiral Clarind would bring the ships into shore to wait out the storm, but the old sea-man had faced storms like this before, and he was determined to make up for the time they were losing. Clarind's only concern was that he had never seen cold winds blow directly out of the west before.

Normally, the winter winds came from the northwest carrying infrequent blizzards down onto Erinia. He feared this storm was the precursor to a harsh winter, and it was still two months before the changing of seasons.

By nightfall, the storm's fierceness had not abated. Sleet made the decks slippery, and choppy waters splashed over the railings, soaking Kristian as he tried to make it back to the main cabin from his spot at the bow. More than once he had worried he would be tossed overboard by the wind and water. He had never seen a storm at sea before, and this one was bad enough to make him pray he would never see another. He forced himself towards the stairs that lead to compartments below, clinging to the support lines running from the sails to the railings. Finally reaching the large cabin at the stern, he fell into a chair to catch his breath.

"Your Highness, I know this weather is exhilarating, but I recommend you stay below before you are thrown over the side of the ship," Alek suggested as he handed Kristian a cup of wine. The cavalry commander had recovered well in the last two days. The rest that had been forced on him by being a passenger below decks had improved his health. He would be fully recovered by the time the cavaliers were needed. The prince smiled as he tried to make light of their situation.

"Oh, you know how it is. I was trying to order the storm to stop, but it was being as insubordinate as you." Kristian downed his cup of wine and sighed as he grabbed a blanket to huddle in. His mood grew darker as he looked at the swaying lamps above his head.

"This storm is never going to end. It's harassing us, keeping us from reaching Belarn. And at this speed … damn Ferral. This is his work. The man has no concept of honor. When we finally get our hands on him, we'll teach it to him as he hangs from the walls of his own city."

Mikhal was sitting quietly in the back of the room. *Who speaks like that anymore? Talking about honor as if it were something real and tangible,* Mikhal asked himself. *Honor is something you do, not something you talk about.* He sneered at the prince's back, but kept silent.

Mikhal wondered if anyone really understood honor. Certainly neither the sorcerer they were about to attack or Prince Kristian seemed to understand nor care. On the one hand, Ferral might disregard any concept of honor to destroy them all, and Kristian might lead them to certain death in the name of it. Mikhal's prince had done little but complain since the storm descended upon them, and his foul mood was beginning to infect the rest of the cavaliers. He hoped the storm would subside soon if for no other reason than to shut the prince up.

Kristian tried to lighten the mood again and get to know the cavaliers better, but he could see the scowl on Mikhal's face. There was an uneasy silence in the room until Kristian decided to get some sleep.

The storm finally broke on the third morning of their travel north. The winds calmed and the waters smoothed, allowing the Duellrian ships to once again cut through the waters toward the Jennd River. The cold temperatures did not leave, however, making work above decks unpleasant and fouling everyone's mood.

Clarind's concern over the early winter provided great insight into the origins of the sudden storm. No one knew exactly what Ferral was capable of, but most sailors and cavalrymen were quick to associate their bad luck with the sorcerer.

Most people throughout Erinia believed ancient Belarn's religion had nearly caused the world's destruction. Whether the worshippers knew it or not, they were in control of very little. The Master of Demons was cunning and could easily twist words and their meaning. They turned their backs on God, thinking they could worship false ones and gain power over others. The Evil One promised them many things in return for their loyalty. Once they were under his sway, he subverted their beliefs even more. He called himself Belatarn and demanded sacrifice as a tribute to his authority over the elements. By offering their own people up to this false god, the people of ancient Belarn believed that Belatarn would ensure great harvests, that commerce

within the kingdom would bring great profits, and that the enemies of
Belarn would be destroyed.

To justify their acts to the people, the priests did not call them sacrifices. People were executed for minor infractions, things that were
easily tolerated in other societies and religions. Not so, with the zealots
of Belatarn who twisted every good thing into something wicked. No
one was safe from the nightly patrols that broke into people's homes
and stole innocent youths for the sorcerers' ritual sacrifices. The killing
was about power and magic and subjugation. It had little to do with
religion.

In the end, mighty Belarn was reduced to rubble by civil war. Perse-
cution by the priests that ruled the kingdom caused many people to flee
the once-proud land. Those that remained were religious fanatics that
cruelly subjugated those too weak to resist. Three hundred years later,
Belarn was finally beginning to show signs of improvement. The kingdom settled most of its border disputes with Erand, and after several
battles, their people were content with a newfound peace.

Unfortunately, there were a few who still believed that Belarn had
been a great power in the new world when it had followed the edicts of
Belatarn. Ferral had beaten most dissenters into submission quickly after murdering his father. Although the majority of the subjects did not
like the resurrection of the long-dead religion, it seemed that Belarn
was destined to send Erinia into chaos once again.

What was worse for those on board was that they remembered
the tales from when Belarn dominated most of Erinia. They shared
the tales passed down from their ancestors. They heard that some of
the priests had controlled the winds much like it seemed Ferral was
doing now. The cavaliers were so passionate about their ancient enemy,
they seemed to remember battles with Belarn as if they had been there.
They remembered how the priests used mists, lightning, hail, and worse
to disrupt the plans of the Erandian army. Those abilities had given
Belarn the advantage they needed to defeat the armies that opposed
them. That was how the Belarnians decimated the Erandian army, and
that was why the cavaliers were created. They constantly patrolled the

borders, forcing the enemy back, until internal strife within the black citadel made the Belarnians weak. Then the Erandians attacked and overcame the followers of Belatarn.

None of the cavalrymen remembered hearing anything mentioned about summoning demons from hell, though. Fear soon spread through the ranks of both the Erandians and the Duellrians as they continued on towards the citadel that had spawned the demon that invoked hysteria and fear into every soldier aboard the fleet.

Sometime before noon, the lead ship arrived at the mouth of the Jennd River. Snow-covered mountains guarded the entrance, the massive ridges rising up into the clouds confusing those that looked at the granite obstacles. The glaring whiteness of the snow and the overcast sky blended so that it was impossible to see where the mountains ended and where the clouds began. A small fishing village lay nestled in a cove close to the river. The huts were also covered with snow, the villagers frantically trying to uncover their boats before it was too late to get on the water and catch anything.

Kristian watched the villagers from his spot in the forward tower, wondering how easy their lives were compared to his. He was beginning to regret his often-hasty comments to his men. He knew his foul mood was having an impact on everyone around him, but he justified his poor manners by blaming it on the storm. Now that the storm had finally passed, he hoped his anger would subside as well.

Instead, he grew even more impatient. They were making far better progress by ship than they would have by land through the winter storm, but he felt a growing sense of urgency rising within him. He feared that if they did not reach Ferral soon, they would be too late to stop the madman from harming Allisia.

How were they to save her anyway? he wondered. *What if he threatened to kill her to prevent them from attacking his fortress? What if she were already dead?* Kristian had no other choice. He would not sit back and do nothing. She was the closest thing he had to a friend, and she was his fiancée. Kristian looked again at the villagers struggling to free their skiffs from the snow and ice that froze them to the beach and wished he was there shoveling with them rather than wasting away on the ship.

The next morning, the Duellrian fleet left the eastern mountains behind them as they entered the northern part of Erand. Progress was good despite the occasional blocks of ice that needed to be avoided. As Kristian and the cavalry officers looked out at their homeland from the upper deck, it was easy to see the storm was even worse on the open plains. Normally, during this time of year, farmers would be working hard to bring in the last of their harvests. Not a single field was visible. There was little hope of salvaging the crops, everything was covered in snow. It was even difficult for the Erandians to pick out the homes they knew should be close to the river. The faint trail of smoke drifting up from a large pile of snow suggested entire homes were covered by the blizzard. The cavalrymen were dismayed by the unnatural storm that had apparently blanketed most of Erand. Many worried for their families and friends as they passed desolate plains.

If Ferral is capable of sending as destructive a storm as this, then what will he have in store for us when we try to tear down his walls? Mikhal thought as he stared in dismay at the area he grew up in.

Their ship suddenly tilted away from the Erandian countryside as the pilot tried to avoid colliding with a large slab of floating ice. "I've never seen ice on the Jennd before," Hanson commented as he watched the ice barely miss the hull. Romlin looked at him; Hanson's realization had been the single thought on all of the officers' minds as they continued to look for signs of life along the river.

"Aren't your parents from this part of Erand, Mikhal?" Hanson asked, turning away from the snow-covered land.

"Yes," Mikhal replied worriedly. He did not know what else to say. His parents did live near here. He strained his eyes to see his parents' home but knew it was too far away to see even if the weather was clear. His father, like so many others in this region, would have been frantically working to bring in as much of the harvest as possible before it was destroyed. He also knew that nothing would have kept him from his crops. He only hoped he had saved enough of the wheat to finally give up and seek shelter.

"I'm sure they're all right," Alek offered to his distraught friend. Mikhal nodded as he continued to stare south toward his home.

That night, Kristian leaned against a railing at the bow of the ship. He looked up at the night sky, hoping to see some stars, but the mist was so thick that it was too difficult to even see the southern shoreline. They tried to stay as close to the shore as possible in case they came across any Erandians with news. So far they had not seen anyone. The amount of snow that had fallen in just a few days was hard to comprehend, and the cold was a bitter cold. It was the kind of cold that could kill a man if he was not well clothed.

"I pray you are safe," Kristian said aloud, wondering what his feelings for Allisia really were. She was a friend, and he desperately clung to the idea that she might be more than that. He needed her.

Kristian was so lost in his thoughts that he did not hear Alek approach him from the main deck. The captain had regained some of his sense of humor now that he was recovered from his injuries. He came to a stop a short distance from the prince and saluted.

"My Lord, I have come to report that the cavalrymen are about to revolt."

Kristian turned to look into the captain's eyes. Shocked by the message, he was unsure of what to say. "What? Are you sure? Why? I don't understand," Kristian stammered as he moved closer to his captain.

"Yes, Your Highness, you see the men are accustomed to the magnificent meals prepared by their own cooks out in the open. They want meals that include something other than what has been caught in fishing nets. Now, I know what you are going to say. 'These men are cavaliers!'" Alek said mockingly in a grand gesture. "I, myself, have attempted to put down this mutiny by crushing those responsible for the outbursts. I have also had my officers set the example for the rest by eating everything prepared for us. I felt this act would be sufficient to quell any uprising, but when Hanson became ill after eating some evil sea creature with more legs than he could count, I began to see that there could be only one solution to the current situation." The captain took a long breath, signaling he was done with his report.

Kristian smiled as he finally caught on. He knew the food served on the ship was awful compared to what they were used to eating, but he could not think of anything witty to say.

"What am I to do?" Kristian asked, playing along.

"I know of only one way to defeat this rebellion," Alek said in quick response. "You must come with me and eat the remaining legs on Hanson's plate, thereby, proving to the men they can survive this ordeal."

Alek grabbed Kristian's arm and started pulling him toward the galley. Kristian let out a small laugh as he followed the cavalryman below. He tried to put thoughts of Allisia and Ferral aside just for a little while.

"But I finally got my stomach back. If Hanson failed to eat it, I doubt I'll even be able to keep it down."

"Nonsense, Your Highness. It will be difficult for you, I know, but that is the challenge of leadership. You must bear your responsibility like a true cavalryman."

Kristian smiled as they descended the steps leading below the main deck, and he hoped his mood might lighten just for a little while.

"Just promise me, you will not share our concerns about the food with the admiral. I would hate to be forced overboard in these cold waters."

There was a true smile on Kristian's face. It was something Alek rarely saw. The commander decided he liked seeing it and hoped his prince's good mood would stay awhile even though he knew it could not. Kristian's concern for Allisia was easy for Alek to see.

THE FOLLOWING MORNING WAS FRIGID. Admiral Clarind's lead ship continued to navigate the ice floats that were beginning to jam the river when a spotter shouted that there was a rider approaching from the south. The man was on a stout horse and carried a spear and shield.

"Hey there! What news from Erand?" a sailor on the bow asked him.

"I have a message for Prince Kristian from the king," the man called back.

Alek heard the man shouting and came closer to the side rail. "What company are you from, soldier?" he challenged.

"I am from the Drakes, not that it's any business of yours. Who are you?" the cavalier shot back.

"I'm Captain Alek Hienren of the Charger Company, and I can't believe that a Drake, even a messenger for the Drakes, would ride a plow horse like that," the company commander responded loudly.

The messenger shrugged. "My horse froze to death last night. If I hadn't found this fat one, I never would have made it here in time. I need to speak quickly with Prince Kristian. Is he with you?"

"I'm here," Kristian called out, climbing up from below decks. "Do you have word from my father?"

"I do, Your Highness. He says, 'The Belarnian attack on Duellr is an open act of war against Erand even though the treaty was not sealed.' He received news of your decision and supports it. He will muster every available unit to move south around the Forsian Sea and meet you at Singhal as quickly as possible," the messenger reported.

"Why doesn't he send the force by boat?" Kristian asked.

"There are no boats," the cavalier replied. "They were destroyed in the storm. You have to understand how much damage this storm has caused us. The army does not have enough supplies to sustain a long march. The blizzard hit us a week before most farmers planned to harvest their crops. It looks like only the southern provinces were spared, and it will take time to get things sorted out."

"We don't have time," Alek shouted back in frustration. "Send out the cavaliers ... we'll need the cavalry support if we're going to have any chance." Kristian looked at him thankfully; it was the first time the commander had said anything to support him.

"I will ride back immediately and give the king your request," the rider promised.

"How long do you expect it to take the army to reach Singhal?" Kristian asked.

"The commanders' conservative estimate is one month," he answered.

"One month!" Kristian shouted in disbelief. "We don't have a month."

"They will push harder than that, Your Highness, but that was the estimate I was told to give you. You will receive regular updates once you reach Singhal."

"Is there anything else?" Alek asked as their ship began to edge away from the shoreline.

"Yes, the king is sorry for your loss. Even though you did not know each other well, he understands that this must be hard for you. He says he misses you and looks forward to seeing you in Singhal. The king will meet you there and together you will bring justice to the Belarnians. Wait for him in Singhal. Do not make a hasty attack. Your father doesn't know if Allisia is alive, but he is certain that rushing in too quickly would not be wise. He warns you to be wary of Belarnian treachery. They will fight in a way that takes advantage of Ferral's new powers."

Kristian threw up his hands in frustration. "Another lecture," he grumbled. "I'm not even at home, and he still manages to lecture me."

"It's sound counsel, Your Highness. Please heed your father's advice," Alek urged. Kristian sighed and then nodded.

The prince waved to the rider, "Thank you. Tell my father we will be at Singhal within a week. We will wait, if we can," Kristian called. "Ride safe."

The cavalier held a hand up high and shouted, "Draaaaaaaaaaakes!"

Alek grinned and nodded in farewell. The cavalier spurred the farm horse on and rode toward the capital. The commander then turned to Kristian. "Your father is right. We'll need their support at Singhal in order to face the enemy at Belarna."

"But we don't have that much time," Kristian insisted. "Allisia doesn't have that much time." He stepped away from the rail and began his frantic pacing again. "And did you hear what my father was really saying? He was telling us to go it slow because he thinks Allisia is already dead or beyond hope."

"Deal out vengeance together," Kristian laughed. "I bet he's thinking more about how we will split up Belarn after the war than what we'll need to do to save Allisia."

Alek approached him, raising his hands to calm his prince. "Please listen to me, Prince Kristian." Kristian stopped pacing and waited impatiently for the commander to continue.

"I don't know how much hope there is for the princess. You saw what the demon could do. It will take a hundred men or more to bring it down. It could have killed her as soon as it flew out the window," Alek said softly.

"And we don't know what Ferral plans to do with her. He could use her as a human shield or kill her while we try to tear down the gates."

"This whole endeavor is for her, Captain," Kristian reminded him. "If we only wanted revenge, we could all take as much time as we wanted and starve them out, but I don't believe she's dead. If the demon or Ferral wanted her dead, they could have done that the night of the ceremony. She's waiting for someone to come. I hope she knows that I would not hesitate to come." Kristian admitted with a resolve that surprised Alek.

"I just don't want you to build up your hopes and then become heartbroken. You will need to be calm and levelheaded if you are going to lead us into battle," Alek claimed.

"Lead you," Kristian repeated, questioningly. "I can't lead you."

"Shouldn't a prince lead his men into battle?" Alek asked. "The company will protect you. I promise that you are our first priority."

"It's not that. I am not afraid of fighting." Alek raised an eyebrow but waited for Kristian to continue. "I thought you and your men hated me," Kristian admitted.

Alek nodded, thinking carefully about what to say next. "You certainly have your days," he said smiling. Kristian smiled back in agreement. "But you're our prince. Even the worst Erandian prince is a thousand times better than a Belarnian one." Kristian laughed until he began wondering what Alek really meant. Alek got the reaction he hoped for. He excused himself and went below decks to get warm.

FIFTY MILES TO THE SOUTH, along the coast of the Forsian Sea, far beyond anything the cavaliers could see, dozens of fires engulfed Brekia, the capital of Erand. People screamed in horror and pain as their city was reduced to charred rubble. Hundreds died in the first few hours of the massive inferno. Those in the army that had not perished in the fires that erupted from several places at once, like a coordinated attack, fought to save their king. Several servants reported seeing a large fireball slam into the side of the tower the king slept in.

Trapped in his private chambers by the intense heat of the fire, the only thing King Emerick of Landron could do was open the doors to his balcony. The old king gasped for air and then looked below to his faithful servants who were desperately trying to push past the flames. Emerick considered jumping to escape the heat and smoke like many others had done, but he knew it was a futile attempt. It was just a different way of dying. An explosion deep in the city echoed through the king's room as he looked over the ruin of his capital. It was the worst devastation any had ever witnessed in modern times.

Whole sections of the city were on fire. The winter winds whipped the flames into a fury. They towered over the tallest church steeples, twisting and turning like fiery serpents. The heat was so intense that hundreds of people were incinerated a block away from the fire. Many more perished in the collapsing buildings. The injured and dying were trying to get out of the city, but there was no place to run. The frigid temperatures would soon kill many of them.

Feeling despair wash over him, he walked back into the scorching heat of his chamber and lay down on the bed. He shook his head in grief and wiped tears from his eyes as he thought about all of the accomplishments his countrymen had achieved. Within a few short hours, everything had been destroyed.

"How could this happen?" he asked God in disbelief. Suddenly thoughts of Kristian flooded his mind. Emerick wondered if his son was alright. Wherever Kristian was, Emerick hoped he was safe. Reflecting on the past and his troubled relationship with his angry son, the king wished he had spent more time with him. Kristian would have to learn on his own now. Most of all, the king wished he had one last chance to tell Kristian that he loved him.

"Please, Lord, watch over my son. Make him the leader he will need to be to save our people." King Emerick of Landron closed his eyes to shut out the heat.

From below the balcony, soldiers and servants tried one last time to rush through the flames to save their beloved king. Several fell crying in pain as their bodies began to burn. Suddenly, a rumbling sound grew from inside the palace. The grand building collapsed, the ground underneath the rescuers trembling. The tower fell in on itself. First the roof and battlements fell. Their massive weight tearing through reinforced floors. As the added weight and momentum continued to fall down, floor upon floor, the outside walls simply sagged in and fell. Hundreds were still trapped inside. There was no chance for them to escape the wreckage. Dozens of rescuers were crushed by the falling rock, smoke, and dust engulfing those that ran screaming from the royal grounds.

The blaze continued well into the evening, killing thousands of Erandians. By then, those that had survived watched from several miles away along various roads leading away from Brekia. Even from their distant vantage points, the survivors could feel the heat of the inferno. Finally turning their ash-covered faces away from the destruction, the remaining citizens of the greatest capital in Erinia moved on to seek cover before the harsh cold of the night killed them. With no food or water and few possessions, their chances of survival looked very grim.

Hours later, one person still remained on a hilltop overlooking the skeletal structures of the once great city. Cloaked and hooded by a dark red robe, she was little more than a shadow. She lifted her head to the sky, pulling her hood down to feel the cold wind on her face. The demon let out a sigh of utter sadness as she looked at the stars that could still be seen among the storm clouds. She had endured her punishment for a thousand years. And after all of those years, the demon still wondered what her life must have been like as a mortal.

She looked up to heaven, her eyes hinting at the forgiveness she desired … but she would not beg for help again. She knew that for the rest of eternity, she would be used by Evil to cause death and destruction. She only wished that this would all be over soon. The demon lowered her gaze from the stars and replaced her hood in shame and then moved back toward the city. There was one final thing that needed doing this night … Ferral would want proof. Then she would rest and try to forget.

11

THE CAVALIERS

The horses stamped their hooves impatiently. Men looked about nervously, checking their gear to make sure everything was prepared for the assault. Some of them patted their mounts' necks reassuringly, lost in the thoughts all men have before they are about to face death; others simply talked to forget their fears. Even Mikhal tried to fight the anxiety rushing up within him as he went from soldier to soldier inspecting them one final time. He had checked them all many times already, but he could think of nothing else to do while they waited for the signal. Mikhal and his men were responsible for securing the docks before the Belarnian guards were alerted. That meant rushing through the town's gate and down the main street in a race to see who could get there first. It was the riskiest part of the attack, but it was Mikhal's plan, and he could not let his friends volunteer for it.

To successfully enter the town, someone had to first open the gate; Singhal was protected by a large wall, and every entrance was protected. That would be Hanson's job. His men would dismount and climb over the northern wall, dispatch any guards nearby, and then open the massive wooden doors for the rest of the cavaliers. Mikhal would lead the charge through the opened gate and head directly for the harbor area. The remainder of the soldiers, along with their commander, would follow Mikhal's men past Hanson's position and head for the local garrison, cutting off any enemy reinforcements that might attempt to reach the docks. Then Alek would meet Mikhal at the harbor, ensuring everything was ready for the Duellrian fleet. It was a good plan, one that Alek and Mikhal had thought through many times before they had disembarked on the northern shore of the Forsian Sea.

The cavaliers had disembarked from the Duellrian ships almost two days earlier; they had left Justan and Admiral Clarind along the border between Erand and Belarn and made their way across the northern plains as quickly as possible. There were no signs of enemy patrols near the sea.

"A good sign that bodes well for the army," Mikhal commented. It meant there was a better chance of them reaching the port without being noticed. At least that is what Mikhal hoped as he looked at the snow-covered walls of Singhal. He also hoped the Drakes' messenger had returned to their king and reported on Kristian's intentions. If the messenger succeeded, Mikhal expected Erand's army would only be a few weeks behind them … and then they could march on Belarna.

Mikhal stood in his saddle, stretching to relieve the tension in his leg muscles, as he continued to watch the walls above the gate for a signal. He could see little through the darkness and wondered if Hanson had even started his part of the mission. Nervously, he checked to make sure the reigns were secure in his left hand and that he had a good grip on his saber in his right hand. Then he looked back past his men to his commander to ensure all was ready.

"Relax sir," one of his sergeants said, riding up next to him. "Remember, you set the example for all of us. You need to stay calm."

"I am calm. I'm just ready to get this started."

"If you cinch down your straps any more, you'll either break them or kill your horse."

Mikhal had to smile. "Thank you, I get the message." But he could not help thinking about Kristian and wonder how his prince might affect things tonight. He rubbed Champion's neck to forget about the reckless prince and focus on the task his men had to accomplish.

KRISTIAN SAW ALEK NOD TOWARD one of his officers in silent acknowledgment that all was ready. All they waited on was a falling torch from the walls to signal their attack. It was hard for Kristian not to interfere. He disliked the plan because he felt it split up the company's forces. They should attack in a massed formation, rushing the walls and drive right past the guards before they had a chance to warn anyone. Kristian had hinted a few times he felt that speed was more important than surprise, but the commander was reluctant to change his plans.

So be it, Kristian thought. *I'll let him have his chance, and if he makes a mistake, then I won't forget.* Kristian was definitely in a hurry to get this raid over with, and everyone knew it.

"They don't know how long this is taking," he complained bitterly to himself. Allisia will be dead or worse before we reach Belarna. He shivered in the frigid night as he thought of her and then tried to put it out of his mind for a while by looking at Captain Heinren's men.

The cavalrymen smiled when he joked with them about how easy it would be to take the town, and they half nodded at his comments about Erand's commitment to honor and duty. The prince thought his words would encourage the soldiers and let them know he supported them, but they seemed a little too worried as he looked around at the gathered men. His concerns over whether the plan might fail grew. They looked nervous and restless. Kristian had thought that well-trained men like the cavaliers would be confident and well prepared. In contrast, these men looked liked soldiers going into battle for the first time.

Truan Langwood came up next to Kristian and patted the neck of his horse. "Now, this is a fine steed, Your Highness," the old warrior said, smiling as he rubbed the horse's muscular neck. Then turning more serious, he looked up at the young prince and said, "Tonight will be easy for them, Prince Kristian, they know that."

"Then why do they look so afraid? They look as if they've never seen bloodshed before," Kristian said as he looked at some of the younger cavalrymen in line.

"Many of them haven't seen battle before, but they are cavaliers. They are the best trained cavalry in Erinia, probably the whole world. They will take the port … they are confident of that. But they also know not everyone is going to make it through the night. These soldiers have families, loved ones that they are afraid they may never see again. And they are a close bunch of soldiers. Soldiers are going to lose good friends tonight. They are concerned about who will take care of their loved ones if they die, and they are concerned about the safety of their comrades … as well they should be." The weathered sergeant pulled his gloves tight over his hands and nodded to the prince before taking his place at the rear of the column.

Kristian watched him go, wondering why the sergeant had spent time explaining this to him. With new insight, Kristian looked again at the faces of the cavaliers. He saw them holding cherished keepsakes or glancing to their comrades one last time. They smiled remembering better days.

Kristian felt ashamed as he thought of his own family. He wondered what his father would be thinking of his son as he prepared to attack Belarn. He had not thought about the possibility that he might never see him again. So many things were left unresolved between them. There were so many things Kristian hoped he could make right once this was all over, but first he had to find a way to rescue Allisia. He thought he had found a way to bring him and his father closer, by marrying the princess. She had seen something in him that no one else had. Allisia had not said so, but Kristian saw it in her eyes; she was willing to give him a fresh start. He hoped it was because she saw potential in him even though no one else did. Looking back toward Singhal, he prayed to God that she was all right.

MIKHAL WAS THE FIRST TO see the small light atop the wall directly above the northern gate. He motioned for his men to make ready as he squinted to see the small flame. A moment later, the torch fell from the battlements to sputter out in the snow. Mikhal looked back quickly at Alek Heinren for permission to move out. After a quick nod from his commander, Mikhal sounded the charge and urged his mount into a full gallop.

The force split into two columns on either side of Mikhal, moving almost silently; the only sounds made were the jingling of a few unsecured harness straps and the crunching of the frozen ground below the horses' hooves. They covered the open ground between their hiding place and the gate in a few heartbeats. They were racing toward the walls, and Mikhal was afraid the doors would not be opened in time. They would have to stop and wait for Hanson's men to open them. He was immediately concerned about his men being exposed to archers and spearmen. He began to doubt whether Hanson had succeeded in taking the gate, that maybe he had misread the signal.

The doors swung silently inward just as he was about to order his men to turn away. Hanson had accomplished his part of the plan. More so, the big southerner had enough foresight to wait until the last minute to open the gates, just in case anyone was around to sound an alarm.

Mikhal leaned forward in his saddle, pushing his horse harder then he ever had before. A moment later, he was through the gate. Wheeling around at the first street corner, he directed his men past him toward the harbor. It was more important for his sergeants and their men to secure the docks and find the harbormaster quickly than for him to be the first one in harm's way. He looked over his shoulder to make sure the rest of the company was heading toward the garrison once his men were past him. He barely caught the gleam of helmets and sabers moving toward the heart of the town before they turned around a distant corner. Mikhal turned back toward his own men and spurred his horse into a run. One of his veteran sergeants nodded, letting him know that all of his men had made it into the small town. Everything was going as planned.

Sprinting dangerously down the icy streets, Mikhal caught up to his men as they turned onto the last street leading to their goal. No lights were on except in a small shack close to a pier.

"That's probably the harbormaster's place," Mikhal called out, as they got closer. Some of the cavalrymen had already dismounted, searching for signs of immediate danger. His men encountered no resistance, though, and began securing the area without having to be told. Mikhal turned his focus to the shack. Two of his men were banging on the door, ordering the occupant to wake up and come outside. A few minutes later, one of his sergeants came to give him a report.

"There are seven warehouses in the immediate area. They've been searched, and no one was found. There's also one tavern close to where we turned onto this street. There were a few drunken people there, but they were told to stay inside or they would be hurt. I had Turngor's squad keep a few men there to watch the place. There are also a few small fishing boats moored along the side of a pier, but they don't look very seaworthy." The sergeant finished his report, scanning the darkness, searching for his men. Mikhal was glad he had such experienced leaders to watch after the younger soldiers. Seeing that all of them were doing what they were supposed to do, he decided to stay out of their way and wait for the situation to develop.

"Thank you, Jamal. The men are doing very well." Jamal nodded and turned to go check on the platoon's progress.

One of the soldiers came out of the shack, leading an old man toward him. The man was almost doubled over from age and looked as if he feared he would be hung at any moment. Wearing nothing more than a dingy tunic, he tried to keep from shivering as Mikhal's men urged him forward.

"This man is the harbormaster, sir." the soldier said as others fanned out to secure the area around Mikhal.

Mikhal looked into the old man's eyes and saw only shock and fright. He ordered someone to get the man some warm clothing and hot food. Then he motioned for the harbormaster to come closer.

"You're the harbormaster?" Mikhal asked politely.

"Yes, sir," the old man answered, unsure of what was happening.

Mikhal patted the man's shoulder reassuringly. "Don't be afraid. I'm Lieutenant Mikhal Jurander of the Cavaliers of Erand. None of us has any intention of harming you or anyone else in the town … so long as no one tries to harm us." Looking directly at the old man he added, "In fact, I bet you could be of tremendous service to us."

"Me?" the master asked suspiciously. He could not fathom how he could manage to help.

"Yes, sir. If you are indeed the harbormaster of this town, I am sure you know every part of these waters."

"Humph," he snorted as he looked out at the bay. "I've worked these waters twice as long as you've been alive. There is no part of it that I don't know better than I know myself … uh, sir," he added, thinking his life might hang in the balance.

Mikhal was amused by the old man's pride and smiled. He knew this man would prove invaluable to the fleet's landing. He had instructed his men that it was imperative they capture the harbormaster alive. Mikhal was going to do everything to ensure that he was well taken care of.

"Are you loyal to your new king?" Mikhal asked. "I want no treachery."

The old man shrugged. "I've never seen him or any other Belarnian king. We're just simple fishing folk. I'm sure that no one will resist if you leave us in peace."

Mikhal nodded.

Suddenly, there was the clash of steel on steel and shouts of warning coming from further down the street. A lone cavalryman ran up to Mikhal and reported that his squad had run into a patrol of Belarnian soldiers. Mikhal fought the urge to run to the fight; he knew his responsibility was to ensure the security of all of his men and not just one squad. He warned the others to keep a sharp eye out for enemy reinforcements and tried to wait for further word from those in the fight. As quickly as the sound of struggle had reached Mikhal, it abruptly ended. He anxiously stared at the dark street corner where the fight had taken place, waiting for news. After a long break in the action, Jamal came running out of the gloom to meet Mikhal.

"There was a small patrol out. They were alerted by the sound of our horses. We surprised them as they came down the street. They're all dead," Jamal announced as he tried to catch his breath. His heart was still beating fast from the excitement. "Darnell has a small cut across his ribs but he will be alright in a few days." The sergeant waited for Mikhal to give him further instructions.

Mikhal nodded and then said, "Well done. Maintain your positions and don't push out any further. Remember we're only to take the docks not the entire town." The sergeant smiled and saluted before running back to his men. Mikhal visibly calmed as he admired the efficiency of his men. They had done their jobs well, and he was proud of them. He only hoped the rest of the plan had gone as well.

An hour later, Alek's officers were gathered within the tavern near the harbor. The three lieutenants and their captain sat at a table looking over a map of Belarn as they ate soup and hot drinks provided by the proprietor. The town of Singhal was secure. Only a small force of twenty Belarnian soldiers was garrisoned within the town with the rest of the security left to the villagers themselves. In the last fifty years, there had not been a single instance where the people had been called upon to repel a hostile force. The quick seizure of key areas within the town had successfully kept the few soldiers on duty from being able to react. Most of the guards were captured as they slept in their beds.

Regretfully, one soldier from Hanson's platoon was killed while securing the northern gate. A single Belarnian guard had hid from the cavaliers as they climbed over the defenses above the wall. Once he saw that most of his friends were captured without a fight, the soldier stabbed the closest cavalier in the back and then tried to jump off the wall and escape.

Unfortunately, the Belarnian ran right into Hanson. He was so enraged by the death of one his soldiers that the southerner grabbed the man and snapped his neck. The Belarnian's body was attached to the signal torch and tossed over the wall.

He was still brooding over the loss of his man as the four discussed how they would conduct their next mission. The Duellrian fleet would be landing within the next few hours and the cavalry officers knew that they would be needed to scout ahead of the main force. The company's sergeant already reported that distant lights out on the Forsian Sea could be seen heading toward the harbor. Alek urged the sergeant to be cautious in case the boats belonged to the Belarnians. The cavaliers were vulnerable to counterattack for the next couple of hours and the commander did not want to be surprised by anything. The sergeant nodded, assuring him that blocking positions had been established throughout the town. No one would get into Singhal without being seen. The sergeant prepared to leave the men to their planning when he remembered something and turned to face them again.

"Sir, I forgot to tell you that the prince wanted to convey his compliments to you and the company for a job well done." Looking at Hanson he added, "He also wanted me to tell you that he is terribly sorry about the loss of Armis." Hanson nodded in grim silence as he tried to think of how he was going to tell the dead soldier's wife that her husband was not coming home.

Mikhal looked at Hanson and frowned. He was relieved that none of his own men were killed and that they completed their mission with just a few cuts and bruises; he remembered all to well what it was like to be in Hanson's predicament. Mikhal had to meet two widows and one grieving mother after his battle with Belarnian forces in southern Erand last year. Mikhal would never forget the deep sorrow on their faces as he told them their loved ones were not coming home. Surely there was enough on everyone's mind already without having to worry about the dead.

Mikhal turned his thoughts toward Kristian's sudden aloofness. After securing the docks, the lieutenant had waited for the rest of the company to search the town and ensure there were no traps waiting for them. Only a short period of time passed, however, before Alek and the prince returned from their reconnaissance of the town. The young cavalry officer was surprised by the prince's quietness as he reported his platoon's success to his commander. Mikhal saw that the prince was aware of everything going on around him, but still, he said nothing as he watched the men prepare for the fleet's arrival.

Mikhal wondered what Kristian was thinking. He hated that a part of him wanted his prince to approve of their actions. Mikhal did not know why he felt this way, especially since most of the time he felt like hitting the young, spoiled prince. No matter how hard Mikhal thought about Kristian and his past actions, he could not understand the man's motivation for some of the things he said and did. It was dumbfounding to hear Kristian praise the men for their efforts one moment and then curse them the next for not doing something the way he wanted it done. Mikhal was concerned about him leading them into battle and was unsure of how Kristian would react at any particular moment. He hoped Kristian would not be in any position to influence things once the fighting started.

FERRAL BROODED OVER THE LATEST information concerning the advance of the Duellrian forces while he sat in his new throne made from the bones of those that had opposed him. The demon warned him they were coming. She had seen ships emerging from the river north of Brekia when she destroyed their capital, and now they had reportedly taken a small town on the eastern border of his country. Enraged by his military advisor's inability to ensure the security of Belarn, he ordered the arrest and execution of the last of his father's trusted officers. It had pleased him to know that he had finally rid himself of those most likely to spread dissent. The feeling of control quickly vanished as more reports were brought to him regarding his enemy's movements.

He was constantly distracted by the wriggling form at his feet. Rebenna had tried to flee the city, to escape Ferral and his demon. The magi had only been able to bring her to his side by hinting that displeasing him could mean the end of her freedom or worse. He knew she feared him now, and it made him smile. He could see the anxiety in her eyes.

Someday, he thought, *all of the world will look at me as she does.* Ferral laughed, reveling in the possibility of countless people groveling at his feet. He would choose who would live and die.

The large doors at the far end of the throne room opened, and a solitary man in polished black armor walked cautiously toward Ferral. General Derout was solidly built; he had served a long time as the prince's personal bodyguard and seen many battles. He pledged a life of service to Ferral and had quickly been promoted to his current position as commander of the Black Guards, Ferral's personal army. Now Derout was ordered to take charge of all Belarnian forces and prepare for battle against the Duellrian army.

A firm, scarred hand rested on the long broadsword that hung from his belt. He stared directly ahead toward his king, slightly jerking his head to the side to fling a single knot of black hair over his shoulder. He tried to focus his stare on the king and not on the new throne as he approached. Even Derout was daunted by the gruesome visage before him. The general could show no outward signs of fear, though. It could be his undoing. Too many of his predecessors had been executed in the last few days because they were weak, but the throne was disturbing even to the seasoned warrior.

Leg bones with feet still attached by rotting cartilage reinforced the old king's seat, completely covering the polished wooden frame. The armrests were bones with hands curved inward at the end in a cruel, mocking invitation to sit. The most horrifying details were the skulls. A single skull was mounted on top of the throne, its empty sockets staring at whoever approached. The mouth was fixed open as if the skull itself was screaming in horror. Wickedly curved horns were affixed to the top of the skull in different places, all of them pointing back to the horrors that filled the wall behind the throne.

Hundreds of skulls were piled against the back wall. Some were so white they appeared to have been bleached by the sun, while others still had bits of rotting flesh hanging from their cheeks. Derout recognized a few of the faces behind the chair. Everyone began to realize that Ferral's reign meant chaos and dark magic. The primary thing running through Derout's mind at the moment, though, was how to survive. The cunning general had his own plans.

Derout knelt before his new king and waited for permission to rise. The sorcerer smiled and motioned for him to stand. "Please, General Derout, stand. There is no need for such formalities between us here. You have been my friend and companion my entire life. You are my most trusted and capable officer, and you have always pleased me, and I am sure you will continue to do so." The general did not miss the emphasis on the last part. The madman's attitude did nothing to relieve him of his fears. "What news do you have on the progress of my army?"

The general took a deep breath before beginning. "My Lord, the bridges have been rigged by engineers to collapse upon your command. Also, stores of grain and meat have been stockpiled. The Black Guards themselves have been assembled and await orders. The regular army is …"

"Stop!" Ferral shouted in anger. "Do not stand there and recite a siege defense to me, you moron. I don't want to sit here in this city, trapped by infidels who mock my powers just because you can't handle them. If you can't do this, Derout, then …"

"No, wait. I have more …," Derout said as he looked pleadingly at Ferral, begging for more time to explain. The general was allowed to continue once his king was calmer. "The regular army will meet the invaders outside the city walls to appear as if we are giving them the advantage of maneuver. From the ramparts, we can watch their army attempt to flank us with their small contingent of cavaliers. We will let them think they are beating us back, and then we will hit them from behind with the Black Guards. Mounted and heavily armored, they are more than a match for the light Erandian cavalry and Duellrian army. They will be surrounded and forced to surrender or die."

Ferral smiled, approving of the plan. "No prisoners, General Derout. Not one of them is to be spared, except for our new friend, the prince of Erand. I want him captured. I want him for myself. Still

…," Ferral pondered the outcome of the battle to come, "more may be needed to ensure complete victory. I will consult my newest advisor and deliver the details to you later." The general nodded and prepared to leave when he was stopped. "Is that all, general? It seems to me there is more you would have me hear if you thought I would not hang you for it. Well, go on, tell me."

Derout looked up at Ferral, judging the madman's stability, trying to decide if it was worth the risk to give him more bad news. He took a deep breath and informed his king of something that greatly disturbed him.

"My Lord, Garnis was killed." The king stared uncomprehendingly at Derout. "He was an officer in the Black Guards. He once served as a personal guard to you, but you recently promoted him and assigned him the task of subduing the mountain villages in the Mercies." Recognition finally showed on Ferral's face as he remembered the soldier.

"A terrible tragedy. I am truly sorry for his loved ones. Now, find the man responsible and kill him." He paused to look admonishingly at Derout. "I would have thought you could handle this little problem on your own."

"That is only part of the problem, My Lord. All of his men were also killed. Stories beaten out of the locals suggest that only one man was responsible for this trouble. It also seems that this man is responsible for the deaths of four other loyal guards and their men. Every time, the stranger is able to escape without a trace. They say he has scars running down the side of his face."

Derout mounted a step to ensure the king understood the importance of what he was saying. "It seems to me that this man has vowed to rid the world of some very capable warriors. I mention this to you because you could also be in danger. I think this man will seek you out." Ferral looked past Derout trying to reason out what he had just learned. It seemed impossible. *Could the boy still be alive?* Ferral pondered. In an odd way, it made perfect sense. He shrugged indifferently.

"It's your responsibility to ensure that nothing happens to me, Derout. I rely on you." He paused a moment and then said, "Prepare your men. It's going to get very cold around here." With a note of finality, Ferral indicated that he was tired of talking with the general. He stood and left the room as Derout and Rebenna knelt before the skull throne. He would now check on his newest guest, Princess Allisia. Tormenting her was becoming one of his favorite pastimes.

12

PRINCE KRISTIAN'S HONOR

Kristian rode alongside Alek and General Aphilan, the commander of the Duellrian Army. Their forces were moving inland away from Singhal. Less than twelve hours ago, the fleet had anchored in the protected bay, and a few ships were able to put in at the docks themselves, but there was not enough room or time to wait for all the ships to unload. Most of the fleet quickly put small boats into the water to carry the foot soldiers into town. The cavaliers had done an excellent job of lighting the harbor with watch fires, and the ships' captains quickly took advantage of the illumination. General Aphilan and King Justan were the first ones to land, and they were immediately taken to the tavern where the Erandians had already laid out maps for them.

Kristian had been aloof the entire time the cavaliers were securing the city. He knew that everyone wondered where he had gone, but he chose to stay out of the way.

Kristian was astounded by the quick efficiency of Alek's company. They had developed an ingenious plan that separated the Belarnian forces and prevented them from reinforcing each other. Kristian thought the cavalry officer was wrong to reduce his strength by dividing his company, but the plan had worked superbly. More times than not, Kristian had gotten into some soldier's way and prevented him from doing his job. Finally, Kristian left Alek and his men to complete the mission while he went to a secluded part of the harbor to think. He sulked because he did not feel like he was contributing to the fight. Kristian could not prove to the men, especially Mikhal, that he had worth.

Kristian knew the cavaliers felt like their prince was thrust upon them, an unnecessary burden, when there was already enough to worry about. The prince was sure he had talent and skill that would help them, but so far the only thing he had demonstrated was that he had poor judgment and was constantly under foot or hoof.

Kristian felt like an idiot for pushing them to follow his plans, especially now that Alek's plan had worked. Worse, a part of him had hoped the commander would be wrong just so that he would be right. The prince watched Aphilan's men move to unload soldiers and supplies as quickly as possible, but time seemed to be flying by, and they still had a long way to go. Kristian finally sighed and decided to sit in on the rest of the planning with General Aphilan and Admiral Clarind.

Again, he felt the planners were being too cautious. He had seen how easily the cavalry company had defeated the guards in Singhal and thought using their speed would be the best plan. His only thoughts were of Allisia, who was still Ferral's prisoner. No one knew exactly what he planned to do with her.

His anger went unchecked during the meeting. It was hard to listen to the Duellrian generals plan a march that would take the army another week to reach Ferral's stronghold. He interrupted them and demanded that his plan be heard out and that some consideration be made for his concept of how to proceed. After all, his cavaliers just demonstrated their outstanding capabilities. Why not use them to force the enemy out of their castle and reduce the likeliness of a long siege?

"Prince Kristian, you promised your father you would wait for him," one military officer reminded him.

"But we have had no reports from him. He may be delayed. It might take him more than a month to reach us. We can't just sit here and wait," Kristian argued.

"This is our primary port. Without it, we have no way to get resupplied. We will have no way to leave. Duellr is not here to take over Belarn. We only came to get our princess back," General Aphilan declared. "We'll leave the larger political issues to you and your father."

Kristian shook his head in disagreement. "I'm here for the exact same reasons you are. I want to see Allisia rescued and taken back to her home. That is all I want." Many Duellrians raised their eyebrows in suspicion, but kept quiet.

In the end, the planners conceded that speed was important. The army could not wait in Singhal for very long. The community could not support them logistically. The army would have to move before it lost its ability to fight. King Justan was especially convincing when he talked of his sister being trapped by Ferral and his demon. The young man regained some of his former composure during the sea voyage. His commitment to seeing Ferral captured or killed was very strong.

A plan was finally devised that balanced speed with force by using a small portion of the army under the control of General Aphilan himself. His force left within a few hours of landing and set out at a blistering pace to reach Ferral's capital as quickly as possible. The remainder of the army, under Justan's control, would set out the next afternoon once the supplies were unloaded from the ships. Admiral Clarind and his fleet would remain in Singhal to protect their landing site and ensure the army had a way to return to Duellr once the siege was over. They also counted on Kristian's father to show up quickly and provide critical supplies if the attack stalled. Alek Hienren reluctantly sent a cavalier south toward the border in the hopes of finding the Erandian army and delivering the new plan to their king.

Once the overall plans were set, Kristian turned to Alek to order him to begin scouting the road to Belarn. The commander cut him short by informing him that patrols were already moving along the major road leading from Singhal to Belarna. The commander's tone reflected what everyone was thinking; Kristian was becoming a nuisance.

Perhaps they would have more readily accepted my plan had I not stepped forward, acting as if I were their supreme commander, Kristian thought afterwards. It was of little importance in comparison to getting them on the road toward Ferral and Allisia.

The Duellrian generals resented Kristian; they considered him an outsider, and he was trying to order them into battle in the name of his cause. Even his own officers had grown tired of his outbursts. Since the voyage began, Kristian had done nothing to prove his competence to his men or the Duellrians. Now the army was preparing to engage Belarn in the largest battle anyone had seen in over five hundred years. Men on both sides were going to die. The authority to commit these men to their deaths was laid upon the shoulders of leaders that the men trusted. These soldiers were willing to risk their lives for the decisions made by those with a lot more experience than Kristian. For the prince to stand in front of them and make demands was insulting. They accepted that he would marry their beloved princess and possibly be their leader in the future, but now, as they were trying to decide how to best deploy their forces, they did not want or need a brash, inexperienced prince interfering.

Kristian ignored them; he was eager to get started. His men would escort Aphilan's infantry to the citadel. He could feel their stares directed at his back and knew he had done it again; they were losing all respect in him … if they ever had it to begin with. Kristian was growing less concerned with their feelings, though, and more concerned about Allisia's welfare. He did not talk to anyone again after that. He simply packed his things and took care of his horse.

Kristian suddenly came out of his deep thoughts as an Erandian scout approached the column. The young cavalier quickly spotted Alek and rode directly toward him and the prince.

Saluting, the scout said, "Sir, Lieutenant Hanson sent me to report that he has pushed his men all the way to the capital. The road is clear, and he has a patrol constantly moving up and down the road checking for ambushes."

"He's at the fortress already," Kristian cursed under his breath. "If he has ridden that far then surely Ferral knows we're coming."

"Excuse me, but I don't think there were any problems. He concealed his men on a small wooded hill that overlooks the city. No one saw us move into position because we moved into the woods while it was very dark, and I'm the only one that has been allowed to leave."

"Very good," Alek replied. "Thank you for your report. Get some fresh water and something to eat. I'm sure you rode as hard as you could to reach us. Go rest a bit and wait for us to get close to Hanson's position. Then I want you to guide us in."

"Yes, sir," the scout replied as he saluted and left for the rear of the column. Turning toward Kristian, the captain looked somewhat disturbed.

"What's wrong? Haven't we surprised them as we hoped? Everything seems to be working out. Now should be the time to spur the men on and secure the high ground before they mount a counterattack," Kristian said.

"Surprise is exactly what we wanted, Your Highness, but this is just too good to be true. We have sailed the largest army anyone has seen in hundreds of years into the heart of our enemy's lands. Now we march toward his capital with the intent of bringing down his walls around him and, yet, not a single person has been alerted to our presence." Alek shook his head slowly in disbelief. "Something isn't right. A plan never works out this well. No matter, we'll be there by nightfall, and at first light we will see what the king of Belarn has in store for us."

"Maybe we overestimated him. Maybe the demon was his only weapon, and he has already played out his hand," Kristian suggested.

"I hope so. But just remember, hope is not a plan to cling to. We should be ready for whatever comes," Alek replied.

As dusk approached, the Erandian cavalry slowly climbed the wooded hill overlooking Belarna. Kristian guided his horse to one side of Alek's men and then suddenly dropped the reigns as he stared in amazement at the size of the city. Built from massive blocks of some black rock, the walls were over fifty feet tall and stretched to his left and right beyond his vantage point. A deep moat, more like a river, encircled the fortress and tied into another river that opened into the Utwan Sea behind the city. Four towers protected the massive walls from siege and scaling. Each was easily large enough to imprison all of the cavaliers. Kristian shook his head, impressed by the magnitude of the walls and towers, but what caught his eye more than the walls was the city itself. No one ever told him about the size of Belarna. He assumed it was a small city, probably not much bigger than one of the southern Erandian provincial capitals and certainly not as big as Brekia. Belarna was much bigger then he realized; it was just as big as Brekia. It was a city-state in its own right, and its defenses looked formidable. Beyond it all, at the far end of the city, Ferral's palace with its twin towers rose into the evening sky.

Kristian's mood quickly changed as he stared at the distant, dark palace. Allisia was somewhere in that evil place. Dark thoughts entered his mind, and he thought of what Ferral might have already done to her. The prince anxiously turned back toward the circle of men that were discussing the next morning's plans. Two soldiers, carrying a limp form, approached as soon as he joined the gathered officers.

"We captured this man at the bottom of the hill. He was wondering around aimlessly. He claims he was looking for us, that he wanted to warn us," one soldier reported to Alek.

Kristian looked the man over. He was weak and elderly and his ragged clothes hung from him in torn strips. The old man appeared to have been severely beaten. He rocked back and forth as he tried to remain standing before the cavalrymen. His eyes were sunken, almost empty, as if they had been pushed back into his skull. One of the soldiers that escorted him complained that he was ice cold. He seemed very near death and Kristian wondered what was keeping him alive.

"How did you know we were here," Kristian demanded.

"My name is Fekalier. I was one of the priests serving as an advisor to the Royal House of Belarn … before Ferral killed his father," he said haltingly. His focus was distant as though he had seen much pain recently. He continued to speak, oblivious to his audience. "I have come to warn you. Tonight the army will leave the city and ride for Erand. You must go and warn your people or they will be killed." He stopped talking abruptly, letting his head sag forward as if it were too heavy to hold up any longer.

"I don't like this," Mikhal said staring at the beaten man. "How did he know where we were? How was he able to make it here like he is?" Mikhal looked to Alek and then at the prince, shaking his head in disagreement. "There is something wrong here. I don't believe what he is saying."

"I agree," Kristian said, looking back to Alek. "He doesn't seem right to me."

"How did you escape old man?" Mikhal asked.

Fekalier slowly raised his head to stare at the prince. Kristian stumbled back as he looked in the man's eyes and saw … a penetrating darkness. They were intact and looked normal, but there was no glint of life in them. There was no spark that would signal hope, resistance, vitality, or life.

"His eyes … look at them," Kristian exclaimed.

Alek leaned forward looking into the man's eyes and shivered. "They're strange, but maybe it's because of the suffering he's endured." Alek paused thinking of what to do about Fekalier. "We'll wait. The rest of Aphilan's men will be here by midnight. We'll wait and see if this army leaves the city before we take any action. Until then, make sure every man is ready to ride at a moment's notice. Keep this man under close guard; I don't want him going back to Ferral to warn him that we're here."

He looked at each of his officers to make sure they understood, and then he added, "We also need to make sure the Duellrians are guided into our hiding place. Now is not the time to tip our hand to the Belarnians."

As an afterthought he turned to Hanson and said, "I want you to send a rider to King Justan and warn him there is a possibility the enemy is heading toward him." Hanson nodded and hurried through the dark to find his men.

Kristian watched Fekalier closely as he was taken down the hill to receive aid. The old man's limp form was dragged away by the two soldiers; the strength Fekalier had mustered in order to speak had left him again. The prince turned back toward the walls of the city, trying to forget about the tortured man and his haunting eyes. He stared down at the massive city, wondering what would happen in the morning. A cold wind pushed him back from his vantage point, forcing him to wrap his coat tightly around him.

He looked up at the sky and saw dark clouds slowly rolling in from over the Utwan Sea. Kristian guessed at what those clouds brought with them and shuddered. He only hoped the impending storm waited a few more days before it hit them. *Hopefully,* he thought, *a few days is all we'll need.* Kristian turned from his view of the city and the dark storm clouds and tried to find a place to get some rest, though he knew sleep would be slow to come.

At the bottom of the hill, the two soldiers guarding Fekalier let their hold on him loosen. They did not like their task. Something was definitely wrong with the old man, and neither of the guards wanted anything to do with him. Finally reaching one of the supply wagons, they motioned for their prisoner to sit while they found him a blanket and some food. Fekalier stood motionless, his head hanging lower than before. One of the cavaliers hesitated a moment and then stepped over to the old man to help him sit.

The guard quickly turned away from him as the stench of death reached his nostrils. The smell was so awful that both men wretched as they stumbled away from Fekalier. The old man turned his head toward the hastily departing guards and watched them disappear around the wagon before he fell lifeless to the frozen ground. His head made a sickening sound as it hit the wagon hitch. Within the black city, Ferral smiled, knowing his enemies were near and that he was ready for them.

KRISTIAN ABRUPTLY AWOKE FROM HIS slumber. Alek was shaking him urgently. The captain leaned close and whispered into his ear. "Something is happening in the city."

Kristian's grogginess quickly left as he stood and followed the cavalry commander back toward the top of the hill. It was still dark, and Kristian guessed he had only slept a few hours. The wind was colder now, and a definite breeze had sprung up out of the northwest. The prince knew that the storm was not going to wait a few more days. They would be lucky if it waited till dawn.

Kristian stumbled through the cold, dark woods along with Alek to a vantage point where they could all see what was going on below. "Now I understand what you were worried about," Kristian commented to Alek.

Easily a thousand torches burned near the northeast corner of the city, close to Ferral's palace. The sound of men and horses could be heard preparing for battle.

"Have we been discovered?" Kristian asked as he looked at the mass of torches burning just inside the walls. The Duellrian forces under General Aphilan's control arrived sometime while he was sleeping, and he wondered if they were ready to defend against an immediate attack.

"I'm not sure," Alek replied. "They're too far away to discern their intentions, but I don't think they are going to attack us."

"Why?" Kristian asked as he and the other officers turned to look at Alek.

"They make no attempt to disguise their actions. If I were attacking an unknown force, in the dark, and on a wooded hill, I would be more cautious. Also, they are at the gate furthest from our position. If they were going to attack, why not use the gate directly below us? From where they intend to leave the city, they will have to ride almost twice as far to reach us, exposing themselves longer to arrows and spears as they round the hill."

Alek hesitated looking back at the blur of motion in the city. "We're ready, in case they move against us, but I don't think they will. They may be riding to attack King Justan near Singhal."

"Could this be the army the old man spoke of? The army that intends to attack Erand?" Romlin asked, concern showing on his face even in the dark woods.

"Possibly, but as we said before, we aren't sure the old man was telling the truth," Alek answered. They all stood among the trees waiting to see what would happen. General Aphilan and his commanders also came up to their vantage point to see what was happening. They did not have to wait long.

The Belarnian army was leaving the gate. The mounted force rode fast, their armor and tack jingling, as they headed away on a road leading to the northeast, away from their hilltop position. If they were planning to attack them the Belarnians were heading off in the opposite direction. Only a few minutes passed before the mounted army was out of the gate, and they still continued off towards the Forsian Sea. It did not take long before the sounds of the army could no longer be heard above the increasing howl of the winter wind. Soon the torches themselves could no longer be seen. They were left standing on the hill looking down into the, once again, dark city.

Kristian was the first to speak. "The old man was right after all. Now is our chance. The army is gone and the entire city lies before us unprotected."

"You're wrong, Prince Kristian, look again at the walls. I can see sentries from here," General Aphilan pointed out quickly.

Mikhal was glad someone else disagreed with his prince's assessment. The Duellrian leader had already proven himself a capable military officer and planner. His experienced leadership was demonstrated by the exceptional way his large force of men entered the woods at night without making noise. His words were spoken quickly but there was a hint of sensible caution in them.

The cavalry officers looked at him admiringly. Aphilan's hauberk and chain mail glinted even in the moonlight. His helmet, like the ones the rest of his soldiers wore, was conical with long protruding guards for his nose and ears. His hands rested casually on the traditional leaf-shaped short sword of Duellr. The general was much older than them, his silver hair hanging down to his shoulders, and his brow was furrowed and wrinkled, but the general of the Duellrian Army carried himself like a true leader. He had that relaxed but alert stance that showed he was ready for anything.

"He is right, Your Highness, this could be the advantage we need, but we must be sure. If this is a trap and we attack now, we will be as exposed as the Belarnians would have been if they had attacked us here." Alek looked around at the other officers to determine what they thought. Some agreed with proceeding with caution while others sided with Kristian.

"This may be our only chance to save our princess, general," one Duellrian officer said to everyone.

"The supplies the Erandians requested were brought forward. It could work," another commented.

"If we don't seize this opportunity, even if there is the possibility of a trap, it may be the only time their army is outside the walls," Kristian argued, looking directly at Alek in anticipation. "If we don't attack right now, we could be looking at the prospect of a siege, which could last months. I don't think Ferral will wait until we bring down his walls before he threatens Allisia. We must act now."

Mikhal looked at the prince in disbelief. He did not understand why the prince was so eager to rush into battle. Mikhal was not afraid to fight, or even die, but he was afraid of letting his men down. He was afraid of uselessly wasting their lives for Kristian's glory and honor. He could not believe Kristian was suggesting they attack before even the majority of the Duellrian army arrived. King Justan and two thirds of the Duellrian army was just leaving Singhal. They would not be able to help them for another few days.

"Captain Hienren, I …," Mikhal began.

The young officer was cut off by the prince, "Well, what is it then general? I speak for my countrymen, and we are ready. Can we count on the Duellrians?" Mikhal looked in shock at his commander. The prince could not do this. He had no right to throw away the lives of his men like this.

The general hesitated, looking at each of his officers before saying, "We are ready. We will attack within the hour, but I ask you, Prince Kristian, to inform our king that we are not waiting for him and that we will surely need his help if things do not go well." Kristian nodded anxious to begin.

As the officers left, Mikhal approached Alek in anger. "Why didn't you say anything? How could you let him usurp your authority? He has no right to …"

"Stop, lieutenant. Remember to whom you are speaking. I am your commander and will not allow you to ever speak to me like this." Mikhal took a step back. He had never seen his commander this angry before. He knew he had crossed the line, but Mikhal had always thought the two of them were closer than this. Mikhal did not know what to say.

Seeing the hurt look on his face, Alek continued in a more comforting tone. "Mikhal, you are my best officer. We've known each other for two years, and I trust you more than anyone else. But you don't understand our true duty."

The commander paused placing a hand on the younger officer's shoulder. "We serve Erand. That means we serve the royal family, including the prince. I can no more tell him what to do then you can give me an order. I didn't say anything because it wouldn't have helped. The decision was already made in his mind before the discussion began. To have started an argument would have only served to discredit us all. The Duellrians would have seen that we lack discipline and that the prince does not have control." The cavalier let go of Mikhal and walked off toward his horse.

"Besides," Alek added, "maybe he's right, this time. Maybe we do have a chance."

"You don't believe that," Mikhal countered. "I can see it in your eyes."

Alek did not say anything as he checked his sword and spear.

"What happens if he kills us all?" he tried one last time.

Mikhal stared at the diminishing shadow of his commander as he walked down the hill toward the rest of the company. Mikhal knew, as well as his commander, that there was little chance of the prince ever being right. He swore, under his breath, and started down the hill toward his own horse, hoping he was the one that was wrong this time.

13

AT THE GATES

General Aphilan's men stood in straight and even lines behind the hill, holding spears and shields at the ready. His attack force consisted of three formations of one thousand men each; another group of five hundred Duellrian soldiers were left to guard the supply trains and act as a reserve. At the front of the formation, the archers stood casually with their long ash bows slung over their right shoulders and arrow cases tightly fastened to their left hips. Behind them were the infantrymen with long, leaf-shaped swords and large wooden shields. All loose gear had been secured to ensure nothing could get caught up or snagged and prove to be an advantage for the enemy. All of their cloaks and outer clothing had been discarded. There would be no need for added warmth, even in this chill weather, once the fighting began. Each man looked to his left and right reassuring his comrades that he would do everything possible to protect his friends during the fight.

The Erandian cavaliers stood at the front of the army, also in three groups. Each of the young cavalry officers and his men would support the advancing Duellrian formations, ensuring no enemy forces would attempt a surprise flanking movement during the fight. The cavalrymen sat on their horses, looking straight toward the gate they would soon rush. Their first priority was to reach the wall as quickly as possible and set the massive wooden gate aflame with the oil they carried. At Mikhal's suggestion, large flasks of oil were brought forward from Singhal. Each of the cavaliers now carried a leather sack full of the stuff. If enough of them could get close to the gate, they might have the chance they needed to secure a foothold in the city. Once inside the walls, they knew they could defeat the Belarnians.

"If we can just reach the wall," Mikhal kept telling himself. If they did not quickly enter the city and reach the palace, they knew that the army would not succeed, and they would all die.

Mikhal sat mounted on his horse in front his men, straightening his plumed helmet for the hundredth time. Gone were the formal uniforms that everyone associated with the cavaliers. They now wore simple chain mail vests under their padded coats. Small round shields were strapped tightly to their left forearms and in their right hands they held eight-foot-long lances with hand guards.

Mikhal fidgeted with the strap on his helmet again. He and his men were in the center and were expected to reach the gate first; Alek had personally given him this task. Mikhal knew his men were the best in the company, but the knowledge did not help him fight the urge to panic. This battle would be much different than the skirmish at Singhal or the border fights he had been involved in. Many of his men would die; perhaps even he would die.

Mikhal had sat on a rock looking at the dark and forbidding city trying to cope with the possibility he would not see his parents or home again. He chided himself several times through the night for being a coward, but he knew that was not what was bothering him. He had always known that his profession would someday call for him to kill or be killed. No, the prospect of killing and being killed on the battlefield was not what frightened Mikhal. It was the possibility that they might fail. Or that he might fail. Mikhal felt a heavy burden weighing down on him. He knew that failing his men was what really bothered him. To think, for even a moment, that some of his men might die because he made the wrong decision terrified him.

Our prince hasn't even considered the consequences of his actions, he complained to himself. *If anything terrible happens, he will be the one to blame.*

He adjusted his chinstrap yet again, hefted his lance to feel the weight of it, and then looked back behind his men to find his commander.

"What are we waiting for?" he asked again. "Let's at least attack before we are seen out here in the open." Mikhal felt exposed and vulnerable standing before the massive city. It was still a league away, and they were protected some by the hill, but the walls were so tall, it seemed to Mikhal that they were easily within range of Belarnian bowmen.

Just then Kristian, Alek, and General Aphilan rode forward of Mikhal's men and centered themselves in front of the nearly four thousand men. Kristian turned and shouted for all the soldiers to hear.

"Men, we are gathered here because of a common need. Monsters live in Erinia. They have crept amongst us and killed your king and stolen your princess. Ferral threatens us with his tricks and wishes us to lie down and let him have his way. Tonight we stand before this vile monster's lair. We will not lie down. We will tear down his walls and rescue the one he stole from amongst us. We will show his people mercy, but we will show him none." Kristian paused to look at the formidable army and smiled. "We will destroy him!"

He tried to shout, but he was drowned out by the deafening cry of the army that was ready to fight. Kristian nodded approval for Alek to begin his attack.

Mikhal strapped his lance into the saddle and raised his saber, signaling the advance. Nothing could be heard above the cheering of the Duellrian men who were ready to kill the person responsible for the death of their king. Mikhal only hoped his men were paying attention to him as he started forward. Looking back, he saw they were riding with him past Kristian. The prince shouted words of encouragement to them, but Mikhal paid him no attention as they prepared to rush the city gate. His men had advanced half way to the wall at a slow trot and nothing happened.

Mikhal raised his saber again and signaled for them to move forward at the gallop. He would reserve the strength of his men and their horses for when it was necessary. They were still more than a couple of minutes away from the gate even if they went into a full run, and he knew this battle was going to last much longer than a few minutes.

Growing anxious, Mikhal knew he could not wait any longer. He lifted his saber a third time and signaled the charge. Mikhal stole a quick look back to see his men urging their mounts on and then let his own horse run as fast as it wanted. They all knew this was the most vulnerable part of the plan. If the guards were alert above, then they would rain arrows and rocks down within seconds and put an abrupt end to their charge. While he was looking back, he saw his commander and the prince riding behind his formation. And though he had only seen them for a mere fraction of a second, he could see the expressions on their faces. Alek rode on silently with a grim look of determination on his face and Kristian rode next to him shouting war cries.

Mikhal turned to look forward and gauge their distance from the gate. They were rapidly approaching the bridge that crossed the moat. On the other side, there were less than two hundred feet remaining before they finally reached the large wooden doors.

Suddenly, fires sparked to life from a hundred different places along the wall directly in front of them.

"Trap!" someone shouted from behind.

Mikhal did not stop, he spurred his mount on; Champion carried him across the bridge an instant later. He felt more than saw or heard the arrows flying by him as he swiftly closed on his target, but something was wrong. No one was behind him. He quickly reigned in his horse at the base of the wall and threw his sack of oil at the door. The leather pouch burst on the wood, spreading oil over a large area.

Mikhal looked back toward the bridge to see his men staring up at the wall directly above his head. Sitting there dumbfounded, fear finally creeping over him, he heard the evil laughter coming from above.

FERRAL LAUGHED CRUELLY AS HE watched the lone rider charge through the arrows and throw something on the gate. "Well done, cavalier, well done," he said as he waved down at Mikhal.

Metal clanked against the stones of the wall as he shouted down at the man. Ferral held a sputtering torch in one hand and the end of a chain fashioned as a leash in the other. The other end of the chain was attached to a metal collar fitted around Rebenna's neck. She looked subdued and beaten. Standing meekly beside her former lover, she looked more like a whimpering beggar than a priestess of Belatarn.

"No Belarnian archers, don't shoot him. This one is braver than his companions. I suspect that if half of their army was as capable as him, they might not all die tonight. Let him return to his men," Ferral ordered.

The demon woman, dressed in her long red cloak, stood beside Ferral and watched the small rider return across the bridge to join his men. Ferral's plan to ensnare the army was working perfectly. She looked on, feeling something akin to remorse as she lost sight of the lone rider regrouping with his companions.

Ferral handed his torch to Rebenna and turned to address the cavaliers. "Welcome to the mighty citadel of Belarna. I bid you welcome and invite you to enjoy your stay." He laughed again, taking great pleasure in his moment of triumph. Another rider broke free of the small knot of cavalrymen and trotted forward onto the bridge.

The man looked defiantly up at his enemy and said, "Ferral, don't play games with us. We already know what you're like. You're a murderer. We have come for Princess Allisia." He struggled to maintain a good grip on the reigns of his horse as he fought back his fear. "Return her, now, and you will save many of your people further harm."

Ferral laughed at the arrogance of the person making claims from the bridge. "Only the prince of Erand could be so bold and stupid to make such a claim." He turned to look at the guards on either side of him.

Waving his hands grandly toward the gathering storm clouds, he said, "Don't you feel it, Kristian of Landron? A new age is upon Erinia. An age I have ushered in. An age that Belarn will dominate for a thousand years."

"We know that evil has been unleashed in the land, Ferral. An evil you created. We're here to stop you and your mad plans."

"Fools! You dare interfere with the wishes of our god, Belatarn? I will crush you for your sacrilege," Ferral said pointing down at Kristian.

"Call your god what you will," Kristian replied evenly, "but there is only one name for the evil you have called upon. Don't think for a moment that God will stand by and watch you destroy his world. He will bring you down."

"Indeed? Then he is planning to do so without the support of the mightiest kingdom in Erinia." Ferral smiled cruelly. He reached down to pick up something from between his feet. It was dark and too far for Kristian to make out what it was. "Tell me, Kristian. How is your father doing? I hope he enjoyed the summer weather I sent him."

"I've had enough of your pointless jokes, Ferral. We all know you're the one causing all of this trouble. Your evil magic has caused this foul weather," Kristian called back.

Ferral acted surprised, putting his hand over his mouth. "You mean you really don't know? I know your father wanted the chance to speak with you one last time. Something terrible has happened, I'm afraid. There was an awful fire, Kristian."

Kristian's heart skipped a beat as a dread feeling began to set in. Ferral's words reached him through a dense cloud forming in his head.

"I wanted him to be more comfortable. I thought a little warmth would help him combat the early winter, but it got a little out of control." Ferral continued, holding the object in his hand higher. "Here, your father really wants to tell you the news himself." The mad sorcerer tossed the object down. It landed on the bridge just in front of Kristian. "Behold, the wise Emerick of Landron! The dead king of Erand."

Kristian looked down in fear and saw a grotesquely scarred head. Blackened and charred, it was unrecognizable. Kristian's instincts told him it was his father, but he could not bring himself to accept it. "It's a trick. You can't fool me so easily. My father has already sent reinforcements. They will be here ..."

"Your father is dead. Most of your people are dead or soon will be. And your land is mine."

"No. You're lying," Kristian shouted.

"Enough," Ferral shouted back. "This game of words is over. I thought I would like you once I met you, Kristian, but I suppose I should have listened to my advisors. You truly are a spoiled brat. It doesn't matter whether you believe me or not. You will be meeting your father before the sun rises." Ferral and his men laughed at the prince, as he stood motionless on the bridge.

"I don't think we will get the chance to meet again, Your Royal Highness, so I bid you farewell. Farewell!" The guards along the wall echoed Ferral's words as they waved to the small force of cavalrymen below.

SUDDENLY, MIKHAL COULD SEE THE silhouettes of men closing on either side of him. Even in the darkness, he could tell there were several thousand armed men forming into ranks on either side of the moat. A chill wind blew past the cavaliers, and Mikhal was forced to huddle behind the neck of his horse in a futile attempt to block the wind. Although his blood was racing, and a moment ago he could feel nothing, he now felt an unsettling cold taking over his body.

"Where did they come from? We saw them leave," Mikhal exclaimed.

"These aren't the same men," Alek shouted.

Alek quickly took charge of his men and ordered them back into even ranks. It was obvious that the Belarnian army was attempting to surround the cavaliers before the slower Duellrian forces could move to protect them. General Aphilan's men were still half a league away.

Ordering a charge, Alek led them toward the furthest point on the right where the Belarnians were still moving into position. Cursing, Mikhal lead his men toward where the forming infantry looked most vulnerable.

The cavaliers rode into the exposed flank of their enemy with their lances lowered. They cut a path through the tightening cordon and broke free of the foot soldiers. Mikhal looked back to see how many made it through and saw an unlucky soldier fall from his horse. The soldier tried to reach an arrow sticking out of his back, but two Belarnians immediately came up and cut him to pieces. The gathering army just as quickly butchered the man's horse. Mikhal could only hope the man was not one of his own soldiers. He was still not prepared to face their deaths.

Alek halted after reaching safety and shouted for his officers to protect the Duellrian flanks, as planned. "We will hold them off and fight our way back to the hill. We should be able to keep the hill until Justan arrives with the rest of his forces."

"No," Kristian shouted. "We have the advantage of speed and skill. Look how many we took down in just one charge. We'll go at them again."

The cavalry commander could no longer keep silent. "What? There must be nearly ten thousand men back there. We're only one hundred. You can't make such a decision."

"Remember your place, Captain Hienren." Kristian stopped himself before he said something more. He sighed in frustration and then added, "Look, we'll never have another chance. They are still trying to get organized, and they're afraid of a mounted attack. We can keep them in disarray until Aphilan can engage them. Allisia needs us. If we give up now, Ferral will kill her." Kristian paused, gauging Alek's loyalty to him. "Do I have to make the order myself?"

"No," Alek shouted back at the prince. "I will lead my men." He closed with the prince and leaned forward so that no one else could hear. "You are our prince. The cavaliers were created to serve you and the king. If your father is still alive, he would never do this. You may have just ordered us all to our deaths. Kristian, you don't know anything about how we should be used." The prince, angry and a little shaken by the exchange of words, sat motionless beside the commander as the order was given.

Alek pulled his horse away from Kristian and called out, "Form into three wedges. I want you to charge past their flanks and force them to extend their formations. Romlin, you will go first and draw them left. Hanson, you will follow and draw them to the right. And Mikhal, I want you to lead a charge through the middle to scatter their lead unit. They're not a regular army. Some of them were carrying only pitchforks and most didn't have any armor … so hopefully they will break and run." The three officers nodded to their commander understanding that speed and confusion were their only chances for survival.

"Don't get caught up among them for very long or they will cut you to pieces," he cautioned Mikhal. "Look for weak points in their formations and take advantage of the ones you find. Move away quickly, and when you're free again, we will regroup here."

"Watch out for archers. Keep your bodies low even after you are free of them," Mikhal warned his men. Alek looked around at his entire command and spotted Truan Langwood. The old cavalier smiled knowingly back at his captain.

"I will follow behind the company, sir, and try to keep them together," the veteran said as he turned to the cavaliers. "Which one of you will bring me the banner of the monster that dares challenge us?" he demanded.

For a brief moment, no one said anything. Then a lone soldier rode out from the formation. He was a young man, one of Mikhal's soldiers. His name was Davil. He looked frightened and pale in the growing cold, but he rode forward and accepted the old sergeant's challenge.

"I will," Davil replied. The sergeant nodded solemnly and motioned for the cavalier to take his place with his men.

Romlin shouted for his men to prepare for the charge. Mikhal also turned and faced his men and shouted, "Davil has made a pledge. Anyone that sees Davil get the banner must protect him with his life." The men shouted in unison praising Davil for his courage.

Then all heads turned as one as Romlin gave the order for his men to charge. The cavalrymen moved swiftly, lances lowered, as they quickly approached the loose formation of Belarnian foot soldiers. Mikhal and his men could hear the large formation of bloodthirsty soldiers cheer as they saw the small group of thirty Erandians move toward them. At the last possible moment, Romlin moved his wedge of horses and men to the left. They scraped the front of the army and pushed the first few ranks of Belarnians back into the spears and swords of their own men. Many of them feared the horses and broke ranks, pushing and shoving to get away from the charging beasts. Others broke from the formation and chased Romlin and his men.

Seeing the point of attack become more apparent, Hanson sounded the charge. His men had seen that the commander's plan could work, and they rode hard; their fear subsided as they pushed toward the right side of the Belarnian army. Hanson began to slow his men's advance to better control his wedge as arrows started flying all around them. The cavalrymen smashed into their enemies again and forced the lead ranks of soldiers upon themselves. Hanson deliberately slowed down his charge even more during his withdrawal to ensure that as many Belarnians followed as possible.

Mikhal watched his friends taunt thousands of angry Belarnians. He smiled, admiring their bravery as the enemy scattered to the left and right, chasing after the fleeting cavaliers. Mikhal stood up in his saddle and shouted, knowing it was his turn to ride and smash the middle, "For Erand!"

His men repeated his shout as he turned in his saddle and raised his lance and then lowered it. Mikhal put his horse straight into a full run. Leaning low, bracing himself against the jarring impact to come, Mikhal centered himself on the large formation before him. He screamed as he chose his target and spurred Champion on into their enemies.

Mikhal's blow cut straight through the neck of one soldier who hesitated a moment too long. The lance caught for a moment as the Belarnian fell grasping at the slender piece of wood sticking out from his throat. His charge had carried his men completely through the lead formation. The Belarnians quickly scattered, leaving many of their comrades vulnerable to attack by Mikhal's men. They started to fan out to either side of Mikhal, thrusting spears down at the confused soldiers.

Mikhal was terrified that he might get overwhelmed while his lance was stuck; he kicked Champion onward and used the momentum of his horse to pull the weapon free. Mikhal lifted the lance and threw it at a Belarnian rushing toward him. The soldier momentarily clutched at the wood jutting from his chest before he fell to the ground, blood bubbling from his mouth. Mikhal quickly pulled his saber free of its scabbard and looked around at his men. Most were similarly engaged in combat. Their momentum had pushed them deep into the ranks of the center formation, much further than he had intended. He knew that if he did not quickly find a way out of this mass of men and steel, they would soon be overwhelmed.

The fears he had thought of earlier came back as he began to believe he might have led his men into a death trap, but he fought down the urge to panic. He found a gap in the fighting to his left and was about to lead his men out.

Suddenly, Mikhal heard a triumphant shout from somewhere off to his right. Davil emerged from a solid mass of Belarnians shouting and waving something in his hand. Covered in blood, the young cavalier looked ready to fall out of his saddle at any moment, but in his upraised hand he held the remnants of a black and red flag.

"I did it! I did it!" he shouted. Mikhal shouted for someone to help Davil and saw several riders break away from their fights to rescue him.

Mikhal saw a glint of steel out of the corner of his eye and turned quickly to see a Belarnian with a crude spear rushing toward him. He could not bring his shield around in time and immediately brought his saber down with all of his strength. His attack broke the spear just

before it went into his side. He brought his blade down again and cut
through the man's scalp.

Seeing his chance for escape fading away, he ordered his men to
make for the spot he saw earlier on his left. Mikhal made a daring attempt to get clear of his enemies; he kicked Champion hard and leaned
low to keep from being knocked down by a chance blow. He cut a couple of soldiers down on his way to freedom. They were trying to grab
the reigns of his horse to stop him, but Mikhal was eventually able to
get clear.

He let out a deep sigh of relief as he kept urging Champion away
from the fighting. Chancing a look back, he saw that most of his men
also made it out safely. He used his saber to point toward where the
rest of the cavaliers were regrouping and then guided his horse in that
direction.

"We did it!" Romlin shouted as Mikhal and his men reached the
safety of the small area secured by the cavalier.

"They barely seemed like soldiers. Most of the ones I saw didn't
even have armor or shields," Hanson offered. "They must have been
pressed into service."

Casualties proved to be far less during the charge than Mikhal expected. He and his men had lost only four. The loss was terrible news to
Mikhal, but he tried to push their faces out of his mind and concentrate
on the battle.

"If we can hold on a little longer, we may just make it," Mikhal
hoped. The young cavalry officer looked around for his commander
and spotted his prince instead.

"Cavaliers, you have proven your worth this day. There is no finer
company of cavalry in the world. Let's ride once more into their ranks
and show them what Erandian soldiers are made of," Kristian shouted
as he waved his saber over his head. Mikhal noticed there was no blood
on his sword, and then he grimaced in disgust as he ordered his men
back into even ranks and awaited orders from Alek.

Alek had also looked at the prince disapprovingly. Kristian had briefly shown them that he had great potential over the last few weeks, but tonight he had chosen to revert back to his usual, uncontrollable self. "Not just yet, Your Highness. Look at how their commanders are whipping their footmen back into tight ranks. They will not be as easily drawn away from the center again."

"At least we have slowed their approach. They seem much more cautious now," Mikhal offered as he pointed at the black mass of soldiers lumbering toward them.

"You're right, Mikhal," Alek remarked, noticing the determined but slower pace of the lead ranks. "I'm surprised they have that much control over their men after what your man did. It was Davil that took the banner, wasn't it?"

"It was," Mikhal turned to congratulate the cavalier but could not find him.

"Sir," Jamal interrupted, "Davil was removed from the ranks. He suffered numerous cuts and was unable to ride any longer. I ordered him to return to the supply wagons to seek aid."

Mikhal looked down at the frozen ground as he tried to figure out what to say. All he could do was nod in understanding. Davil was a good soldier. His courage in capturing the flag bolstered the spirit of the entire company. Now he was badly hurt, and Jamal made it sound like he might not see the sunrise.

"Here they come!" someone shouted from behind Mikhal. The cavalier scanned the distance to judge the progress of the Belarnians. They had gained a lot of ground while the Erandians rested. The deep sound of Belarnian war horns reverberated through the night. It worried some of the cavaliers that had never experienced the sound of the march-horns. It was followed by the chants and screams of thousands of angry Belarnians as they rushed toward their hated enemies.

Alek rode forward so that everyone could hear him. "They have seen how well we can fight. Those bastards won't rush in to pull us down again." Many of the younger cavaliers laughed nervously. "But now we've got to use the combined force of our entire company to ensure we're not taken down piecemeal by these murderers of women and rapists of sheep." They all laughed and cheered.

"We'll charge them again, but this time in full force. All elements focus on the center to put fear in them. At my command, we will shift our momentum to the far left. I noticed that side is slower to react than the rest of their army. We will rake their front and turn to smash back into their flank. Does everyone understand?" The entire company shouted their acknowledgment in unison.

"With any luck, Aphilan's men will finally join the fight," he added, jokingly.

Mikhal barely had time to turn and make sure his soldiers were ready before his commander sounded the charge and led them toward the enemy. He tried to keep them centered on his captain as they rode toward the middle of the large army, looking back constantly to ensure his men were in a tight formation. Mikhal could see the front rank of foot soldiers and peasants begin to slow and stop as they feared a direct assault. Belarnian commanders tried to bring archers closer to the front to slow their charge, but at the last possible moment, Alek veered to the left.

Pitchforks and spears reached out to knock Mikhal's commander from his horse, but he was too fast for them to follow. Hanson's soldiers were on the side closest to the Belarnians as the cavalier shifted to the left. His men knocked many down with just the momentum of their horses. Hanson tried to maintain the speed of his charge, his men using their lances to force the Belarnian mob back, while the rest of the cavaliers headed toward the far end of the army. The front ranks were either crushed by the horses or cut down by Hanson's men. Several hundred Belarnians ran away just to keep from being trampled in the panic.

When they finally passed by the end of the formation, Mikhal signaled for his men to turn back into their enemies in a wide arc. As his men again faced the army, he saw Hanson and his cavaliers break free of the Belarnian front ranks and move into position behind him. The cavaliers crashed into the weaker side of the opposing army just as they tried to get back into a defensive posture. Mikhal was surprised at how great an effect their horses had on the foot soldiers. Easily a hundred were killed in the first few moments as the cavaliers used their momentum to push toward the flag of some Belarnian commander.

The officer, dressed in black armor, turned toward the advancing cavaliers and ordered the men closest to him into a protective ring. The rest of the Belarnians between the black, helmeted commander and the charging Erandians were, unfortunately, confused and shocked by the cavalry charge. Unlike their commander, most of them wore nothing more than ragged clothes and had no armor protection. They ran as fast as they could to get away from the thundering hooves of the cavaliers, creating chaos throughout the entire left side of Ferral's army.

It was during the charge that Kristian decided to follow the cavaliers deep into the flank of the enemy.

"No, Prince Kristian, stay with me!" Alek shouted. The prince either did not hear or chose not to heed the commander.

Kristian saw Mikhal lead the daring attack and urged his horse through the gap in the enemy lines. He did not check his horse's speed and ran into the back of one of the cavalier's mounts. The horses faltered and Kristian thought he might fall. He struggled to maintain control of his horse.

A Belarnian ran forward then, seeing an opportunity to bring a few of the cavaliers down, and grabbed Kristian's reins. Kristian saw the man's panicked expression as he frantically tried to pull the horse to the ground. The prince of Erand hesitated for a moment, knowing he had to kill the other man, but now that the time had come to test his mettle, he found it hard to raise his saber.

In that brief instant, Kristian knew his adversary had been pressed into service. This wasn't a warrior. This was an ordinary man that had been forced to obey the commands of an evil ruler. *Was he justified in killing the man?* Kristian wondered.

He let the saber fall but put little force behind the swing. The cut sliced through the man's left eye socket and nose but failed to kill him. The Belarnian screamed in panic, seeing parts of his eye and nose fall off in his hands. The man's blood covered his face, hands, and even parts of the prince's horse.

Kristian raised the saber again, realizing he had botched the attack and could not leave the man like he was. This time he brought the blade down with all of the force he could manage. The force of the swing almost threw him from his saddle. The impact of the blow helped steady him, though, as his sword came down hard on the man's exposed neck. The blow did not completely sever the man's head, but his spine was cut and the man's screaming suddenly stopped.

Kristian raised the bloody sword, breathing heavily and looking for other threats. There were a few more Belarnians nearby but they decided not to attack him, fearing either the horse or the men with their lances and swords. Kristian was glad. He regained control of his horse and guided it through the closing gap. Kristian quickly reunited with Alek, and the two backed away from the front ranks of the Belarnian army.

"That was not a smart move, Kristian," Alek rebuked the young man. "You had no one to protect your other side and could easily have been overwhelmed."

Kristian nodded in agreement. He would be more cautious the next time. The prince looked at the blood running down the groove in his saber. He felt a sick fascination and was a little relieved at having finally killed another man. Kristian had not been certain he could do it when the time came, but he had done what thousands before him had done. And he realized he did not like it; a sense of dread began to creep over him.

"We've got to pull them back before it's too late. Sound the horn. Regroup. Regroup!" Kristian shouted back at Alek. A cavalier pulled out his horn and sounded a few short notes. Mikhal saw one of Romlin's men drive his lance into the Belarnian commander as cavaliers pushed through the remainder of the protective circle. Several Erandians shouted in triumph, feeling the outcome of the battle shift in their favor; the remaining Belarnians were running back to the protection of another unit.

For a brief moment, there was an eerie silence on the battlefield. The cavaliers looked around them in relief, thankful for the momentary respite. Mikhal saw Kristian next to his captain just outside the fray. He was breathing heavily and looked distraught and confused. He clenched his saber desperately as he looked around in disbelief. Mikhal noticed that this time Kristian's sword was covered with blood.

Good. At least the prince has finally learned the price of winning a war. How brave and noble do you think killing is now, Your Highness? The words were only thoughts in Mikhal's mind, things he could not bring himself to say out loud.

Suddenly, the mass of soldiers around them seemed to close in. The Belarnians regained control of their army and were attempting to trap them. Mikhal looked around in despair as he saw all possible escape routes vanish. He pulled hard on Champion's reigns, trying to calm his horse. The lieutenant heard the signal for them to pull back, but it was difficult to see a way out of the mess. Mikhal could see the looks on many Belarnian faces. "They know they've got us this time," he spat at them.

A single snowflake fell to the ground in front of Mikhal, and he shivered, feeling the cold wind blow even harder than before. The distance between the cavaliers and the cautious Belarnians was slowly closing.

"A few seconds more, and then they'll be close enough to launch arrows at us," Mikhal warned his men.

The sound of horns echoed across the battlefield just as the enemy prepared to assault the cavaliers. Mikhal thought it was Alek's second call to pull back and regroup, but as he prepared to make his last stand, the cavalry officer could see his enemies turn away from him in confusion. The horns gave out a much more musical note than the sharp, gruff sounds of the Belarnian march-horns. Screams and shouts of alarm rose from the far side of the battlefield and the Belarnians forgot about the cavaliers as they fought to keep from being over run by the Duellrian army. Aphilan's men had finally caught up with the Erandians and were rushing into the larger army, hoping to free the cavalrymen.

Mikhal could see hundreds of arrows arcing down toward Ferral's men like a heavy downpour of rain. The soldiers could hear the hissing of the massive storm even above the sounds of battle. Hundreds of unprotected men fell in an instant.

Alek saw their opportunity for escape and ordered those around him to charge. "Now, men. Ride! Ride now!" he shouted as he led them toward a smaller group of Belarnians.

Mikhal saw his commander and shouted for his men to follow him. He spurred his horse after Alek and the remaining cavaliers did not hesitate. They forced their horses to run over those still barring their way to safety and then turned toward the rear of the Duellrian army for some much needed rest.

THE BATTLE RAGED ON FOR over an hour. Of the one hundred Erandians present for the initial charge, only fifty cavaliers could still sit in the saddle and carry a lance. Saved by the Duellrian attack, they had regrouped and rested while their allies managed to push the larger Belarnian army back against the moat. But the weather grew worse as they fought, and the Duellrians began to lose their momentum. They were able to hold their position but could not keep the Belarnians pinned against the edge of the moat. An inch of snow was already on the ground, forcing soldiers to move more cautiously on the frozen, snow-covered battlefield.

Alek saw that the Duellrians were losing their advantage and ordered his three officers and their men to help by attacking the exposed flanks. The commander hoped their harassing tactics would keep the enemy worried enough about their vulnerable sides that they would pull some of their forces away from the front.

Duellrian archer units launched their last volley of arrows into the center of the large mass of men near the moat. The scene was one of violent chaos.

MIKHAL LOOKED BACK TO SEE how many of his men had fallen during the last pass. "Three. Three more good men," he said, despairingly. So far, Mikhal had lost fifteen men during the battle. He wondered how many more he would have to watch die before he was also pulled from his horse and killed.

Mikhal reigned in to rest and scanned the winter gloom for signs of the rest of the company. He could see Hanson and his men also pulling free of the army, racing toward a place where they could regroup. The southern Erandian only had twelve uninjured cavaliers with him. Mikhal also looked for Romlin. Earlier, the lieutenant had struggled to rally his men against a large force of pike men, but Mikhal could not find him. He did, however, see Alek and their prince talking with General Aphilan.

Even from where he was sitting, Mikhal could see that Kristian was ordering more people into the fight. The prince pointed to a group of Duellrians and waved his saber mightily in the air. The soldiers he was talking to quickly ran off toward a small group of Belarnians.

"How many more brave men will you send to their deaths, Prince?" Mikhal asked as he looked in dismay. The Duellrian army started to give ground to the much larger enemy force.

Mikhal saw Aphilan give the signal for retreat as they began to lose control of their formation. Trumpets began to sound across the battlefield for the second time as Duellrians and Erandians hurried away from the Belarnians. Mikhal looked up at the walls of the city to see Ferral still laughing at Kristian's failed rescue attempt.

Anger swelled up within Mikhal as he thought of the terrible costs they had all paid only to fall back. He called for Jamal saying, "Bring me a torch. Quickly."

"What are we going to do?" one of his soldiers asked as he stared at Mikhal's grim face.

Mikhal did not bother saying anything as he grabbed the flaming torch and turned toward the fortress. He kicked Champion hard and rode off, leaving his men behind. They began to understand what their leader was planning to do and shouted war cries and charged after him.

Mikhal and his small band of men raced for the bridge, passing groups of Belarnians that were resting or cheering at the retreat of their enemies. They crossed before anyone realized what was happening. Mikhal reached the large wooden doors blocking their way into the city before his enemies could stop him.

A moment later, Mikhal thrust his burning torch at the oil soaked doors. His men added their remaining sacks of oil and the flames began to grow. There were only a few bags left, but they were enough to help the flames spread across the entire door. Mikhal sighed, enjoying the small victory as the fire began to burn into the wood.

14.

A NEW ERA

Ferral turned away from the smoke rising toward him. He threw his torch at a guard, shouting in uncontrollable anger. "Where is that fool Derout? My men are floundering about like fish." Ferral's eyes bulged, and he fumed as he stared back down at the Erandian cavalry.

"I don't know who you are, little man, but I will make sure you die this night." Mikhal raised a clenched fist in defiance up toward Ferral, but his companions stopped their cheering when they heard the sorcerer shouting at them. The cavalrymen urged their leader to flee before it was too late.

"Do you hear me? You and your small, pitiful group of men will die the worst deaths." Ferral laughed hysterically pointing down at the cavaliers. "I will come for you, and I will bring death with me, but it will not come too quickly. You may scream in agony, cry for your mothers, but your deaths will take hours." The mad sorcerer laughed again, dismissing the cavaliers as he motioned for the army to surround Mikhal and his men.

Over a hundred soldiers answered the call of their king. They rushed to take the bridge before Mikhal could escape. After blocking his escape route, the Belarnians slowly approached their enemies in even ranks with their spears lowered.

Ferral smiled again. Turning to the demon, he asked, "Where is Derout?"

The demon woman took a few moments to answer Ferral; her attention was drawn toward Mikhal. She looked at the cavalier with deep sadness and longing before turning to face the man that controlled her. "Derout is a capable man. He will come."

"But when? If he does not come soon it will be too late."

"And there are more Duellrians coming. They will be here by midday," she replied looking east where the sun would rise in a few hours.

"More? How many more?"

"Thousands more," she answered calmly, still watching Mikhal. "The larger portion of the Duellrian army received word of the battle, and they haven't stopped to rest. They've been marching all night."

"No. This can't happen. The outer door has been breached. My pathetic army can barely keep this smaller force at bay." Ferral looked at the demon. "You will stop them."

The demon looked at him in surprise. "Why Ferral, you're becoming used to your new authority, aren't you?" she answered, mockingly. "Have I not shown you things that should have allowed you to defeat this army by yourself?"

"You've only shown me a few tricks. Snowstorms? Ice in the water? I have blanketed Erand in snow. I have even brought in a storm to make it harder for the damned Erandian cavalry to charge, but they continue to beat my forces."

"I like the cold and snow. It's fitting weather for tragedy and death," the demon replied.

Ferral shook his head angrily, "I want real power. I need more than what you have shown me. Even my witch could learn what you have taught me." Ferral pulled hard on Rebenna's chain sending her flailing toward the stone floor. "I didn't raise you from the depths to learn things I could have learned from this harlot. Your master did not give you to me so that I would lose."

"He is your master, as well, Ferral. For all eternity."

"I gladly welcome him as my master. I have committed myself to him, but you continue to deny me that which I have always sought," Ferral fumed. "None of our master's plans will come to fruition if I am defeated tonight. Show me what I want to know," he demanded.

"You have the scroll. The power you seek is written there for you to learn," she teased.

"I've already tried. I had some success but not on the scale that the scroll promised. I need your help. There is a phrase that I have never fully translated," he whined.

The demon smiled again, enjoying Ferral's tantrum. "Surely you know that our master will not simply give you what you want without a special sacrifice?"

"The princess? Now?" A look of disappointment and dismay crossed Ferral's face as he contemplated the demon's demands. He was growing fond of the young girl from Duellr. He had even thought of keeping her for himself. Ferral was tired of Rebenna. She served his needs out of desperation; she only wanted to stay alive. Truth be known, Ferral was sick of her. She always tried to squirm away from him because she was terrified of his new powers, but Allisia was completely different. The Duellrian princess struggled to escape his grasp because she hated him. He could see it in her eyes. She loathed being near him and would rather die than serve him.

"Kill the princess, and I will teach you the words you can not speak," the demon promised reluctantly.

Ferral wanted Allisia too much. *If I could subdue her just enough to keep her here,* he thought, *I could enjoy her beauty and youth for years.* A smile broke out on his face as he dreamed of the day when he would take Allisia to bed.

"A sacrifice?" he asked as if he did not understand the demon.

"Yes, Ferral, our master won't give you what you seek unless you continue to pledge obedience to him and drink the blood of a victim you kill in his name. Princess Allisia was brought back to you for that purpose. The power you would have gained by taking her life on the new moon at the end of next month would be much greater ... but if you feel you can not wait, you can perform the ceremony now. It will just be more ... painful."

"Very well," Ferral said as he looked back toward the palace where Allisia was still imprisoned. "Bring the princess here," he ordered a nearby guard.

He turned to Rebenna, yanking on her chain and bringing her closer to him. The witch was trembling from the cold but glad that the princess was about to be murdered and not her. She threw her arms around her lover, kissing him passionately. Rebenna knew her only chance of surviving the nightmare that she helped build was by pleasing the madman at all costs.

"I shall choose the victim and the time, demon," Ferral claimed as he returned Rebenna's kisses.

He grabbed her hair, pulling her head back to kiss her neck. He suddenly paused for a moment, thinking about what he was about to do and the power he **was** about to obtain. "I choose now, and I choose you, lovely Rebenna." He whispered as he flicked a blade up to her neck.

"No ... Ferral, please ... I," Ferral showed no sign of remorse as he quickly moved the **bone** blade she had found for him across her slender throat. Rebenna gasped for air as her lungs filled with blood. She reached out to Ferral in panic as blood flowed down her gown, soaking her clothing. She choked on her own thick fluids trying to cry out for help. Ferral embraced her, smiling and saying something, but she could not hear him.

She could feel Ferral's teeth sinking into her throat, hungrily sucking her blood from the gaping wound, as she began to black out. Although she knew she was very close to death, she still felt the sharp pain of his teeth and could feel the last of her life flowing out from her body into his mouth.

Rebenna no longer struggled. She no longer felt the pain. She could not even blink her eyes, but she could still see and think. Rebenna saw her blood dripping from Ferral's lips and bearded chin. He picked her limp form up and carried her toward the ramparts. He struggled to lay her on the black stone and then raised his hands chanting. The demon was whispering in his ear. Then he pushed her body over the edge to fall on the cavaliers below.

Rebenna's vision blurred as she fell toward the bridge and Mikhal's men. Colors faded into black and white as she sensed more than felt or saw that she had hit the ground. She thought she saw Ferral looming high above on the wall waving to her as her vision turned to black.

"It's not the princess. I remember seeing her in the palace, on a balcony, one night. That's not her," one of his men called out. Mikhal turned his head away from the woman's crumpled form and shook his head.

"No, you're right. It isn't the princess," he confirmed.

"But we are going to look a lot like her if we don't get out of here soon," someone shouted, pointing to the Belarnians still marching toward them.

Mikhal looked to his left and right, trying to find a way for them to escape. To the south, the moat curved in toward the city as it headed around a corner; the route looked too narrow for an escape route. But to the north, the ground between the wall and the water continued on out of sight in the snowy darkness.

"We'll go that way," Mikhal ordered his men.

Ferral fell to his knees in agony as the power he begged for coursed through his body. The sorcerer clutched at his robes, every part of his skin feeling as though it were on fire. He screamed in terrible pain.

"Is this what you sought, Ferral? You're so eager to control the magic that you will do anything, kill anyone," the demon claimed as she watched Ferral cringe in pain. Her face was livid with uncontrollable emotions.

"Finally," she told herself, "the fool has started something he doesn't know how to control." The demon felt sympathy for those living in the dark times about to come, but she was also relieved that her chains to this world would soon be destroyed. The king of Belarn lay on the floor of the rampart convulsing as the evil flowed into him, filling him with awesome power that no man was intended to have.

"Yes," Ferral hissed through clenched teeth. Even as he felt his body and soul melting into the black stones beneath him, he knew the power he was gaining was what he had always sought. He would rule the world with the knowledge he now possessed. Those who stood in his way would meet the same fate he planned to soon deliver upon the fools struggling against him below. He smiled at the thought of watching Kristian die horribly. Then the pain reached a new height, and he screamed in agony.

Ferral's back arched to the point that bones in his spine popped. The air was forced from his lungs as the power finally took hold inside him.

The demon looked at Ferral, mildly satisfied. A part of her hoped the sorcerer might die as she stared down at his limp form, but she knew he was still alive. Their master would not allow his tool to be destroyed so easily. "No, Ferral, you're not dead. You may wish you were, but you are not." She held out her hand to assist the stricken sorcerer, but Ferral would not move.

"No …," he struggled to say, "I don't wish I were dead. I have seen what you have … I have seen things. I have seen things that I thought could never exist." His eyes opened wide as he began to comprehend the full extent of his new powers. He stared at his hands and legs, moving them as if he did not believe they were truly whole. Then he smiled.

"Where is the princess," he demanded of the guards standing close by. They rushed away, eager to escape the madness surrounding them.

Mikhal urged his horse into the gloom surrounding the fortress. Snow and wind blinded him as he tried to find a way for him and his men to escape. He looked back once to see how many men were with him, but he could see nothing in the storm.

In front of him, he briefly saw the reflection of something shiny off to his right. It was the moat waters, and there was another bridge ahead. Mikhal shouted in excitement, pointing toward the stone structure. He crossed quickly along with the rest of his men and then halted on the other side of the water to rest.

"God has truly watched over us tonight," one of the soldiers acknowledged.

"Or maybe it's just you, sir," another soldier offered to Mikhal. "You are the luckiest man I have ever met, and I'm glad that I have stayed close to you tonight." The remaining men in the group laughed, enjoying their momentary safety.

Mikhal reached down and patted his horse's neck reassuringly. "Well, Champion, you've saved me more times than I can count. I promise that if we survive this mess, you will see no harder tasks the rest of your life than to run free in the pastures." The horse stamped impatiently despite numerous cuts on its shoulders and withers. Mikhal shook his arms to relieve the tension in his muscles and then stood up in the stirrups to get a better look around him.

In the distance, he saw a small hill rising into the snowy mist. Through the darkness he could see small stone buildings and statues breaking up the hill's silhouette. Mikhal's good mood quickly evaporated as he realized he was staring at a Belarnian burial ground.

"Not exactly the type of thing you want to see during a battle, is it?" a soldier asked nervously.

"No, it isn't," Mikhal replied. Something inside him was shouting a warning, but he did not understand it. He knew he should run, but he could not. Something was wrong, he could feel it.

"What is that?" one soldier asked pointing to a dim light beginning to appear from behind the burial grounds.

Mikhal leaned forward in his saddle, straining to make out the single torch in the storm. He gasped as several other flaming brands suddenly joined the first. "It's a column," Mikhal realized, and then he lowered his head in defeat. "It's the same army we saw leave before the attack, the departing force that convinced Kristian to move against Ferral." He turned to face his soldiers. "They've been waiting here beyond our sight the entire time. We've been tricked. This has all been a trap. We must warn the Duellrians before all is lost."

"Well, sons of Erand, I hope you enjoyed your break," Jamal declared as he motioned for Mikhal's exhausted soldiers to get in line.

"We're ready," the veteran sergeant reported to Mikhal after quickly inspecting the men. Mikhal felt an overwhelming sense of gratitude; he was the best cavalier Mikhal had served with.

The young cavalry officer nodded grimly as he looked at the few remaining faces still with him. They were tired beyond comprehension from the fighting and stress, but they had a glimmer of hope in their eyes. Twelve mounted Erandians leaned into their saddles, preparing for the word to move. Each of them looked at their leader ready to do everything they could to prevent the Belarnians from destroying the Duellrians. Mikhal wished he shared their confidence, but he could not.

Feeling as though he had somehow failed them, he reluctantly nodded for Jamal to give the order. He leaned forward like his men, ready to make one more charge. Jamal checked his saddle harness, ensuring it was tight. Once he was satisfied, the sergeant raised his saber and shouted, "Ride!"

MIKHAL STOOD BENT OVER AT the waist, his hands barely able to hold onto the reigns. He fought to control his nausea, but wretched again as the cold wind brought the smell of fresh blood and smoke to his position behind the Duellrian army. Mikhal wiped the spit from his mouth and chin as sweat ran down his face despite the bitter cold.

Every time he attempted to watch the battle to estimate the amount of death the Belarnians now brought upon the Duellrians, his vision narrowed and he became dizzy. All but two of his men were lost in the ride from the bridge back to General Aphilan's position. They were forced to ride closer to the Belarnian cavalry than they wanted because of the moat and had to fight the advancing threat before they were finally able to break free. They were the Belarnian Black Guards, known as much for their devotion to Ferral as for their cruelty.

It only figured that the Black Guards were involved in Ferral's trick. They were the best trained and equipped of all the Belarnian forces, but they were not as good in battle as the cavaliers. They relied more on their fanaticism, numbers, and heavy armor than skill. All Black Guard soldiers reveled in the murderous tasks their sorcerer king gave them.

Mikhal's sergeant, Jamal, led half of Mikhal's men against the heavy cavalry, attempting to delay their advance while the rest of Mikhal's men sprinted on to warn General Aphilan. Mikhal remembered the reluctance reflected in Jamal's eyes. The man knew they were all going to die. It was madness to even think he and five other lightly armored cavaliers could halt a mounted force of over five hundred, but Jamal knew there was no other way to save everyone else unless a few sacrificed themselves.

Mikhal remembered seeing him look down at the ground, contemplating his fate for a moment before a determined looked passed over his face. He shouted for Mikhal to keep riding as he pulled in those soldiers close by and told them of their desperate need to slow the enemy. They immediately realized what he wanted them to do. If they did not make their stand now, no one would survive this hellish night.

With little more than a final wave and a half smile, Jamal and his men charged into the front ranks of the Black Guards. The sudden impact of horses and men threw the attackers into disarray. Horses screamed and soldiers shouted in anger and pain as the six quickly cut a small path into the Belarnians. Mikhal lost sight of them among the black-armored men that were eager to kill their sworn enemies. He could barely see the glint of torchlight reflected off the surface of polished sabers clashing with broadswords somewhere in the middle of the chaos.

Mikhal did not wait to see the outcome. He knew that Jamal's sacrifice would only provide him a brief moment. He did not plan to lose the chance given him.

The first person he was able to find was his prince. Kristian was conferring with some of the Duellrian officers, discussing the best way to finish off the remainder of the Belarnian army. Mikhal's charge to the gate had emboldened the men. The Duellrians renewed their attack, and now they were on the verge of victory. It was obvious to Mikhal that Kristian was excited. Mikhal took a small amount of joy in the fact that his news would quickly spoil Kristian's mood.

Wearily, he dropped from his horse and approached his prince. "I have terrible news. The Belarnian cavalry we saw leave earlier hid just beyond our sight. They're riding toward us now. We have only a moment to prepare for their attack," Mikhal abruptly stopped unable to say more. He was surprised at how exhausted he was. Finally feeling as though he had done as much as he possibly could, he sat down in the snow trying to catch his breath.

Kristian looked down at him, doubtfully. Mikhal expected to see despair spread across his face, but instead he saw suspicion. "Are you sure?" Kristian asked, looking into the young cavalry officer's eyes. "There have been no other reports. We're close to finishing off these vermin. If we pull men away from the fight now, we could lose everything."

With the little strength he had left, Mikhal pulled himself off the frozen ground and stood defiantly in front of his prince. Fuming, trying to find the words that could possibly match his furry, Mikhal sputtered, "My men are all dead. Dead!" He poured his hatred of his prince into his stare. "This has all been a trap. You convinced us to attack early, and that is exactly what they wanted us to do. Five hundred Black Guards are about to hit our right flank. I advise you to warn General Aphilan."

Still doubting him, Kristian turned and called for Alek to dispatch a patrol to scout out the new enemy. "We'll soon see if there is a new threat," Kristian said, turning away from Mikhal to watch the dwindling battle at the gate.

"Fool," Mikhal shouted back at him. "We'll all die because of you."

"What is it? What's wrong?" His commander asked riding up beside him. His helm was severely dented over his left eye, and blood trickled down into his mustache.

Mikhal quickly told him of the new danger, warning that more than a patrol was needed. "They're Black Guard cavalry ... about five hundred of them." Alek saw the grief in Mikhal's eyes and instantly believed him.

His commander left quickly, calling for all remaining cavaliers to join him. Mikhal saw the ragged remains of his company come together under the banner of Erand and ride off toward the new threat.

FERRAL SMILED CRUELLY AT PRINCESS Allisia as she was dragged out of the tower door to stand in front of him. Allisia was terrified. She thought everyone might forget about her when her countrymen had finally arrived. For the last two hours, she had worked desperately to bust the lock on her door and escape. She finally managed to open the heavy wooden door only to find two guards arriving to take her to Ferral. She screamed in horror as they took her out of the palace, thinking they had come to take her to her death. Ferral threatened several times to cut her throat and offer her blood to his god, and now Allisia thought the time had come.

Ferral often visited her to give little snippets of news about the approach of her kingdom's army. He always seemed in control of the situation and hinted he had a special surprise in store for her on the day the fools arrived to challenge him. Allisia always tried to act defiant, showing no outward signs of fear, but she panicked as they took her across the courtyard toward the walls.

The guards opened the tower door and shoved her back out into the cold; Ferral and the demon were standing before her, expectantly. She screamed again, sensing it was finally her time to die. Then she looked out and saw the chaotic battle below. The Belarnians were easy to spot with their black and red banners, but Allisia thought Ferral's army looked to be in desperate shape. They were pushed back against the moat and were fighting to stay in control of the bridge. She looked down, noticing that the heavy iron and wooden doors were completely destroyed. Black smoke washed over the top of the wall making it difficult to see the figures directly below her, but it looked like they were trying to erect a hasty barricade to block the open gate.

The madman reached over and grabbed her wrist pulling her to him. His breath smelled horrible, like he had eaten rotten meat. "Look, do you see? The death of your countrymen and your young prince is at hand." Allisia saw hundreds of bodies littering the snowy ground. Death was truly everywhere, but as she looked again at the battlefield, she still thought Ferral's army seemed defeated.

In fact, most of the fighting in front of the ruined gate had already ended. A small force of cavalry, that she supposed were the cavaliers that Ferral often cursed, were locked in battle with a much larger force of Belarnian cavalry. A thousand more Duellrians were on their way to help the Erandians, though. She also saw General Aphilan's standard; he was leading another group of five hundred soldiers into the fight. The Belarnians would soon be surrounded and destroyed. Perhaps Ferral had not yet realized that he was defeated.

Defiantly, she turned to Ferral and said, "Looks more like death has come for you." She stared at the disgusting man before her, trying to hide her fear. Her jaw went slack, however, as she saw the dried blood clinging to his bearded chin and clothes. *Would he kill her now that he was defeated? Would he kill her just to ensure her countrymen could not feel good about their victory?* she wondered.

Ferral simply smiled. "Even were my followers to fail me, I would still crush my enemies. This battle was merely for my enjoyment." He turned to look at the demon woman. Reassured now that he had the power he had always sought, Ferral said, "I alone can destroy those you love, Allisia."

Allisia forced out a laugh. She thought he was lying, trying to cause her to despair one final time before he killed her. Allisia learned many things about Ferral in the time she was held captive. She knew that even though he was faced with defeat, he would strike out as many times as possible before the end. His soul was corrupted by the evil he wished to control, he could not bear seeing anything good happen. She expected him to kill her soon and then retreat to hide from those who had come to save her.

"You're sick. Look to yourself to see death. Something as disgusting and evil as you defies God by still breathing clean air," Allisia shouted.

"What an amusing comparison, Allisia." He held out his arms in a grand gesture, encompassing everything around him. "For to look on me is to see death. I am the earthly power of my god, and he has given me the strength to shape this world to his liking. Look at those below my walls and see the future of all Erinia."

Ferral lowered his hands and pointed to those struggling on the battlefield. He hesitated, turning to face Allisia once more. "All will die except you, lovely Allisia. You alone shall live to the bitter end of time and see the fate of our world. You will have the honor of seeing everything crushed below the feet of my army." He faced those struggling below. "And all souls of hell shall do my bidding."

KRISTIAN HEARD ALLISIA'S SCREAM COMING from somewhere along the fortress wall. He broke away from the fighting and pushed his way onto the bridge. Mikhal had recovered somewhat and followed him toward the sounds of struggle above. He was not interested in helping the prince do anything, but the frantic screams of someone in danger urged him to follow Kristian.

Kristian looked up to see Ferral still standing atop the walls, looking down at him. Beside him was the demon woman that had taken Allisia from her home. He knew he had heard Allisia and panicked when he could not find her. "Where is she, you monster?"

"She is here, Kristian. Don't worry over her, she is my betrothed now. Once she heard you and the rest of the little bugs with you were about to be destroyed, she quickly decided to join me." Kristian heard Allisia shout for him over the top of the madman's laughter.

"Allisia!" Kristian struggled to find her but could see nothing behind the darkening curtain of black smoke and snow. "I will kill you. I swear that I will kill you no matter what happens."

Ferral's voice came down to them through the snow and smoke. "Tonight is a special night. It is the beginning of a new era. The beginning of my empire on Erinia and soon the entire world." There was a pause, and then suddenly the ground seemed to vibrate beneath their feet.

"You are finished, Ferral. Your army is defeated. Release her now," Kristian demanded.

"Oh, but you have not met my new army. They are the most devout of all servants. And you shall soon become one of them." Mikhal saw the figures above clearly illuminated by a brilliant flash of lightning. Ferral's body was consumed by the blinding light before he fell back. The hairs on the back of Mikhal's neck stood up, and he felt colder. He turned to make sure no one was coming upon them from the far side of the bridge, but they were alone. Still, something was wrong. Mikhal continued to look around worriedly.

Kristian tried to gather men around him just as everything seemed to go completely silent. An invisible wave of pressure passed through him and his ears popped. The blast forced him to his knees. The horses screamed in panic, moving nervously from side to side. The prince of Erand put his hands over his ears as the moans of thousands of horribly wounded soldiers filled his head. The sound was deafening, and he thought he would go mad, but the sound ended as quickly as it began.

Mikhal and Kristian scanned the area for signs of approaching enemies; there was nothing but silence. Soldiers on both sides stopped fighting to see what was going on. Then, through the snowy mist, a lone figure near the castle wall stumbled toward the two Erandians. Mikhal raised his saber, prepared to defend himself but hesitated as the person came closer. It was the woman Ferral had thrown from the top of the wall. Blood covered her broken body and there was no way she should have been able to stand. It was as if her body was held up by the strings of an unseen master. Her eyes were dull and looked beyond the two men.

"This isn't right. What's happening?" Mikhal shouted. He turned around to witness other impossibilities rising from the frozen ground. All over the battlefield, the grizzly shapes of the dead stood up and slowly ambled toward the living. Belarnian, Erandian, and Duellrian … Ferral's spell had brought them all back, and they were all moving slowly and silently forward.

Kristian was suddenly thrown from his horse as the terrible form of what was once Rebenna grabbed his reigns. He struggled to stand, looking for his sword but could not find it. Kristian quickly grabbed a Belarnian broadsword, swinging desperately to keep the creature at bay. The sword stroke severed the thing's grasping hands as it came at him. The force of the blow threw it back against the low wall of the bridge where it lay crumpled for a moment before it again managed to stand and come for him. He started to go into shock. The creature would not die.

Had Mikhal not come up and jammed his saber into the back of its neck Kristian would be dead. The cavalry officer tried to pull his sword free, but the point had gone up into the skull and was stuck. Mikhal sent the dead thing back to the stone floor of the bridge, giving him the chance he needed to reach Kristian.

Mikhal remounted and pulled the dumbfounded prince on behind him. He kicked his horse hard, hoping to get free before it was too late. Mikhal looked back for an instant to see Rebenna rise again with the saber point jutting from her forehead. He shook his head in disbelief as he rode through a clearer portion of the battlefield. To either side of him, figures reached out bloody hands trying to pull them down.

ALLISIA LOOKED AT FERRAL IN horror. The mad sorcerer was bent over, coughs racking his entire body. Blood trickled down from his ears and nose as he held onto the bulwark for support. "Die! All of you shall die," he gasped between spasms of pain. Allisia backed away from the evil man, unable to comprehend what he had done. The demon turned from the chaos below to smile at Ferral.

"Our master is pleased, Ferral. Even he did not foresee how much ruin you were capable of. I, for one, thought it would take much longer for you to destroy everything, but you have surprised even me." The beautiful demon smiled in pleasure, seeing the pain tear at Ferral. She knew that eventually the power would consume him. He could not control it, and her master would be able to accomplish what he had sought for a millennium. The demon pulled down her hood and turned back to the bridge to see the two men struggling below with Rebenna.

Allisia also leaned forward, fighting the screams in her head. She knew that Kristian was down there and prayed he would somehow escape. She clung to the small hope that he might survive. He had really come for her. Allisia watched her hopes of escape vanish when Kristian was whisked away to safety by a cavalier.

"At least he is safe," she acknowledged. Allisia let out a brief sigh of relief as she turned her attention to her own countrymen.

THE DUELLRIAN ARMY WAS STILL nearly a thousand strong. They had somehow managed to destroy most of the Belarnian army. Their spirits were high after the destruction of the massive doors, and their courage enabled them to defeat a much larger enemy. They had killed or wounded at least eight thousand Belarnians and were preparing to push the remaining soldiers away from the bridge and enter the fortress. As they fought what they thought was their last battle, an invisible wall of pressure past through their ranks. Mortally wounded men struggled to stand back up and then approached those close by. In the first few moments of chaos, men were pulled down by groups of mangled corpses. Their screams filled the oppressive silence as the dead ripped the living apart.

Commanders reluctantly pulled their remaining soldiers into a protective ring as they realized they were now faced with the horrible challenge of fighting those they had already killed once, as well as their fallen comrades. They forgot about taking the bridge as they fought to keep their own men from running blindly into the darkness. The wind abruptly died as though it could no longer be forced to blow where the dead walked. Snow continued to fall in heavy sheets, blanketing the ground and limiting Allisia's view of the army.

She could barely see her people. They were surrounded by a much larger force that slowly stumbled toward them. Thousands of the dead converged on those that were unable to quickly withdraw. They formed a wall of spears and pikes to keep the grisly forms at bay, but it was not enough to hold them back. The dead pushed past the weapons or pushed each other onto them in a frenzy of hunger. There was a loud clanging of armor and weapons, followed by the growing sounds of terrified men being torn apart.

Allisia saw groups of the dead break off from the rest to attack the Belarnians as well. Whatever Ferral had done to raise these foul creatures had tasked him too greatly. He had broken the laws of nature, bringing all nearby corpses back from the dead, but he could not control them. She saw the Belarnians run for safety through the ruined gate as many of their own comrades were yanked from the crowd by the bloodthirsty creatures.

She looked down at Ferral who was fighting to stay conscious and kicked him in the chest. "You're mad! Insane!" she screamed.

The demon slowly approached her, enjoying Ferral's added pain. She longed to see the young girl crush the worm, but her master was not through using Ferral. No one knew what else the sorcerer might do to hasten the end of the world. The demon grabbed the princess by her cloak with a firm hand and dragged her back to an uneasy guard.

She dropped Allisia at his feet and said, "Watch her. Make sure she does not escape or harm herself." The demon looked into the man's eyes. "You have seen what your king can do?" The nervous man nodded quickly. "Then do not fail him or you may suffer their fate," she warned, pointing at the dead below them.

The demon pulled her cloak close to her and headed for the tower door. She turned a final time to the men on the rampart. "Your king is now the hand of Belatarn. He has created an army that will raze this land and ensure Belarn's control over all the other kingdoms. Make sure he is kept safe." As an afterthought she added, "And you better reinforce the damaged gate. They're hungry enough to push past that fire and destroy everyone within these walls." She smiled as she left them, prepared to do her part in creating destruction this night.

15

BOUND BY DUTY

"What do we do, General?" a confused and shocked officer asked the black-armored warrior. Derout looked across the battlefield, watching the nightmare shapes tear apart his countrymen with their bare hands. Screams of dismay and pain rang out time and again, making it hard for the Black Guards leader to think.

He knew Ferral was somehow responsible for the catastrophe that was threatening to destroy his army, as well as the Duellrian force, but the king could not be found. Ferral had not told him of his plans, and he was just as shocked as his enemies to see the dead walking. He ordered his cavalry to break off their attack and regroup; he had to think about what to do. There was a gaping hole in the main gate; the dead were streaming through the breach, and the lower districts of the city were in danger of being overrun. He also saw an opportunity to destroy his ancient enemy, the Erandians. The Belarnian general was torn for a moment, unsure of what would appease Ferral more, saving the city or destroying his enemies. Derout waved his heavy sword in the air shouting curses at the remaining cavaliers. He wanted to be the one that destroyed the Erandians, not Ferral's dead creatures.

"You and your families will be our slaves forever. Remember that, you Erandian dogs, if you live." Derout laughed at the sight of men and horses fleeing the battlefield.

"Our king has already destroyed the enemy," he called out to his men. He suddenly turned around in his saddle feeling a sharp pain in his right leg. Looking down, he saw one of his own black-armored soldiers tearing through his shin guard.

"What are you doing," he demanded.

The figure looked up. The flesh on one side of its face hung down from the cheekbone. Derout saw its eyes and gasped. It moved with fierce determination and obvious hunger, but when the general looked into its eyes, he saw no emotion. The thing continued to tear at his straps and armor, trying to satiate its need to kill the living. Derout kicked the dead man away and brought his heavy sword down on its head. Its skull was cleaved in two, but the thing fell to the ground still trying to grab his sword. The general looked around once more before ordering his men toward the enemy's marshalling area. A thousand more of the things were ambling toward him and his men. Derout would lead the dead toward his enemy's supply wagons; if he could trap them on the hill until the dead arrived … Derout laughed. It would be like ants swarming over a carcass.

MIKHAL AND THE REMAINDER OF the cavaliers regrouped on top of the small hill where they initially planned their attack. Alek and Hanson were still alive, but there were few others. In all, there were less than twenty.

"We'll all be dead soon," Mikhal said, looking down at the small ring of Duellrians trapped by the creatures.

Some of General Aphilan's men tried to establish a small, protective formation to block the dead while the remaining Duellrians forced their way toward the high ground where the cavaliers were resting. The clamor of steel and curses echoed across the frozen battlefield as they fought to survive.

Mikhal turned away from the fighting below to look around him. Kristian was nearby, sitting on a snow-covered log with his face in his hands.

"No. This is not real. This is not real," the prince kept murmuring over and over again.

Mikhal could hardly believe it himself. The image of the broken woman trying to pull them both from his horse was vivid in his mind. He moved stiffly toward his commander, more afraid than he had ever been in his life.

"Mikhal, forget about what happened for now. I need you with me." Alek shook his young officer hard. He pointed toward the city "The Duellrians will pull free. We must be ready to accept them. Prepare a group of men to stand ready on the western side."

Mikhal looked at him questioningly, "But ... they will come from the east. The ground over on the west side is too steep and frozen for even those monsters to climb."

"Just do it," Alek shouted pointing to the west, "and take the prince with you. Protect him." Alek left him standing there dumbfounded, already heading for Hanson's position.

Mikhal slowly turned away, confused by his commander's decision. Reluctantly, he approached the stricken prince. Mikhal pulled the grief-ridden man off the log and looked at the few cavaliers standing nearby. "You four men, come with me." Mikhal then dragged the murmuring prince to the far side of the hilltop, the four cavaliers walking silently behind.

The Duellrians finally broke through the ring of dead, but they paid a heavy price. Nearly half their numbers were pulled screaming from the formation as the army pushed toward the hill. In the end, someone shouted for everyone to run, and they all forgot about an orderly retreat as they struggled to find a way through the gauntlet. Groping hands reached out and snagged kicking men by their arms and legs. Screams of horror and pain filled the night air.

Mikhal could hear their pleas for help clearly, even over the howling wind that had picked up again with new malice. He scanned the steep hill below, wondering what he was supposed to do. His four men were hastily sharpening their weapons, preparing for the terrible battle ahead. Mikhal and some of the others had retrieved Belarnian broadswords, favoring the heavier steel for the butchering that was to come.

In a sudden panic, Mikhal went back to find his horse in a wooded part of the hilltop. It was standing in the midst of several other horses as far away from the dead as it could get. Even the animals sensed that these monsters were unnatural. He stood next to Champion, gently rubbing the horse's nose and tried to remember how they had come to this end.

After several minutes, Mikhal went back to where he had left Kristian. The dumbfounded prince had not moved since Mikhal had dragged him away from the center of the hill. The prince held on to a frozen branch for support, rocking forward and backward, as if he would be sick. He continually shook his head in disbelief as he watched the slaughter of those caught by the dead; Kristian was not the only one unable to cope with what they were witnessing. Many cavaliers and Duellrians were shouting and cursing … all of them were in shock. Mikhal ignored the panicked men and tried to think of how he and his four men might help their commander if he asked for it.

Perhaps five hundred Duellrians escaped the slaughter. Those that did make it back to the hill stood exhausted inside the protective ring of cavaliers. General Aphilan was panting, winded by the long climb up the hill. He tried to listen to the urgent words of his remaining commanders but had difficulty hearing them above his own breathing.

"We must flee, now," one captain urged. Blood covered the entire left side of his armored chest. He had barely escaped the dead.

"He's right. We lost over half our men just reaching this hill. If we wait, they will encircle us again, and then it will be too late. The blocking force can't hold them back forever," another officer claimed.

"We were so close to finishing them off," a cavalier moaned.

Aphilan motioned for silence. "If we wait here, we will die; these creatures can't be destroyed." He looked at the gathered soldiers. "We need to regroup and then move toward King Justan and the rest of our army. That will give us time to think about what must be done next."

"But what about the princess?" one of the officers asked.

Aphilan looked down at his frozen boots. "For now, she remains the prisoner of that evil man. Dying on this hill won't help rescue her." The Duellrians bowed their heads in sad acknowledgment.

They had come vowing to rid the world of the king of Belarn and save their princess from his mad schemes, but they failed. No one knew how long she might survive inside the citadel, but there was nothing they could do. They had underestimated Ferral's power, and they would be lucky to escape.

"The monsters were distracted by the breach in the main gate. I saw hundreds of them trying to get inside. It should take them some time to find us here in the dark. Count your unit's strength and prepare to march. We will rendezvous with what's left of the reserve at the backside of the hill and then send word to Justan. He should only be half a day's march behind us." Aphilan looked around for Alek. "Are your men ready to ride, captain?"

The exhausted commander nodded wearily. He was ready to leave this nightmare far behind. "Then order your remaining men to their horses. We leave as soon as you're ready."

"Then leave now. The cavaliers will be on your heels," Alek shouted as he turned and called for Hanson and Mikhal. Aphilan gave the order, and his men quickly shuffled back down the hill.

Only a few moments later, the cavaliers turned their heads in alarm as they heard shouts and screams coming from the bottom of the hill. They were just getting into their saddles, ready to catch up to their Duellrian comrades, when the sounds of battle rang out. Hanson rode up to Alek, Mikhal, and Kristian to find out what was happening. Then a figure stumbled toward them. It was a Duellrian soldier and he was badly hurt.

"Those bastards. They cut us off," he moaned.

"What's happening? What are you talking about," Alek demanded.

"The Belarnian cavalry … they ambushed us. The reserves are lost. Most have lances sticking out of them at the bottom of the hill. General Aphilan is dead. They rode in hard and cut us down. Their general laughed and cursed at us and then rode over us. There are only a few of us left down there not seriously wounded. The dead will quickly finish them off. Leave while you can." The soldier fell to the ground sobbing.

Mikhal stood frozen, staring at Alek, waiting for guidance. He no longer cared what happened and was ready for whatever fate might await him. He looked expectantly at his commander, waiting for him to give the order to charge the Belarnians one last time. "The Belarnians are withdrawing, but they are staying close by. I think they are luring the dead toward our position," a cavalry scout reported.

Alek looked at Kristian. Alek's eyes were filled with regret as he summed up his prince one last time. He quickly approached Kristian, grabbing him roughly. "You have led us poorly, Your Highness. There were times when I hoped you would learn from your experiences, but for the most part you have done poorly."

Kristian looked up as if from a dream, suddenly realizing what Alek was saying. "Time and again I let you make mistakes because your father charged me with finding the man in you … I didn't find him."

Alek looked around to ensure no one else was listening. "You always thought honor was what made someone a man. A man makes himself better by doing what's right and that brings honor to him. Things like duty, love, respect … and sacrifice are what transform an ordinary person into an honorable man. Remember this final lesson, Kristian. If you're lucky, you'll get one final chance to become a better person." The cavalry commander turned away from the dumbfounded prince to address his soldiers.

"We've been cut off." Those eager to escape heard Alek's words and shouted in dismay.

"This is not a new situation, cavaliers," Alek responded. "We fight and die to protect our king and country. Charging through the dead will be suicide; our mounts are exhausted, and we can't leave our Duellrian comrades behind. Soon the dead will smell us out, and they'll come up the hill to get us. When they do, the Belarnians will have to withdraw back into the city or be pulled down the same as us. And when that happens, we will have one last chance. We'll either break through them before they can overpower us or we'll hold this hill until the rest of the Duellrian army arrives. They are less than a day away."

Alek raised his saber, calling for men to form a line on the south side of the hill. "I won't give you a choice. You will not run. You are cavaliers. Form a barrier between the cliff side and that fallen tree. I will take half of you to protect the east and south sides where the dead will likely come from. Hanson will take the rest and guard the north side … they will also be our reserve." Alek nodded and ordered his soldiers to the perimeter.

"For Erand," many shouted with passion. Consigned to certain death, they ran to take up defensive positions across the snowy hill.

Mikhal moved next to Alek and asked, "What about me? What do you want me to do?" Mikhal was hurt that Alek had not given him a more important assignment.

"Mikhal, I give you the hardest and most thankless task." The older man smiled, placing a hand on his friend's shoulder. "I need you to stay in the center with our flag bearer and three others. Take the four you had earlier, if you like." Alek paused, looking back at Kristian. "Protect him. Make sure Kristian survives."

Mikhal shook his head, refusing. "No, I won't do it. We have a fight coming. My place is with our men."

"Yes, Mikhal, you will do it. I'm ordering you to do it." The commander sighed and then relaxed by smiling and whispering, "Please … he is still our prince. We are defeated here, and we are all probably going to die anyway, but if there is a chance you might make it through the fight and get back to help, then you must take it and get him out of here." Mikhal continued to shake his head defiantly. He began to tremble, unable to control his emotions.

Alek continued, "He must survive. Maybe he can get to Justan's forces and warn them. And there is the princess to think of."

"Above all else, I want someone to carry word of our deaths to our king and the ones we love." Alek looked straight into Mikhal's eyes. "Yours is the hardest task, Mikhal. Remember every cavalier that has fallen. Don't forget us. Good-bye."

He left Mikhal standing there, forcing him to accept the order. Mikhal reflexively opened and closed his fists trying to hold in the tears that began to fall down his cheek. The four soldiers he had taken charge of earlier stood apart from the others that were even now frantically preparing for the army of dead. They waited impatiently for Mikhal to give them guidance.

Trying to regain some composure, Mikhal took a deep breath and approached his four cavaliers. "We are to protect the flag and our prince at all cost," he said so vehemently that the soldiers took a step back. Then they stiffened with pride at their seemingly vital role. Mikhal involuntarily flinched, no longer able to comprehend how soldiers, even the well-disciplined cavaliers, could accept such orders without resenting their commanders.

I would rather die standing next to my comrades than live to ensure his escape, Mikhal thought as he looked at the distraught prince. He moved forward toward the top of the hill, caring little whether Kristian followed, but he did follow. Little was left of Kristian emotionally, and that which remained was capable of little more than accepting simple orders.

Mikhal heard the reports coming in from the ring of protectors as he stood in the center of the combined forces of the surviving Erandian cavalry and Duellrian infantry. "The Belarnians are withdrawing. They are moving off to the northeast," one soldier exclaimed.

"I see the monsters below. They are milling about as if unsure of which way to go. Maybe they will attack the Belarnians," another wished.

"No, look ... they're surrounding the hill. They'll be here soon," Hanson called out. "Any ideas on how to get out of this one, Mikhal?" he shouted jokingly behind him.

Mikhal could not answer.

Truan Langwood limped slowly over to Mikhal and then tapped him on the shoulder. Mikhal tried to smile reassuringly, knowing that the veteran soldier was about to say something important. He pulled a portion of torn black cloth out from his coat and handed it to Mikhal. "It probably sounds overly dramatic, but what I am about to say is very important." He paused to ensure Mikhal understood. "You must make them understand what we are about to do. You must make them aware of our sacrifice."

Mikhal nodded gravely, accepting the order, even though he wished he could just die with everyone else. *What was there to live for?* he asked himself. *Everyone was gone … or soon would be. Ferral had won.*

"I'll probably die anyway. It will just happen in the worst possible way, protecting him," Mikhal complained as he looked quickly over at Kristian.

Truan ignored the complaint and continued, "I saw Davil. He's dead. I think his wounds were worse than we thought. He was at the bottom of the hill and never made it back to the reserves where he could get some aid. He was … he was stumbling around the wagons. He had already turned into one of those things." He paused, sighing to relieve some tension. "Well, anyway, I looked for the Belarnian flag he captured but couldn't find it." Truan pointed at the cloth now in Mikhal's hands. "Take this one and always remember what happened here."

Mikhal examined the old fragment of cloth that Truan had been carrying for nearly twenty years, ever since the Battle of Marker. "So the story is true?" he guessed.

Truan smiled and moved back toward the defensive line. Mikhal stood silently, gripping the banner in his hands. The respect and gratitude he felt for his comrades had never been stronger.

THE STRONG WINDS AND SNOW continued unabated after hours of relentlessly hitting the eastern shore of the Utwan Sea. A few inches now covered the frozen ground where thousands of soldiers fought and died. The white powder should have covered their bodies, like a blanket, giving them some comfort in their final sleep, but Ferral had corrupted nature. The sorcerer king broke the barrier separating the living from the dead. Now, all those that died within the vicinity of the Belarnian fortress were walking again. They staggered around the battlefield, the only thought entering their foggy minds was the need to kill, to tear the living apart. That need could never be satiated.

The dead sensed those around them with a life force and were drawn toward them, driven forward by a searing pain that demanded they destroy every living thing. They were unable to discern the Belarnians from those they were created to kill and were pulled toward a strong force of life within the citadel. If the Belarnians had not called off their attack and re-entered the city to repair the destroyed gate, most of the inhabitants of Belarna would have become a part of the growing army. The monsters were incapable of understanding what they had become and focused all their efforts on those that were easiest to reach, Ferral's innocent subjects that hid within homes near the destroyed gate.

More than one hundred of the dead entered through the ruined doors before a barricade could be erected. They began breaking into homes and killing people even as Belarnian soldiers hunted them down. The soldiers were losing the race against those transforming into the dead and those they destroyed. A containment strategy was quickly adopted, and the lower half of Belarna was sealed off.

The vast majority of the dead saw their opportunity to kill Belarnians dwindle once the gate was blocked and turned their attention to the Duellrian army. The creatures blocked General Aphilan's escape and killed five hundred of his men before the survivors broke out and fled back to the hill. The things saw the survivors flee to the snow-covered hill to hide, but it would do them no good. The dead would find them; they sensed the living.

Derout's blocking tactic served two purposes. First, he prevented his enemies from escaping back toward their reinforcements. Second, his men served as bait that lured the dead toward the bottom of the hill.

The creatures were drawn directly toward the spot where the Belarnian general had wanted them.

It did not take them long to surround the entire hill. The dead found access on three sides, but the west side was too steep. They moved determinedly up the slopes, desperate to kill the living. Small groups of the dead broke off to finish any remaining wounded that had been ambushed earlier by Derout's Black Guards.

A soldier screamed as he was ripped open by the slow moving hands of those who wanted his life. He could do nothing against their attacks, his wounds were too serious. He was forced to watch them mutilate his body until he could no longer feel any pain and died. Within a matter of minutes, the man joined the army of dead and clambered up the slopes, seeking to destroy his former comrades.

Mikhal and Kristian watched as cavaliers and foot soldiers used everything available to stop the advance. Heavy swords and axes worked best at severing limbs, but the effort barely kept their attackers at bay. They worked relentlessly, seizing every advantage to keep the dead from breaking though to the center. Men fought valiantly, swearing to send them back to hell by chopping them to bits.

After only a few minutes, one of the staggering monsters broke through, heading directly for Kristian. Hanson ran up in front of Mikhal swinging a sword as he shouted in anger. His blow cut a dead Duellrian foot soldier in two, but the parts kept moving feebly. Hanson did not stop and moved away from Mikhal, seeking others that were attempting to push their way past the defenses.

Soon an entire group of creatures was able to kill defenders near the fallen tree. Again, they came directly towards Kristian. Mikhal rushed forward, swinging his sword wildly. His force knocked one of the creatures to the ground, and he turned to face the others. He saw one of his men jam a spear into the ribs of a monster. The wooden pole stuck in its rib cage and would not come free. As the soldier struggled to pull his weapon out, the dead converged on him and pulled him screaming to the ground.

Mikhal gasped, backing away. A hand grabbed him by the shoulder and spun him around. Reflexively, he raised his sword ready to bring it down on his attacker's head but stopped at the last instant; it was Alek.

"You must leave, now. Find a way down on the west side, if you can. It is too steep for them to climb up, and you may be able to escape." Alek said a final good-bye to his friend.

Mikhal wanted to say something but did not have the chance. There was no time to say anything else. The cavalry commander ran off, ensuring the gap on the south side was closed.

Reluctantly, he turned back to Kristian and his two men. "Move to the west side and find a way down for us." They stood there, confused.

"We can't leave them. Our comrades are here, and this is where we should stay, no matter what happens," one of them said.

"This is an order. We have our mission and that is to ensure our prince survives and that word of this battle reaches King Justan and our people." He looked at them threateningly, clinching his sword tighter. "Now move."

"No, he's right. I deserve to die more than anyone else. We should stay and face our fate," Kristian admitted.

Mikhal did not hesitate. He hit Kristian on the head with the pommel of his sword. The prince fell to the snow fighting to maintain consciousness. Mikhal reached down and pulled him back to his feet.

"I have my orders!" He shouted at all of them. He pushed the staggering prince over to the drop off on the west side. The cavaliers looked at Mikhal as if he were a madman.

"No. I will not leave," one soldier challenged. He turned and ran toward a group of dead that broke through the southern defenses again. He shouted in senseless rage as he jumped into their midst.

Mikhal did not stop to watch the outcome. There was no time to waste. Mikhal went to the edge where the ground dropped off vertically for nearly twenty feet. It was difficult to see anything below in the darkness and blinding snow, but Mikhal thought he saw a ledge where the dead could find no access. He moved over to his right, looking for a way down.

The one remaining cavalier with them helped his prince along the edge; Kristian moaned in confusion and pain. The cavalier supported his prince with one arm as he prepared to face the approaching dead with the staff that held their flag. "They're getting pretty close. The line's almost overrun."

Mikhal hesitated, unsure of what to do. The small distance he had moved away from the rest of his comrades had already begun to influence his thoughts. His friends' screams and curses filled the darkness and made it difficult to think. He knew that in a few minutes, they would all be dead.

He had just seen Hanson pulled down. The things slowly surrounded the big southerner; their circle grew tighter and tighter despite the numbers that he cut down with his sword. Then his friend was gone. There were only fifteen cavaliers remaining now. Mikhal heard Alek shout one last time for them to escape before he was overrun by the things and lost beneath a swarming mob of creatures. Alek's screams filled Mikhal's mind. He looked left and right for a way to escape, fear and panic suddenly taking hold of him. He wanted to live.

"Jump," Mikhal said.

"What!?" the shocked cavalier cried. "It's over twenty feet. We'll break our legs."

Mikhal stepped over the ledge without waiting to see if Kristian or the soldier would follow. He hit the ground below them hard, feeling the air leave his lungs and a sharp pain in his legs. He would have fallen off the small ledge if the soldier and Kristian had not jumped off right after him and landed on either side, flattening him.

There was a brief moment of silence as the three felt their bodies for injuries. Their relief was short lived, the ledge crumbled underneath them. They fell a few more feet before hitting the steep slope of the hill. The snow cushioned their fall but also kept them from stopping as they continued to slide, gaining speed.

They had little time to worry about whether they would die. They stopped sliding once they hit a patch of thorn bushes. They quickly jumped up, holding their weapons before them and searching for the dead. Mikhal and Kristian both held broadswords they had taken from the battlefield. The soldier held what remained of the broken staff.

"Do you see any?" the cavalry soldier asked them.

"No … wait. Yes, I see them." Mikhal pointed off to the left where he could see one of their supply wagons standing eerily alone in the predawn gloom. "I see a few of them wandering around on the other side of that wagon."

"I see them," Kristian remarked soberly. "I see the damned things." Mikhal shot him a glaring look, reminding him to keep his voice down.

"There are only three of them," the younger cavalier said. Mikhal remembered that his name was Garin.

"Thousands more are close by, and they'll be here as soon as they're finished killing our friends," Mikhal replied in disgust. "But we need supplies if we're to have any chance of making it back to the rest of the Duellrian force. I think they're about a half day's march from here, and we will never make it in this freezing storm." He tried harder to assess their situation and come up with a plan.

The dead were wandering aimlessly around unlike the ones they had just encountered at the top of the hill. They seemed to lack the purpose that drove the others to destroy the living. Mikhal could see much clearer now as dawn approached.

"Look … beyond those three, thousands more are coming!" Kristian exclaimed.

"We'll not make it to the wagon now," Garin said, defeated.

"No, look. They're just like those other three. They're stumbling, barely able to walk," Mikhal observed.

"It's like their drunk," Garin commented.

"Even drunk men, even dead drunk men can kill," Mikhal snorted.

Suddenly, as the first rays of the sun broke through the storm clouds and shown down upon the battlefield, the dead fell lifeless to the ground. Mikhal gasped in surprise as the monsters dropped like discarded puppets. He did not know what to do. The snow continued falling, covering the ground and the thousands of dead that again littered it.

"No," Mikhal said full of remorse. He looked around frantically. Everywhere he looked the dead had fallen. Mikhal could not see a single living person other than themselves.

Mustering what energy he had left, he ran back up the hill to his friends. He passed thousands of bodies, tripping over them in his desperation. The young cavalry officer abruptly halted at the top. Bodies lay everywhere; not a single person was alive. Every single soldier that had sailed from Duellr was dead. Even the horses, even Champion was dead.

Mikhal stumbled over to the vantage point where they had all first come to spy on Ferral's city. Looking down across the battlefield, he saw thousands more littering the plain. Nothing moved except a few war banners.

16

THE FROZEN LANDSCAPE

An hour later, Mikhal, Kristian, and the last remaining cavalier, Garin, were leagues from the battlefield. They limped and staggered along the snow-covered road, their torn and wet clothing little comfort against the cold. Their bodies were battered and bruised from hours of fighting and running, and each of them secretly wished the others would suggest a break. They knew that stopping, however, could mean losing any lead they had over possible pursuers.

Actually, none of them knew whether they were being followed at all. The three sprinted from the hill toward the wagons once it seemed that no one else was going to attack them. They dodged the bodies that covered the ground until they reached a supply wagon and then quickly moved to the back side, trying to hide as best they could. Mikhal and Garin climbed in, looking for additional cloaks and food. The three made packs out of blankets to hold the little food and gear they had found that was not destroyed during the battle. The three had waited a long time after the sun had risen and the dead had fallen before deciding to join King Justan and the rest of the Duellrians. Mikhal had wanted to wait, hoping they might find other survivors … but there were none.

Iᴛ sᴇᴇᴍᴇᴅ ᴛᴏ Kʀɪsᴛɪᴀɴ ᴛʜᴇʏ ran for hours before the pace finally slowed, but even then the three survivors did not rest. They continued marching east at a hard pace, hoping to reach Justan before noon. But when noon passed and the day continued on toward dusk, the three began to worry.

"Maybe the storm slowed them down," Garin suggested.

"That's probably what happened. No one could have moved far in that blinding snow," Mikhal admitted.

But Kristian felt something was terribly wrong. Nothing had gone right since he had left Erand. They were harassed by peasant villagers, his future father was savagely murdered, his betrothed was kidnapped by a demon, and his entire campaign to defeat Ferral and rescue Allisia was crushed in one evening.

Kristian felt shame and self-loathing. His decisions cost thousands of men their lives; worse his taunts and challenges probably caused Ferral to unleash his magic upon them all. The single worst part of the night was that he had survived.

"I should have died on the hill. I should have died several times last night, but they wouldn't let me." His self-pity turned to anger, and he focused it on the one officer left that was responsible for keeping him alive. Mikhal Jurander.

Of all the cavaliers, Kristian knew, Mikhal would like nothing more than to see him dead, but he followed his orders and protected him. Mikhal had protected him from the Belarnians, the demon, the dead, and from himself. *I would have died like everyone else had it not been for him.*

Kristian stared accusingly at Mikhal's back.

The three continued in silence, resting little as they searched for signs of the Duellrian army. An hour before dusk, they found the remainder of Justan's forces. Kristian stood at the top of a small rise less than a league away from a column of horses, men, and wagons. Their movement was slow enough that Kristian had a hard time discerning if they were moving at all. The sound of a banner flapped in the wind, and something was definitely wrong.

Thousands of Duellrians lay frozen in the snow. There were groups of men everywhere, sitting motionless, huddled together as if they tried to keep warm during the blizzard. Kristian saw others still sitting atop fallen horses holding on to lances and reigns as though the freezing death came so quickly that none had time to react. Their faces were shiny, almost blue, their eyes and mouths slightly open, hinting at the extreme pain they felt before they died.

"More of Ferral's work," Mikhal said as he picked his way through the frozen column. Kristian simply shrugged in defeat. He was not surprised by what he saw. After all, he was the one that forced Ferral's hand and unleashed the power within the sorcerer. Kristian knew now that they were all meant to die. What he was seeing before him was only the beginning of worse atrocities to come. It was not even surprising to see Justan standing frozen among a circle of stiff defenders. Their drawn weapons stood out from their blue hands as though they meant to ward off an enemy that was no longer there.

Kristian walked up to the young king who had seen nothing but misery since Kristian and his cavalry escort arrived at the Duellrian court. The man, no older than Kristian, had seen his own father's head ripped from his body and his sister kidnapped by a demon. His face had the same expression of fear on it as when Justan had first seen Ferral's hideous monster.

"There's no sign of fighting," Garin exclaimed, examining the ground. "There aren't any footprints or anything."

Mikhal agreed. "There aren't even any battle wounds on the dead." The cavalier frowned, knowing what had most likely happened. "It was the demon."

The three looked closer at Justan, and they were puzzled. His arms had been ripped off of his body after he had been frozen. Both arms lay on the ground, one pointing toward Belarn and the other arm back toward the port of Singhal.

Kristian threw his hands up in defeat. "It would have been better to die and have my shame die with me than to survive and see everything else destroyed." He did not see Mikhal come slowly up behind him.

"Garin," Mikhal said, "don't go far, but see if there is anything we can use from their supply wagons. We'll end up just as frozen as these men if we don't get warm soon." The younger soldier nodded gloomily. Mikhal understood how the young soldier must be starting to feel. How could he keep the soldier's spirits high enough to make him want to live if the prince kept speaking of the death they all thought about?

Mikhal viciously turned on Kristian once Garin was out of sight. "I'm not going to keep secret the fact that I hate you. I hold you responsible for all of their deaths. I would like nothing more than to see you dead, but it's more important that we get back to Erand as quickly as possible and warn your father of Belarn's treachery."

"Get back? To my ... father?" Kristian asked in credulity. "My father is dead. And just how the hell are we supposed to get back to Erand, anyway? We have no food, no water, no warm clothes, and we're in the middle of Ferral's country in the worst snowstorm I've ever seen." Kristian shook his head in defiance. "I'd rather die than make it back to Erand where everyone will see how I have disgraced them."

Mikhal lost control of his emotions and grabbed Kristian. Shaking him, Mikhal threatened, "You will make it back, and you will face your shame. My friends deserve that and much more. More than you can ever repay, you pitiful excuse for a man."

Mikhal took in a deep breath of air to calm himself, but it did not help. "They fell at the rising of the sun. Did you see it, Your Highness? The sun rose, and the dead fell."

Kristian stared at Mikhal, his own anger beginning to rise. Mikhal continued, "Only fifteen minutes after they destroyed the last of my friends. Fifteen minutes more is all that we had to hold on to survive.

If I hadn't been ordered to protect you, I might have been able to help them hold off the monsters for that short amount of time."

Kristian snorted. "It wouldn't have taken them five more minutes to finish us regardless of what you did. You would have made no difference. Besides, I didn't ask you to protect me."

"Those were my orders, and unlike you, I know when to shut my mouth and do what is needed. Now, you are going back to Erand."

Kristian refused the demand. He shoved the young officer away from him, pulling his sword out of his belt. Mikhal saw the look in Kristian's eyes and carefully backed away. *Maybe it would be better to kill him now,* he thought.

He had little time to think on it before Kristian lunged at him. The thrust was half-hearted and meant to scare Mikhal more than hurt him.

"If you think I am going to Erand with you after everything that has happened … then I'll just leave on my own," Kristian declared.

Mikhal pulled his own sword out and looked at the thousands of frozen bodies around him. *More brave men dead because of my prince,* he thought.

"If you think that your royal blood is going to save you from getting the lesson you deserve … then you're gravely mistaken. When you pull out a sword and threaten someone, you'd better be prepared to use it."

He caught Kristian by surprise, swinging his blade around fiercely, knocking the other's sword away. Kristian was spun around by the force of the blow but quickly recovered. The hatred in both men exploded as they faced each other; neither wanted to face the grim reality that was forced upon them. Each blamed the other for their personal losses.

Mikhal hated Kristian because his selfish decisions had killed all of his friends. Kristian hated the young cavalier because he represented everything he had wanted to be but was never allowed. Kristian had always wanted to be like Mikhal. He wanted to be a great leader, strong, and mentally tough. More than anything, Kristian wanted to be respected by his men. Kristian's jealousy and self-pity turned to rage.

Kristian's unrecognizable shout of anger echoed off the frozen wagons and dead that surrounded them. He rushed in, forcing Mikhal back. Mikhal stumbled on the form of a Duellrian curled up in the snow. He fell onto the body, feeling the chill of the frost on the soldier's skin. He looked up in time to see that Kristian was not hesitating. The prince swung his sword downward, aiming for Mikhal's head, but the cavalier rolled away untouched.

Kristian tried to keep Mikhal away through the shear force of his anger, but Mikhal moved in past his sword, pushing the prince back to the center of Justan's ring of protectors. They closed once briefly. Their blades caught in each other's cross guards, and they exchanged blows with their fists as they tried to free their swords. Kristian tried to take back the offensive, but he was not as skilled or experienced as Mikhal and was eventually forced to the ground. The fallen prince looked for his sword, but it was out of reach.

Mikhal exerted enough pressure to draw blood as he pushed the sword point into Kristian's neck. Kristian did not move or show any sign of fear as Mikhal stood over him, ready to finish him off. "Thousands have died because of you! Thousands," Mikhal shouted in fury.

The cavalier could no longer keep his sorrow in. His grip on the broadsword loosened as he began to sob. The tragic knowledge that he had lost all of his friends in just one night forced him to his knees. He silently asked God for help, raising his hands up pleadingly toward heaven. He knelt beside Kristian a long time, wondering what to do. Finally, Mikhal stood up and looked at Kristian in disgust.

"I'm not going kill you, Your Highness. That would make it too easy on you." Mikhal wiped away the tears on his cheek and then put away his sword.

"The whole world will know that I was the one to unleash Ferral's madness. You're right … it's all my fault. Thousands have died because of me, and I will never be able to forgive myself. How am I ever going to face our people and tell them what I did?" Kristian asked, panting for breath.

Mikhal's anger would not subside. "I don't know or care. You have a lot to answer for."

Kristian paused and then slowly nodded in agreement. "I deserve it. I deserve to die more than anyone else."

Then Mikhal looked back toward Ferral's city and sighed, "It's not all your fault. We all pledged to help the Duellrians rescue Allisia. We were all fools to think we could just show up and demand her back. Not even you could have seen what Ferral was capable of. The sorcerer has even more to answer for than you."

"But I knew he controlled a demon," Kristian said as he stood up. "For a man to be able to control that much evil … I should have foreseen what would happen."

Mikhal shook his head, confused. He had lost control of his emotions and was not sure who was to blame for what any more. "It was a risk we all took in coming to Belarn. They have always worshipped the devil. I'm as much a fool as you are … more the fool because …" Mikhal was going to continue but thought it better to stop.

Kristian finished the cavalier's thought. "Because you think you're better than me. Because you have always been watching and judging me, and you knew that I would fail."

Mikhal looked away from his prince, focusing instead on Justan's frozen form. The kneeling blue corpse shouted silently at them.

"When you decided to attack without word from your father and without waiting on Duellrian reinforcements, you overstepped your authority as a leader. When you say 'charge,' men follow those orders trusting in your better judgment as their superior. Hundreds of good men died because you refused to leave the bridge when we should have regrouped with Aphilan's men. And when you recklessly left your position to get into the fight, I saw several follow you, leaving their position to protect you. How many died to ensure your survival? When you volunteer your men for something, it has always been for the wrong reasons. It should never be for the sake of honor or fame. Only after considering the lives that you are responsible for and the outcome of your decisions should you make such a decision."

He reached down and grabbed the prince's sword. "You already know that your position grants you great authority, but you've never understood that with that authority comes great responsibility." He handed the sword back to Kristian and then walked away.

Kristian responded quickly. "No, you're wrong about one thing." Mikhal turned, looking at him doubtfully. "I may have dreamed of honor or becoming a great hero, but when we attacked, the only thing I could think of was Allisia." Mikhal did not answer.

"What am I supposed to do with this?" Kristian raised the Belarnian broadsword Mikhal had returned to him.

"There are only three of us, and we'll need even your sword if we want to survive." Mikhal looked directly at Kristian. "I trust there will be no more outbursts? Remember, there are still many more lives at stake." He added, "And I don't want you to say anything negative in front of Garin. He's young and looks up to you."

Mikhal snickered and then continued, "He's probably the one loyal follower you've got left."

Garin suddenly reappeared from behind one of the abandoned wagons, holding a few supplies. "This is all I could find. A water cask. It's completely frozen, but still fresh. I found a heavier sword to replace this broken staff. And here are some better coats to replace our wet ones." Garin looked questioningly at the other two seeing for the first time the uneasiness between them. He could see the bruises that were already appearing on their faces from the struggle. His puzzled look went unanswered.

Mikhal took two of the long coats and handed one to Kristian. Silently, they put the new clothes on over the top of their wet ones. They were glad for the extra warmth even though the tight fit forced their cold, wet clothes against their bodies. Kristian started to shake violently and the hairs on the back of his neck stood up as the temperature around them suddenly dropped.

He looked around in the gloom of dusk for signs of danger but could see none. The prince turned to Mikhal, seeing that he was also feeling the eerie chill. Mikhal quickly finished harnessing his sword over his new coat and walked back toward the ring of dead defenders. Garin followed uncertain of what to expect.

Just as the two approached the center, Justan's head began to move. The dead king's skin cracked and muscles stretched and snapped as he forced his head to turn toward the living men. His blue eyes were glazed over by a film of ice, but somehow he was able to tell that the living were near. Mikhal and Garin stopped abruptly in their tracks, watching in horror as their one-time comrade struggled to reach them.

"Watch out!" Garin shouted to Kristian. The prince backed away slowly from the image of horror in front of him, pulling his broadsword free.

Kristian felt a searing cold flash up his leg and looked down to see the grinning face of another dead soldier pulling on him. He quickly kicked his leg free and ran to his companions. "We have to get out of here now before they all wake up."

There was no arguing that, Mikhal thought. The three Erandians quickly began maneuvering their way through the rising forms of the frozen men. Mikhal turned back once after they cleared the milling mass. He thought he heard the scream of a horse or the shout of a man as they ran from the awakening army. What he saw only made him panic more.

Mikhal saw the Belarnian cavalry fighting with the frozen dead not far from where they were. "The Belarnians have caught us." He turned back to Kristian and Garin, urging them to move. "Run. Maybe, if we're lucky, they will be slowed down by the dead." The other two did not bother to look back, already hearing the growing sounds of battle behind them.

17

THE STRANGER

The three trudged along through the darkness in ankle-deep snow. Cold, miserable, and hungry, they all wanted to stop and rest, but they had heard the sound of men shouting through the woods. They knew Belarnian patrols were looking for them, but so far it seemed as though they had successfully eluded their pursuers. It had been three hours since they fled Justan's frozen army, but they were exhausted, and it was hard to tell how long they had been moving. None of them could remember how long they had been running from their hunters, but it seemed like an eternity. Garin was the first to see the twinkling light through the trees.

"Wait," he whispered urgently. "There's a light ahead. It might be an enemy camp." Mikhal climbed a small rise to inspect the area.

"No. It looks like a single campfire." He looked for a way around the light. "But just to make sure, we should skirt the area so that we're not seen."

Kristian was reluctant to speak to Mikhal. The two had not spoken to each other since their fight, and the prince was determined to not provoke the cavalier, but they were all exhausted.

"I understand our situation. We should keep moving and forget about the fire, but … maybe it's someone who could help us." He could feel the anger swelling within the cavalry officer already.

"Oh, thank God you said it first, Your Highness," Garin exclaimed. "I'm frozen and exhausted. I was afraid to be the first to say it, though." He looked pleadingly at Mikhal. "Sir, we've been on the move for over a day now. We're frozen. Our clothes are soaked from sweat. And I can't feel my feet." Mikhal looked back toward the fire again.

Kristian added hopefully, "Maybe there's food and water." Mikhal did not lash out like Kristian expected.

Instead, Mikhal thought hard about the prince's words before answering. "Here's what I'm thinking. You're right that we need rest and warmth. We have been through more than anyone should be expected to face in a lifetime, but we are still in Ferral's lands. Even if that fire does not belong to one of his soldiers and we are lucky enough to get some comfort and escape again before the Belarnians find us, they will certainly find this place and torture the person it belongs to … just to get information on us. For our safety, as well as that of anyone who is down there, we should just keep going." He looked at Garin. "What do you think, Garin?"

The young soldier lowered his head in disappointment. "Sir, I will do whatever you say."

"No," Mikhal said immediately, "there are only the three of us, now. We must all agree on any decision, and it should be based on all of our feelings." He looked expectantly toward the soldier.

There was an unexpected gleam in Garin's eyes. "Thank you," he replied quietly. Kristian suddenly realized how much the younger soldier admired Mikhal; Garin would do anything for him. Kristian also remembered how he had wished others would look at him the same way. That would never happen now.

"The truth is that I am close to falling over," Garin offered. "I am not going to make it much further. I think a couple of fingers and toes are useless; I can't feel them anymore. And if I am needed at some point to help fight, then I need to rest." Pointing at the fire he added, "If the Belarnians see this fire, they will likely torture the person anyway, even if we don't stop. We should take advantage of this opportunity … it may be a long time before we get a chance like this again."

Mikhal waited a moment before nodding. They decided it would be better to look at the campsite more before just walking out into the open. Garin and Mikhal crept around the opening in the trees in opposite directions while Kristian stayed at their original location. They made as little sound as they possibly could, but their fatigue made it very difficult to maintain any stealth. All three had stopped breathing when Garin accidentally snapped a dead twig under his foot.

The three began to relax a little when no signs of alarm were raised by the loud sound in the night. When the two returned to Kristian, they reported what they saw.

"Nothing … I could not see anyone around the fire." Garin was puzzled. Why would anyone make a fire and leave it unattended, especially in this terrible weather?

Kristian asked what they were all thinking, "Where do you think …."

"I'm right here," a soft whisper responded from behind them. They spun around, reaching for their weapons.

"Stop," the voice hissed. "If I had wanted to kill you, I would have done it when I first heard you wondering around like cattle." The three still held onto the hilts of their swords, unsure of what was happening.

"If you had tried to kill us, you would have found that our horns are shaper than most of the other cows," Mikhal responded threateningly.

"Perhaps," the stranger chuckled, still hidden somewhere in the trees nearby. He finally moved out of his crouched position in the darkness and slowly approached them. They could see little of the man in the darkness. He was of average height and build and did not look overly dangerous.

"Who are you and what are you doing here?" Kristian demanded.

"I have more right to ask that question than you. Weren't you try-ing to spy on me?" The hooded man looked at each of them. "On any ac-count, I mean you no harm. It's easy to tell that you are in need of some comfort. I'll share whatever I have in exchange for the latest news."

The three finally relaxed after hearing him promise food and warmth. "We're lost merchants from a caravan that was raided on the road near here yesterday," Mikhal offered to the stranger.

"You're nowhere near any road," the man replied.

Kristian added, "We've been running for our lives, afraid the raid-ers might come after us. We haven't even stopped to see if they are still following us."

The black-cloaked man cocked his head to the side as if he found it hard to believe the incredible story. At last, he shrugged and said, "I don't care what happened." He waved his hand, indicating the woods around them. "No matter what your story, the Belarnian patrols have already been through the area. I don't think they will return before sun-rise."

"You've seen the patrols," Garin blurted out. Mikhal nudged him as a reminder not to give anything away about their true situation.

"Don't worry. I like the Belarnians little more than you obviously do." The stranger could tell he had hit a nerve with that last comment and quickly changed the subject. "Come down and warm yourselves. I have extra water and some dried food. You are welcome to your share." He motioned for them to follow as he started down toward the fire.

"I'm sorry I gave us away earlier," Garin apologized. They all started walking behind the stranger toward the fire.

"The twig didn't give you away, friend." The stranger called back. "Breaking branches is a common sound in the woods. Many animals snap twigs, and old trees drop dead limbs all the time. It was your whis-pering at the very beginning that alerted me." He turned back toward the three as they arrived at the fire.

"Only humans would start talking when an animal could commu-nicate with just a look." Mikhal and Garin both raised their eyebrows at the wood lore their new companion seemed to know.

They looked around one final time for signs of danger before they gave into their exhaustion and fell to the ground beside the fire. There was a lean-to made of fallen limbs and bows of pine nearby. A layer of snow was piled on top of the shelter to keep the fire's heat close to the ground.

"Thank God for this little mercy," Garin exclaimed in relief as he took a cup of warm soup from the stranger. The young soldier smiled as he sipped the broth, staring at the blaze in front of him.

The stranger sat in dark contemplation as the three relaxed on blankets, letting the warmth of the fire carry them away from their worries. For over an hour, the man said hardly anything to them. He mentioned once that the weather in the mountains to the west was much worse. That was all he said. Kristian began to wonder whether it was safe to really trust this stranger, but soon his fatigue got the better of him, and he fell into a deep sleep.

It could only have been a few minutes later, he thought, when he was rudely awakened. Kristian, still groggy, had forgotten about their predicament and looked around the fire, confused by the sudden activity. "What is it? Where am I?" He vaguely saw Mikhal's face illuminated by the glow of the fire.

"The stranger is gone," Mikhal said, scanning the darkness past the campsite. He looked into the woods, wondering what their new companion might be up to. "He didn't say anything. He just got up and walked off."

It all came back to Kristian, their flight through the woods at night, his fight with Mikhal amongst Justan's fallen army, fleeing from the dead … the horrible night when Ferral changed Kristian's world forever.

He sighed in despair. "Maybe he's just looking for more firewood," Kristian suggested. He was a little annoyed at being awakened so soon. "Besides I am so tired right now I could care less. I'm going to need more than a few minutes sleep if we're going to continue all the way back to Erand on foot."

Mikhal was unmoved. "That's something only a prince could say. You've been snoring for the last three hours. Don't whine to me about not getting enough sleep." Kristian grimaced surprised at how long he had slept. He hadn't moved a muscle, could he really have slept that long?

"Someone is coming," Garin whispered urgently.

"Get up," Mikhal ordered Kristian as he moved away from the fire, sword in hand.

Kristian stood slowly trying to stretch out the soreness in his back. Soon, he also heard the sound of hooves in the distance and moved with more haste. Worried, he strapped on his sword belt and turned toward the sound.

The sound turned to rolling thunder as a Belarnian scout crashed through a thicket into the campsite. Reigning in his horse, the lead soldier seemed surprised to have finally found the three fugitives. He grinned as he pulled up a horn that was hanging from his neck and blew a single high note. He let go of the horn and pulled free a wicked-looking hatchet. It was curved and spiked and looked well used. The scout backed his horse away from Mikhal and Garin to keep them centered.

Five more mounted Belarnians quickly entered the clearing and fell in with the lead scout. They laughed to each other, looking forward to the reward they would receive for taking back the three bodies as proof of their deeds. They pulled out their weapons and adjusted their helmets as they confidently prepared to attack.

"This is a lucky night," one of them exclaimed, grinning fiercely. "Good luck for us, at least," he added, jokingly.

Suddenly, there was a blur of movement behind them. A black shape jumped out of the trees and passed by the arrogant soldiers, the stranger's sword moving silently through one of the riders. The man landed softly on the ground, rolling under their reach. As the black-cloaked apparition stood and faced the Belarnians, the one who had praised their good fortune fell from his horse. A gash across the back of his neck had severed his spinal cord. He lay motionless on the ground.

The remaining patrol members did not wait for the stranger to attack again. They charged, leaning forward in their saddles and holding their weapons high. The sudden flurry of activity confused the weary men. Kristian stood his ground, hoping to stay where he could see his attackers better but none came directly at him.

He saw their new companion run at the nearest attacker holding a two-handed, slender sword high over his head. Quicker than Kristian could follow, the stranger stepped away from the downward blow of the mounted Belarnian and used his own blade to knock the soldier from his saddle. He then moved swiftly over to finish the scout.

Kristian also saw attackers move to strike Mikhal and Garin. They blocked the blows of their adversaries using what little strength they had left. With each exchange of steel they were forced back further and further away from the center of the clearing. Kristian uprooted himself from where he stood and ran to join them.

As he moved across the clearing, he saw a flash of steel. He looked to his right and saw another scout charging toward him with his sword pointing forward ready to strike. The mounted soldier shouted in excitement, gathering speed. Kristian tensed, waiting for the attack and hoping to dodge the charger and foe, but before the man even got to him, he fell from his horse and landed on the ground with a loud thud. Kristian once again saw the black-clad stranger standing behind where the horse had been and knew the man had somehow managed to save him.

Kristian forced himself out of his crouch and sprinted off toward his companions. Mikhal was now managing to force his opponent back even though the Belarnian was mounted high above him. His skill at fighting and his own anger allowed him to get past the futile swings of his enemy. The young officer was finally able to strike a blow when the other was unable to control his horse. As he struggled to pull it back into the fight, Mikhal thrust upward with his sword. The blade found a seam in the armor and slipped into the Belarnian's side.

Garin was worse off. The little strength he had regained quickly left him. He twisted his ankle on a loose rock and fell heavily. His enemy moved in for the kill even as Garin was trying to pull himself back up.

Kristian screamed in fury. He rushed up to the Belarnian, swinging his sword downward. The man cried in pain and shock as his sword arm fell to his side severely wounded. His misery was short lived. Kristian came back around with the sword and cut him down.

The three Erandians looked around for other attackers, but the last member of the patrol moved away from them. He spurred his horse on, trying to get away, but was unable to escape the reach of the stranger's sword. The first scout to find the campsite was the last to fall.

The Erandians found each other and quickly asked one another if they were injured. Seeing they had all escaped serious injury, they turned their heads in disbelief toward the stranger. The man cleaned his blade with a small cloth and replaced the weapon somewhere within the folds of his cloak. He moved to the fire and added another log.

"That's all of them. They've been combing this area for over an hour. When they finally found the fire and approached, I went to check on them." He sat down on a log near the fire. "You're safe again."

The three slowly walked back to the fire, keeping their eyes on the stranger. No one could move faster than this man did, they all thought. They sat down across from him staring in amazement.

The man in black finally pulled back his hood and scarf, letting the fire warm his skin. The Erandians immediately noticed the scars that ran across the man's face. Three pink scars ran down from his right temple across his cheek and ended at his chin.

He saw them staring at his face and turned away for a moment. Realizing that hiding his face solved nothing, he shrugged and faced them again.

He ran a hand through his short brown hair, shaking out the ice and said, "My name is Cairn." That was the only new thing he was prepared to tell them about himself. They waited impatiently for more clues, but he was not forthcoming about any further details; Cairn just sat there, quietly lost in his own concerns.

18

TRUE LOVE

Smoke and haze filled the night air surrounding Belarn's capital. Blazing fires stood in stark contrast to the thick black columns of smoke where several blocks of the lower districts lay in ruins. Ferral could not stop the dead from entering through the ruined gate; he lacked control over the creatures he had raised, and so they poured in through the broken doors Mikhal had set ablaze. Those that lived near the gate were startled awake as a hundred lifeless monsters broke into their homes through windows or shattered doors. People screamed as the dead tore them to pieces, their cries ringing out across the city even as defenders franticly tried to erect some type of barrier to stop the rising tide of dead from overwhelming their city.

The infested areas grew silent as the dead started their transformation. Soon, a thousand new creatures began to wander the lower streets of Belarna searching for more victims. Derout finally gave up on saving any of those in the lower portion of the city and quarantined the entire district. He ordered bordering neighborhoods set afire to prevent the monsters from moving into new areas. The plan was effective, and their advance was halted. The terrified screams of those still alive but trapped by the walls of fire echoed through the streets up toward the battlements were Ferral's general surveyed the damage.

Derout shook his head in disappointment.

"What a waste," he complained. His decision had saved the city, but even the cruel general had difficulty blocking out the tormenting sounds of those burned alive or ripped apart by the dead. Derout bitterly hated the Erandians and would gladly use deception and trickery to destroy all of them, but he did not want to be responsible for the deaths of his own countrymen. In that, he was different from Ferral. They both craved power and would stop at nothing to obtain it, but Ferral wanted to use the power to destroy the world for his unholy god. Derout simply wanted power to place himself above all others. He turned to his men along the wall, trying to ignore the endless screams of pain that accompanied the towering infernos that consumed a large portion of the black citadel.

Shortly after his decision to give up a part of the city, a barrier was constructed to keep the dead from penetrating further into the heart of the capital. The creatures moved slowly away from the intense heat, back through the shattered gate, and out onto the lifeless battleground. He was unsure of how many he had destroyed or how many he had saved. The general only knew that his actions had prevented the rest of the city from falling to Ferral's creatures.

Derout frowned and shook his head as he looked at what remained of his army. A third of their number was dead because of the battle against the Duellrians; they now served the sorcerer-king as slaves in his transformed army. Another third had joined them after fighting futilely against the advance of the creatures attacking the unprotected citizens near the breached gate. Until Derout had ordered them to torch the houses, they had tried to contain the things with just their spears and shields. Now, they massed beyond the repaired gate, trying to regain access to the living that they could sense behind the black walls. The general watched his men pour hot oil and loose burning arrows at those below in a futile attempt to stem the attack. There were thousands of the things, and more seemed to be coming from behind the hill where Kristian's army had made their last stand.

"At least they're dead," the general consoled himself. It felt good to know that the cavaliers were destroyed, that his Black Guards had helped defeat them once and for all.

He felt a nagging sense of uncertainty, however. Derout was troubled by a message he had received just as the predawn light moved slowly across the macabre scene below him. The dead fell to the ground lifeless once again, and then a mounted messenger carefully approached the citadel. Derout had ordered a large patrol to finish off any Erandian or Duellrian survivors. A single courier from that patrol returned with news that the remainder of the Duellrian army was found only ten miles from the fortress. The rider described the frozen bodies they saw from a distance, and the three men searching the dead. As the patrol closed on the three, the dead began to awake. In the confusion, the three survivors escaped into the forest.

"At least seven thousand more dead soldiers are approaching the capital," the scout reported.

"They're drawn to the strong presence of life protected behind these walls," Derout said, frowning. "It's that or they are drawn to their master."

Derout did not know what evil magic Ferral used to devastate the remainder of the Duellrian army. He did not care if they were dead; they were his enemies, and he was glad his own men would not be wasted hunting them down. The news of the three escaping, however, did not sit well with him. It would not sit well with Ferral either.

"They'll probably freeze during the night, anyway," he hoped. His instincts told him that somehow they would survive. He turned away from the wall, reluctant to tell Ferral the news. The sorcerer-king was too powerful and could no longer be trusted … Derout would have to be cautious. He turned away from the smoke and death surrounding the walls of the city and reluctantly started toward the palace.

ALLISIA SAT MOTIONLESS ON THE dark, cold floor staring past the horrors surrounding her. She showed no outward signs of fear or distress, but on the inside, she was screaming hysterically. The princess wished for someone, anyone, to help her.

But who is left? she asked herself. Her father was dead. Kristian was dead. At least half of her people's army was destroyed. Who else was there left that could reach her? She pulled deeper down within herself to escape the terrible things she had seen … the things Ferral continued to make her watch.

"It has to be a nightmare," she murmured. "Nothing can be as horrible as what I've seen. These things can't be real," she kept telling herself.

She prayed continuously since the nightmare had begun, but no one answered. Allisia's mind raced from one frantic thought to the next as she silently pleaded for someone to help her. She somehow sensed the presence of someone new entering the room, but was unable to free her mind of the terrible shapes surrounding her.

DEROUT SNORTED AT WHAT HE saw. The Belarnian throne room had been transformed into a macabre trophy room. Remains of several men littered the floor or hung limply on chains from the massive columns. Their reanimated limbs shook in a vain attempt to reach out across the room toward the one living captive among them. He barely recognized the Duellrian princess chained among the dead. She sat on the floor with her hands hanging above her.

She stared blankly across the room at the monsters trying to reach her. The beautiful girl's face had turned pale. Her auburn hair was now a tangled, dirty mess. Allisia's gown hung loosely from her shoulders, torn to shreds.

Derout's attention was drawn away from her by the sound of violent coughing. Ferral was being attended to by several servants. They scurried around him like rats, checking to see if anything could be done to please their master. The sorcerer-king lay on a makeshift cot near his throne of skulls and bones. He continued coughing, his body shaking from the effort. Blood trickled down one corner of his mouth. As Derout approached his king, Allisia felt a little warmth leave, and she fell even deeper into the abyss. She wondered if anyone would ever help her.

Ferral tried to sit up as his general approached. "Yes, I'm afraid my entertainment got a little carried away," he said, nodding towards Allisia.

"I barely pulled her away from them in time. A few moments more, and they would have torn her apart." He smiled to himself, pleased to have found something new and amusing to do with the princess. "I guess I left their chains a little too long."

He fell back into the arms of an older priest, coughing as he tried to laugh at his own joke. He pushed away from the attendant violently, snarling in anger.

"What news do you bring?" he asked anxiously through spasms of pain.

Derout hesitated before finally stepping forward. "My Lord, the army of dead broke through the ruined gate. Before they could be destroyed, they killed a thousand Belarnian citizens. Thankfully, I stopped them from demolishing the rest of the city." The words pushed Allisia even deeper down into the dark place she was trapped in.

More deaths … more horror.

"And how, General Derout, were they destroyed? My legions of dead feel no pain. How did you destroy them?" Ferral asked inquisitively.

"With fire, My Lord," Derout responded, confidently.

"Fool, those soldiers are mine as much as you and your men are. How dare you destroy them without consulting me!" The sick king lashed out at the nearest attendant. Ferral used a servant to pull himself up and then edged closer to Derout.

Derout backed away from him, fearing the man's new powers. "But, My Lord, they were destroying the city. I had to destroy them to ensure the rest might survive."

"Don't think on your own again, Derout. My plans go far beyond the well-being of this one city. Besides, alive or dead, they would have served me. Now they are useless piles of ash."

"There are plenty more to add to your numbers now, Ferral," a beautiful voice interrupted. The battle-weary general backed even further away from the dais as the demon-woman approached the king. Her hood fell back to reveal a calm, smiling face.

"The remainder of the Duellrian army has been destroyed. Unfortunate timing caught them on the open plains during a fierce winter storm."

The words pierced Allisia's heart like a lance. Darkness filled her as she realized that her brother was also dead.

Ferral sat a little straighter. Smiling he said, "At least something went right. Is her brother dead?"

"Yes," the demon replied. Allisia would have cried, but the news barely registered in her mind.

"And their fleet … is there anyone left to oppose me," the sorcerer pressed.

"No one," the demon assured him. Derout shifted uncomfortably.

"What now, Derout?"

"Not all of them were destroyed. Not yet," Derout murmured. He flinched as Ferral's eyes turned black with fury.

Quicker to reply than she meant, the demon said, "He speaks of only three men, Ferral. Three ragged, exhausted men who more than likely died last night."

"And as of yet, the body of the one man I wanted found and brought to me is still missing!" Ferral fumed. He looked hard at the demon, judging her loyalty. "Who are these three survivors?"

"I don't know their names," she stated indifferently. "What do you care about three worthless men? You have the ability to conquer any kingdom you wish now that you control the greatest army in the world."

"I control very little," the mad sorcerer declared as he was helped from the cot over to his throne. "The pain of raising them was terrible. … I didn't know it would …."

The demon cut him short, turning around to face him. Her eyes seemed to smolder as she said, "All powers have a price, Ferral. Being a leader like General Derout," the man inadvertently took a step back at the mention of his name, "means sacrificing your personal life for the well-being of your soldiers. Becoming the greatest sorcerer to ever walk the earth means you sacrifice your soul. I can assure you that it will hurt for quite some time."

She turned slowly away so that Ferral could not see her face. Looking Derout in the eyes she added, "Yes, Ferral, it will take you some time to recover from what you have done." She smiled wickedly at Ferral's general as she moved to leave.

Ferral did not seem to notice the look she gave Derout as she started to leave. He countered, "I suppose the same holds true for other things as well."

"Like what?" she asked, continuing down the hall.

"Like love." The mere mention of the subject made the demon involuntarily wince. The movement was barely noticeable, but Ferral had seen it and wondered if he had finally found her weakness.

"Surely, if someone truly loves another there must be some sacrifice? Some test to prove to the other that their love is genuine?" He smiled, leaning forward to hear her response. Ferral knew he had found out something intriguing about his reluctant demon. She pulled her cloak close about her. It was the first time she had ever seemed bothered by the cold. The knowledge that she was in some way vulnerable excited him. The demon paused, seeing brief images of her mortal life flash before her eyes.

She abruptly pushed the confusing memories away, saying, "No, Ferral, you're wrong. Love has no tests. It is patient and kind. Love does not envy or boast. It is not proud. It is not self-seeking. Love always protects, always trusts, always hopes, always forgives … true love will not fail." She emphasized her words slowly, deliberately, as she looked at Allisia. The young girl was chained to the column, surrounded by the grasping hands of the dead.

THOSE WORDS BROUGHT A GLIMMER of hope to Allisia as she continued to push the nightmarish images of the battle out of her head. "There were only three," she told herself. "Fighting against the hordes of this evil sorcerer ... one of them might be Kristian," Allisia hoped. It was the one glimmer of light penetrating the darkness in her mind. Allisia reached for it and embraced it.

"BUT HOW CAN I CONTROL those things I created?" Ferral asked uncomfortably, suddenly wanting to change the topic. "Everyone that dies immediately fills their ranks, at least when it is dark. During the day, they just lay around rotting."

"As you regain your strength, you will obtain more control over them. They wander about seeking the living because they have no will guiding their purpose. And not every person killed will join their ranks, only those within the borders of your own kingdom." She could see the question on his face.

"You are not all-powerful yet. The farther they get from you, the more difficult it will be to transform and control them. Unless ..."

"Yes?" Ferral asked eagerly.

"Unless you send someone forward that can assist you in controlling them." The demon put on her best smile and turned to look at Ferral. "There are things we have discussed. Don't forget about your plans to destroy the older kingdoms to further your quest for power. Send me along with your new army, and I will see that your will is done."

"My new army? What about Erand?" Ferral asked her. "After hundreds of years, Belarn is poised to once again conquer those fools. I had plans to send them east, not west."

The woman came close, whispering in his ear, "They're no real threat. They will fall easily. Send your remaining men after them, if you like, but the dead are far more powerful than the living. Send me out to control the dead, and I promise you the Holts and Atlunam will not be able to stand against me," the demon said.

"The Holts are so far from here that they are of no concern to me.

Not yet, any way. And the Atlunam will not interfere. I have … leverage over them," Ferral bragged.

"They are a very real threat," the demon said, becoming angry. "They are more ancient and powerful than you think. If they unite, all of our plans are for nothing."

"Ha!" he shot back at her. "There will never be peace between them. Let them fight and kill each other. We can deal with them once I have destroyed Erand and Duellr."

The demon snarled. "The dead are of no use to you right now. They cannot go beyond the boundaries of your power. Give them to me, and I will conquer both kingdoms at the same time you are ravaging the eastern lands."

"Very well," he said after a brief pause. The demon was right. He would have to learn more from the scroll Rebenna had brought him if he wanted to completely control the dead. He had plans for his new army, but he did not need them yet. Ferral had always had a grand scheme, even before the demon started advising him.

Ferral's concern was growing, though. *Can I truly trust the demon?* he wondered. He could do little without her, but she was like an addictive drug. The more Ferral called upon the demon to use her powers to aid him in his schemes, the more dependent upon her he became. She was not subservient to him the way he expected. He did not think her plans were always the same as his.

If he were able to create a creature that he could use to channel himself through, he would be able to control the army wherever he sent it. He would no longer need the demon. The mad king would first have to learn how to make such a creature, and then he would have to experiment. Before he could do that, he had to find out who he could trust, he looked back and forth at the demon-woman and Derout, his eyes narrowing in suspicion and greed.

FROM BEHIND THE THRONE, WITHIN a dark alcove, the slim and pale servant girl with dark hair watched and heard everything they said. Her eyes moved slowly over the prisoners chained to the columns. To her dark and confused mind, they seemed like tortured, undernourished peasants. She felt pity for them even though she would never be able to break free of Ferral's control to express her feelings. She also wondered about the beautiful girl chained among them. The prisoner was little different in age than she had been many years ago ... before Ferral ...

For a moment, the girl thought she might remember what had happened to her, but she could remember nothing. The dead servant girl could not remember her past.

She looked closely at the peasants reaching out toward Allisia. Their limbs were too thin. Their faces had no eyes, no flesh. Yet, they moved as if they were human.

A voice screamed inside her mind. They were dead, kept alive by Ferral's evil magic. She looked at her own hands and then her body. She examined closely how the shadows leaped across her pale skin with the flickering of the torchlight. Was she the same as them? What had happened to her that made her what she was? Her mind could not go back that far into her past. She screamed silently as doubt, fear, and horror bounced around inside her mind without release.

She tried to scream louder, wanting to shove people and knock things over, wanting only to be noticed. To know she was not like them, that she was alive. Her mouth barely twitched, revealing none of the pain that she was really feeling. No sound came from her closed lips.

What did I do to deserve this? she asked herself. She had the sudden notion to run away, to flee Ferral's evil citadel, but she knew she would never be able to get past the palace doors. Her master would never allow it.

Ferral motioned for her to bring him a cup of wine, and the dead girl immediately floated silently across the floor to his side, ready to serve.

19

SEPARATE PATHS

"Well, Cairn, you've proven to be a valuable friend," Mikhal said, impressed by their new companion's skills. "I don't know what your plans are, but I think I should at least inform you of the situation to the north." Cairn only shrugged nonchalantly.

Looking hesitantly around, Mikhal leaned closer to emphasize his concern. "Belarn is under the control of an evil sorcerer. A battle was recently fought seeking to bring the mad king down, but the armies opposing him were destroyed. He brought the dead back to life to fight them." None of the news seemed to affect Cairn at all.

"I've heard many stories. Wars come and go. So long as you don't get involved, the forces are usually too worried about each other to harass someone like me."

Cairn's casual attitude annoyed Mikhal.

"It must be hard to remain so stolid … holding back your emotions so you don't act against the atrocities that you see." Cairn tilted his head slightly toward Mikhal while he stirred his soup. "It must be hard to pass by murderers and do nothing about it." Kristian and Garin both put their bowls down, alarmed that Mikhal might provoke the one person helping them.

Cairn smiled knowingly, showing no sign of being offended. "Angering me will reveal nothing, lieutenant. Over the years, I've learned to keep my feelings in check ... it helps me stay alive." The three looked at each other in alarm. How did Cairn figure out who Mikhal was?

"I'm sorry, but I'm not an officer. I'm not even in an army. We're simple merchants that were ambushed by the men you just helped us kill."

"We just told you that," Garin blurted out. Mikhal tried to lend as much credibility to their story as he could muster, but it was obvious that Cairn already knew more about them then he had let on.

Cairn shrugged indifferently placing his empty bowl down by the fire. "You can pretend to be whoever you want, but you can't hide your accent, manners, or training." Mikhal kept a steady face as Cairn talked, but Kristian and Garin could only hang their heads low, submitting to the truth.

"Besides, the patrol had already been through this area looking for you. They said the three they were looking for were Duellrian, but it's obvious you're Erandian."

"And you are a Belarnian, from the sound of your voice," Mikhal shot back. He was determined to push Cairn and find out just what his intentions were. Mikhal had lost too many friends; he had a hard time trusting anyone now. "If you knew we were Erandians, why did you help us against your own countrymen? Now, you're in the exact situation you seemed to want to avoid."

Cairn took a long time before answering. He looked around at the bodies of those they had just killed as if judging his own character. Finally, all he could do was give an already all too familiar shrug. "I wanted to share my fire and food in exchange for news of what has happened. Therefore, you were my guests and my responsibility to protect. I could have let them kill you and probably would have had you not stumbled into my camp, but I made a decision to help you, knowing that you were being pursued. I see little difference in what would have happened to me if they had known I helped shelter you or helped you by killing their men. Either way, they will be after me if we don't part ways soon." He stood, reaching for his bowl. Cairn cleaned the bowl with a cloth before he put it back into his pack.

"Just the same," Mikhal offered, "you could have saved yourself a lot of trouble if you had not helped us. Whatever your reasons were, thank you."

Cairn seemed agitated by the gratitude Mikhal showed him. He could only think of someone he had been unable to help a very long time ago. He silently pulled his hood back over his head and walked away from the fire.

Kristian tried to remind Mikhal of their current troubles. "But what do we do? We should keep moving if we want to out run the patrols. And if we ever hope to get back …," Kristian said as he looked at Cairn suspiciously, "to our country, we need to stay as far ahead of our pursuers as possible." Garin nodded in agreement, but Mikhal only glared at him.

"Why would you want to go back to Erand?" Cairn asked casually as he packed his gear. "I can't imagine why anyone would want to go back … after what happened." The three immediately stood, fear and concern etched in their faces. They stood rigid as they waited for Cairn to give them more information. Seeing them standing there expectantly, he realized they had not heard.

"After what? What has happened in Erand?" Kristian demanded to know. His voice wavered; he felt a chill in his body that made his heart pound. His head suddenly throbbed, and everything sounded muffled. He waited for Cairn to say more, afraid of what he was about to hear.

"The Erandian capital was destroyed over a week ago. I don't know the whole story, but from what others have told me, a massive fire left the city in total ruin. A wall of flame swept through the streets, destroying the army barracks, homes, and even the palace. Thousands were trapped inside the city walls. Most of the army was destroyed ... even the king was killed."

"Liar!" Kristian shouted as he leaped over the campfire, lunging for Cairn. "You're lying. It isn't possible. These things can't be true." Mikhal and Garin came rushing to his side, holding him back. All three looked horrified and waited expectantly for Cairn to continue.

Cairn was confused by the young man's reactions. "Steady friend, I meant no harm. I'm only relaying the news every merchant and traveler in southern Belarn is talking about."

Cautiously, Cairn told them everything he knew. "They say a terrible wind carried the flames from one side of the city to the other in less than an hour. Few had warning before they were trapped. The army was decimated. The king, your king I guess, was trapped in the palace. It collapsed, killing him and the many people trying to save him. Thousands more died that night in the terrible cold. With little shelter to protect them from the storm, they froze to death. I suppose the Belarnian army will move south now to block the border roads. You won't get far if you're trying to get back to Erand." Cairn looked ashamed and tried to turn away from them, "I'm sorry that I had to be the one to tell you."

Kristian fell to his knees, crying. Cairn felt a knot in his stomach, a feeling of pity that he rarely felt. "Perhaps, it isn't true. News often gets distorted when it's passed over such great distances."

"No, it's true." Kristian said through clenched teeth. "God! I feel the truth of it in my soul. That madman told me himself, but I refused to believe him. What else can you do to us?" he shouted into the night.

"Father, I'm sorry!" He cried between gasps for air. "It's my fault. I failed you. I failed everyone. I'm sorry!" Kristian fell on his stomach, burying his head in his arms, trying to hide from the world. He wanted to forget all the horrible mistakes he had ever made.

Kristian despaired, "How do you make sure someone knows you truly love them despite the way you treated them ... after they're gone?" His voice was barely a whisper.

He felt as if God, his mother, and now his father and people were looking down on him from above, judging him for his actions. He was not sure what they would do to him if they were given the chance, but he wished he was with them instead of being left alive to face the cold, bleak world Ferral had created.

Cairn hesitated but knew he could not hold the rest of the news back from them. There was much more they needed to know. "I'm sorry, but I must warn you of something else. I overheard the scouts talking earlier when they were searching for you. The Belarnian army plans to control all movement heading east. They're going to hunt down people in Erand like wild dogs, chasing them into the hills to the north and east. If you try to go back, you'll be captured. It won't be long before all of Erand is under their control. Duellr will be next, I suppose. Or perhaps the Holtsmen to the west."

Kristian buried his head even deeper into his arms.

Mikhal watched as Garin also sank to the ground. His knees had given out as he too realized that many of those he loved were probably dead. Mikhal remembered Garin had a beautiful, young wife whom he had just married prior to setting out for Duellr. She had been taken in by one of the soldier's wives while he was away. If what Cairn said was true, there was little chance she survived.

There was little chance the remainder of the cavaliers were alive either. Their quarters were in the center of the military district where Cairn said the fire started. Mikhal walked off into the woods, unable to comprehend how so much destruction could be brought down on them so quickly. He stopped a short distance from the firelight, leaning against an old tree.

What about my parents? Have they survived the destruction Ferral unleashed upon our people? He could not help but think that somehow they were all right. They lived a half-day's ride from the capital and would have been in little danger from the inferno.

The cold would have been enough to kill them, he worried momentarily. Still, Mikhal had a strong, confident feeling they were alive and doing their best to survive.

His thoughts turned instead to how the fire could have started. Was Cairn right? Had Ferral somehow been able to destroy their entire kingdom while he was fighting a battle at the very gates of his own fortress? A powerful image of the beautiful woman in the red cloak entered his thoughts. Her long blonde hair floated in the night wind, her cloak flapping behind her. She stood on a snow-covered hill overlooking a massive city engulfed in flames. The city was their capital, Brekia.

He watched as the demon stood there motionless, listening to the sounds of devastation carried up the hill by the wind. Screams of pain and horror and shouted orders filled his mind ... the demon's mind. The vision continued as he watched thousands of Erandians break through the closed gates and escape into the night.

He mentally turned his thoughts back to the woman on the hill. It was the demon-woman that had killed Allisia's father. She seemed to sense his presence and turned toward him in his mind. Her face was solemn and somehow familiar. A tear streaked down her face, ruining her beautiful complexion as she reached out for him. There was a longing, a need, coming from her that Mikhal could sense. It was so powerful that his entire body tingled with excitement. She continued to reach out, arms open wide for an embrace that he could not give her. Then she was gone.

The young cavalier stood within the trees a moment longer, tears running silently down his face. He wondered how many more innocent people would die before their nightmare was finally over. He did not know the answer but made a commitment right then, among the snow-covered trees, to find help. He would find others willing to fight Ferral for the death and destruction the madman had brought down upon all of them. He would find a way to kill the demon.

KRISTIAN SAT ON A LOG staring blankly into the brightest part of the fire. Thoughts of his parents constantly flowed in and out of his mind. He remembered the time his mother held him close after he fell from his horse. She had comforted him like any loving parent, soothing his fears and brushing the dirt from his clothes. He remembered vowing to his father that he would someday be a cavalier, defending the kingdom from those that meant to harm their people. His father had nodded, gleaming with pride for a son that tried so hard to honor his parents. They had shown him love and support, but then things had changed. He had changed. He could barely remember those cherished memories … mostly he remembered his failures, his spiteful actions toward those around him.

Kristian remembered the times he was forced to study, separated from other children. He was told that he was being prepared for the difficulties of ruling, but he did not care. His mother had recently died, and his father neglected him as he spent more and more time with his council. Kristian had no one to talk to and lashed out against all forms of authority. His tutors soon came to despise him.

He even pushed his father away. At the time, Kristian had believed his father was insensitive to the needs of his only child. The king refused to let him do anything that would bring him into contact with others his own age. *Perhaps*, Kristian thought, *it was to protect him.* He had never stopped to think how the death of his mother had affected his father. Kristian had not been able to see beyond his own selfish demands.

Kristian rebelled and grew more independent, abandoning his dream of becoming a cavalier. He became a loner that no one could reach. His father may have realized he was partly to blame, but by the time he tried to make amends, it was too late; there was a rift between them. Kristian moped through his adolescence, creating a barrier between himself and everyone else. To forget his troubles, he pushed himself hard. He swore that no one would be better than himself in anything. From riding and fencing to manipulating the fools in his father's court, Kristian wanted no man to be better than him. But he had truly not even known what it meant to be a man. In his attempts to reach perfection, he isolated himself even more. No one liked the egotistical, self-serving boy that Kristian had become.

Soon, there were no teachers dedicated enough to stay and help; his only form of learning was through reading old texts, and it seemed those accounts were often flawed. He was always impatient, unable to control his temper when people did not immediately get him what he wanted. His anger continued to flare as he approached manhood. Kristian's father tried to calm him, but nothing seemed to reach the boy who had spent his time ruining friendships rather than making them.

Tears fell freely down Kristian's face as he remembered every person he had wronged. All the servants in the palace, most of the guards assigned to duty near the king, and especially his father. He remembered the terrible mistakes he made in leading Captain Hienren and his men on their doomed quest. He acknowledged the fact that they were all dead because of him, and he would never be able to change that.

His sorrow deepened with the realization that he was alone. Mikhal hated him and Garin did whatever the young cavalry officer wanted. Ever since their confrontation yesterday, Mikhal had made it perfectly clear how he felt about Kristian.

"Your opinion doesn't matter, and your wishes will be considered last in all things," Mikhal told him when they were alone.

How was Kristian supposed to go on, knowing the cavalier would be constantly watching his back, that no one trusted him? How was he to survive his entire life with no kingdom or home? He laughed at himself. How was he supposed to go on living with the knowledge that his failures had caused so many deaths?

"Maybe it would be better to end my life now and hope God forgives me and takes pity on me," Kristian said looking up toward heaven.

Even in his deep depression, Kristian knew he could not do that. He knew what must be done.

"I can't abandon Allisia," he swore. She was his only hope for personal salvation; she was probably the only person still alive that might give him a second chance. The only way to regain any part of the honor he thought he once had was to fight back against Ferral, as difficult as it was going to be. Surviving the cold winter and Ferral's monsters would not be enough. To become a man in control of his own life, he would have to dedicate himself to earning the trust and respect of those around him, especially Mikhal Jurander's trust. He would take on any burden to save Allisia and his people from Ferral.

Mikhal represented all the things Kristian had aspired to be, but failed to achieve. The prince realized that where he was unable to take the advice of others, Mikhal was able to listen. Where Kristian shouted out orders and expected immediate results, Mikhal issued plans based on the advice of both his superiors and subordinates. He was patient, knowledgeable, and showed genuine concern for others.

Allisia was the only person stubborn enough to give him a second chance. Kristian knew she did not love him, but he could not let her remain trapped and tormented by Ferral. His concern for her was genuine, and he knew some of his recent demands were motivated by his feelings for her. Kristian knew that was something Mikhal would never accept no matter how many times he might say it.

What if Mikhal was right? What if everything I have done was simply for some stupid notion of glory, for a quest that was never my right to undertake? he asked himself.

Have I really done any good at all? Is Allisia better off now then before we started all of this? Kristian began to get sick. *Do I truly care for her, I mean, how much time did we actually spend together? Not much time at all,* he realized.

But the more Kristian contemplated his feelings for her, the more he was certain he knew the answer. Kristian did care for Allisia. She had given him a second chance at friendship, and that was something no one else had ever done for him. For that reason alone he had to help her. He put Mikhal out of his mind, his personal struggle with the cavalier was nothing compared to what he would have to do to bring Ferral down and find Allisia.

AN HOUR LATER, THE FOUR of them were ready to part ways. The Erandian survivors were still weak and cold, but now each of them was focused and determined to do what they had promised. They knew there was little chance of getting through the Belarnian lines back to Erand. Even if the three did succeed in getting safely home, they knew there would be few people able to help them rebuild and fight back against their oppressors.

Kristian was faced with two important challenges. His people needed him. They were likely scattered and confused. Kristian was no longer a prince but a king responsible for the welfare of his people … if they would ever accept him.

But Allisia needed him, too. He knew the Duellrians would never confront Ferral again. If Kristian did not figure out a way to fight back against the sorcerer and save her, no one else would.

The Erandians needed hope, though. They needed to know that Kristian was not abandoning them. They needed to know that he was doing the only thing that he thought he could to help them. Mikhal, surprisingly, agreed. The two of them wanted to get word to their people so that they would not lose hope, but felt their chances of defeating Ferral would be better if they went west or south. Mikhal brought Kristian and Garin close to him. Reaching into his coat, he pulled out a torn piece of black cloth.

He said, "One of my men, Davil, was brave enough to take a banner like this from the Belarnians. Wounded and weak, he was ordered back to the supply train where he could rest. He was later killed, and the prize he fought so hard for could not be recovered." He paused to hand the cloth to Garin who examined it closely.

"On the hill, I thought we were going to die. I thought we were all going to die, but as I watched the dead move closer to our lines, Truan Langwood gave me this. I had always thought his story about capturing a war banner and saving the day was just something to amuse the younger cavaliers, a story to make soldiers laugh." Mikhal smiled as he remembered the dozen times or more he had heard the old soldier retell his story.

"I guess, in part, he did try to make us laugh, but underlying the humor was a feeling that all cavaliers share. We want to be the best.

We want to serve our country no matter the sacrifice." Garin nodded in solemn agreement.

Mikhal paused, trying to hold back the anguish. Finally, he continued, "Take this back to Erand and show it to everyone you encounter. Tell them of all the heroic deeds you witnessed. Don't forget a single one of our comrades that died to ensure that their prince ... I mean king, survived." Kristian bowed his head in silence, wishing those sacrifices had never been made.

Mikhal concluded his speech by saying, "Try to get back home. Let them know their king is calling on all people throughout Erinia to oppose this evil. Bring our people together and give them comfort. And lastly, raise an army of our own countrymen. Prepare them for our return."

Garin looked at the banner in his hands and stammered, "It was easier to fight the dead then to do what you are asking of me now. I don't know if I can do it. I'm too young."

Kristian stepped forward, resting a hand on Garin's shoulder. "I think you can. You have to try, please. I have only known you a short time, Garin, but your dedication and endurance are as strong as any cavalier I've ever met. I need your help." The young soldier stood a little straighter. "Get back home as quickly as possible. We'll send word when we can." Garin nodded and shook hands with Mikhal, and then he bowed deeply to his new king.

"I will not fail you, My King." Before Kristian could say a word of thanks Garin trotted out of the clearing. At the very edge of the trees, standing on a small rise, he pulled another banner out of his coat. He held a blue and gray flag high in the air. It was the cavalier's banner that Garin had carried throughout the battle against the Belarnians. He held it high in the early dawn for just a moment and then turned away in a hurry. Kristian watched him until he was completely out of sight.

"I just hope I don't fail you," the new king of Erand said to himself. He joined Mikhal by the embers of the fire, helping him pack the last of their provisions.

CAIRN APPROACHED THEM JUST BEFORE they were ready to leave; he had already finished packing his gear. "If you're serious about taking on Ferral again, travel south for a day, perhaps two, and you'll reach a road. Take the road west toward the mountains until you come to a river that flows toward the south. Follow that river." The swordsman shifted uneasily, perhaps unsure of whether he should be telling them this.

He continued, "Keep close to the river and head south toward a great forest. There are people living within the woods that might help you."

"The spirit folk!" Kristian exclaimed. "They're just a myth."

"They're no myth. I've seen them," Cairn responded.

"You've seen them? I've heard they are fairies or elves with powerful magic," Mikhal commented.

"They're not elves or spirits … they're just men and women like the rest of us. Their heritage is older than any kingdom in Erinia. They are masters of the sword and bow," Cairn answered.

"Why would they help us? I'm not sure we're going to find anyone to help us," Kristian added.

Cairn shrugged, "I'm not sure you will either, but I know they are real, and it's the best place I can think of for you to start."

Kristian stuck out his hand, offering Cairn his thanks, afraid to ask the swordsman what was really on his mind. Mikhal was not as shy, "Will you come with us? We could really use someone like you."

Cairn looked uneasy. It was as if he was listening to someone else speaking, someone only he could hear.

"You've been a great help," Mikhal added.

His words did not help ease Cairn's conscious. He knew they would ask this of him, but he had already made up his mind. It was made up six years ago, he could not afford friends.

Cairn finally said, "I can't join you." Then he turned back to his horse, climbed up, and surveyed the woods. He gave them a final, silent good-bye and then left.

20

ALONE

The cell was cold, damp, and dark. The smell of rotting straw mixed with sweat hung heavily in the air. Allisia shivered, trying to fight off a growing sense of despair as she sat in the corner as far away from the barred door as she could get.

She tried to stretch out her sore muscles. The bruises on her arms and legs from where Ferral had kicked her still hurt. He had only beaten her twice, preferring to play tricks on her mind. He wanted to break her spirit more than her body.

Her shock had finally subsided. It returned occasionally when Ferral let some of his new experiments loose in the dungeons. The door to her small cell was locked and barred from the inside rather than the outside. The mad sorcerer found it quite amusing that she was forced to lock herself in to keep the dead away. He had put her down in the dungeon as another form of degradation, giving her a false sense of hope by placing the locks on the inside of the cell. It was her choice to make; should she try to escape knowing the dead might be outside the door or lock herself in the small cell and hope Ferral might return to help her?

She often heard them, their feet shuffling down the corridor. It was completely dark in her prison, but they always managed to find her. They would pound and scratch on the door, trying to use bars and chains to tear the door apart. Just as they were about to break through, Ferral would call them back to him using his new powers, and she would be left alone, wondering if it was safe to open the door. In the end, Allisia decided to leave it barred. No food or water came during the time she was alone in the dungeon, and she began to grow weaker, but she refused to abandon hope.

Allisia prayed to God for salvation. She prayed that Kristian was safe and that the things Ferral told her about her brother and her people were lies. It was hard for her to remember what had actually happened. It was hard to understand what was real and what might be a dark thought in her mind. She clung to the possibility that either Kristian or Justan was one of the survivors.

Ferral was obsessed with the fact that three men had survived the battle. She had heard him order his commanders to use the entire army to find and kill the fugitives. His anger at not finding them quickly was enough to give him the strength necessary to control the dead. Allisia saw him walk among them untouched, flaunting his power. Their grossly disfigured bodies swayed precariously as they stared in dumb silence at their master. The servants and priests that were required to be near Ferral were also protected from the monsters by his magic. The king of Belarn had threatened many times to let the creatures loose on those that failed him. It was enough to keep the remaining citizens of Belarna silent and obedient.

She had no idea why Ferral put her down in the dungeon. Maybe he saw the glimmer of hope in her eyes when she heard that some had escaped the battlefield. Or maybe he just wanted to lash out at someone to inflict pain and misery for his own pleasure. She did not know. Allisia realized her best hope of surviving and eventually escaping rested solely upon her own shoulders. So far, she had no plan or even any advantage to use to her benefit. As long as Ferral kept her in the dark and guarded by the dead, she would remain his prisoner.

Footsteps echoed off the corridor's walls outside her cell. Allisia sat motionless, trying to stop even her breathing lest it give her away. The sounds stopped in front of her door, and the handle clanked as someone tried to open it. The princess pulled her knees up to her chin as she waited for her tormentors to leave. But they didn't.

"Princess Allisia," a ruff voice called out. She sat in the dark, afraid Ferral was playing another trick on her. The voice called again. "Princess Allisia, are you in there?"

Afraid to answer, but longing for someone, anyone, to talk to she answered, "Who is it?"

"It is General Derout. I have brought you some food and water."

The sorcerer's right hand, she thought. *The man responsible for the deaths of thousands of my countrymen.* Allisia did not move out of her corner. "How do I know this isn't another one of your master's tricks," she challenged.

"I'm alone, except for a serving girl. And he's not my master. I'm no dead man to be ordered around like a puppet." There was a pause as the man thought of something else to say. "Other than that, you will just have to trust me." The voice broke off waiting for her to reply.

Allisia stood slowly on wobbly legs and moved toward the door. Her muscles ached from the cold and wet conditions, but she forced herself forward. Swallowing down her fear, she grasped the locking bar and pulled it back. She quickly went back to her corner waiting to see what would come through.

Powerful rays of light burst through the crack in the door as it was pushed open. The light blinded her and even as she sank into her corner trying to hide from the light, she knew he could see her. The general entered and stood in front of her. The servant girl with long black hair dimmed the lantern then, and Allisia could see the big armored man, his single top knot of hair resting over his massive shoulder.

"Princess Allisia, I'm General Derout, and I want to help you," he declared.

She yelled back at him, defiantly. "I haven't been here long enough to fall for that one," she laughed, her voice cracking from dryness. The small and gentle servant girl knelt beside her and handed her a cup of water. Allisia grabbed it quickly unable to hold back any pretense of control. She drank it quickly gulping down every drop.

When the cup was empty, it was refilled and placed beside her on the floor. Then a pale hand gave her a bowl of bread and fruit. When the princess reached out for the food, her hand touched the other woman's fingers. A cold chill rushed through Allisia instantly. She gasped pulling back her hand in shock.

Allisia looked up at the face of the beautiful, young woman. She was little older than the princess, not even twenty years old. Her black hair was pulled back through a scarf and hung over her shoulders in long wavy curls, but her skin was very pale and cool, and her eyes seemed distant, almost empty. Allisia flinched reflexively away from the other girl who did nothing as she waited for the bowl to be taken out of her hands.

"She will not hurt you," Derout said. "Yes, she is dead. Well, mostly dead … I think. The girl was one of Ferral's earliest experiments. He has never come closer to maintaining the appearance of beauty over death. I suppose his current plans don't call for the subtlety of something as wonderful as this little girl."

"What … what is wrong with her?" Allisia asked still reluctant to accept the bowl of food. The girl continued to wait patiently with no sign of concern on her face.

"She was near death when Ferral cheated her of her chance to escape him. He used his limited knowledge of the black arts to sustain her. Now her soul is trapped between this world and whatever lies beyond death." Derout stepped closer squatting down between Allisia and the dead servant girl.

"He has always been fascinated by death and ways of controlling it. To him, control over the dead is a symbol of his power. It's his way of exerting control over his neighbors, over the other kingdoms in Erinia. But after creating this girl … so many years ago, Ferral lost the knowledge of how he had been able to create her or more like her. He has been searching for the means to create monsters to serve him ever since. When he regained the favor of Belatarn, Ferral acquired the knowledge and power necessary to create his new army. He now has an army that will destroy our world."

Allisia was truly saddened by the other girl's fate. She was also afraid. In an odd way, she thought Ferral's crime of trapping this poor girl's soul in her body, where she was neither alive nor dead, was much worse then making puppets out of the soldiers that were already dead. They did what Ferral wanted, but felt no sorrow or pain. Did this girl feel things the same way Allisia did?

"It's horrible that she is a prisoner in her own body. Unable to truly live or fully die," Allisia commented sadly. Finally, she took the bowl and thanked the pale girl.

"Why are you doing this? I'm sure your master would kill you if he discovered you were helping me."

The experienced warrior shrugged and sighed, admitting he did not completely understand his motivations either. "I'm not ashamed of what happened to your people or my part in their deaths. Kingdoms will always be at war. I'm a warrior, after all. And I strongly believe it's Belarn's destiny to be the greatest kingdom in Erinia. But," he hesitated looking back toward the door to ensure no one was listening in. "He has gone too far with his use of black magic. I used to think his resurrection of the ancient cults would revive our culture, unite our people. Their passion for this old god, along with Ferral's magic, would create a drive in them that would give us the power to sweep across the land and reclaim what was once ours."

The man in charge of the elite Black Guards and the Belarnian army raised his head, the vision of his people conquering other lands filling his mind. "I thought we would crush the Erandians and the Duellrians and claim your lands for our own. Then we could influence the old kingdoms of Mesantia once again.

"Belarn was once the most powerful kingdom on earth, you know.

People throughout Erinia bowed low to the earth out of respect as we rode through their towns."

"You mean fear," Allisia corrected. "Fear that their lives would be sacrificed to an evil and false god."

The general raised an eyebrow as he looked down at her. He shrugged, "Probably, but our ability to influence so many others through sheer force was incredible. No kingdom has ever done that besides Belarn. None."

"Being remembered as the one kingdom that destroyed everything in its path is quite an honor, I'm sure." Allisia was angered by his rhetoric and was certain she did not want his help. She turned away, looking at the girl who stood motionless by the door. Derout would not let the conversation die.

"We were strong and proud centuries ago, and we'll be that way again ..."

"But?" Allisia asked in feigned curiosity.

"But Ferral has succumbed to the powers that Belatarn gave him. He has learned how to do things that a man was never meant to know. Soon it will consume all of us. There will be nothing left worth conquering."

Allisia could not deny that Ferral had lost his grip on reality. His atrocities stretched the very fibers of nature and threatened the lives of millions, but there was more behind Derout's offer for help then what he was telling her. "Why are you really helping me, Derout?"

The warrior leaned toward her, excitement filling his voice. "Ferral is not only consumed by magic. He's also consumed by your beauty." Allisia sat upright, the disbelief plain on her face. "In part, he wants to possess you because you are betrothed to the Erandian prince. Ferral enjoys tormenting you because he knows the young Erandian fool can do nothing to stop it. But," he said as he looked at her slender neck and long hair, "he also wants you for himself. You're beautiful and innocent. For now that is enough to captivate him. Later, he will try to take one or both of those things from you. Eventually, you may end up like this little girl." Derout nodded toward the servant, chuckling.

Allisia hated the man in front of her now more than ever before. It was obvious he was only seeking an opportunity to increase his own power. She would only be able to count on him for help as long as he could profit from the experience. He was cruel and cared for no one but himself. The princess began to tire of the conversation. "What do you want?"

"For now … nothing. When the chance presents itself, I will help you escape. In the chaos that will ensue, I will kill Ferral and take his throne of bones for myself. Then Belarn will become the great kingdom it was destined to become."

Allisia was skeptical. "What makes you so sure my escape will cause so much trouble?"

Derout smiled, showing long, yellow teeth. "Losing you will torment him. It will be a personal insult, and he will do everything in his power to get you back. His focus, his power, his demon bitch will all be concerned with just one thing … getting you back. And that will be my chance."

She felt a darkness begin to wash over her. Someone else was entering the room. Allisia looked beyond the general to see the sorcerer-king, himself, standing in the doorway. No one else was with him. None of the dead things accompanied him. Yet, there was an oppressive weight in the musty air. Allisia found it difficult to breathe. He also looked different to her. He stood without assistance, finally recovered from casting his terrible spells. But his head was bent forward as though it was too heavy for his neck to support and his eyes were ringed by dark circles. He seemed lucid, yet, haunted. The costs of his new powers were obvious. They were sucking the life out of him.

Derout stepped close to her face, his foul breath hitting her full force. He was still unaware of Ferral's presence. "Just remember who helped you, little princess. You will soon have no kingdom to go home to. Your only hope of survival will be through me … you better be grateful," he said, sticking his tongue out toward her in a grotesque gesture of sexual desire.

She cringed away from the man. Derout looked a little hurt, but then he smiled, "At least I won't turn you into a rag doll to be used whenever I want." He started laughing and just as suddenly stopped again.

He finally seemed to sense the danger he was in and turned around faster than Allisia thought possible. The general waited anxiously for Ferral to speak, not knowing how much the sorcerer had overheard.

Ferral smiled wickedly as he stared at Allisia. "Even if I had not sensed you were up to something, Derout, and followed you down here, I still would have known of your plans." He looked at the servant girl, giving her an appraising smile. "I see everything she sees."

"My Lord, you misunderstand. I was only trying to add to her torment by tricking her into trusting me." He licked his lips nervously, the moisture gone from his mouth. "I did it for your pleasure," he pleaded.

"Don't attempt to save yourself by sinking to even new lows, Derout."

The general had known Ferral for years. He also knew how ruthless he would be in passing judgment on him. It would be better, he thought, to save himself now while the king was alone and unprotected. Swiftly, Derout pulled free a dagger from his belt and rushed his king.

Allisia watched the events unfold in front of her as if she were watching a bizarre play. The cruel general raised his hand to thrust the dagger deep into Ferral's chest, but just as he brought his blade down, with all of his strength, the servant girl sprang into action. The small and delicate girl jumped up involuntarily and stepped between Ferral and Derout's dagger.

Allisia gasped as the long metal knife entered the girl's chest and buried itself to the hilt. Derout tired to pull the weapon out and continue his attack, but his hand began to ache. His fingers curled up like wilted pedals on a flower. Sharp pain filled his body as the crippling affect spread up his arm. Unable to control his muscles, his body began to shake, and then he fell heavily to the floor. Ferral laughed, enjoying the scene.

He slowly approached Derout's stricken form. Paralyzed, the general could do nothing but blink his eyes and gasp for air. Ferral stepped over him and turned his attention to the dagger hilt protruding from his servant's chest.

Effortlessly, he pulled the blade from her body. He examined it for a moment then let it drop beside Derout's paralyzed form. The Duellrian princess watched in horror and shock as the girl looked down at the hole in her breast. The girl saw that there was no blood coming out of the wound and was able to show emotion for the first time in many years. The feelings came slowly as realization finally sank in that she was not human. She looked at the ghastly hole in her breast, down to the sharp dagger on the ground and, surprisingly, back to Allisia.

The girl's eyes opened wide in shock and fear. She opened her mouth to scream, and at first nothing came out, but her pain and sorrow could not be restrained by Ferral's powers any longer. Her voice finally came to her, and she filled the room with a terrified shriek. Her blood-curdling scream frightened Allisia and surprised Ferral.

The girl finally turned to him and begged for answers. "Why? Why?" she screamed in agony. Then she gasped. The dead servant girl remembered what had happened.

"JULIA," HER MOTHER CALLED OUT, "there is a long line at the well. I guess everyone is getting what they need for the celebration." She grabbed a large vase and handed it to her daughter. "Can you quickly walk down to the shore and get me some water?"

Julia frowned. "I just put on my new dress," she complained. "I don't want to get it dirty right before he sees me."

"I'm sure he won't notice anything other than your pretty face," her mother replied. "Besides, with your grace, I am also sure that you won't get a spot on that dress." She nodded toward the Utwan Sea. "We live closer to the shore than anyone else. Go to the creek and fetch some fresh water."

"Fine," Julia answered, giving in.

The girl walked along the path that led from her home toward the sea. There was a small creek with fresh water nearby that emptied into the Utwan. Few villagers ever came down the small path her father had made into the side of the hill, and it sometimes made Julia feel uneasy to walk here alone.

"But it's a lovely day and not very far," she coaxed herself.

She smiled, thinking of what her betrothed might say to the rest of the village during the feast. He was usually very shy, but he always knew what to say to make her happy. *Perhaps today, he will say something so eloquent and romantic that we will not have to wait another month for the wedding ceremony. Perhaps the elders will allow us to marry today*, she hoped.

"Cairn and Julia are a perfect match," most of her parents' friends would say. Her mother would agree. They were both dreamers.

Julia wanted to see as much of Erinia as she possibly could see before she and Cairn settled down to make a family. The young girl had an adventurous spirit, and she normally talked her love into doing things he might not normally do. Cairn always felt slightly uncomfortable around others, especially if people were gathered in large crowds, but he would do anything for Julia.

He might even find the courage to say something wonderful without being nervous, she hoped.

Where Julia was outgoing, Cairn was intuitive. The young boy easily grasped complex problems, solving many of the village's most unique challenges. He was also gifted with the speed and agility of a mountain cat. Cairn might not have a warrior's fighting spirit, but he was not afraid to tackle risky jobs.

Julia remembered how he climbed up a thin rope and then hung upside down for half an hour just to rig a new pulley system. Fixing the grist mills hauling system earned him the respect of many of the men in the village, including her father.

The two had been close since they were little children, and they always knew they were meant for each other. With Cairn's increasing reputation within the village, they had no problem openly declaring their love for each other. Her parents did not object.

Julia knew it was Cairn's happiest memory. Her love had worried

over what he would say to her parents for a week. When the time came
to talk to them, he did not have to say much. They already knew what
he wanted and welcomed him with open arms.

Splashing and a cursing voice abruptly interrupted her daydream.
Julia was startled by the unfamiliar voices.

"How long can a kid hold his breath?" a young, gruff voice asked.

"Much longer than I like," replied an equally young but melancholy
voice. "Hurry up and get it over with. We need to start back toward the
capital before my father suspects something."

"Yes, Your Highness," the first voice acknowledged.

Julia was horrified by what she heard. She wanted to run and tell
her father, but felt drawn down the path. Julia crept through the trees
until she could see the waters of the creek leading toward the sea. A
group of Belarnian soldiers sat on their horses watching one of their
men holding a small boy under the water. By now the boy was no longer struggling to reach the surface. His body was limp, his fingers floating to the top of the water.

Julia gasped out loud at what she saw. She quickly realized what
she had done, but it was too late. The soldiers turned their heads and
quickly found her. She saw each of their faces. She saw the hate that
filled their eyes. Julia took a step back up the trail.

One face in particular frightened her more than the others. A young
man, perhaps thirty years old, smiled warmly at her. He pulled long
strands of hair from his face and then smoothed out his mustache.

"Hello, there young lady," the prince of Belarn called to her. "Do
you know who I am?"

Julia stood there frozen, afraid to run.

"Do you know who I am?" Ferral asked again with more force in
his voice.

Julia nodded quickly, still afraid to say anything.

"Then you understand that we are here conducting royal business.
This incident has nothing to do with you or your family. You could say
I am doing God's will," he smiled at her again.

"Yes, Your Highness," Julia stammered. "I … I didn't see anything, and if I did it was none of my business."

Ferral laughed, "Ha. That's very good … very good. What's your name?"

"Julia, Your Highness," she replied quietly.

"Julia," Ferral repeated. "A beautiful name for a beautiful lady." He waved a hand up toward the path she had come down. "You may go."

She stood there meekly, afraid that one of the prince's men might shoot her in the back with an arrow. Julia found it hard to breathe and was about to cry.

"Go!" Ferral barked at her.

Julia sobbed for a brief moment before starting up the path. She held her breath for a long time, wondering if she would soon be killed. When it seemed the prince and his men would not come after her, she started to run. Julia ran as fast as she could back to her home.

Ferral sat there watching her until she was out of sight.

"Your Highness, you really don't think she will keep quiet, do you? There is a village just up the hill. By the end of the day, over a hundred people will know what happened," the man in the creek said.

"I know, Garnis," Ferral sighed. "She was just so beautiful, and I didn't want to see her die … just yet." The prince frowned, considering what he would have to do to keep his murder secret.

"What do you want us to do, Your Highness?" Garnis asked.

"Ride into the village and kill everyone," Ferral ordered.

"Everyone," Garnis repeated to make sure he had heard correctly.

"Yes," Ferral acknowledged. "Julia has given us a way to cover up our little incident. We'll claim she was the daughter of the nursemaid we killed back at the castle and that she kidnapped my brother. When we finally caught up to her she drowned Aron in the creek and then fled to her village. We were too late to save him, the poor child, but we hardened ourselves and destroyed all of those that harbored the young girl."

Garnis smiled; he was one of Ferral's most devout supporters.

"Why he decided to have another child now I can not fathom. My father will actually thank me for killing them," the prince added. Garnis remounted and got his men ready for the attack. Ferral reached out to slow him down. "I want her for myself, Garnis."

"The peasant girl?" Garnis asked.

Ferral nodded, lust filling his eyes. "Bring her to me unharmed."

"We'll need to scout out the village then and make sure we develop a better plan. These men," he nodded to his soldiers, "aren't known for their precision in attacks."

"That's why I like you, Garnis. You know exactly what you and your men are good for. You will be handsomely rewarded when I am king."

Garnis bowed deeply. "Just keep me near you, Your Highness. I would hate for you to become angry with me someday. With your noble ambition to take the thrown and your ability to cast spells and all … I quickly learned who deserved my loyalty. May Belatarn bless me."

"Spoken like a true believer," Ferral responded.

WHEN THE SOLDIERS SHE HAD seen earlier in the day came rampaging into the center of the village, she knew there would be no escape for anyone. She was so afraid of what the prince and his men might do to her and her family that she had not told a single person, not even Cairn. Her promise not to tell anyone what she had witnessed meant little to them. Julia knew they were there to erase any possible evidence, as well as, witnesses of the small boy's murder.

As the carnage got worse and Julia realized they were not just there to kidnap or kill her, but to massacre the entire village, she tried to step away from everyone else. Julia hoped the leader of the Belarnian soldiers would recognize her and focus his anger on her instead of the innocent people she knew. It was hard to find the courage to move away from the tables where her father and mother were still cowering. Most of her friends and neighbors were in shock and could not comprehend what was happening. Even Cairn stood dumbfounded until she began to move.

Garnis was on top of her quickly. He rushed in and grabbed her before she was more than a few feet away from her parents.

"You've caused us a lot of trouble, girl. You're the lucky one today, though. The prince wants you for himself," Garnis told her.

"No," Cairn shouted as he jumped and leaped from table to table trying to save her from Garnis and his men. He knocked the leader from his horse and fell on the ground next to her.

The wind had been knocked from her chest, and she could not get enough air in to warn Cairn to stay back. Julia already knew what her fate was. She did not want the one that she loved to suffer something worse. Julia reached out to him, but it was too late. Cairn was already starting to stand. He meant to face Garnis and defend her.

The idea was somehow noble and foolish at the same time. Even Julia understood how uneven the fight would be. Garnis was a trained killer. He felt no remorse. The bigger man was also heavily armored and carried a large sword. Cairn had no armor and no weapons. Julia could not let him die for her.

Had I warned the village, she thought, *perhaps none of this would have happened.*

Julia struggled to her feet and jumped between the two men. There was a lot of pushing and shoving. She saw angry men with wide, toothy grins. She saw Cairn's concerned face and then the big man hit him hard with his spiked glove. Cairn fell heavily to the ground, blood covering the side of his face. Then she felt a sudden ache in her breast.

When she looked down to see what had happened she was surprised to see the dagger sticking out of her chest. Garnis seemed just as surprised as she did. He even seemed confused and upset. She knew things had not gone quite the way the man intended. The lieutenant rushed over to the younger soldier that had stabbed her. He struck the man heavily with his glove and then stabbed him in the face with his sword.

He then walked casually back to her and pulled the dagger out of her breast and let her fall. Julia's vision began to narrow and blur. She had difficulty breathing.

I don't feel any pain, she thought. She did not even feel her body fall heavily to the ground.

Her hand lay next to her face, and she saw the blood that covered her fingers. Her blood. "Remember me," she whispered to Cairn, "I love you."

Julia saw him laying next to her, his face a bloody ruin, like her dress. She wanted to reach out to him, to hold him one last time, but she could not. Her life was slipping away fast, and she would never hold him again.

"CAIRN! CAIRN!" SHE SHOUTED OVER and over again. "I remember what you did," the servant girl screamed at Ferral.

"I remember what …" Julia was crying so much that the words caught in her throat. "God, why have you let this happen? Why?" Julia crawled to where her master stood. He looked down at her and smiled cruelly. She reached a shaky hand up to his boot and then pulled hard on his clothes.

"Please, kill me. Kill me!" She clawed at the sorcerer's robes, sobbing. Allisia reached out hoping to comfort her, but Ferral snapped his fingers, and the girl fell to the floor as lifeless as Derout.

ALLISIA SAW THE TEARS STREAKING down the girl's face as she laid there on the floor staring mutely back at her. While Ferral was focused on the two still forms before him, Allisia searched for the dropped dagger. Thinking quickly, she reached out to hold the girl. She was lifeless and Allisia would have thought she was finally dead if she had not suddenly blinked. The servant girl's eyes shifted in and out of focus unable to center on anything. Then they finally lost the spark of life in them and faded once again back to a dull gray color.

Ferral roughly pushed Allisia aside with his boot as he examined his two victims. He raised his hands as if lifting an invisible weight, and they came off the floor. Floating effortlessly, Derout and Julia left the room at the direction of the sorcerer's hand.

Allisia sat motionless, staring at the madman. "I hate you," she said vehemently.

"I hate you!" she screamed in rage. Ferral finally seemed to notice her and bowed.

"Allisia, I'm sorry I have neglected you for so long." He gasped, feigning surprise at the poor conditions of her cell.

"I think you have been humbled enough. I will send for you soon, and you can live in luxury once more. However," he warned turning on her, "do not forget that I hold more than your life in my hands. I hold your soul." With that he left the dungeons, laughing to himself.

Allisia moved her hand to the side, revealing what she had been able to hide from the king. She picked up Derout's dagger and put it within one of the pockets of her ragged dress. She knew that if she were going to survive, the only person she cold depend upon was herself. Allisia wished she was not alone as the forgotten lantern began to dim. She wished her father and brother were alive. She wished her country's soldiers had not been slaughtered. She also prayed Kristian was alive and thinking of her. Then the lantern's light completely faded and she was left alone, again, in the darkness.

21

ONE REMEMBERING

Cairn rode throughout the day, traveling north. He had seen nothing of significance during his ride and began to doubt Kristian's warnings. It was not hard for him to believe the king of Belarn would use treachery, every kingdom used deceit to win, but he could not accept what Kristian and Mikhal had told him. The dead could not come back to life.

Cairn had seen many things in his wanderings. Many incredible sights that could have been supernatural, but he had never seen anything as far-fetched as an army of walking dead. He had never seen a ghost or spirit, except the ones constantly haunting his dreams.

"Do you still remember me?" she asked again, a slight hint of amusement in her voice.

He remembered what Kristian told him about Allisia being held captive, and he was reminded of his own past. Cairn began to wonder if he had made the right choice. Were the last six years worth seeing Garnis and the others dead?

Is hatred and revenge enough to sustain me for the rest of my life? Cairn asked. He rode north through the woods, wondering if he was not making another mistake by turning down the Erandians.

"Why did I ever think that seeking revenge would ease my pain?" he asked himself harshly. After six years of searching, hunting down, and killing the last of the marauders, he felt even more pain than before.

Shouldn't I feel exhilarated by what I've done? Where is the sense of fulfillment from killing those responsible for her death ... for my parent's deaths?

These questions constantly plagued Cairn's troubled mind, and he could not find the answers. If anything, he felt emptier now than he had in a long, long time. He was lonely and had no sense of purpose.

Now that it is over, what am I supposed to do? Where should I go?

He wandered, seemingly with no direction until he realized that he was traveling toward the one place he vowed to never return; he was heading toward home.

Cairn had barely slept since his encounter with Garnis. The cold weather had little to do with his inability to find rest. He had searched for the cause of his suffering and could not find one. So he rode on as he always did, looking out for just himself, taking few risks except when it helped ease his troubled mind. Cairn deliberately made few friends so that he would not have to answer questions about his past.

The three Erandians had not cared about his past or his scars. There had been an immediate need for security, but there was also an unspoken need for companionship. Cairn joined with them, for a very short time, and they could have been friends. In the end, when they asked him to join their cause to defeat Ferral, he quickly turned them down. His excuses were unbelievable, but he did not apologize. Cairn had enjoyed their company, but he was reluctant to make lasting friendships.

I can't let them know what happened. That's a memory and burden that only I am allowed to have. If the night were to happen over again, Cairn reasoned, he might have stayed with them, but it was too late now, and he would have to live with his decision like so many others he made.

Cairn made camp near the edge of the woods as dusk spread over the land, covering everything in a gray haze. He settled himself in at the base of a hill where the light of his campfire would not attract any more patrols. He took time to look after his horse, combing him and covering him with an extra saddle blanket. Cairn could not comprehend how the sturdy horse managed to survive the bitter cold of the Mercies, but he was grateful for the strong horse. Ka'ap was a precious gift and his one constant companion.

"It's just us again, Ka'ap," Cairn spoke to the horse, patting him for comfort. After he finished taking care of the horse, he prepared a soup with vegetables and dried meat. He ate in lonely silence, staring at the fire. He must have been more tired than he realized because he fell asleep, the bowl of soup still in his hands.

That night Cairn dreamed about the past. His dreams were usually filled with horrific memories from his past, and he would struggle to wake up before he cried out, but this dream seemed incredibly real and was filled with one of the happiest memories of his life. He walked down the one road in the village, smelling the various scents of bread, meat, and pies coming from the homes on either side of him. He smiled, remembering that it was almost the day of celebration. Tomorrow would be the Day of Salvation and a great feast was being prepared. Tomorrow would also be the day he would be announced as Julia's betrothed.

Cairn hurried on his way, saying hello to familiar faces as he approached her family's home. Stone's Brook was a small village far north of Belarna, though it was still within the kingdom's borders. There were fewer than thirty families that lived in and around the town. They were mainly farmers and traders doing business with Belarn and the smaller communities to the north. Most homes and shops were combined in a simplistic but neat manner. The one road going through town was constantly grated and mixed with gravel to keep the dust down. It was a small town, but the people were good, and it made him smile as he continued down the road.

Cairn waved at Fandel, the storekeeper that sold Cairn's father the best jarred fruit in the area. Fandel was sweeping his small entryway like he always did late in the afternoon. Life was slow here, but Cairn did not mind. Julia often dreamed of adventures in far away places, but they would probably never leave. Cairn was happy to just stay where they were.

Cairn slowed down to admire the flowers Julia's mother had planted in the front yard of their modest home. She took great pride in her garden ... the colors and scents always reminded him of his love for Julia. Instead of knocking on the front door, he crept around back to his love's window. Julia seemed to have sensed that he was coming and was already waiting on him.

"We don't have much time. I don't have long before Mama comes to check on me," she said, giggling as she looked back over her shoulder. "I think she suspects we're up to no good every time I'm out of her sight."

"I'm not exactly the best example of an honorable man, am I?" he added jokingly.

"Oh, Cairn," she admonished. "We've probably kissed fewer times than any couple in town."

"Yeah, but a few of those times were pretty good." That made her blush, Cairn noticed. "Still, our parents wouldn't approve of me sneaking over here the day before the ceremony." Julia leaned out over the windowsill to watch the setting sun. The pale sky was turning from orange to pink as the sun fell below the horizon.

"It's beautiful," she commented dreamily. Her mind wandered as she thought of the future. "Cairn?"

"Yes, love." In his dream, she was as beautiful as she had ever been. Her dark hair fell over one shoulder in long waves. Her piercing blue eyes always held him spellbound.

The dream continued.

"Do you still promise to take me away from here, to see more of Erinia?"

"The entire world, if that is what you want," he pledged happily.

"All of it?" she asked astonished, her eyes widening. Julia loved to tease him.

"Yes, if that is what you want." There was a hint of despair in Cairn's voice.

Julia took a moment before answering. She smiled and said, "No, I don't want to see all of it."

"Why?"

"Because there would be nothing left to dream of."

Cairn's constant loneliness began to intrude in upon his dream, and he said, "You can always dream of me."

She looked at him, deep love and admiration briefly reflected in her eyes, and then she smiled. "But do you dream of me, love? Will you always think of me?"

Grief filled him, but he managed to smile and say, "Always, Julia. Always." She smiled, beaming with pleasure as she bent down and kissed him gently. Cairn smelled the flowers that scented her hair as they embraced. He held her tight, not wanting the dream to end. Finally, she said goodnight.

"What will I do now? I have kissed you more times than I have fingers. I'll never be able to keep track of them all." Her excitement forced him to smile. Then she was gone.

Cairn was suddenly transported to a new scene. He sat at a table with his father and mother in the town's square. The entire village was at the feast celebrating the salvation God had given them on this day. Everyone was happy, glad to be with their families, friends, and neighbors. Cairn looked anxiously across the square, searching for Julia. She saw him first and stood up at her table, waving to him. He finally saw her and waved back nervously. Something did not feel right. Julia looked frightened, more nervous than he had expected. *She probably thinks I will make a mess of my speech*, he thought.

Cairn knew everything that was about to happen, but he was only a spectator to the events unfolding within his dream, the same events that had occurred six years ago. Cairn knew when the food was going to be passed. When the prayers to God would begin and end. He dreaded what was to come next.

A call went out for silence as Julia's father stood on top of his bench. The crowd turned toward the respected man as he raised his cup. Cairn's parents smiled and hugged him as they all waited for the announcement. He winced as Julia's father began to speak and wished there was some way to stop him.

Cairn tried to wake himself, knowing what was about to happen, but the dream continued. He sat helplessly at the table, listening along with everyone else. "Today is a proud day for me." Cairn heard him say. "Today I wish to announce that my daughter, Julia, will be wed to the son of Netanyal of Stone's Brook." He raised his cup again in toast, and the gathered folk cheered also raising their cups.

Cairn suddenly jumped up and frantically scrambled over his table toward Julia, knowing he had already waited too long. The crowd seemed to ignore him as they drank in his honor. Drinks and bowls of food were spilled as he jumped from one table to the next, but they did not see him. They also seemed oblivious to the sound of thunder rolling down on them from the south. Just as he was about to reach Julia's table, the horses came over the hill and entered the village. The villagers screamed in shock and fear, but he was still one table away from her.

Julia had not realized what was happening and smiled at him, giving him that special smile, sadder though than any he remembered. Then the villagers panicked, finally seeing their doom ride toward them, and Cairn was nearly knocked from the table as people ran in every direction, trying to escape.

The marauders rode into the village just the way they always did in his dreams. Most of the villagers fled from them, running toward the woods. The men dressed in black armor did not let them escape; all paths out of the village had already been blocked off. The Belarnian patrol began destroying the homes and buildings, setting fire to everything they saw and killing everyone they could find.

Cairn desperately tried to reach Julia. She was still by her table, calling to him frantically. Cairn finally broke free of the other villagers and sprinted toward her. Before he could reach her, one of the soldiers saw her standing there, stranded and alone. The rider shouted to some of his fellow men and raced toward her.

Cairn saw Garnis racing toward her and tried even harder to get to her first. He heard her scream out his name in fright as the black-armored man bore down on her.

"No. Stop," he heard himself shout through tears of grief and pain.

"Wake up! Wake up," he pleaded with himself knowing it would do no good. He had been so young, so naïve. Cairn kept running, almost reaching them, as Garnis grabbed Julia roughly and pulled her up onto the saddle in front of him. He said something to her then, and Cairn could see the horror on her face.

Cairn jumped off the table, reaching out for the man. He shouted in fury and blood lust, hoping that just this once he would kill him. His speed was enough to carry him into the soldier, knocking all three of them to the ground. The breath was knocked from his lungs, and he struggled to focus on the soldiers approaching them. Cairn and Julia were surrounded.

He saw each of the men in great detail in that brief moment. He saw their faces and their evil grins. He heard them joke about what they would do to Julia. He saw the blood-red crosses on their breast-plates. Then the one he knocked off the horse came at him. Cairn would later learn that the man with dark, curly hair and neatly trimmed beard was Garnis. He was tall and strong, much older and experienced than Cairn. The smears on his chest plate were different than the others he saw, the bloody handprints still left a vivid impression in Cairn's mind. The smears were fresh; Garnis had been specially selected for some-thing. The rest of the patrol held back at Garnis's command.

His spiked glove came down in a backhanded blow that smashed into Cairn's face. The force of the blow sent him reeling to the ground. Through the haze and cloudiness of his mind, he heard Julia shout at them. He looked up at her through the sweat, tears, and blood. He silently pleaded for her to run away. His love did not hear him, and she continued to fight past them toward where he lay. He closed his eyes to block out the images, but it did not help. His mind had replayed the horrible scene almost every night since that day.

Cairn heard her scream one final time. He looked up to see one of the men holding her close. There was a look of disbelief on the soldier's face as he let go of her. The lower-ranking soldier looked apologetically toward Garnis. Apparently, he spoiled whatever plans Garnis had for her.

Julia fell slowly to the ground beside Cairn. Her hand weakly reached out for his as her beautiful blue eyes began to dim. He looked from her ashen face to the soldier and the knife in his hand and back to his love. Julia's blood flowed swiftly from a small hole in her chest where the soldier had clumsily stabbed her. The front of her special blue dress was a bloody ruin.

"No!" he screamed as blood dripped down his ruined cheek and pooled on the dirt road. There was a look of sadness on her face as the men pulled him away. Her beautiful eyes faded, and she died.

"No," he screamed again finally able to break free of the nightmare.

Cairn shot up out of his blankets, looking for signs of danger. Seeing none, he wiped the sweat from his forehead. The dream was as real as ever. Cairn began to shiver almost immediately in the freezing cold. He packed his things and put out the fire, resolved to leave this place as quickly as possible. The sword master was alone again with the dark, more afraid of his memories than anything else in the world.

"*Remember ...,*" her voice trailed off in his mind.

A FULL DAY HAD PASSED since the Erandian survivors separated. Garin had said his farewells quickly, vowing to inform their fellow countrymen of what had happened, of what Ferral had done. He also vowed to send orders back to the remainder of their country's army. Kristian and Mikhal wanted the kingdom to consolidate its forces and aid in the struggle against Belarn. Kristian did not know Garin well, but it did not take the new king long to miss the added sense of security and companionship he felt from having the young soldier with him.

Garin's attitude was optimistic despite their hardships. Even after the deaths of his friends and possibly his new wife, the cavalier pushed on. Garin's absolute devotion to Kristian made Mikhal's attitude toward him even worse. His skills as a hunter and a fighter were invaluable; he always took up the duty of rear guard, constantly looking over his shoulder for signs of danger. Garin also insisted on carrying the few supplies they had, proving he was as devoted and loyal a man as any. Kristian wished he could do half of what Garin was capable of.

Kristian was torn by his decision. *Did I do the right thing?* A part of him kept insisting he was betraying his countrymen, abandoning them when they needed someone to protect them from the Belarnians. Kristian thought of their plight, knowing hundreds were dying because of the invasion and harsh weather.

How could he be expected to get back if the Belarnians blocked all of the roads and were hunting for him? Garin was their only hope of getting news back to their people. It would take Kristian at least a month to get to Erand on foot. He would still have to raise a force to fight the Belarnians and would be no closer to saving Allisia.

Cairn had mentioned the spirit folk in the large forested area in southern Erinia might be persuaded to help him save her and destroy Ferral. If he could accomplish both, somehow, he would solve all their problems. Not to mention regain some measure of purpose in his shattered life. He quickly developed a headache from the constant stress.

Finally, Kristian shrugged. The decision was already made. He prayed he could save his people, as well as Allisia as quickly as possible. Kristian and Mikhal had charged Garin with establishing a formal resistance movement against the Belarnians in Erand. That problem was out of his hands.

"For the moment," Kristian chided himself, "I need to concentrate on keeping up with Mikhal."

The two had only each other to rely upon now. Kristian knew the cavalry officer was reluctant to trust him, but Mikhal had no choice. The cavalier could not do everything himself. He could not lead them south, as well as, protect them from danger that might approach from the north. He would never be able to stay awake all night standing watch.

Kristian did everything he could to show Mikhal he was dependable, mostly by copying what he saw the other doing. He wanted to prove his worth, a challenge he did not think he would ever win when it came to earning Mikhal's approval. Kristian was not sure if he was doing the things he saw Mikhal doing correctly; he was not even sure why he was doing half of them, anyway, but at least Mikhal had not said anything negative in the last few hours.

That first night, when Kristian and Mikhal were alone, they had split the watch in half. Although he was exhausted, Kristian was able to stay awake and alert the entire time. Nothing eventful happened, and in the morning, the two shared a small breakfast of dried meat that Cairn had given them along with some nuts and roots Mikhal had found. After eating, they quickly packed their few things away in silence and headed south.

The winter morning had been quiet, but they were still concerned about their chances of escaping Belarn. The one conversation they had focused on how lucky they were not to see any more of Ferral's creatures. The talk had forced terrible memories back to the front of Kristian's mind. He had already been so weary and cold when the dead had risen and attacked that it almost seemed like a nightmare rather than reality. Mikhal's comments forced him to accept that they were real.

Kristian tried to bury the horrible memories and his failures by focusing his attention on his surroundings. He carefully examined their heading and the trail they were making in the snow. After awhile he began to understand Mikhal's methods. They did not head straight south but spent extra time searching out areas where there was less snow or where the snow was hard packed. Looking behind them Kristian could only see a few feet past where they had been. Beyond that their footprints were too distorted by their chosen path to be easily spotted. Kristian realized this was little help in completely covering their tracks, but knew Mikhal was doing everything he could to prevent them from getting discovered by another patrol.

Kristian tried to pay attention to the woods, as well. The ground was clear of underbrush, but some snow drifts were forming. This made security a little easier; they could spot others from a long way off, but it also forced them to hide so that they were not seen. Kristian's alertness paid off when he spotted a trail of gray smoke rising off to their right.

By late afternoon, they reached a small rise; smoke rose from just beyond the hill. "You're going to check it out alone?" Kristian asked Mikhal after seeing him adjust the strap on his sword. The cavalier said nothing, but gave him a stern look.

He sighed. "What do you want me to do?"

"Be quiet for starts." Mikhal was as angry with Kristian as he had ever been. The cavalier was tense, worried about what they might find on the other side of the hill. He took a deep breath to calm himself.

"Well, at least it doesn't sound like there is a patrol over there," Kristian offered in a much lower voice.

"But they've been hunting us all night, and they might be asleep. That could just as easily be a Black Guard unit over there," Mikhal countered.

Kristian decided to go along with whatever Mikhal decided to do. He was afraid of making any further decisions on his own, fearing it would spell certain doom for them. The cavalier's gut feeling told him to be extremely cautious, but his curiosity pushed him into action. They needed food.

"I'll go in for a closer look while you stay here," Mikhal told him. Kristian wanted to go along and was about to argue when Mikhal added, "If it's something more than I can handle, you can either move to a better spot to aid me or run … if necessary. It's at least better than both of us being surprised or caught in an ambush."

Mikhal's admonishing look silenced any complaint Kristian had. Kristian doubted he would be any help if there was an ambush on the other side of the hill.

He followed Mikhal for a short distance, staying far behind the cavalier. He made sure he never lost sight of the young officer but was far enough away that he would not be detected at the same time as Mikhal.

When they reached the left side of the hill, Kristian moved behind a snow bank. Mikhal nodded to him, his glare warning Kristian not to make any mistakes, and then he crept around the hill into the clearing.

THE SMOKE WAS COMING FROM the chimney of a small cottage. Kristian was immediately relieved. It did not appear as though there were any patrols in the area. Then he saw the open door to the cottage, and he knew something was not right. He scanned the clearing for the owner and began to notice other alarming things. Carcasses littered the snow. From his hiding place, he could not tell what they were, but he was sure they were not human. For a moment he feared they had run right into what they had wanted to avoid, Ferral's dead creatures. Kristian looked back to Mikhal.

The cavalry officer was creeping toward the open door. He, too, saw the gross display of blood and gore in the front yard. Already exposed, he decided to investigate and find out what had happened inside the small cottage. One look inside was all he needed. Mikhal ran back to Kristian seemingly in panic. His stealthy approach was forgotten as he climbed over the snow bank to reach Kristian.

"There's a dead man inside. He's strung up over the hearth and his guts are all over the place." Kristian cringed. He knew the innocent man was somehow dead because of him.

"The dead … are they here?" he asked afraid to hear the answer. Mikhal shook his head.

"No. It was definitely a Belarnian patrol, probably the Black Guards, by the look of the mess." Mikhal sucked in air trying to calm down. "I've never seen such cruelty."

"Are they still around?" Kristian asked, looking around nervously for signs of danger.

"I don't think so. The body looks like it has been there for at least a day. I think we're safe, but it concerns me that they're already ahead of us. If they're this far south, it will be much harder for us to leave the woods."

"What should we do?" Kristian asked him. Mikhal looked around slowly, trying to get a sense of the place. Finally, he shrugged.

"I think that if we hurry, maybe we can find a few things in that cottage that will help us. Although, after seeing what I've seen, I doubt there is anything left worth scavenging." Kristian nodded in agreement, and then they quickly stood and ran toward the cottage. Neither of them wanted to waste time discussing a plan. They quickly approached the door, Kristian trying to prepare himself for the sight of the corpse inside.

Mikhal stopped by the door, waiting for Kristian's nod. When he was ready Mikhal walked determinedly inside. The poor man's body was immediately visible. He was an older man. It was hard for Mikhal to tell just how old he was because of the condition of the remains. The body was suspended half way between the floor and the ceiling. His hands were bound and secured to the rafters. His feet were similarly tied and secured by other ropes to the hearth. Kristian's gaze was drawn to the man's face. His eyes and mouth were wide open as if framed by the murderers in a grotesque expression of horror and pain. What answers did they possibly try to pull from his lips? Whatever the woodsman had said must not have been what the Belarnians wanted to hear. There was blood everywhere.

Mikhal forced himself to look away. Once they were more accustomed to the sight, he pulled Kristian over to the side. "All of the rooms are probably the same. But we might find something useful. Why don't you go into the bedrooms and see if there are any clothes that would be more suitable for us." Kristian swallowed and then nodded unable to say anything. He stepped carefully around the hanging body and went through a door to the back of the house.

Just then Mikhal sensed movement near the door. He quietly pulled his sword free and moved next to the opening. *It was a trap after all*, he swore to himself.

A shadow appeared in the doorway, and the Erandian prepared to bring his blade down. A large head pushed itself through the entryway.

Its dark, round eyes stared inquisitively at Mikhal as if asking him what had happened here.

Mikhal sighed in relief, lowering his sword. He smiled as he reached out a hand to reassure the horse that everything would be all right.

THEIR OUTLOOK HAD CHANGED DRAMATICALLY after finding the woodsman's animal. It was an older workhorse not used to carrying people, but it was still in good shape and helped them make better progress through the snow. Kristian had found some fur-lined clothes in one of the bedrooms, and Mikhal had managed to salvage some dried meat and biscuits. All of their new belongings were packed into a few blankets and loaded onto the horse's back.

For the remainder of the day following their encounter at the cottage, the two took turns guiding the horse through the woods while the other rested on top. Near dusk, they found themselves at the end of the tree line. Kristian looked toward the south and west, taking in the fairly flat, open terrain with a little apprehension. They would be even more vulnerable out there. There was nothing to do about it, so they waited for the sun to go down before continuing on. Kristian wanted to get as far away from Belarn as they could. They would rest for a while, letting it get very dark before they started out into the open.

Still afraid of being spotted by patrols, the two survivors did not risk a fire. Instead, they dug into the snowdrifts around them making low walls to block the wind. They ate in silence, reflecting on everything that had happened and what needed to be done.

THAT NIGHT THEY BOTH RODE. The horse seemed ready to carry the added burden, and it seemed able to spot areas where the snow was not as deep. They found the road Cairn had mentioned just as the sun was rising.

"Follow the road west until you get to the foothills of the Merciless

Mountains. Cross the river and then travel south until you reach the Great Forest," Cairn had instructed them.

"How do we know if it's the right road?" Kristian asked.

Mikhal snorted. "Do you see any other roads?"

They should have missed it completely; it was buried in the snow. Luckily, a strong wind had blown enough snow off part of it that they heard the horses' hoofs skid on the frozen surface. In one direction, it headed off toward their homeland, a place as cursed as any in the world, its people scattered after the destruction of their citadel and death of their king.

The urge to turn left and see the devastation for himself was strong for Kristian. He wanted to hear from his people what had happened and hopefully, see where his father lay entombed. Kristian knew what was in store for him if he went the other way. His quest was seemingly impossible, and he could not imagine finding others willing to help him against Ferral. He was tempted to just turn east and head for Erand, but he also knew there was very little he could do there to help either Allisia or his own people. There would be no viable force coming from Erand or Duellr for some time. He regretted not being able to help his people or atone for his mistakes, but his instincts told him to go west.

Grimacing, he looked down the road to his right. "Well, Lieutenant Jurander, we've made it."

Mikhal simply nodded. "We've made it, so far," he added, scanning the horizon for Belarnian patrols. Kristian noticed that even Mikhal looked remorsefully to the east.

"I'm thinking the same thing. I don't think we can help them, though," Kristian said.

"No. We can't help," Mikhal commented. "We'd be dead before we even got to Erand. I just hope we didn't send Garin to his death. But," the cavalier sighed, "if you're committed to ending this and killing Ferral, we must find new allies. For once … we have something in common," Mikhal said.

"What do you think we'll find out there?" Kristian asked. "I mean, who do you think we'll find—others that will believe what we say and join us?"

Mikhal shrugged. "I don't know. If Cairn is right, there should be people sympathetic to our cause within two days ride of here."

"And if they aren't there any more or they don't want to help us?"

"Then I suppose we will have to keep looking." Mikhal tried to look behind him to see Kristian. "Are you ready to start this quest, King Kristian?" His tone was full of contempt.

Kristian ignored him and surveyed the land again, hoping to see a hopeful sign somewhere in the snowy landscape, but there was nothing. Finally, he nodded, more determined then before, and answered, "Let's go."

Mikhal turned the horse he had nicknamed "Old Man" west along the snow-covered road.

THEY SPOKE LITTLE THE NEXT day. In unfamiliar territory, with the threat of enemy patrols still in the area, neither of them felt like talking. Mikhal was too preoccupied with maintaining a good pace and keeping a look out to say anything. Kristian knew the reasons Mikhal did not speak to him and, for awhile, he did not mind; he was more worried about how they were going to survive. The cavalier might know something about what to do, but he certainly was not going to share his thoughts with the man he hated.

The battle had been almost five days ago? he tried to remember. The memories were already so foggy in his mind that it was hard to remember the details of what happened. *What had Ferral said?* Kristian thought he would never forget the words of that evil man. Ferral had held onto Allisia, shouting down from the black wall, but Kristian's constant fatigue made it hard to recall things. He suddenly felt shame as Ferral's words came back to him.

I should have known we were in danger, Kristian told himself. *I should have understood Ferral's powers and warned the Duellrians to wait for the rest of their army instead of being the one to push them into attacking early.*

Kristian shook his head in grief. An important lesson was learned about Ferral, but the knowledge came at a price no one should have had to pay, except Kristian. Tears began to well up in his eyes. He vowed to never quit until he had made everything right, but he feared more than anything that there was no way to make amends for what he had done.

Kristian tried not to linger on his own misery for too long, he was beginning to think he might go mad. His mind raced from one frantic thought to the next. Images of Allisia being tormented by Ferral frequently surfaced, and he tried not to think of her too much. He was already worrying so much that he was getting sick every time he imagined her face. At the end of every thought, however, his mind drifted back to her.

No one else had ever cared to listen to him or tried to understand his feelings. Allisia had not agreed with him, and she convinced him to see that he, too, was to blame for his behavior. Allisia was a stubborn girl, and Kristian liked that part of her.

During their first conversation, she had admitted their marriage was not what she wanted, especially since Kristian was the self-centered fool he appeared to be.

Kristian smiled despite the painful memory. He remembered how she sent people out to discover who he really was. It made him feel good to know someone went to that much trouble just to understand him. She was open and direct, but Allisia was also kind and considerate. No one had been that honest to him in a long time.

The truth hurt, and he had lashed out at her with terrible insults, forcing her to walk away. No one had done that before either.

He instantly realized that she might be the best thing that could ever happen to him, but she was abandoning him, and he could not stand to see her go. Kristian apologized to keep her from leaving the garden. His actions in the courtyard could have been enough to ruin their relationship forever, but he refused to let her go away angry.

Kristian tried to say he was sorry again, adding as much sincerity as he could muster. He had never been forced to accept that he was wrong before. Allisia expected more of him, and in a way his father never had. It was as if she knew the true character of him that was trapped deep within and demanded that he share that side of his personality with her. She finally accepted his apology and promised to see him again to talk more about their future.

He remembered every word they spoke to each other from when they had first met up to the final night in the courtroom. Kristian also remembered her every expression. He felt terrible every time he remembered how she smiled or laughed or became angry. He had let Allisia down more than anyone else. She deserved to be safe. She was his only friend.

Kristian wondered if he loved her, but more importantly, she was someone he trusted and he could not fail her. It was hard to accept that Ferral was holding her prisoner in his fortress. He did not want to think that she lay alone in some dark corner of a cell and her only memory of him was the way he had initially treated her.

His mood began to darken even more as he thought of everything she had been through in just a few weeks. Allisia witnessed the brutal murder of her father right in front of her and had then been taken captive by the demon. She was forced to watch as Ferral's dead creatures slaughtered her countrymen. And now, Ferral claimed her as his war prize, saying he would marry her and kill Kristian.

Everything he was about to do, this quest to raise a new army and his desire to kill Ferral, was to make sure that did not happen. He took in a deep breath to try and calm himself.

Kristian tried to stop worrying about her for just a few moments by looking at his surroundings.

In the distance, he could see low rises in the landscape, the foothills of the Merciless Mountains. They grew out of the darkness ahead, slowly taking shape in front of him. They looked so far away that it was impossible for Kristian to tell how long it would take to reach them.

Couldn't they go faster? he wondered anxiously.

THEY REACHED THE FOOTHILLS EARLY in the afternoon on the ninth day after the battle. The weather had gotten worse the closer to the mountains they got. Strong, cold winds blew ice and snow at the two, stinging their faces. Each looked at the jagged peaks off in the distance to their right in awe. Kristian had heard of the mountain range called the Mercies, which lured many into its high valleys with the hopes of riches and then trapped them forever in its cruel winter clutch. He never imagined they would look so forbidding. Even now, he could see more dark storm clouds rolling down the mountain peaks, rapidly approaching where they stood. He laughed out loud at their poor luck as he remembered how cruel the weather had been the night of the battle.

"At least it's a natural storm," he commented to Mikhal. "It doesn't seem to have the cruelty to it that Ferral's storm did."

"I think you'll change your mind about cruelty once it hits us," Mikhal replied, sarcastically.

They continued to watch silently in dismay, as the clouds grew darker and closer throughout the day. In a rush that almost swept them from their horse, the fierce winds finally caught up to them … and with the winds came a blanket of snow. The Erandians dismounted, grabbing hold of Old Man's reigns for support. Kristian had never witnessed such destructive storms before, and now he had seen two in less than two weeks.

Kristian shouted over the wind so that Mikhal could hear him. "I think I was wrong, these mountains are cursed after all. It certainly wasn't a coincidence the night of the battle." It was hard to see Mikhal's reaction, his face was hidden deep within a fur-trimmed hood, but he thought the cavalier was nodding in agreement.

"I've been thinking the same thing. I saw that madman standing on top of his black walls chanting." The cavalier looked around him at the swirling mists of snow. "This is definitely not natural. Look," he said, pointing toward the hills to the north, "the storm winds are blowing directly south instead of to the east, and it is too early in the season for northern gales." Mikhal even thought he saw odd colors swirling within the clouds where they met the mountains.

"Evil magic is at work here." It was Kristian's turn to nod in agreement. Neither had believed much in the ancient stories of sorcerers using magic to defeat armies, but it was hard for either of them to deny those stories now.

"How do we know which way to go? I can't see my own feet," Kristian complained as he stepped cautiously forward through the blizzard.

"I don't know, but I can't see any shelter either. We should keep moving until we find a few trees or a settlement. Anything to at least block the wind."

They continued westward, hoping to find some place to take a break, but the storm died out as quickly as it had come. At first, the companions did not notice the change in the weather. Their ears rang from the howling wind, and their fingers and toes were numb from the biting cold. Then Kristian looked up and saw a star twinkling through the clouds. The storm had gone on for an entire day. He looked to Mikhal who was trying to pry his frozen glove away from his hold on the reigns.

Mikhal's first thought was to check on the horse. It was shaking badly, and its ragged breath was difficult to hear. "I'm afraid Old Man's done for." The cavalier tried to rub some warmth into the horse's neck and then patted him. He loved horses almost as much as people. "I'm sorry, my friend. We didn't take very good care of you. You served us well when we desperately needed you, and when you needed us we completely ignored you."

"What should we do with him?" Kristian asked. He could see that Mikhal was truly upset. The young king had watched Mikhal closely and learned another important lesson. He began to understand, in part, what being a cavalier meant. A horse was just as important to one of the riders as a sword. The two, horse and cavalier, fought together and lived and died together. Mikhal was trained to care for his horse just as he was trained to look after all of his soldiers. And now, with his inspection of Old Man complete, Mikhal determined the animal would not last much longer. Part of Kristian felt shame for not having paid closer attention to the horse.

Mikhal shrugged. "He's shaking badly from the cold. It looks as though he has frostbite on one of his front legs. His eyes are nearly frozen shut, and his lungs are raw from the freezing winds. We should say one final thank you and kindly end his misery, but I can't even bare to mercy kill the poor beast. I've done too much killing lately." Kristian nodded, understanding. Neither of them had the heart to end the horse's pain.

Just then Old Man moved forward as though it understood what was being discussed. It nudged Mikhal, pushing him. He looked at the suffering animal questioningly. It nudged him again.

"What does he want?" Kristian asked puzzled.

"I don't know." Old Man nudged Mikhal again. He laughed in surprise. "I don't think he's ready to give in yet." Both of them smiled as the stubborn workhorse moved ahead of Kristian.

The two shrugged as they struggled on through the snow with Old Man plodding on ahead of them. "Hopefully, we'll find the river running south soon," Mikhal commented.

"Or maybe a nice village with a tavern or an inn with a hot bath," Kristian joked.

Mikhal stopped to look at him sternly. "As I recall, King Kristian, the last time you directed people to stay at a village, we were chased out by an angry mob. Besides, the last thing we want is to draw attention to us in an area where they might decide to turn us over to the Belarnians." Kristian nodded silently, accepting the rebuke. He had only been joking, trying to lighten the mood, and it was not worth mentioning. Something else was nagging at him.

"Why is it you only address me as "King" or "Your Highness" when you're mocking me? Do you hate me that much?" Mikhal kept walking and did not turn to look at him.

"I need to know ..." Kristian stammered. "I need to know where I stand with you. Why are you helping me if you would rather see me dead?"

Mikhal stopped but still did not face Kristian. "I wish you dead no more than I wish myself dead."

"I'm not sure that makes me feel any better after what we've been through."

"We have our differences," Mikhal offered, trying to be civil. "Like I told you before, you have a lot to answer for, but we have more important things to worry about right now. I don't have the political savvy that you have, and we'll definitely need your gift for words if we're going to convince anyone to take on Ferral. I have some … leadership experience, but it will only be good if we get another chance at taking on Ferral. I promise that I'll support you. You're my king, after all. I'll serve and protect you, but I'm not going to let you forget what happened."

Kristian stared at Mikhal's back dumbfounded. "You don't have to remind me. I'll never forget." *Would things ever be good again?* he wondered. Then he realized that this was only the beginning.

"You're wrong about something, though. You're not giving yourself enough credit. You fought better than anyone else that I saw. You have courage and skill and … people respect you for your bravery." He could not tell if his words had any affect.

Mikhal kept walking on through the snow, trying to ignore the compliment.

22

RESPITE

The next morning, they found the mountain stream running across their path. The water was fresh and clear, and it ran down out of the foothills, winding its way toward the Great Forest that was somewhere to the south. The shock of the cold water running down Kristian's throat revived him and made him feel better than he had in several days. Refreshed, he cleaned himself the best he could in the icy waters. Once he was done, he surprised Mikhal by volunteering to look after Old Man.

They were both amazed by the animal's stamina. Many other beasts of burden would have collapsed by now, but their newest companion was determined not to be left behind. Old Man favored one leg and often coughed, trying to rid his lungs of the cold that must have soaked into his every bone. When Kristian examined the horse, he also noticed a small trickle of blood running down out of its muzzle.

"This can't be good," he commented. "How long will he hold out?"

"He's much stronger than I thought. He's hurt, but there's still a lot of life left in him. He might make it as far as the forest," Mikhal offered.

In fact, when the horse also took a drink from the river, he, too,
seemed to regain strength. The horse was eager to start the next part of
their journey by the time the two Erandians were ready to turn south
in search of the forest and people who might help them. It was as if all
three of them were ready to leave the terrible memory of the things
they had seen in Belarn behind them. They repacked their belongings
and quickly moved off in search of the legendary spirit folk. They continued traveling throughout the day, using the stream as a guide to keep
them on track.

Toward late afternoon, Kristian noticed their surroundings were
beginning to change. The dark storm clouds that had menaced them
almost constantly since the start of the war in Duellr were breaking
up. Rays of soft light penetrated the malevolent clouds, warming him.
His mood improved as he took deep breaths of fresh air. He smelled
several pleasant scents that he had almost forgotten existed. The dark,
pungent scent of earth mixed with the smell of pine and cedar overwhelmed Kristian's senses. A warm, gentle breeze coming out of the
south brought other smells, as well. Kristian smelled grass and leaves,
and he suddenly opened his eyes wide to take a closer look around him.
The snow was melting. After less than a day's ride south from the Mercies, they had ridden out from under Ferral's domain. Already, patches
of grass and mud were standing out against the white landscape.

"I've never been so glad to feel the warmth of the sun in my entire
life!" Kristian exclaimed.

Mikhal nodded. "I was beginning to think I would never feel my
feet again." He filled his chest with fresh air and let out a deep sigh. "Oh,
how this heavenly smell brings back memories of home. I remember
walking in my father's fields, feeling just the same as I do now. It should
be harvest any day now. Why, I would—" Mikhal cut himself short.

"What's wrong?" Kristian asked.

"It's not right for either us to feel so good when our countrymen are
oppressed." Mikhal lowered his head in shame.

Kristian wanted to do something to ease Mikhal's worries, but he was afraid of once again saying something to offend the cavalier. He took his time trying to come up with the exact words he was looking for. "I'll never be able to let go of my guilt or forget what our people are going through. I know that our people are suffering and dying, but if we were with them right now, we could do nothing for them. The most I could do would be to encourage them to fight the cold and hope for a day when we can all feel safe again."

Mikhal turned in the saddle to look at him, he felt encouraged to say more. "We've faced a lot of danger, and we're definitely going to face more before the end. I don't think our people would begrudge us the comfort of a warm day or a short period of peace as long as we don't forget them or why we are out here to begin with. Besides, this weather will help speed us on our way."

Mikhal was looking straight at him. He paused a moment and then gave his king a half-smile. The cavalier nodded and then veered their horse around a deep bog. It was the first time Kristian had seen him smile since the battle.

"That was spoken well enough," Mikhal commented. "Why can't you always speak like that? You know how I feel about the things you've said and done. Hell, most of the time I only had to indirectly serve you, and I found even that to be unbearable. I was always far enough away from the inner circle that your decisions rarely affected me. But I have heard you say some … some of the most pompous things I have ever heard."

Kristian nodded in sad acknowledgment.

"If you just took the time to think through your thoughts and say something like what you just said to me or made decisions based on all the advice given you … no one would ever doubt you."

"I understand." Kristian paused, knowing how Mikhal felt about him, but he was still unsure of how to explain himself. "I … I don't know why I've acted the way I have. I want to blame my mother, my father … but I can't. I hated them for so long. Actually, a part of me hated everyone I saw or spoke to for a very long time."

"Why?" Mikhal did not understand what Kristian was saying.

Kristian shrugged. "I felt like I was forced to spend my entire life separated from everyone else. I couldn't do the things other children were allowed to do like play games or explore the countryside. I was trapped by books and scholars and even my own parents. And I hated them for that."

"They only meant to prepare you for the great burden of being a king," Mikhal countered.

"I know. I began to understand that just as we were preparing to leave the city for Duellr, but I couldn't face my father. We had barely spoken a word to each other since our argument over the arranged marriage." Kristian stopped for a moment, thinking of his father. "I just could not say that I was sorry, and I hate myself for it. I hope he forgives me."

"A father loves his son no matter what foolishness he may do. I'm sure he loved you whether he was able to say it or not," Mikhal added. "He was a great king, and I was proud to serve him." Kristian smiled still sad.

"I will spend the rest of my life trying to be as good a king as he was," Kristian claimed.

Mikhal snorted. "That will take a lifetime, Your Highness." Kristian chided Mikhal for mocking him again, but the cavalier ignored him and pushed the conversation forward. He needed to know more about the man he was serving. The young officer needed to know more to justify his own feelings of guilt for abandoning his comrades on the hill. Mikhal would no longer follow someone blindly.

"I thought I heard you say you were arguing with your father over your arranged marriage to Princess Allisia. Didn't you want to marry her?"

"No, not at first. I thought he was trying to send me away so that he wouldn't have to argue with me any more. I thought only of my own selfish desires, and I refused to leave the city. I spoke harshly to him, and it hurts now to remember what I said, but once I met Allisia, I began to think my father knew what was best for me after all."

Kristian laughed as he remembered. "Actually, I still don't know if I love her. I think I do, but I've never been in love before."

"Only a prince could fall in love in one day," Mikhal remarked sarcastically.

"It was more than a day," Kristian argued. "Even if it was only one day, it was the best day I've ever had. She's the closest thing I've had to a true friend. I suppose she is my only friend. She didn't just try to please me by telling me things I wanted to hear. Allisia matched my temper with her own stubbornness and forced me to hear how she felt about our marriage. Through her words, I began to realize how frightened we both were of being married to someone we didn't know.

"I spent as much time with her after that as I could. It wasn't hard to forget my troubles with my father while I was with her. She made me feel at ease and welcome, and I wanted to be with her as much as I could." Kristian sighed, missing her.

"She's beautiful." Mikhal admitted. "You must be in love to talk so much about her after only knowing her for a few days." The image of the beautiful woman that turned into the demon suddenly jumped into his mind. He unconsciously flinched, wondering about his own feelings.

"Yes, she is beautiful and … I think I love her. More importantly, she's my friend. I can't leave her in Ferral's hands. She deserves something far better than that."

Mikhal agreed with him.

"Well then, Your Highness, we must make sure we steal her back from Ferral as quickly as possible." They both nodded as the last rays of the sun fell below the horizon.

"Please don't call me that any more. It makes me uncomfortable." Mikhal could tell that Kristian was pleading for him to let up.

"Then the next time you hear me say it … it will be with true respect." Mikhal saw a glimmer of hope in Kristian's eyes. "Don't be too comforted. It will take a lot to earn my respect. It may take you a lifetime."

THAT NIGHT THEY RISKED A fire. The two Erandians found a small copse of cottonwood trees on a hill overlooking the stream. Hidden among the old river trees, the two talked for a while, eating their small portions of dried meat and biscuits. They were both surprised to find out they were the same age. Kristian thought Mikhal was at least three or four years older than him just because of the way he carried himself. The young king had seen the cavalier make several hard decisions while facing death and wondered how someone the same age as he could be capable of handling so much responsibility.

When he had commented on this to Mikhal, the cavalier replied, "Well, I suppose I've made some very difficult decisions lately, but I think part of my ability to react quickly is because of my training. It isn't easy being a cavalier; it takes a great deal of time and often pain to become one of us."

"Did you know that I wanted to be a cavalier?" Kristian admitted. Mikhal shook his head in surprise as Kristian smiled, remembering how he used to spy on the elite cavalry soldiers as they practiced maneuvers near the city. "I wanted to ride and fight and ..."

"Yes? Go on, why didn't you become one of us? Many Erandian princes have joined us in the past." Mikhal was intrigued by Kristian's admission.

Kristian smirked. "My father wouldn't allow it. I had to train by myself miles from the city just to make sure he didn't find out. I would practice for hours with a horse or a sword. I thought I would have been a good cavalier." Kristian smiled, but it quickly faded as the realization of how he had actually turned out came to him.

Mikhal sensed it and said, "I'm sure there was a part of him that would have loved to see you lead our army in battle against Ferral." Kristian laughed at him. Mikhal looked at him, wondering what was so amusing.

"Sorry," Kristian offered as he regained control of himself. "I just thought it was funny that after all of the mistakes I've made, you would say something like that."

"Say what? Look, just because you rush in and make decisions rashly doesn't mean you don't have the potential to be a better leader … the kind of leader we need." Kristian shook his head, disagreeing with him. "You have to because our people need you. You just have to remember to take into consideration the consequences of your actions. It may seem you're wasting valuable time, but in the end, you save time and lives by making a clearer plan."

Kristian shook his head again. "Did you just hear yourself? You're the great leader we need. Maybe it's your training that has given you the ability to quickly decide what the best course of action is, but I don't have that training or experience, and I certainly don't feel like I'll ever be able to think like that. Not after the mistakes I've made."

"Well, I'll never be the kind of man that can moderate all the different opinions people have. I'm no politician," Mikhal declared.

Kristian paused a moment considering something. Then he asked, "Maybe thinking about things for too long can be just as bad as rushing in when you don't know the real situation?"

Mikhal agreed. "Yes, exactly. You understand better than you claim." Mikhal leaned closer to Kristian. "You know, being timid is just as bad as being an impatient and demanding fool." Kristian immediately knew what the cavalier was getting at but did not know what to say. Mikhal waited for a response.

"I don't know what you mean by that," Kristian claimed.

"I mean that some of the qualities you had before the battle were just as necessary to being a good leader as your new-found traits of caution and concern. A leader must accept that his decisions will risk lives, maybe even cause people you care about to die, but you can't let that keep you from making the right decision. And just as you said earlier, the longer you wait in making the decision you already know is right, that many more lives are put at risk by your delay. Sooner or later you're going to have to make important decisions again."

"Just before we started the invasion, I wondered if my harsh feelings toward you were justified," Mikhal admitted. Kristian's eyes opened wide in surprise. "The men were coming around to you, and you seemed genuinely concerned about their welfare. You weren't as elusive as you had been during the ride to Duellr. I thought maybe I was wrong about you."

"Then you got to see me for what I really am," Kristian tried to finish for him.

Mikhal did not know what he felt. Kristian was responsible for the deaths of his comrades. He was responsible for the massacre of the entire Duellrian army, but the cavalier wondered if the outcome would have ended any differently. Mikhal wondered what he would have done if he were in Kristian's position.

He sighed heavily, shrugged, and then offered, "Don't be too hard on yourself. That's my job."

Kristian went to sleep wondering how much longer he would have before he was expected to make those decisions. The talk with Mikhal confused him. "Be cautious. Take necessary risks. Take in the situation around you. Don't hesitate in making the right choice!" The words continually echoed in his mind.

He finally fell asleep after hours of worrying about what might soon come up and force him to be a king. He wished that time would never come, but he knew it would come all too soon.

LATER THAT NIGHT, MIKHAL ROLLED around in his blanket while Kristian kept watch. Kristian was concerned about his companion rolling into the fire, but he was hesitant to wake him.

The cavalier dreamt of a beautiful woman with long hair the color of wheat. She walked amid a field of blue wildflowers, stopping to smell a few as she went. When she sensed Mikhal was watching her, she turned to him and smiled. The smile melted his confusion and doubts away and left him with a warm feeling inside. He waved back to her reassuringly, and then she continued walking away.

Mikhal could have happily spent the rest of the night watching the beautiful woman in the peaceful meadow, but his mind kept pushing the dream along. The woman in her flowing gown of white was somehow familiar to him, and he pushed ever deeper into his mind to solve the mystery. Storm clouds grew overhead as he stared at her fleeting shape. The sound of distant, rumbling thunder served as the dream's eerie melody as the vision changed from a peaceful meadow full of flowers and tall grass to a nightmare landscape of fire and death.

Mikhal stood out over a large body of turbulent water. Across the water in front of him was a land engulfed in flames. The land shook and fountains of liquid fire shot out from the mountains overlooking a once magnificent city. Above the deafening sounds of the land sinking below the waves, he could still hear the cries of thousands of people. Mikhal heard the piercing screams of those in the fire and water even though he covered his ears. One voice stood out from all the rest. One so beautiful and yet so full of sorrow and pain that it made Mikhal cry. He was safe, far enough out in the water that he had escaped the catastrophe, but her voice called out to him even as she certainly must have perished. Her voice called to him. Mikhal shook his head to forget her awful cries and woke suddenly.

He was shaking. The dream seemed so real that he was not sure where he was. The campfire startled him, and he jumped back, afraid he was still in the dream and that he was about to share the beautiful woman's fate. When Mikhal finally realized where he was, he sat up, looking around for Kristian. The young king was standing a fair distance away, pretending not to have noticed the cavalier's actions. Mikhal shook his head to clear out the ringing in his ears.

The dream seemed so real, he swore.

The woman had been so beautiful that he still longed for her even after waking. Mikhal knew it was the demon-woman.

23

FERRAL'S POWER

The cold wind swept across the plains of Belarn, making a sound much like a moan. Nature, itself, was tired of the abuse it was feeling from the tight control Ferral held over the land. The weather had no choice except to obey his commands, and so it cried out as it ran through the hills and valleys of the once beautiful country. The only other noise on the lonely plain was the squeaking of rusted chains and hinges from the countless cages that swung in the strong winds. Inside the iron prisons laid the remains of those that had somehow displeased the sorcerer. Rotted limbs hung limply out through the bars as a silent reminder to all those passing through Belarn.

The spell the sorcerer-king cast two weeks earlier had affected them as well. They were accused of heresy or treason for trying to abandon their king. He had them executed and then placed in the cages lining the road between Belarna and Singhal. During the day, the corpses slowly rotted in the cold sun. At night, they reached out feebly through the bars toward the citadel, hungry for the living that sought shelter inside the walls.

Travelers throughout Erinia heard the tale of Belarn's evil king and his powers over nature and the dead. Most chose not to believe the nightmarish stories, but all took extra precautions while traveling. No one felt safe, and all felt betrayed as the weather continued to worsen in the east.

Those that did not believe in the legacy of Ferral's ancient god or were too frightened to stay and watch the destruction of their city fled. It was not surprising to see hundreds fleeing through sewer grates or climbing down from ropes and running away from the black fortress. There was little time to get away from the dead before they came back to life at sundown.

At first, the guards fought them, forcing them to stay. It was rumored Ferral had executed their only hero, General Derout, and was assuming direct control of the armies. He decreed that anyone attempting to leave the city was to be immediately killed and the bodies kept preserved for his black arts. Those that guarded the gates thought their king's order would be enough to keep people from fleeing, that and the constant threat of the dead that pushed against the outer gates every night. But the exodus increased significantly every day. The first hundred or so that attempted to escape were caught and killed like the sorcerer ordered, their bodies carted away for some awful purpose.

Soon afterward, the guards were mobbed by rushing hordes of frantic people. The gates were finally closed for good in an attempt to keep them from leaving, but every day, guards on the ramparts reported people heading away from the fortified city heading south. A few guards were likely making a large fortune smuggling people out of the city when their officers were not around.

Finally, the army gave up on enforcing the mandate. They tried to cover up the city's plight by reporting to Ferral that all was in order. Ferral simply nodded, accepting the information; those selected to tell their mad king the lies would scurry away quickly afraid of what would happen if he ever found out the truth.

On this day, as the sun faded beyond the Utwan Sea and the Merciless Mountains further to the west, Ferral ordered an assembly of all the army's officers. They were to wait for their king in the large courtyard between the inner wall and the palace. Hundreds of torches lined the walls and balconies of the courtyard as the deep shadows and the setting sun threw the area into darkness.

Most were nervous and afraid that their king was going to unleash the living dead upon them. They were herded into the courtyard by those that reverently worshipped their king and the god, Belatarn. Mad with blood lust, the faithful servants jabbed at their comrades with spears and swords threatening to slaughter them if they did not move to obey their king's summons.

They waited in fearful silence for Ferral's arrival. They were jolted from where they stood by the deafening boom of a large drum. It sounded three times to announce his appearance.

The king walked out onto a balcony above them, just out of range of any spear thrown from the crowd. With his thin frame hidden within the folds of a great black and red robe, he looked like **Death** itself. He waved solemnly to those below, a look of disappointment **on** his face. The drum's reverberating sound finally ended, leaving **an eerie** silence behind.

Ferral raised his hands and smiled. "Welcome, welcome, great warriors. I gratefully thank you for coming on such short notice." His smile dropped as quickly as it had appeared.

"Today we celebrate our victory over Erand and Duellr. Their lands are in ruins, and their people scattered throughout the frozen wastelands of their once proud kingdoms. Now all know my power and speak the name of our country and our god with great fear. You have helped us in our quest to make all those in Erinia remember the great Kingdom of Belarn. I salute you."

With a dramatic flare, he pushed his robe back and waved his hand in the air. It was a prearranged signal for those behind him. Men in armor appeared on other balconies above the soldiers. They were the generals and commanders that had lead their army in the battle.

Ferral motioned to those around him. "These are your proud and heroic leaders. All of them are fearless and dedicated to our cause." Few in the courtyard could see the soldiers hidden in the darkness of the open doorways behind their commanders or the sharp spears they held at their backs.

"They've all pledged eternal allegiance to me and vow to serve Belatarn unwaveringly. They wish to follow the lead of our greatest hero ... General Derout, who also vowed to serve our cause by making the greatest personal sacrifice." Ferral stepped to the side to let another figure come forward.

Soldiers and officers gasped as Derout slowly appeared on the balcony. They had all heard that Ferral killed him, but there he was standing next to the king. Then realization began to sink in as those close enough to see finally made out the gaping wound on Derout's throat. The officers tried to back away from the balcony's ledge as they realized what Ferral had planned for them. Ferral's loyal servant's lowered their spears and forced them back out to where the crowd could see them.

"General Derout is the man responsible for the total annihilation of the Duellrian army. He is the greatest hero of the Belarnian Empire. He volunteered to be the general of my ... newest army. The Deathmarch Army." Derout opened his mouth wide to shout. No sound came out, but the effect was enough to make those gathered cringe in fear.

"And now, his subordinate officers and aides have also volunteered to serve in the vast ranks of the new army. You have been invited to witness their beautiful transformation ceremony." Ferral laughed hysterically as he threw his hands out to his sides.

Suddenly, sharp points protruded from the chests of the army leaders. They braced themselves against the railings of the balconies as their eyes widened in shock. A few turned on their attackers trying to deal out some vengeance for their betrayal, but they were easily subdued and gutted. The men that had just stabbed their generals quickly threw ropes over their necks, as well as, their own. They picked up the kicking and squirming bodies of the officers and with a shout of loyalty to Ferral threw the bodies over the railings. With another shout, pledging eternal service, the fanatics jumped from the balconies to hang beside those they had killed. The men in the courtyard below shouted in horror and pushed at the gates to get out. They looked up to see their officers swinging just above their heads; their bodies jerked a little and then stopped. Ferral laughed in pleasure through the entire bizarre show.

"Now you will be the few worthy enough to witness the power I control!" Ferral shouted. With a grand sweeping gesture, the sorcerer pointed at all of the swinging bodies. At first nothing happened, and there was a hushed silence in the courtyard. Then the bodies began to jerk again, reanimated by the dark magic Ferral commanded. Some soldiers panicked, beating on the barred gates, begging for someone to release them. Many others knelt down bowing to their lord, acknowledging his powers. They chanted his name over and over again. He raised his hands for silence.

"We have crushed all who opposed us, but some have escaped. The prince of Erand, himself, escaped and fled west. He realizes his father is dead and his entire kingdom is in ruins, and now he likely hopes to raise a new army." A few scoffed at the absurdity of the Erandian's quest, but Ferral was not amused. The crowd fell silent.

"You have all proven your ineptness in catching three lone survivors. Were you not needed to fulfill another part of my plans, you would be sharing the same fate as your commanders." They looked at each other in alarm. Were they to be transformed into the living dead after all?

"Do not worry," he said with a reassuring smile. "I have a greater task for you. You now have a task that will lead you to glory and riches beyond your imaginings. You will march tomorrow to take control of the occupied lands to the east. Make the Erandians your slaves. Do not stop until you reach the Tarin Ocean." The gathered soldiers grinned again as the thought of booty filled their minds.

"The Deathmarch Army will leave under the control of our beloved heroes." He pointed down at the dead officers that struggled to reach the living below even as their necks stretched from the ropes. "They will seek out 'King Kristian' and any foolish enough to follow him. They will destroy everything they encounter and will not stop until they have eliminated every threat to our cause."

He stepped to the edge of the balcony and added, "Soon I will control all of Erinia. We will make the people of these lands our slaves. They will feed the hunger of our god and live to pleasure us with their pain. And when we are ready, we will sail across the Tarin and storm the old lands of Mesantia. The entire world will know of me, Ferral, the king of Belarn. Ferral the great sorcerer and the prophet of Belatarn." With his fervent words the gathered soldiers shouted out his name. He hushed them again, smiling.

"I also wish to announce that a wondrous day is quickly approaching. As you all know, the lovely Princess Allisia is without a family now, without a home. I have decided to show her compassion and love by taking her as my wife. On Sun's Day, during the longest day of the year, we will celebrate the Duellrian holiday with a great feast for all of my loyal servants." Cheers rang out from the army.

Ferral raised his hands, sending small sparks of blue lightning out from his finger tips into the night sky. The army shouted in awe and fright, bowing to their king. Ferral laughed in genuine amusement and then left.

KRISTIAN COULD SEE FAINT LIGHTS flickering among the trees as the last rays of the sun began to fade behind the endless green canopy of the forest. They had ridden hard another five days before finally reaching the Spirit Woods. They had, at first, wondered how they would go about finding the secretive people.

"Well, at least we won't have to search the entire woods for them," Mikhal commented.

Kristian wondered whether the mysterious people would welcome them or hunt them down. He knew little of the secretive people. They could all be sorcerers, like Ferral, evil and twisted. They could be fairies that might curse him or imprison him just for sport.

"How do we know they won't just kill us for intruding upon their sanctuary," Kristian wondered aloud.

He looked over at Mikhal who also noticed the burning torches hidden among the trees. The cavalier did not seem worried. In fact, Mikhal appeared ready to walk right up to them. So Kristian shrugged off the bad feeling and stepped off toward the gathered flames in the woods.

Suddenly, streams of arcing fire filled the night. Their smoky trails curved down from the balls of tiny light back to where the torches had been. Kristian and Mikhal froze in their tracks, staring at the flaming arrows. Cursing, Mikhal grabbed Kristian and pulled him a step back. An instant later, the flaming arrows landed with dull thuds in the grass where Kristian had been standing a moment before.

Six arrows were aligned in a perfect barrier, blocking the Erandians path to the trees. The fires consumed most of the wooden shafts creating a small wall of orange flame. It was a dramatic sign that they were not welcome. Mikhal turned to Kristian.

"Well, I don't think they want us to come any closer." Kristian shook his head in disgust. They had traveled a hundred miles or more on foot since the battle. To have come so far … he was not going to give up so easily. Kristian had to try something more. The Erandian king stepped around the wall of fire, waving his hands over his head.

"Hello," he shouted. "We mean you no harm. We've come a long way seeking aid and support. We need your help." His words were cut short by the hissing sound of more arrows racing toward him. They were not lit, and he could not tell where they were coming from in the growing darkness. He looked around alertly, but remained where he was.

Another six arrows landed before him. They ringed him in a half circle forcing him to back out. He stood motionless, unable to comprehend why the woodsmen refused to listen to him. A heavily accented voice spoke out from somewhere within the shelter of the trees.

"You are not welcome here! We have no aid to give you. Now go."

The hissing sound filled Kristian's ears, and he cringed, afraid that this time arrows would pin him to the ground. They hit one after another right at Kristian's feet, constantly forcing him back until he was standing next to Mikhal again. The voice called out again in anger.

"Fool! Heed our warnings and leave. The next flight will not be so far off the mark." Kristian did not want to think about how much closer the woodsmen meant to put the arrows. Disappointed, he waved one final time, acknowledging their warning.

He turned, and the two Erandians walked back over the hill. "Now what do we do?" Kristian asked in disbelief. "We finally found them, and they refuse to even talk with us."

"Could you blame them?" Mikhal countered. "Two armed men in rags claiming they need help? We look more like bandits than anything respectable."

Kristian grimaced, disgusted at the turn of events. He looked back over his shoulder as the shadows deepened over the forest, hiding any trace of the woodsmen and the shelter he hoped to find.

Mikhal gently pulled on his sleeve, "Let's go back up the river a bit. We'll camp there and try again in the morning. Maybe if we show them how persistent we can be, and they realize we are no threat, they'll change their minds."

LATER, THE TWO FOUND A small depression close to the river. Bitter gusts of cold wind blew down from the north onto the grassy meadows, reminding them of the evil they had narrowly escaped. They could find no wood to build a fire and were forced to curl up in their coats for warmth. Mikhal took the first watch while Kristian tried to put their bad luck out of his mind.

Sleep came quickly for the Erandian king, but he was plagued by nightmares and twisted memories. The young man was haunted by ghastly images of himself. A cruel and evil specter, dressed as he had been during the battle against Ferral, taunted him with his failures. Laughing, the image danced through the mists of the battleground, pointing his sword toward the action. Where he pointed, Erandians rushed forward to die. Kristian shook his head in disbelief.

"No!" he screamed. "It wasn't like that." Ghosts of those that followed him, obeying his ridiculous orders, floated past the ethereal image of himself. They would not speak, but their silence deafened Kristian. Everywhere he turned to escape the nightmare forms, he ran into another soldier that had trusted him only to die a grizzly death.

Kristian backed away from them all, but they closed in upon him, tightening their circle. His dead comrades reached out for him, their eyes pleading for him to save them. Kristian screamed in horror, and they vanished. Slowly, an image of a solitary man replaced all of them. Stately and proud, he refused to let the burden of his death bring him down. His stern gaze fell on his cowering son.

"Father?" Kristian called out. The ghost said nothing. "Father, please, I … I'm sorry. Please forgive me." The dead king would say nothing. His image faded slowly in the mist, leaving his son alone in an empty and terrible place. Kristian wept in sorrow.

Mikhal woke Kristian and quickly hushed the confused Erandian. When Kristian saw the worried look on Mikhal's face, he immediately became more cautious. "Riders. Less than a mile from us, approaching from the north," the cavalry officer whispered.

"North?" Kristian gasped. "It must be a Belarnian patrol."

There were eleven of them. Most wore various scraps of leather and mail armor, but one appeared to be a Black Guard. Each rode upon a dark horse, making it difficult for the two Erandians to identify their progress. It seemed the patrol had stumbled upon their trail somewhere near the mountains and followed them south toward the forest. Riding single file, they lazily approached Kristian and Mikhal's small depression. Kristian was afraid Old Man might whinny at the approaching horses and give away their hiding spot. He motioned toward the place where they had left the horse to graze. Mikhal nodded, cursing silently.

But Old Man did not make a sound, and the patrol continued past the depression. They were so close that Kristian could see the expressions on their faces. They were tired, exhausted, and their slack faces indicated the patrol had searched long and hard for them with little success.

If they only knew how close they are, he thought.

Just then the lead soldier, the Black Guard, halted. Reigning in his horse he said, "Wake up, you lazy whore's sons. There are lights in the trees ahead." The leader pointed toward the woods, and the others roused themselves, excited by the possibility that they might have found their prey.

One soldier in the middle of the patrol pulled out of the column and faced his comrades. His horse came close to stepping on Kristian who was hiding in a small bush. He cringed, trying harder to push himself back into the darkness.

The soldier closest to Kristian spoke out. "What about the tales of these woods? People say these forests are full of evil spirits that devour humans and drag their victim's soul to hell." The leader rode up next to the superstitious man.

"And who are we to be frightened by evil spirits? Our king controls the spirits themselves. Who is more evil than he?" He looked through the gloom at his men. "I would much rather face whatever may be holding those torches than report back to Ferral that we let the Erandians go because we were too frightened to enter the woods in the dark." The others backed up their commander with grunts and nods.

"But what if they are just woodsmen, Jorn?" The reluctant soldier asked his leader. "We're far from Belarn, and these people have done nothing to interfere with our king's plans. Why slaughter them needlessly? We could ask them for information or for some food." Others nodded, thinking about how long it had been since they had eaten something other than stale rations."

"Do you think it's them? Do you think it's the cavaliers? I mean it's a rather large reward Ferral's offering," a soldier called out from the rear of the column.

"Not unless they've found others to help them. I count six ... no seven torches," another replied. "Either way, we'll have some fun. If it's

the Erandian king and his survivors, we'll butcher them and get our reward. If they're just woods folk, well then, we'll just butcher them, too,
and take whatever we can."

"Forget about the reward and booty for now. Worry more about
what Ferral and that demon will do to us if we fail," the one called Jorn
shot back, looking at each member of the patrol. He turned his full attention to the reluctant one in the middle. "As for you, I'll be watching
you. I always knew that the High Hill people were traitors and cow-
ards, supporting the king only when it benefited them. You better be at
the front of the attack, so I don't mistake you for an Erandian dog and
slit your throat." The soldier quickly backed his horse away but saw the
determination on Jorn's face and reluctantly moved to the front of the
line.

"Maybe there are women with them. Young women," one Belarnian
said excitedly, breaking the silence.

"What do you care how old they are, Moric? It never stopped you
before," the leader snarled.

Jorn pulled free his broadsword and returned to the front of the
column along with the superstitious soldier. "Now, stop your crying,
children. I see people in want of a lesson in terror. And if you find the
Erandians with them, make sure to keep their heads for proof or you
won't get any reward. Ride them down!"

With that they charged out of the depression where Kristian and
Mikhal were hiding and headed for the dark forest. Kristian pulled
himself out of the bush looking for his companion.

"Over here," Mikhal called. Kristian rushed over to where the cavalier was.

"What should we do now?" Kristian asked.

"This is the best chance we'll have to lose them. I didn't think they
would get this close, but if we move quickly, we can use this diversion
to our advantage." Mikhal pointed to the west. "Maybe we can cover
our tracks by crossing over the river and heading that way," The cavalier
offered.

Kristian shivered just thinking about the prospect of swimming through the mountain-fed stream, but he could not think of a better plan. Finally, he shrugged, securing his pack and nodding that he was ready to move out.

They started out of the depression, heading in the opposite direction of the Belarnians. They hoped their tracks would be harder to find mixed in with those of the patrol. After traveling a mile from their campsite, they would try to find a good place to cross the river. As they climbed the small rise leading out of their protected hide site, they heard the sounds of battle coming from the woods. The two looked back over their shoulders to see flaming arrows streaking through the night. They could not see where they were impacting, but the screams and shouts of Belarnians indicated just how accurate the forest archers were.

Mikhal smiled. "You see? Their welcome was much less pleasant than ours." He squinted through the darkness, trying to make out the results of the battle. "I hope they all die." Kristian finally pulled the cavalier down off the hill afraid someone would see them if they stayed any longer.

"What about the horse?" Kristian asked as they ran down the backside of the hill.

Mikhal paused. It was hard for him to leave a good horse. "We'll have to leave him. I don't think he could make the fording, and he will never be able to out run the patrol. It will be a lot more difficult for them to track us if we're on foot." Kristian did not like the possibility of facing mounted Belarnians while they were dismounted, but there was no time to argue.

Mikhal let the reigns go and urged Old Man to leave. The horse stood there mutely but did not follow them as they started searching for a way to cross the river.

THE TWO STOOD BY AN old, solid oak, trying to catch their breath. Mikhal scanned the dark waters of the river, trying to find a good place to cross, but where they stood was too high to just drop in without making noise or getting hurt. So they squatted down, looking for a way to the bank.

Just then the two heard the approaching sounds of a horse plodding through the tall grass. Kristian thought it might be Old Man, trying to find them. They hid behind the tree, just in case, but it was too late. Two Belarnians came into view from the south. The riders saw them and abruptly halted.

One raised his hands pleadingly, "Please, please don't shoot. We're sorry … forgive us for intruding upon your lands. We surrender." The other soldier sat slumped in his saddle hugging himself.

Kristian and Mikhal stood there unsure of what to do. *They think we're woods folk,* Kristian knew. Then recognition seemed to dawn on the soldier's face as he saw the Erandian's hesitation.

"Wait," he growled, "You're … the Erandian scum. It's my lucky day. Fewer of us left … a pity for sure," he said to himself, "but more reward for me!" He turned over his shoulder to call out, "Over here, over here! I found the Erandians by the river." A shout from somewhere behind him echoed back. The shout gave the Belarnian a measure of courage; his comrades were on the way. The Belarnian pulled out a spiked mace and charged.

Mikhal had no time to get his sword out. He dived under the falling ball just as it crunched into the tree where his head had been. The cavalier came up on the other side of the Belarnian, pulling him from his horse. He was caught off guard and fell heavily to the ground at Mikhal's feet. Seeing Mikhal locked in a struggle with the one, Kristian rushed the other soldier that still sat slumped in his saddle.

An arrow protruded from the man's unprotected abdomen. He held onto the shaft with one hand as he tried to turn his horse away from Kristian. Kristian could have easily caught him, but he saw the wound and pain on the man's face. It was the same soldier that had tried to warn his companions and turn them away from the woods. Kristian hesitated, wondering what would happen if he just let the man go. By the time he looked back, the Belarnian soldier was already too far away to catch. Kristian quickly forgot about him and turned to help Mikhal.

The Erandian officer was shouting curses as he continued to pummel the Belarnian scout with his fists. The man struggled against the weight of his armor to get up but could not get away from Mikhal's flailing arms. Just then another Belarnian galloped out of the darkness right next to Kristian. Sword raised high, the grinning soldier was ready to cut him in half. Kristian reacted instantly. He pulled free his own sword, continuing the swing outward until it hit the soldier's horse. It screamed and ran forward a bit before it reared, throwing its rider against the oak tree.

The Belarnian grunted as he hit the solid wood and fell further down the sharp bank into the water. The Belarnian shouted as he splashed about in the shallow water.

"Damn, it's cold," he said gasping. Without thinking, Kristian jumped off the embankment. Shouting a wordless cry of rage, he landed on top of the soldier, thrusting down with his sword. It glanced off of his opponent's black armor. It was the patrol's leader, Jorn. The man was in knee-deep water, but the weight of his wet clothes and armor made it hard for him to get his head above the surface. The man's arms waved about franticly, and his hands finally grabbed hold of Kristian's shirtsleeve, desperately trying to pull himself up. Kristian held him down firmly, fighting Jorn. He pushed down with all of his weight on the man's head. Several moments passed before Jorn stopped fighting. Kristian looked hurriedly back to the tree.

"Mikhal?" The cavalryman stood up, looking back toward the sound of his king. "Hurry, before more come." The cavalier turned toward his unconscious opponent, kicking him one more time, and then he ran jumping away from the embankment landing close to Kristian.

"What are you doing?" Mikhal asked, looking at Kristian in confusion. Finally, Kristian let go of Jorn. The Black Guard did not come up.

Kristian gasped, "He held his breath for a long time." Already exhausted, he started for the other side of the river. It quickly got deeper, and they were forced to swim. They panted and gasped, trying to catch their breath, but the water was so cold their lungs refused to work.

"We've got … to reach … other side quick … or we'll never make," Mikhal was cut off by the sound of shouting behind him. He did not bother wasting effort to look back; instead he tried even harder to reach the far side.

Kristian was the first to find his footing again. He quickly pulled himself out of the water, falling down at its edge. He looked back across the river for an instant to see chaos. The remaining Belarnians were scrambling away from the river as quickly as they could. One scout fell from his horse, two shafts sticking out from his back. Another screamed in agony, clutching his stomach. The woods folk had dealt swiftly with the Belarnians. Kristian pushed himself off the ground and helped Mikhal out of the frigid water; both were shaking uncontrollably.

"We'll be dead soon if we don't get warm," Kristian said between clenched teeth. Mikhal shook his head in agreement.

"Maybe crossing wasn't such a good idea," he admitted, shaking badly. Pain kept him from saying more. Wearily, he motioned for Kristian to get up the bank and seek cover. They helped each other up the steep slope and fell to their knees at the top.

Mikhal was trying to catch his breath as he searched the darkness to the west. "I don't know where to go, but we have to keep moving. If we rest here, we'll die from the cold." With renewed determination, he stood up. The cavalier pulled his king off the ground, and the two started off with no idea of where they were going.

KRISTIAN HAD NEVER FELT CLOSER to death. He had not eaten in two days. He had walked for what seemed like an eternity. His joints were swollen from the freezing water and fighting, but he had to keep walking. They had narrowly escaped the patrol, but it seemed they had only escaped one type of death to encounter another one, a much slower one. They stumbled through that first night and the next morning and only kept warm by constantly moving. Their bodies ached from the pain.

Kristian began to fear that if he survived, he would be crippled for life. It had been three days since they had first reached the boundary of the Spirit Woods, and they still had not been able to enter or find anyone willing to help them. Somehow in the darkness, they had become disoriented. Mikhal had wanted to stay close to the border of the woods, but they lost sight of the trees and walked along aimlessly. They had no food or water and were getting desperate. They were too weak to change their situation.

It mattered little to Kristian now. He had been reduced to little more than a walking puppet, much like Ferral's army of the dead. His mind wandered from one thought to the next, constantly changing and never focusing. He was no longer aware that Mikhal was walking limply next to him. He just kept moving because that was all he could remember to do.

Mikhal was in no better condition. The cavalier had fallen several times. Once he had tripped over a partially buried rock and banged his knee on another. He limped from the stiffness of the injury but no longer felt the pain. His eyes stared out past the horizon searching for something that he could not find.

Unlike his companion, though, his mind was focused … so strongly focused on one thing that his soul screamed for escape. He was in the golden field again with the beautiful girl. She ran through the flowers and tall grass teasing him, daring him to catch her. He smiled at her antics. Mikhal's heart ached as he watched her dance before him. He knew she was the demon from another life. There was no mistaking those depthless blue eyes or their penetrating stare. As much as he wanted to turn away and run from this waking nightmare, he continued to concentrate on the girl. She dipped behind a hill, waving as she disappeared. He quickly ran after her, afraid he might lose her.

Mikhal stopped at the top of the hill looking down on a magnificent sight. A sprawling metropolis spread out below him in a wide valley. *A hundred thousand people must live here,* he thought. The houses were constructed of white and gray marble, their red tiled roofs dotting the valley floor. He also saw larger buildings, obviously designed for administrative work and worship. The height of these larger buildings made Mikhal stagger in awe. They stood higher than any tower he had ever seen. Detailed designs were painstakingly carved into every imaginable corner of the marble. Legendary heroes loomed over nearly every building and street corner. And despite the great wealth of the city, there were no walls or fortifications. The girl called to him, spoiling the moment. She was down at the outskirts of the city, waving for him to follow her. Mikhal quickly forgot about the magnificent city and ran down the hill after his love, once again entranced by her beauty.

When he got to the street where he had seen her, she was gone. The street itself was dark and miserable, a sharp contrast to the remarkable sights he had seen from the top of the hill. The warmth of the sun was hidden behind dark storm clouds and the breeze made him shiver. Mikhal slowly walked down the street calling for his love. She did not respond. At an intersection, he saw a gathered crowd. All of them were dressed in fine clothes. Silk and other precious materials were loosely draped from their bodies. Many dressed provocatively, displaying as much of their skin as they could. Mikhal noticed that everyone's hair had the same fair color … like his loves and like his own.

Mikhal wondered what his connection to these people and this place might be until his attention was called back to those on the far side of the street. Everyone pushed for a glimpse of something beyond Mikhal's view. The men, women, and some children laughed and cheered. Mikhal was curious to know what it was they were looking at.

He crossed the street to where barrels were stacked by a tavern. The white stones had been stained by dirt and grime over the years, but Mikhal could still see the workmanship that had gone into building this simple tavern many years before. The cavalier climbed atop some wobbly barrels, leaning against the tavern for support. He immediately wished he had never crossed the street.

At the opposite corner of the intersection, the crowd was watching slave traders show their prized possessions. Hands bound together and naked, the slaves stood motionless on a makeshift stage. Mikhal had never seen people like those the traders were selling. Their skin was dark, as dark as the storm clouds above the fine city. Their hair was cut short, even the women's hair was short, and they all had a lean muscular look to them. A young slave was brought forward to the surprisingly loud cheers of the gathered people. The trader pulled the slave to the front by a rope tied around his neck. The young man stumbled but caught himself quickly, his muscles rigid as he tried to hide his emotions. He remained silent and continued to stand motionless on the stage.

The people shouted out prices quickly. Several argued over the worth and cost of the slave. Eventually, only one person was able to keep bidding higher. His love stepped away from the crowd, handing the slave trader a few gold coins. She grabbed the rope that was dangling on the stage and gently guided her new servant off. The beautiful girl seemed to feel Mikhal's stare and turned to face him. Her wicked smile quickly fell from her face as she saw his disbelief, but only for a moment. The girl Mikhal knew to be the demon smiled again, pulling her slave behind her.

In his dream, Mikhal fell from the barrels as a tremor from the earth shook the city. People in the middle of the street cringed, unsure of what to do. A statue of a beautiful goddess fell from its pedestal crushing a man. The delicate glass torch that was held in the statue's outstretched hand shattered on the paved street. A loud boom rocked the foundation of the tavern next to Mikhal even as the earth stopped shaking. He looked up from where he lay to see a column of dark smoke rise from somewhere deeper in the city.

Mikhal's nightmare was abruptly halted as his body fell to the earth again … this time for real. He did not feel the pain nor call out for Kristian's help. His mind refused to let go of the dream; he demanded answers to his questions. Kristian heard him fall, but continued walking, unable to comprehend what had happened. A few feet later, he also fell to the ground, exhaustion finally taking over.

Delirious, Mikhal looked out past the grassy meadow where he and Kristian lay. In the distance, he could see many small columns of smoke rising up into the sky. And then he closed his eyes, hoping to find his love again.

Breinigsville, PA USA
19 August 2009
222569BV00002B/66/P